T0359841

Romantic Suspense

Danger. Passion. Drama.

Ambush On The Ranch
Tina Wheeler

Cold Case Disappearance
Shirley Jump

MILLS & BOON

AMBUSH ON THE RANCH
© 2024 by Tina McCright
Philippine Copyright 2024
Australian Copyright 2024
New Zealand Copyright 2024

First Published 2024
First Australian Paperback Edition 2024
ISBN 978 1 038 93906 7

COLD CASE DISAPPEARANCE
© 2024 by Shirley Kawa-Jump LLC
Philippine Copyright 2024
Australian Copyright 2024
New Zealand Copyright 2024

First Published 2024
First Australian Paperback Edition 2024
ISBN 978 1 038 93906 7

MIX
Paper | Supporting
responsible forestry
FSC® C001695

Published by
Harlequin Mills & Boon
An imprint of Harlequin Enterprises (Australia) Pty Limited
(ABN 47 001 180 918), a subsidiary of HarperCollins
Publishers Australia Pty Limited
(ABN 36 009 913 517)
Level 19, 201 Elizabeth Street
SYDNEY NSW 2000 AUSTRALIA

Cover art used by arrangement with Harlequin Books S.A.. All rights reserved.

Printed and bound in Australia by McPherson's Printing Group

Ambush On The Ranch
Tina Wheeler

MILLS & BOON

Tina Wheeler is a retired teacher and award-winning author. She enjoys spending time with her large extended family, brainstorming with writing friends, discovering new restaurants and traveling with her husband. Although she grew up near a desert in Arizona, her favorite place to plot a new story is on a balcony overlooking the ocean.

Books by Tina Wheeler

Ranch Under Fire
Ranch Showdown
Ambush on the Ranch

Visit the Author Profile page at
millsandboon.com.au.

I sought the Lord, and he heard me,
and delivered me from all my fears.
—*Psalm* 34:4

To my sister, who is always there
to encourage, advise, chauffeur or offer her
home-improvement skills. Her generosity is boundless.

Chapter One

Help! God, please help me! Janel Newman -dodged one pine tree, then another. Her lungs burned with each breath as she pumped her arms harder, forcing her feet to run faster in the cowgirl boots she hadn't fully broken in yet.

A bullet whizzed over her shoulder, splintering bark off a tree in her path.

Panic struck, and she jolted in a new direction.

Every muscle resisted her effort to move another inch. She ached from head to blistering toes. How much more of a beating could her body take before it failed, leaving her a helpless target?

Racing toward a copse of overgrown bushes, she spotted a boulder barely visible in the dense Northern Arizona forest. When the moment was right, she circled back around the huge rock and crouched as low as her tired, cramping legs would allow. With only enough energy left to breathe, she leaned against the hard granite for support.

Why hadn't she minded her own business? None of this would have happened if she'd driven straight to work instead of making that U-turn.

The encroaching sound of pounding footsteps warned he was coming closer.

Fear consumed her.

He suddenly stopped, and silence hung heavy in the air. She strained to listen. Where did he go? In her mind, she pictured the murderer scanning his surroundings from beneath his sunglasses.

She pulled her elbows in closer—a desperate attempt to shrink lower behind the boulder, the only thing between her and certain death.

His footfalls started again, and he drew nearer. He was coming straight for her.

Her thumping heart echoed in her ears.

She shoved aside the intense urge to run because he'd shoot the second she stood.

Life. She was choosing to live—if God wanted her opinion on the matter.

The man who wanted her dead stepped even closer.

His shadow fell over the boulder onto a patch of snow inches away from her boots. She froze, afraid to move, to breathe, to even think.

Seconds later, the sound of someone else traveling through the forest carried on the chilly breeze. The shooter's shadow disappeared as he ran in the newcomer's direction.

She waited and waited, then pushed off the rock and sprinted away. Her destination: the trees with the widest trunks, hoping they'd provide protection.

A shot rang out.

The bullet missed, and she continued fleeing as fast as she could. A grunting sound made her glance back long enough to see the shooter trip and fall. Hoping to take advantage of the situation, she fought to quicken her sprint. She had to get away.

Out of the corner of her eye, she thought she saw a horse in the distance. Was she hallucinating? Or did her pursuer have an accomplice coming to join the hunt?

* * *

Zach Walker glanced about as he quickly guided his chest-nut-colored quarter horse through the dense forest in search of a suspected murderer: a man wearing a black hoodie who'd escaped into the forest seconds after a landscape worker had been shot and killed. Their suspect had a twenty-minute lead, but the sound of two gunshots gave them a general direction to home in on.

The other Mounted Fugitive Retrieval Team members were riding toward that area from different parts of the forest. Zach, a Sedona rancher, was the only fully trained volunteer, sworn in and given a badge. He could perform the same duties as any other county deputy sheriff when needed.

After covering another half mile, Zach pulled the reins to halt Copper. He pushed back the brim of his hat and listened for sounds of movement. A breeze carried the scent of pine, and the sun's rays filtered through the thick branches of evergreen trees. The signs of a peaceful winter day belied the threat that could strike at any second, around any turn.

Another gunshot fired, and the forest sprang alive with the flapping of wings from birds soaring off their perches. Copper bobbed his head.

"Let's go, boy."

The pair adeptly navigated the terrain with a sense of urgency, closing the gap between them and the shooter. A petite blonde emerged from the shadows fifty feet away. Her presence surprised him. There was no good reason for her to be here.

He was about to yell to her when another shot startled Copper and propelled the woman in a new direction. Zach's pulse raced as he dismounted and secured his horse behind a boulder. He removed his Glock from its holster and peered around the jagged granite concealing his position.

The woman glanced back over her shoulder, and he caught a full view of her face. *Janel? From church?* Was the fugitive trying to shoot her? As he watched, her sweater caught on a branch, and after jerking it free while still trying to run, she smacked into a sturdy tree trunk. She bounced off and collapsed into a heap on the ground.

Zach cringed. He desperately wanted to help her but couldn't risk moving closer. Not until he'd dealt with the shooter. Suppressing his concern for Janel, he quietly radioed a quick update to his team.

A bullet whizzed through the air, high above her still body.

The sound of boots crunching a pine cone on the forest floor gave away the shooter's location. He must not have detected Zach's and Copper's presence.

Zach needed to draw the man away from Janel before he risked engaging in a confrontation. Coming across a rock the size of an orange, he threw it at a towering pine. The branches swayed, and another shot discharged.

Taking cover behind a bush, he waited for the shooter to step out into the open. The team was working on the premise that this shooter and the fugitive were the same person. Through his radio's earpiece, he heard the team converging on his GPS coordinates. They would be here soon.

Another footfall revealed the shooter's new position. Zach held his weapon tight as he shifted to the other side of the bush to get a better view. All he could see of the man hiding behind a tree was part of a black hoodie and reflective sunglasses... and the pistol he lifted.

Zach identified himself as a sheriff's deputy. "Drop your weapon!"

The fugitive aimed.

Zach fired.

A jerking motion and guttural response told Zach he'd hit his mark—the man's shoulder.

Copper snorted and pranced in place.

Voices in the distance, accompanied by hooves stomping over dirt, sent the man fleeing.

"I see him!" a deputy shouted. "Average height and build, still wearing the hoodie."

"He's heading north," another responded.

Zach rushed back to Janel, keeping an eye out for the shooter in case he tried to sneak up on them. She moaned. A slight utterance, but it signaled she was alive. His breathing relaxed.

"Help's on the way." He crouched and pushed strands of her long hair away from the goose egg growing on her forehead. This was all too surreal. During their many conversations at church, she'd mentioned more than once that she wasn't into hiking or camping, so what was she doing deep in the forest?

Her lids fluttered open, and she stared up at him as she lifted a hand to her head. Her sky blue eyes held no recognition. "Where am I?"

When she tried to sit up, he stopped her. "You might have a concussion."

Zach radioed for medical assistance while continuing to glance about for any sign of danger. From what he heard next through his earpiece, he suspected the fugitive was racing toward the freeway. While the mounted team headed in that direction, the lieutenant gave the all clear for EMTs to move in.

"My head hurts. A lot." Janel closed her eyes again and repeated, "Where am I?"

"You're in the forest near Flagstaff. Do you remember why you're here?"

She gave a small groan. "No. I don't."

"Do you recognize me?" He hoped so. Zach first met Janel six years ago at a fall festival they both spearheaded. He'd been impressed by the Sedona art gallery owner, who had the business connections to secure donations and find vendors. It hadn't taken long for them to develop a casual friendship. She was kind and generous, not to mention beautiful, with her heart-shaped face and flawless complexion. He would have asked her out if she hadn't been dating an instructor at the university in Flagstaff. Was her boyfriend nearby?

Janel peered up at him, her lids partially open. "*Should* I recognize you?"

"We're friends from church." He prayed her memory issues were temporary. The possibility of brain damage worried him. "Try to relax. The medics will be here any minute now."

His gaze shifted to her Western outfit beneath the heavy brown sweater. Why would she trek through the middle of nowhere wearing a knee-length denim skirt and cowgirl boots? None of this made any sense.

Janel wasn't the type of person murderers chased down to kill. She must have been in the wrong place at the wrong time. Zach placed his hand over hers. Was she safe now? Or were her troubles just beginning?

Chapter Two

By late afternoon, the stabbing pain in Janel's head finally lessened to a relentless ache. Sitting back in a cushioned reclining chair, she stared up at the blue curtains that separated her from the other patients in the emergency department. The doctor had urged her to rest, but she couldn't. She feared if she fell asleep, her returning memories would slip away again. It was bad enough she still couldn't recall the past two days. She almost died and didn't know why.

"You'll feel better before long." The calming voice belonged to Zach.

He'd been standing vigil close by since she'd arrived by ambulance, even waiting there while she underwent tests. The doctor would be back soon to go over the results.

She glanced over at Zach, and another memory flickered through her mind. They were working at a church festival they cochaired. He handed her a plate of cookies for the bake sale and joked about how they were safe to eat because his sister donated them, not him. "We made a lot of money that day," she murmured.

Zach tilted his head. "What?"

"The fall festival. We brought in a lot of money for the food bank."

He eased into a smile. "We did. When you're all better, we can plan the next one."

She agreed and settled back in the chair. Zach made her feel safe, and not just because he stood six foot three, had broad shoulders and a commanding presence in his official uniform. He was a solid connection to her normal life. Their conversations at church were always easygoing, nothing too personal, and she enjoyed his company. He made her laugh—during less serious times. And now he'd put his life on the line for her.

Zach lowered his large frame into the cushioned chair beside her. He was ruggedly handsome with his thick dark hair and square jaw. "Have you remembered what happened this morning?"

"I'm afraid not. I can't get over the fact a murderer shot and killed a landscape worker and then tried to kill me." She bit her lip, thinking about what Zach had told her when she questioned him earlier. "I'm so grateful you were there. You saved my life."

"I was doing my job," he responded in his usual humble manner, then added, "I'm glad I was there, too."

She nervously brushed her fingers over the denim skirt covering her legs. "I wish I knew why I was in the forest. It's not like I'm dressed for a hike. Not that I have the interest or time to go on one."

"Could you have made plans to meet your boyfriend at one of the camping sites? I tried to reach him at the university, but no one answered the phone in his department."

The mere mention of the man she'd wasted over five years dating made her headache worse. That was a memory she would have liked to keep hidden in the back of her mind. "We broke up last month."

"I'm sorry," he said, his tone sympathetic.

"It's for the best. I need to focus my energy on the gallery, instead of the drama that comes with dating and breaking up."

Because she didn't trust her instincts, she feared she might attract another man like Todd.

She should have realized earlier that their relationship was doomed. He worked tirelessly, ensuring he remained on the tenure track, while she kept busy trying to attract new customers to her gallery, Red Rock Artistry. He lived in Flagstaff, and she lived farther down the mountain in Sedona. But they never argued, and she trusted him, so she was blindsided when he fell in love with a former student. Obviously, he wasn't spending all his free time writing articles for academic journals.

The curtain opened and Janel's fraternal twin sister peered in at them.

"Karla! You're here." Relief washed over her. It had only been a week since they last saw each other, but right now, it seemed like an eternity.

Zach stood, surprise flickering across his face. His gaze shifted from one sister to the other.

Janel was used to this reaction. They both strongly resembled their mother. Strangers often mistook them for identical twins until they stood side by side, and then their slight differences became apparent. Karla was two inches taller and had hazel-colored eyes. Janel's were blue.

"Your assistant manager called me from the gallery." Karla rushed over in the signature black turtleneck sweater and black jeans she wore with her blond hair, the same color as Janel's, tied up in a ponytail. "Are you all right?"

"I'm fine." She was too embarrassed to admit she lost a fight with a tree and hit her forehead.

"Deputy, are you guarding my sister?" Karla's tone was gruff. She was older by ten minutes, but it might as well have been a decade. She had been looking out for Janel since they were toddlers.

Zach held his hat in his hands and answered, "There's no reason to believe she's in any danger here, ma'am."

"Karla, this is Zach Walker. He's the deputy sheriff who saved me. He's also my friend from church. I told you about him."

"I'm sorry I sounded harsh." Regret flickered across her face. "My sister's safety is my top priority."

"Completely understandable." His gaze traveled between the sisters again. "I'm surprised we haven't met before."

Janel didn't want to bring up the touchy topic of her sister not attending church or the fact she thought Sedona was too small. "She lives down in the valley, in Scottsdale. We usually get together there."

"We can talk about that later." Karla examined the bump on Janel's forehead, then turned to Zach. "Who did this to her? Have you caught them?"

"Not at this time." Zach's tone remained professional. "But we know he's headed north, and the Fugitive Retrieval Team is hot on his trail."

The doctor stepped through the opening in the curtain and joined the group. Janel was relieved to see the man with the answers. Based on the touch of gray at his temples, she had guessed him to be in his early fifties. She'd instantly liked him when he first examined her; he spoke in a soothing voice while avoiding the use of scary-sounding medical jargon.

"Miss Newman, how are you feeling? Any changes since we last spoke?"

"My head feels like someone's tapping on it with their knuckles instead of a hammer, like it did an hour ago. I guess that's progress."

The doctor glanced at Karla and did a double take.

"This is my sister," Janel explained. "You can speak freely. We're all eager to hear the test results."

With a nod, he began, "I confirmed you have a concussion. Your headache, any dizziness and most, if not all, of your memory loss should be temporary, but you must relax and let your brain heal."

Karla studied her when the doctor mentioned memory loss.

"Should," Janel repeated. "Are you saying I may never re-member what happened today?"

"That's a possibility, but nothing to worry about. It's not un-common for patients to forget the event that caused the injury."

"Is it normal to forget two days?" Janel hoped it wasn't a symptom of a more severe condition, while she tried to ignore the growing look of concern on her sister's face.

The doctor gestured toward Zach. "The deputy sheriff said you were running from a gunman. Your memory loss is un-derstandable when you consider your brain is trying to recover from both a concussion and an extremely traumatic situation. Keep in mind when you first regained consciousness, you couldn't remember who you were."

"How long will it take for the rest of her memories to re-turn—if they do?" Karla asked.

"Each case is different, but it's been my experience that she might remember more over the next few days." He turned back to Janel. "Unless your subconscious doesn't want you to, or if you try to get back to a normal routine too quickly. Also, there may be moments when you have trouble focusing or you feel confused as your memories return. That's normal and won't affect your brain's ability to function and store new memories."

"That's a relief. When can I go home?"

"Soon, unless your symptoms worsen. Do you have any other questions?"

Janel shook her head, then looked to her sister, who said, "Not right now."

"When you get home, you'll want to schedule a follow-up appointment with your regular doctor." He stepped toward the curtain. "I'll be back shortly with your discharge papers."

Janel thanked him before he left. She still couldn't wrap her head around the fact she'd lost two whole days. "I don't know how I'll relax if I can't stop wondering why I was in the forest. It's driving me crazy."

Karla planted a hand on her hip. "Something unexpected

must have taken you there. When I spoke to Charlene, she said you had left work to go to the bank and planned to come straight back."

The mention of her assistant manager's name had Janel thinking about her gallery and the trouble they were facing. But then her throbbing headache reminded her of the doctor's recommendation to relax.

Attempting to do so, she watched her sister and Zach discuss the businesses closest to that part of the woods.

Keeping his word, the doctor returned about fifteen minutes later. After he cleared her to leave, Karla announced she would drive Janel home.

Zach offered to walk them to the parking lot, which made Janel feel safer. "Sheriff's deputies will step up patrols in your neighborhood, just in case, and if anything out of the ordinary happens, call me right away."

Karla took the business card he offered. "We will. I'm taking the rest of the week off to stay with her."

"You don't need to do that," Janel protested, not wanting to be a burden.

"I want to. You're family. Not to mention you would do the same for me." Karla collected the paperwork from her and then they all stepped into the hall. Because Janel wasn't admitted to the hospital, there was no need for a wheelchair.

Outside the emergency department's automatic doors, the cold winter weather enveloped Janel while the hum of Flagstaff's rush hour traffic reminded her of the late hour. It would take longer to reach her house near Sedona. At least forty-five minutes, maybe an hour.

Zach scanned the lot, filled with cars. "Where did you park?"

"The back corner. Stay here, and I'll get the car." Karla took a step and Janel touched her arm to stop her.

"I want to go home. It'll be faster if I walk with you." Facing two troubled expressions, Janel tried to assure them that she'd be fine. "I haven't run into a single tree since we left the building."

Karla relented. Zach smiled at her remark, but he stuck close to her side as they passed by a parked ambulance in the circular drive.

Her sister guided them toward the first row of vehicles. Before advancing between a truck and a delivery van, she held up her key fob. "My car's been sitting awhile in the cold. I'll start the heater."

Karla pointed it toward the far end of the lot and pressed the button.

The ground quaked as a hot blast shot through the air, sending metal flying, and knocking Janel off her feet with a powerful force.

Instinctively, Zach caught Janel in his arms before she hit the asphalt. A fiery cloud blanketed the sky as he whisked her away between the oversize vehicles parked in the front row. Karla regained her balance and rushed after them.

"Stay low and out of sight," he instructed as he shifted into a crouched position to keep from being seen by whoever planted the bomb in Karla's car. He placed his hand on Janel's shoulder and looked her in the eyes. "Are you hurt? Did anything hit you?"

"No," she murmured. Clearly stunned, she sat on the cold, hard ground, hidden between the truck and delivery van. "Did someone just try to kill us?"

"It looks that way." He coughed on the acrid smoke wafting through the air, then turned to Karla, who sat next to her sister. "How about you? Are you all right?"

She removed a cell phone from her pocket. "Shaken, but okay. I can't believe someone blew up my car! I'm calling 911."

"Tell the dispatcher you're with me and ask to be connected to Lieutenant Yeager with the sheriff's office." Zach removed his Glock from his holster, then left Janel in the care of her sister to peer around the truck for anyone who looked like they didn't belong.

A young couple rushed from their car to the safety of the group gathering outside of the emergency department's doors. Security guards spoke in their communication devices while spreading out through the lot. EMTs scanned the area for potential victims of the blast. Zach hadn't seen any.

Movement in the bushes that separated the hospital from the administrative offices caught his attention. He shifted to get a better view and spotted a man of average height and build in a black hoodie and distinctive oversize sunglasses with mirror-blue lenses. Somehow, the fugitive had escaped the sheriff's deputies, who were still heading north.

Zach yelled toward the crowd, "Get back inside! Now!"

A shot rang out, and he dropped low behind the truck. A bullet whizzed over his shoulder and hit the van behind him. The side mirror landed on the asphalt with a noisy clatter.

Screams erupted from the stragglers still outside the emergency department's entrance, and this time, the guards yelled for them to hurry back inside.

"Zach!" Janel's voice rose in panic.

He turned and leaned toward her. "I'm okay."

"What are we going to do? This guy is going to kill us." Fear had Janel's hands shaking. The shooter must think she can identify him, or he wouldn't have risked coming to the hospital.

"Have faith. I'll get us out of this alive." Zach's words reminded him to pray for guidance. The danger they faced was escalating, and they needed help.

Karla handed him her phone. "It's the lieutenant."

Wasting no time, he grabbed the device and rattled off, "We're being shot at. It's our fugitive. Same black hoodie and sunglasses." Sirens in the distance announced help was coming, but would they arrive in time? "I need to get Janel Newman and her twin out of here. He just blew up the sister's car."

"The sheriff's office has a lobby full of reporters waiting

for a press conference," his friend and supervisor stated, his voice pitched higher than normal. "I'll need time to find a safe location to hide them."

Zach's family had experience with this type of situation. His brothers had both hid women in danger at the ranch. The shoot-outs and bombing that followed led to the family equine business losing longtime customers. They were struggling financially, and it was up to him to find the solution to turn things around since his father had retired and left him in charge. Any additional trouble, resulting in further loss of revenue, would ruin them.

Feeling the weight of this decision on his shoulders, he chose to put their futures in God's hands. "I can take the sisters to the ranch."

"I was hoping you'd say that." Lieutenant Yeager sounded relieved. "I'll call your brother Cole to warn him you're coming in hot before I update the sheriff. We'll do what we can to help."

After disconnecting the call, Zach handed the phone back to Karla. "We're leaving. I need you both to do exactly as I say and try not to make a sound."

He peered through the truck window, looking for their shooter, who was no longer standing in the same spot. Then, after assuring himself that his SUV was where he'd left it, Zach motioned for the sisters to follow. "Stay low."

Janel pushed to her feet and hunched between him and Karla. They wove like a snake between and behind vehicles. Another shot fired.

The bullet pinged off a streetlamp three feet away.

Zach jerked back, then thrust out his arm to halt their progression.

The wail of sirens grew louder. Help was much closer. But the fugitive could still shoot and kill them at any moment— even once the deputies arrived. After a minute elapsed without gunfire, Zach continued forward, rounding the bumper of a compact car. He glanced back toward the bushes but didn't see any movement.

"Let's go!" They hustled while hiding as much as possible behind one car, then another until they reached his SUV. He could hear Janel's footfalls behind him.

He stopped the sisters once again, this time to look under the car's carriage. His key fob wouldn't turn on the engine, or he would have done so earlier to check for a bomb. Not seeing anything, he opened the driver's side door and searched the inside.

Confident the SUV was safe, he ushered them into the back seat. "Stay out of sight."

After closing their door, Zach climbed behind the wheel and turned over the engine. Shifting into Reverse, he realized he had held his breath while turning the key. Breathing normally again, he backed out, shifted into Drive and then sped out of the lot onto the busy road, just as a parade of sheriff's vehicles stormed the parking lot through the other entrance.

He checked the rearview mirror and caught sight of a white sedan careening out of the hospital's administrative parking lot. The same area where the fugitive had recently hidden behind the bushes. The sun reflected off the driver's mirrored sunglasses. "Hang on! He's following us."

Hearing Janel and her sister buckling up in the back seat, he pressed on the gas, swerved around one car, then another, until he reached the intersection. With a green turn arrow displayed on the traffic light, he pulled the steering wheel into a sharp U-turn. The fastest way to his family ranch outside of Sedona would be the interstate, not the switchbacks down the mountain.

They raced out of town, increasing the gap between his SUV and the sedan that had missed the U-turn. Zach kept the engine roaring while his gaze constantly checked the rearview mirror. He couldn't count on maintaining their lead on the long stretch of interstate.

With a sign for Kachina Village looming ahead, a plan developed. He swerved onto the exit and drove into the quiet neighborhood. After several turns, he found what he was looking for: a cabin with no cars parked out front and a boat stored on the side. He maneuvered the SUV into position and backed up beside the boat, which would allow for a quick exit.

"What are you doing?" Janel asked.

"Hiding until the coast is clear." Zach reached for the folded sun shade he had left on the passenger seat, then flipped it open. After securing it in the front window, he called the lieutenant and filled him in on the white sedan. "It has an orange flower decal on the front bumper."

"We had a report of a stolen vehicle matching that description. Stay put until you hear from me."

Zach disconnected the call and turned in his seat to check on his passengers. Janel had a deer-in-headlights expression. "We shouldn't be here too long."

She nodded, not looking convinced.

Karla squeezed her sister's hand. "No one can say you're boring."

A smile tugged at Janel's lips. "Not funny."

"Kind of," her sister replied with a shrug.

Janel's eyes suddenly grew wide as she pointed to the passenger window.

Chapter Three

Stunned into silence, Janel, sitting in the back seat, could only point toward the tinted passenger side window. The white sedan rolling down the residential street was about to pass by in front of them. They hadn't seen it sooner because they had parked beside a boat on a trailer, which blocked their view. The murderer was only ten feet away.

"Down!" Zach ordered in a low voice from the front seat, clearly concerned that the SUV's darkly tinted windows and sunshade fully covering the front window might not be enough to hide them.

Janel unbuckled her seat belt and slid down onto the floorboard. Her sister followed her lead, the stress of the moment showing on her face.

From her position behind the passenger seat, Janel watched Zach. He sat perfectly still, watching and waiting.

Loose gravel on the residential road crunched below the wheels of the sedan as it slowly drove past them. Janel feared the shooter would recognize their vehicle and shoot Zach, then her, then Karla.

If they lived, she'd thank Zach for backing in when he parked. Their position hid the license plate. The shooter surely must have seen it during the chase in Flagstaff.

She strained to hear every sound. The rattle of the sedan's engine slowly faded. The murderer had turned a corner and was now driving down the side road.

With each second, he drifted farther away. You'd think her heart would stop thundering and her breathing would return to normal, but no. She felt lightheaded, the way she had in the emergency room.

She reached up to touch the goose egg on her forehead. *Relax.* The doctor's instructions echoed in her mind. This couldn't be what he had envisioned. A silent chuckle racked her body, and she feared she was losing her mind. Tears slid down her cheeks.

"He's gone," Karla murmured. "Everything's okay now."

"Is it?" Janel glanced at her sister. "For how long?"

Sirens coming from the nearby interstate gave her hope. After a couple of long, frightening minutes, Zach turned to speak to them while holding up his phone. "The lieutenant just texted. A deputy reported seeing a white sedan speeding away from this location."

"What now?" Janel focused on his familiar warm brown eyes, which further eased her fears.

"I contacted my brother Jackson. He runs a Northern Arizona task force. His group volunteered to watch the roads between here and the ranch to make sure we're not followed. We'll sit here until they're all in place."

"It's good to have connections." Karla climbed off the floor.

Janel rose and peered out the windows, double-checking to make sure it was safe to leave her hiding spot. Her legs cramped as she stretched them. "Zach, are you sure you want to take us to the ranch? There's a murderer after me. We'll be putting your family in danger."

"My family has had plenty of experience fighting bad guys." Zach sent her a gentle smile, which she returned as she eased into her seat. She'd heard stories about the shoot-outs at his ranch and hoped that kind of trouble wouldn't follow them there.

Silence settled over the SUV as incoming storm clouds altered the golden hue of the sunset to create a powerful image in the sky. With time ticking by at an agonizingly slow pace, it soon became apparent that the murderer wasn't returning. With nothing to do but wait, Janel's thoughts bounced between past and present, although the past two days still eluded her.

Janel had to admit she felt better knowing Jackson's team would look out for them when they drove to the ranch. She'd met Zach's brother at church. He'd married a woman he had protected while working for the DEA. From all accounts, they were a happy couple with a long lifetime together to look forward to.

Once upon a time, Janel thought she'd be living a fairy tale with Todd, but it all went wrong. His cheating proved he wasn't the man she thought he was. Did she miss the signs from day one? Did he say what she wanted to hear, so she'd be available until he found someone better? Why didn't she see through him?

Todd wasn't her only misstep. She and Karla had grown up surrounded by Western art. Their mother became a famous Sedona-based artist after her divorce, and their father was a museum curator in Scottsdale. Eight years ago, Janel opened her gallery, a place where she could display her mother's paintings, along with the works of other Southwestern artists.

No one expected a larger gallery to open down the street. When sales dropped, Janel convinced herself that this was a temporary condition. The newness of her competitor, Sedona Imagined, would soon wear off. Only it didn't. Before long, she was forced to reduce the number of hours for Charlene, her assistant manager.

Janel had been excited when she came up with a plan to boost sales. It included building an addition to the gallery: a room where she could hold painting classes. Her father's new wife wouldn't allow him to lend her the money, and Karla didn't have any to spare. So, she turned to the bank. The biggest mistake of her life. If only she could forget *that* again.

"Buckle your seat belts." Zach's remark jerked her out of her thoughts and reminded her they had to venture out into the open, away from the shadow of the boat stored beside them.

She did as he said and drew in a deep, settling breath. He turned over the engine and headed down the street. They passed several cars, most likely driven by people who lived in the cabin community. No one gave them a second look. He knew what he was doing, hiding here.

When they reached the interstate, her pulse picked up along with the speed of the SUV. She kept an eye out for the white sedan, despite knowing Jackson's team was making sure they weren't followed. Karla looked out the back window while Zach focused on the road ahead. No one spoke as lightning lit up the night sky miles away.

Janel took her cues from Zach. As long as he acted like they were out of danger, she could believe they were. For now.

Forty minutes later, Zach drove under a wooden arch: the gateway to Walker Ranch. A porch illuminated up ahead called to them like a beacon.

With darkness blanketing the pasture, the horses were nowhere to be seen. She spotted a barn beyond the white wooden fence and pictured them resting for the night. As they neared the house, a garage door lifted with the familiar sound of grinding gears.

Zach drove inside, rolling closer to Mr. Walker, who stood beside an open door, waiting for them. The older, distinguished-looking cowboy pushed the button to close the garage once the SUV was safely parked.

Janel exhaled, louder than she'd intended. She felt like an intolerable weight had been lifted off her shoulders.

Karla grinned. "We made it."

"Thanks to Zach and his brother." She would be forever grateful.

"Let's get you both inside." Zach pushed open his door. "You must be hungry. I know I am."

She wasn't ready for food, but she was more than ready to leave the SUV. She climbed out and headed toward Mr. Walker, who gently touched her shoulder.

"Thank you so much for taking us in." Janel's voice hinted at the exhaustion she felt. She could only imagine how tired her eyes looked.

"It's no problem at all, little lady." He offered his hand to Karla. "Welcome to our home."

"You have quite the family. I can honestly say we are alive thanks to your son here." Karla gestured toward Zach, and his father sent him a proud nod.

Mrs. Walker waved them into the kitchen. "You're here!" She pulled Janel into a hug like her mother would have if she were still with them. "We were so worried about you. Cole told us all about your sister's car exploding. How terrifying."

"Terrifying sums it up." Overcome with emotion, Janel felt a tear slide down her cheek. Mrs. Walker had always been kind to her. She'd even brought meals over to the house when she'd heard that the twins were losing their mother to cancer. That was three years ago, and Karla had been around more during that horrible time. "Mrs. Walker, you've met my sister before."

Janel stepped aside as Zach's mother took Karla's hand between hers. "Of course, I remember."

This family was beyond kind.

Fear twisted in Janel's gut. "Mrs. Walker, I think we should leave. I don't want to put your family in danger by being here."

Zach's mother wiped a tear from Janel's cheek. "Nonsense. God made all three of my sons law enforcement officers, and everyone in this family can shoot a gun and hit their target.

Now, let's get you two settled in so you can rest. Dinner will be ready soon."

She escorted the twins through the kitchen, which smelled of warm rolls baking in the oven, and into the spacious living room.

Karla collapsed onto a comfortable brown leather sofa. "Janel, how did this happen?"

"I wish I could tell you. I just don't know." Janel sat beside her, the hopelessness of the situation ripping her apart. She spotted Zach watching them from the dining room and asked, "How and why did he blow up my sister's car?"

"Well, we know he stole the white sedan after leaving the forest." Zach sat on the edge of a wing-back chair. "My best guess is he heard the news reports on the radio about you being taken to the hospital. Once he was there, he spotted Karla arriving and knew she had to be there to see you. You two look a lot alike."

"Where did he get the bomb?" Janel asked. "I doubt he found it inside the trunk of the car he stole."

"I suspect he had easy access to one and picked it up on the way."

Fear and confusion had Janel's headache pounding again. "But how did he know she would drive me home?"

"He wouldn't have known for sure." Zach rubbed the pad of his thumb over his chin. "If you saw his face and can identify him, blowing up Karla's car would serve as a warning—if you didn't die in the explosion."

If she could tell the murderer she couldn't identify him, would he believe her? Would he go away and leave her alone? Probably not.

After breakfast the next morning, Zach sat at the kitchen table across from Janel and Karla, who had changed into jeans and long-sleeved shirts his mother had rounded up for them. He gulped his third cup of coffee, needing every drop. His father and sister, Lily, had volunteered to divide up the night into shifts where they watched their recently installed security monitor. But between the rain pelting the ranch all night and jerking awake at every unusual sound, he still didn't get much sleep.

His brother Cole stepped into the room, and Zach introduced him to Karla, adding that he was Sedona's lead detective.

"Is this a personal visit or professional?" Karla asked.

"Both." Cole poured himself a cup of coffee and leaned against the counter. "Janel, how are you feeling this morning?"

"Tired." She touched the goose egg left behind after she collided with the tree. The swelling had gone down, but not completely. "My head doesn't hurt nearly as much as it did yesterday, though. The over-the-counter pain relievers your mother gave me are helping."

"That's good. And your memory?" Cole watched her closely. "I heard you lost two days."

"I'm certain I took cinnamon rolls to the gallery yesterday or the day before. I'm hoping that means I'll remember more soon."

A wary expression flickered across her face. Zach could understand if she feared those returning memories. A murderer was trying to kill her, and no one knew why.

Cole's gaze shifted to Zach. "Have you discussed the gallery?"

"Not yet, but I agree with you. The two events must be related." Zach never believed in coincidences. He opened his phone, which contained the app that would allow him to view the security monitor. His deep-seated fear was drawing a murderer to the ranch. Both Janel and their equine business depended on a safe environment.

"What two events are you talking about?" Janel asked, making it apparent she hadn't remembered the burglary yet.

Karla tapped a fingernail on the table before reluctantly answering her sister. "Janel, your gallery was broken into early

Monday morning. Four VanZandt bronze statues and Mom's paintings were stolen."

Her jaw dropped. "Mom's... No. That was her legacy."

"I drove here immediately after you called yesterday morning. That was hours before you ended up in the forest and lost your memory." Karla's gaze shifted between Cole and Zach. "In my job as an insurance investigator, I've been looking into a recent string of burglaries. At least one art thief, maybe more, has been hitting galleries and private collectors in New Mexico, Arizona, Colorado and Utah. The most valuable items were taken each time and only enough to fit in the trunk of a car. Janel is my sister, so I won't be working her case."

Zach had seen how brave Janel was after her mother's cancer diagnosis. She took on the role of caretaker while working remotely. Then came the depressing months following the funeral. But she picked herself up and focused on her business. Now this. He wanted to fix everything for her. The truth was, he wanted to go out with her, but he couldn't enter another rebound relationship. He refused to risk his heart like that ever again.

Visibly upset, Janel reached up and touched the bump on her head.

"Is the gallery burglary similar to the others?" Zach knew about the break-in; his brother had mentioned it the other night when he began his investigation. What Karla was sharing was new information.

"I don't know yet," Karla admitted. "The guy I'm looking for wears black from head to toe, including a ski mask, and circumvents the alarm system by cutting wires and jamming the backup signal. A security guard in Santa Fe changed his routine one night and walked in on him. He was overpowered and tied up."

"There are two big differences between those burglaries and this one." Cole had their full, undivided attention. "If Zach's fugitive is the gallery's burglar, he shot and killed someone. And, according to the security company, Janel's code was used to disarm the alarm. Only the cameras were jammed or turned off."

"That's not possible. No one knows my code but me and my assistant manager." Janel glared at the brothers after they exchanged knowing looks. "Charlene would *never* steal from me."

"Janel…" Zach kept his voice calm, projecting both his role as a lawman and as her friend. "Cole has a job to do. It would help if you told him all about Charlene and why you trust her."

"Okay." After composing herself, she began. "Charlene is so competent, she's the only person I've had to hire. She has an art degree and one day, when she has enough money for a down payment, she'll open her own gallery. There isn't anything she doesn't know about the business."

Janel must have realized she'd just provided Cole with a motive for Charlene to steal, because she rushed to add, "I've known no one who is more trustworthy or more reliable. Charlene handles large money transactions, private information and valuable merchandise. And I've never had an issue with her. Not once."

Zach's mind raced over the possibilities. He knew one thing for sure: if Charlene was innocent, suspicion would fall on Janel. "Could anyone else have gained access to your alarm code?"

"Todd," Karla answered for her sister. "Did you change your code after you two split?"

"No, but he wouldn't steal from me, either."

Karla sent her an I'm-not-so-sure-about-that look. "He wasn't who you thought he was, and I saw you enter your code without hiding it from him."

Janel held her head in her hands before releasing a long, slow breath. "You're saying the burglary, the murderer chasing me in the forest and the car bomb are most likely connected. Todd called me two weeks ago, trying to get back together. A man who claims to have feelings for you doesn't steal your mother's paintings and then try to kill you."

Her ex called her? Zach felt an ache in the pit of his stomach as his own past reared its ugly head. A few years before he met Janel, he dated a woman who had recently broken up with her boyfriend. Everything went well for six joyful months. He was beginning to think they had a future together when she dumped him to go back to her ex. She'd failed to mention that this other man had been calling her, promising to be faithful.

Zach had learned a valuable lesson: don't date anyone coming out of a long relationship, especially not a woman still communicating with her ex when he's trying to win her back.

He forced his mind off the past and pictured Janel's gallery. He'd been there several times. "How long have you had your security system?"

"About ten months. Our father paid to have the system upgraded after Karla told us about the string of burglaries."

"Did you select your code or use one the security company gave you?" Zach asked.

"I chose it, but the technician who installed the system walked me through the steps."

Karla leaned closer. "Did he watch you enter it, or did he step away?"

"I don't know." Janel pressed fingers against her temple. Her headache must have returned. After a few seconds, she dropped her hand and locked gazes with Zach. "I paid this company to protect my inventory. One-of-a-kind art. It never dawned on me they might steal from me."

He worried this discussion might be too much for her. The stress could delay her recovery, and he cared for her too much to see that happen. "We don't know that they had anything to do with the burglary."

Cole's cell phone rang, and he left the kitchen to take the call.

While he was gone, Zach asked if her code might be easy to figure out—like her birthday.

"No. The security panel has numbers and letters, so I used our mother's childhood nickname. She never shared it with anyone but us." Janel gestured toward her sister. "And of course, I told… Charlene!" Her eyes widened. "What time is it?"

Zach checked his cell phone. "A quarter to nine. Why?"

"Charlene's on her way to work. It's not safe. That murderer figured out which car belonged to my sister. He probably knows about the gallery—especially if these events are connected. He might be waiting there for me—with a gun."

"Charlene has blond hair like we do," Karla added. "He could mistake her for Janel." She unlocked her smartphone. "What's her cell number? We might be able to reach her before she gets there."

Janel groaned. "You know I don't memorize numbers. They're in my Contacts, and I lost my phone yesterday." She turned to Zach for help. "If he kills her, it will be all my fault. We have to find her and warn her!"

Zach shook his head, stiffening both his back and his resolve. "We're staying here. I will not risk your life."

Chapter Four

"The police should be at the gallery by now." Janel's foot shook with impatience while sitting at the ranch's kitchen table. Zach had called his lieutenant over two minutes ago. "Why didn't I think to close the gallery after the explosion?"

"You have a concussion. Besides, you were dealing with a lot yesterday," Zach reminded her.

"We all were," Karla added. "Now, try not to worry. I'm sure Charlene's fine." Her tone was reassuring, but the concern in her expression belied her words.

"I can't relax. That…murderer blew up your car. He's determined to kill me and may have planted more bombs." She sent a worried glance Zach's way. "I watched a news report last night on Karla's phone. They named my gallery."

"I understand your concern, and I've always admired the way you care for others. It's one of your finest qualities," Zach stated calmly. "As for Charlene, the Sedona Police Department increased their patrols around your gallery last night. No one reported anything out of the ordinary." His phone rang, and he checked the screen. "I'll be right back."

Just because no one saw anything when they drove by her gallery didn't mean there wasn't another bomb. Trepidation churned in her gut. "I can't take this waiting any longer." An idea occurred to her. "Can I use your phone?"

"Why?" Karla held it close. "You can't call the gallery. Charlene might rush inside to answer the phone. If there's a bomb…"

"I wouldn't endanger her like that." The mental image was too much for Janel to handle. She pressed her hand to her now throbbing forehead. "I only want to check the security camera footage. If it's even working. The burglars managed to shut it off when they broke in."

Karla handed her the phone.

After logging into the security website, Janel was relieved to see the inside of the gallery pop up on the screen. Charlene was standing at the glass door, turning the key in the lock. She tugged the door open.

Janel held her breath, her heart thundering in her chest.

Karla squeezed Janel's arm like a vise.

One. Two. Three.

Nothing happened. No explosion. No hidden madman shooting.

Afraid to relax too soon, Janel remained frozen in place.

Charlene punched the security code into the pad hanging on the wall. Meanwhile, her boyfriend, Robert, a tall, good-looking man in his late thirties, turned the Closed sign to Open.

After walking behind the counter, Charlene locked her purse away in a cabinet beneath the cash register as two Sedona police officers rushed into the gallery, glancing about for trouble. They took the assistant manager and her boyfriend totally by surprise. Soon, a sheriff's deputy joined them. Janel wished she could hear what they were saying.

Moments later, when it became obvious Charlene was safe, Janel exhaled, releasing the mountain of stress that had built up inside her. Janel reached for her sister's hand, still gripping her arm. "You can let go now."

Karla rubbed the area she had squeezed. "Did I hurt you?"

"Nah." Fingernails breaking the skin was nothing compared

to the fear of possibly seeing a bomb kill someone close to her, not to mention the destruction of her livelihood.

Zach stepped back into the kitchen. "Everything's fine at the gallery."

"Thank you for sending the police and deputies." Janel held up her sister's phone. "And, as you can see, my cameras are working now. I'm not sure what that means for your brother's investigation into the burglary."

"I'll text him after I tell you some good news you don't already know." Zach's mood was lighter as he slipped back into his seat at the table. "The fugitive's white sedan was found abandoned and burned outside Las Vegas."

"Burned?" Janel lifted a brow.

"To eliminate fingerprints and DNA evidence," Karla supplied.

Zach acknowledged her statement as fact with a nod. "There was enough left of the car to confirm it was the one stolen in Flagstaff yesterday. Unfortunately, we haven't located any video showing the driver's face without the hoodie and sunglasses, so we still can't identify him."

"We could pass each other on the street one day, and I won't know it's him." The phone felt heavy in Janel's hand. This was the first time she'd logged into the security monitoring website since being told about the burglary after her memory loss. She peered into the screen again and noticed the walls where her mother's paintings once hung were now bare. A sense of loss overwhelmed her. She'd only felt that empty one other time. The moment her mother had passed away.

"I'm calling Charlene." She closed the website and located the gallery's number on the phone. When her assistant manager answered, Janel blurted, "I was so worried about you."

"I'm not the one who was almost blown up yesterday! Are *you* safe?" Charlene's heightened sense of alarm was evident in her voice. "I tried to reach you several times, but my calls went straight to voicemail."

"I'm fine. Karla and I are staying at Walker Ranch."

Zach cringed, and Janel realized too late she probably wasn't supposed to reveal her whereabouts. Too late now. "I lost my phone. You'll need to call my sister to reach me." Janel touched the screen. "I'm placing this call on speaker. Karla and Zach, the deputy looking out for us, are in the room with me. It turns out the guy who tried to kill us is hiding in Las Vegas, but I think it would be wise to shut the gallery for a few days, just in case." It was the safest decision for everyone.

Karla shook her head at the same time Charlene rejected the idea. "We can't afford to close the doors. Besides, my boyfriend took the next week off to act as my bodyguard. And since it doesn't sound like we need one now, he can chip in and help. We've had a steady stream of customers since your story hit the news. Some are townies wishing you their best, others are tourists or reporters hoping to overhear private information. At least most are buying postcards, small prints or bookmarks."

"That's wonderful. I think." Janel winced as she touched the sore spot on her forehead. After being chased by a murderer twice, she had a hard time believing he was gone for good. The lives of every person who entered her gallery were her responsibility. "Please thank your boyfriend. I feel better knowing he can act as security if it becomes necessary." Robert had served in the military and carried a concealed weapons permit for his gun. He was levelheaded and polite.

"I'll go to the gallery to help," Karla offered. "I just need a ride."

"That can be arranged." After checking to see if anyone else wanted a refill, Zach topped off his mug.

Janel told Charlene, "Karla will head to the gallery to help you. I have to go now, but stay safe. If anything happens, call the police."

After she disconnected, Zach said, "Cole wants directions to Todd's cousin's RV. According to Todd's neighbor, he's spending a few days there."

"I can't tell him where to find the RV, but I can show him."

"Out of the question." Still holding his coffee mug, Zach stepped to the table and towered over them. "We don't know if your ex hired the murderer to break into your gallery."

Janel rolled her eyes. "I sincerely doubt he knows anyone dangerous."

"You can't be sure of that," Karla countered. "Maybe his new girlfriend has connections to the underbelly of society."

Janel stifled a chuckle. "Do you hear yourself?"

"It's not funny when it could be true," Karla shot back.

"You're talking about Todd. Besides, they broke up. He told me so when he called."

"He claims they broke up. Don't forget, he lied and cheated. Now, let's address the matter at hand." Karla gestured to Zach. "Can you give him directions on how to get to this RV?"

"I don't think turn left at the burger joint and right at the wooden bear statue is going to help, and that's all I've got." She shrugged, knowing it wasn't what anyone wanted to hear. "The RV park is on private property, and I don't remember his cousin's name. Zach, it would be best if you drove me, and Cole followed. I could point to the RV. Todd doesn't own a gun, and the murderer is probably still in Vegas."

"We can't count on that, but as long as we don't stop and get out of the car, your idea works for me. You'll have the both of us protecting you." Zach reached for his phone. "I'll call Cole."

Ten minutes later, Zach's sister, Lily, was driving Karla to the gallery while Janel stepped into the ranch house's open garage. The feeling that she should duck hadn't left her yet. How long would it take for her to feel normal again? With the murderer's identity still hidden, would she always be afraid of strange men walking up to her?

A dark cloud hovered over her both figuratively and literally, with another storm approaching. Janel climbed into the passenger seat of Zach's SUV and pulled her long sweater over her jean-clad knees. He had offered her a coat to wear, but they were only going for a drive in a heated vehicle. No need for anything bulky.

When they approached the gate, several quarter horses stood next to the white picket fence as if greeting them. She waved, and a smile tugged at Zach's lips. If he wanted to think she was silly, that was okay with her.

She settled into her seat, preparing for the long drive. After twenty minutes of meaningless small talk, Janel finally shared, "I still don't remember the gallery burglary, but when I was on the security website this morning and saw my mother's paintings were missing from the walls, I almost broke down crying."

"No one would blame you if you did." His understanding sliced off a sliver of her emotional pain, but there was still so much left behind.

She had been worried about losing the paintings to the bank and was fighting to make sure it wouldn't happen. Now they were gone—stolen.

"I've lost so much. My mother, her paintings and maybe next, the gallery. Time and time again I've prayed, but nothing I try helps. I feel like God has abandoned me."

Zach took his eyes off the road long enough to look her way. "God hasn't abandoned you. New, wonderful beginnings can spring from terrible circumstances. I've witnessed it many times. I promise, He has a plan for you."

"I hope you're right." Janel admired the confidence Zach exuded. Confidence she never had. "Is becoming a deputy sheriff your new beginning? The last I heard, you were in charge of your family's ranch and heading search and rescue missions."

"If you remember, we had a shoot-out and bombing at the ranch. The sheriff took notice of how I helped in those situations." Zach's smile warmed her heart. "That, along with finding a lost hiker last spring, led to a call from the sheriff. He asked if I would be interested in becoming a member of the Mounted Fugitive Retrieval Team on either a full or volunteer basis—my choice."

"I remember hearing Cole and Sierra had dated, broke up, then reunited when he saved her from a crazed bomber." She studied the sharp lines on Zach's handsome face. They'd been friends for so long, she hadn't considered how easy it would have been to fall for him if she hadn't been dating Todd. And now that she wasn't dating her ex, she didn't trust her instincts. Was Zach as good a man as she thought, or was he only showing the best side of his personality at church functions?

Her mind returned to the danger she'd faced the day before. "I'm glad you took the sheriff up on his offer. I can't imagine going through this with a total stranger."

"I admit I would have tried to trade places with anyone else assigned to protect you." After a brief pause, he added, "Breaking in a new cochair for the fall festival would be difficult work." His chuckle became contagious.

Soon she was laughing. "You can't just take a compliment, can you?"

"I guess not." He gestured toward the road. "Am I turning anywhere soon?"

"Take the next right onto the dirt road. The street sign has been missing for years."

"How many times have you been out here?"

"Three or four, for day trips. Todd likes to fish. I don't, so I would read a book in an Adirondack chair while he went out on the pond in a boat." Another example of how she and Todd had nothing in common. Why hadn't she recognized how incompatible they were? She snuck a peek at Zach and felt an emotional tug. Would she always question her judgment where men were concerned?

He steered around a corner. "Now where?"

"Continue down this road." The pine trees reminded her of the fear she'd felt the day before in another part of the forest, many miles away.

They headed closer to the hills, and she hoped she wouldn't

see Todd. Ever. With the Lord's help, she would forgive him one day, but it would take time.

Minutes later, they curved their way around to a panoramic view of storm clouds heading toward the large pond the locals referred to as a lake. Recent rains and melted snow had filled in the water lost during their long, hot summer.

"I can see how hard it would be to find this place if you didn't know about it, especially with a missing street sign." Zach checked his rearview mirror.

Janel glanced at her side-view mirror and only saw Cole following them. "After you enter the park, drive toward the pond, but go slow enough for me to hunt for the armadillo."

"An armadillo?"

"Not a real one." She rolled her eyes, and he chuckled again. But the gravity of the situation soon returned. She was here to point the way for Cole. He was going to ask her ex questions that would make it obvious that he was a suspect in her burglary. Would he be angry with her? Should she care? What if he was involved?

She had been so busy defending Todd she never took the time to consider the possibility that he was involved in her burglary. A mutual friend had told Janel that he was late with his last mortgage payment after dating a woman who was high maintenance. Was he feeling the crunch financially? There were so many things about him, both past and present, that she didn't know.

"You all right?"

Zach's voice caught her attention.

"There!" She pointed to the ceramic armadillo sitting out front of a blue RV. "Turn right, then drive slowly down the road."

Cole called and Zach answered, "I'm handing you to Janel."

She nervously gripped the cell phone in her hand while she scanned the area for Todd. "We're almost there." The SUV rolled closer and closer. "It's the one with the burgundy trim on the left."

"Thanks," Cole said. "Now, you two get out of here before your ex sees you."

Zach navigated back to the road they came in on, and Janel tried to relax, but something didn't feel right. After rounding the first hill, she heard a loud pop and jerked around in her seat.

A huge spiderweb of cracked glass stretched out from a bullet hole.

Feeling her eyes grow wide, she yelled, "Someone shot at us!"

"Get down!" Zach pressed on the gas. Several glances in the rearview mirror confirmed his suspicion. They had a second assailant. This one on a hill, shooting his high-powered rifle from a kneeling position like a hunter. He was much larger than the fugitive they had encountered yesterday. Instead of a black hoodie, he wore aviator sunglasses and a camouflage jacket.

"But he was just in Las Vegas! He came back already?" Janel had slipped down in the passenger seat but kept stretching to see her side-view mirror.

"He has an accomplice." Before speeding into the next curve in the road, Zach caught sight of the shooter, pulling a helmet over light brown hair, then pushing his ride out from behind a bush and climbing on. "This one's driving a motorcycle down the hill."

"Oh, great!" Janel cried out. "How are we going to lose a shooter on two wheels?"

"We're not." His SUV had over a hundred thousand miles on the odometer. This wasn't the time to see if it could hold its own in a race. It also wasn't the time for a gunfight. Janel might get caught in the crossfire.

As they rounded the hill, he surveyed the landscape for a quick escape. Not a single side road yet, but that might work to their advantage. A side road would be too obvious.

"Over there!" Janel pointed to an area where the tree line thickened on the far side of a meadow. "Can we hide behind the trees?" The wide stretch of gravel leading up to the grass would allow them to drive off the road without leaving an obvious trail.

"Hang on!" He swerved to the right, gripping the steering wheel tightly as they bounced over uneven terrain. A *vroom* in the distance warned that the motorcycle would round the hill at any second and the driver would have a clear view of their position.

Zach's cell phone rang, and he connected it through the SUV's onboard screen with a single touch.

"I heard a gunshot," Cole yelled.

"Rifle shot! We're being chased by a shooter, wearing camouflage and driving a motorcycle. We went off-road where the forest thickens after the hills."

"I'm heading that way now."

"Call it in." Their connection ended, and Zach pressed harder on the gas while Janel gripped the center console with one hand and the SUV's grab handle with the other. He drove between two tree trunks and made a sharp left to avoid hitting an overgrown bush that had lost its leaves with the cold temperatures. They continued to weave around nature's obstacles, unable to find the perfect place to stop.

"The storm is getting closer." Janel's voice was difficult, but not impossible, to hear over the SUV's roaring engine.

Swerving around a boulder, he noticed the dark clouds. They were floating toward the nearby hills. The last thing they needed was to get stuck in a downpour.

A flash in the forest behind them, possibly sunlight reflecting off the motorcycle, sent Zach's pulse skyrocketing.

Locating a clear path to a copse of evergreens, he floored the gas pedal, climbing the mound to reach a potential hiding spot.

The SUV sped faster and faster.

At the top, he tried to circle around the bushes but couldn't.

The other side of the mound turned out to be a cliff, where floodwater rushed down a creek roughly fifteen feet below them.

Zach slammed on the brakes, but not soon enough.

They skidded over the side.

And dropped.

Janel screamed, and Zach's stomach leaped into his chest.

They landed with a jolt, and water splashed high into the air.

"You okay?" He spared a quick glance in her direction.

Wide-eyed, she nodded.

The SUV turned ninety degrees as they began to float downstream. Last night's rains had made the creek too deep to wade across.

"Water's coming in through the door!" Janel urgently lifted her boots off the floorboard.

Sirens screamed through the forest. Help was coming, but they weren't close enough.

They couldn't sit here a second longer.

"We have to get out," Zach yelled to be heard above the sound of water and debris crashing into the SUV.

She unbuckled her seat belt, then unlocked her door with a click of the power button. She pushed on the handle and then with her shoulder. "It won't open!"

"Come out on my side," he instructed and lowered his window. "There's an undertow, so stick close to me."

"Should we crawl onto the roof?" She shifted closer to the middle console, and a bullet blasted out the passenger window where she had just sat.

Chapter Five

"He's going to kill us!" Janel scrambled over the SUV's center console as Zach crawled out through his window. Waiting for him to clear the threshold so that she could follow sent her thumping heart into overdrive. "Hurry!"

A second bullet fired with a bang and shattered the back passenger window. Fear reverberated down her spine.

Zach reached inside, grabbed her upper arms and pulled her out into the chest-high raging waters. She gripped his broad shoulders as the frigid temperature assaulted her senses, and the undertow kept her boots from gaining purchase on the rocks below. The ping of another bullet made her shudder.

Using the SUV's door as a shield, they each took hold of the window frame to keep from being swept away. Janel leaned toward the closed back seat window, daring a quick glance at the shooter. He sat on his motorcycle up on the cliff, ready to take aim.

She panicked and ducked.

Water hit her face.

A bullet whizzed over the SUV, inches from where she'd been seconds ago.

He must have seen her.

The helmet and sunglasses he wore had kept her from getting a good look at his face. An empty rifle case hung loose over his shoulder, answering the question of how he'd managed to carry the weapon while driving his motorcycle.

Releasing her grip on the SUV with one hand, she wiped her face while kicking her feet to stay in place.

Last night's rainwater that had flooded the banks of the creek ripped apart the shrubbery and sent it sailing downstream. Zach batted away branches threatening to smack against them. Leaves clung to Janel's arm as she reached for the car again.

The SUV groaned and shifted position as it tilted with the weight of the water, filling it up like a fish tank. Her teeth chattered from the cold. They couldn't stay here long, but venturing out into the open would make them easy targets. A sense of hopelessness weighed down on her.

Zach gestured toward a sharp bend in the creek about twenty-five feet away.

She studied the area where the water turned away from the cliffs, which were a series of rock faces, some with enormous gaps between them. The shooter couldn't follow them easily on the motorcycle if they moved downstream. He'd have to backtrack into the forest, travel in a parallel direction and then find another path to the creek. That would give them time to escape.

Zach leaned close enough for her to hear him ask, "Can you swim?"

She nodded, despite knowing the feat might be too much for her. The current was strong, but they couldn't stay here, freezing and treading water, hoping help would find them in time. The SUV was unstable. If it dropped below the waterline, they would have nothing to hide behind. "How do we get there without him killing us?"

"When I start shooting, you swim as fast as you can. After you turn the corner, find a spot where he can't see you and get out on your right side. I'll catch up with you." Zach pulled his gun from a shoulder holster.

Could he swim and fire his weapon at the same time? An image of him fatally wounded and drowning flashed through her mind. Terror struck her. "Don't die on me, Zach Walker!"

He looked her in the eyes and promised, "I won't."

Did he really believe he would live? She tried to read his face, but he turned and held his gun above the SUV's roofline.

"Wait!" The drenched sweater she wore over the shirt she'd borrowed was too heavy to swim in. She slipped it off her shoulders and pushed it inside the SUV through the open window. "Ready."

With the sound of his first shot, she jerked into action. She pushed away from the sinking vehicle with her feet and swam through the murky water, summoning every ounce of energy she could muster. More than once, she shoved floating branches away from her face and felt the sting of their scratches.

A bullet whizzed overhead, and Zach fired back two shots.

She pushed aside her trepidation and swam hard. *Don't look back.*

Knowing she was out in the open with a gunfight taking place over her shoulder, she wanted to duck but knew she'd see nothing below the surface. Instead, she kicked faster and worked her arms harder. *God, please save us.*

After she turned the corner, she let the swift flowing water carry her another thirty feet. She could no longer see the shooter on the cliff, which hopefully meant he couldn't see her, either. Her mission now was to find clear access to dry land. When the flooded shrubbery reaching up out of the water thinned, she stopped floating and fought against the current to swim ashore. More gunfire rang out in the distance.

She crawled up onto the bank, her breathing rapid and shallow. After shifting into a sitting position, she wiped the dead grass and dirt off her hands, then pushed wet hair away from her eyes and listened. The seconds between shots lengthened. Her fear for Zach was overwhelming.

Janel could hear multiple police cruisers now but couldn't see them.

With the roar of the raging waters and high-pitched sirens filling her ears, she barely detected the motorcycle's engine as it came alive and took off. Surveying the scenery, she spied Zach swimming down the creek, less than twenty feet away. *He's alive.*

"Over here!" Janel jumped to her feet and waved both arms until he spotted her. When he was close, she grabbed his soaking wet coat and tried to help him up out of the water. It soon became clear he had the situation under control, so she stood back and watched this tower of strength rise out of the creek. He was here, with her, and they were safe.

Dripping wet, he took her hand. "We need to find cover in case he comes back."

With those words, her brief solace disappeared. They weren't out of danger like she'd thought.

They rushed toward an enormous tree and hid behind its wide trunk. Freezing from head to toe, Janel slumped to the ground and curled up in a ball, wishing she were invisible.

Zach remained standing, scanning their surroundings. Seconds later, the sirens traveled in a new direction. "Looks like the deputies spotted him."

"I hope so." Her aching legs cramped. She stretched them out, but when the wind swept over her wet clothing, she shuddered and curled up again. The tree's rough bark scratched her back. "Do you think he's gone for good?"

"Maybe for the moment, but we still need to be on high alert."

If these men weren't arrested soon, she'd always wonder when they would show up to finish the job. Would they ring her doorbell at home first? Walk into the gallery with a gun? Approach her on the street with a knife? "You said this shooter wasn't the fugitive you were chasing near Flagstaff. The one who tried to kill me and blew up Karla's car."

"That's right. This guy is much bigger." Lines furrowed in Zach's forehead as he looked down at her from where he stood, leaning against the tree and keeping an eye out for the shooter.

"Do you think your fugitive, the murderer, came back from Vegas? Assuming he's the one who burned the stolen car there. Could he be here, too?" Her teeth clenched as she tried to rub the chill off her arms. The long-sleeved shirt she wore was still wet, and the outside temperature kept dropping. "Don't sugar-coat anything for my sake. I want to know what I'm up against."

"Okay. I promise to always tell you the truth. Yes, it is a possibility. If he's smart, he'll stay away, but he could be out there, looking for us. All we can do this second is remain vigilant."

"And pray we're rescued before someone shoots us." She shuddered from both the cold and the all-too-familiar feelings of fear haunting her. While staring out into the forest, searching for danger, she jumped at every shadow flickering in the wind.

Minutes later, her vision turned hazy, and a memory returned.

Her mind floated back to yesterday morning—before she was running for her life. Although the sky was bright then, her mood was dark. She drove her metallic blue hatchback slowly through a neighborhood she didn't recognize. Keeping her eyes trained on two men down the street, she kept her distance, afraid to be caught...

Zach watched the waves of the splashing floodwater dip and roll like a roller coaster as it raced down the creek. Sirens that signaled the pursuit of the shooter had faded away. An encouraging sign. The chase was nowhere near them.

Still standing behind the tree, he inhaled the aroma of pine while studying the dense landscape around them. Not seeing anything out of the ordinary, he checked on Janel, who sat on the ground beside his legs. The dazed expression on her face frightened him. His first thought was the frigid waters had aggravated her concussion. He crouched and placed his hand on her shoulder. "Janel, can you hear me?"

She jerked and looked up at him with dull, clouded eyes. "I remembered something."

That would explain the shocked appearance. Concerned about her emotional well-being, he sat and took her hand in his. "Do you want to tell me?"

After a quiet moment, she drew in a deep breath. "Yesterday morning, at least an hour before you found me in the forest, I sat in my car and watched two men in an old truck pulling a trailer filled with tree branches. I stayed far back at the street corner, where they were less likely to notice me."

"Why? Do you know them?"

She shook her head. "No. I don't even know why I was watching them."

"What did you see?" He noticed her hand was feeling warmer and color was slowly returning to her face. Talking appeared to be helping.

"The driver parked along the curb in front of a Victorian house, then he and another man climbed out of the truck."

Zach raised his brows. The shooting took place behind a Victorian. "What did these men look like?"

"The driver had red hair. He was lanky and wore jeans and a long-sleeved shirt with a logo. I got the impression that he was in his late twenties, maybe early thirties. The other man wore black jeans and a..." Her gaze locked on Zach's. "A black hoodie that covered most of his face. He's the man who chased after me."

"A redheaded landscaper was shot and killed near the forest where I found you. He had a trailer attached to his white truck."

"The truck I remember was white." She shuddered, most likely from the cold, but possibly from anxiety, as well. "We thought I might have witnessed the murder, but it didn't feel real until now."

"This could be the traumatic event preventing you from

recalling most of the past two days. Only…" He struggled to make sense of what he knew.

"Only what?"

"The shooting happened in the backyard, not the front. Did you park and follow these men?"

"I don't know. Maybe." She nervously bit her lip. "I'm not sure I can handle remembering a murder. I've never seen anyone die before. My mother passed away quietly during the middle of the night when Karla and I were both sleeping."

Zach cradled her chin with the palm of his hand, wanting her to trust that he was here for her. "You're stronger than you think. I've seen that truth many times already."

"Even if you're right, with two shooters wanting me dead, I'll need a strength greater than mine."

He squeezed her hand, knowing she meant God. "He'll see you through this, and so will I."

She placed her other hand on top of his. "Thank you. Thank you for being you and being here for me." After a brief pause, she looked up at him. "Zach, how did this shooter know we would be on this road?"

"That's a good question. Your ex would have known if his neighbor called him after talking to Cole, or Karla might have said something to Charlene while helping at the gallery."

Janel shook her head. "Considering the circumstances, I'm willing to consider the possibility that Todd might be involved in the burglary. He could have hired these shooters—but not Charlene. She wouldn't do this to me. To anyone."

The unexpected sound of an engine made them both jump to their feet.

Gun in hand, Zach spied around the tree trunk but couldn't see any vehicles. "Stay here. I'll check it out."

He could tell she wanted to protest, but she relented and nodded her understanding. When he left her, she was leaning against the tree, rubbing her arms. Their clothes were still damp, and the chill was bone deep.

Cautiously traveling along the grassy bank, Zach scanned his surroundings for the source of the engine noise. Near the bend, he spotted Cole and a deputy carrying a boat down the cliff on the opposite side of the creek. He wished there was a bridge, but rowing a boat was better than swimming.

Waving to his brother, Zach noticed the storm clouds were drifting even closer. He ran to Janel and grabbed her hand. "It's time to go home."

"Home…" Relief flickered over her face for a brief second. They both knew she would return to the ranch, not to her own house.

By the time they turned the bend in the creek again, Cole and the deputy were lowering the boat where the water appeared less treacherous and then took turns climbing inside. Zach placed his arm around Janel's damp back as they waited impatiently.

While the muscular deputy helped row, Cole barked orders each time the current took control and turned the boat downstream instead of across. Water splashed everywhere.

Once the boat reached them, Cole jumped out and Zach helped pull it up to the bank.

"It's about time you got here." Zach slapped his brother on the back.

"I've been a little busy." Cole smiled, then turned to Janel. "Ready?"

"As ready as I'll ever be." She waited for Zach to climb inside and reach for her hand. "Did I mention I'm not a boat person?"

"No worries. I've got you." He guided her to the middle seat.

Janel cringed as they rocked. "Now I remember why I don't fish."

"You're doing just fine." Zach sat protectively close to her while Cole pushed the boat back into the turbulent waters, then jumped inside.

They rocked furiously, and Janel grabbed hold of Zach's arm. He had to admit, if only to himself, he didn't mind.

Out in the open, away from the canopy of trees, the winds ushered in the storm. He clamped his teeth shut to keep them from chattering. Janel shivered. They both needed to change into dry clothes as soon as possible.

Lightning lit up the sky and thunder clapped thirty seconds later, which meant the rain was maybe six miles away. Zach kept a nervous eye on their surroundings. The water rushing around them picked up speed. The nearby storm dumped more rain into the creek. They needed to reach land before a flash flood drowned them all.

Chapter Six

"Faster!" Zach used his hand to help row the boat through the frigid water. They worked hard to reach the opposite bank before the rising floodwaters had a chance to swallow every inch of flat, dry land, leaving them no place to run ashore. His lieutenant emerged from the path that led up the side of the cliff. He rushed to the water's edge and grabbed the boat's bow, allowing the deputy to disembark.

The two sheriff's officers fought against the fierce current to steady the boat while Zach climbed out, taking care not to send Janel flying overboard. With Cole's guidance, she shuffled up to the front.

When she reached out to him, Zach placed his hands on her waist and lifted her high into the air with ease before setting her down on the grass, away from the water's edge.

"This way." Lieutenant Yeager led them to the path while the deputy dealt with the boat.

Zach took one last look at his sinking SUV. The water had reached the top of the windows and was splashing over the roof.

"We'll fish her out for you." Lieutenant Yeager stopped walking long enough to emphasize a point. "Cars come and go. The important thing is you two are alive, an amazing feat when you think about it. You evaded a motorcycle in a forest while driving an SUV."

"He's right," Janel said, smiling up at him. With her deep blue eyes, cheeks pink from the cold and strands of damp hair framing her heart-shaped face, she looked like a porcelain doll. "You saved my life—again."

Zach stared back at her in awe. By the grace of God, she had summoned the courage and strength needed to survive the harsh elements while still suffering from a concussion. "You swam like an Olympian."

A blush rose from her neck.

"Let's get going," the lieutenant said, yanking them out of the moment. "You two must be freezing."

After the brief climb, Yeager removed two emergency blankets from his official vehicle.

"Thank you." Janel wrapped the heat-reflective plastic sheeting over her shoulders and hugged it tightly to ward off the cold.

"Any update on this new shooter?" Zach asked his supervisor, while wishing he had warm clothes to offer Janel.

"We're bringing in a drone to assist in our search." Yeager scratched his bearded chin. "Did you get a good look at him?"

"Just enough to see he's bigger than the murderer who wore the black hoodie and had an average build. This guy is taller, looks like a football player, has light brown hair, wears aviator sunglasses, along with a camouflage jacket, and drives a black motorcycle."

"Cole passed on the information about his clothing." The lieutenant, a friend since the first search and rescue they worked together, walked a few yards away from Janel and waited for Zach to join him. "The background checks you asked for on the gallery's assistant manager and her boyfriend came back clean. No priors for either of them. Robert Matthews received an honorable discharge from the army ten years ago. Since then, he's been working in real estate."

Army? Zach lifted a brow. "Any special weapons training?"

"Only the usual. There's nothing in the report to suggest he's one of our guys."

"Ja... Miss Newman will be glad to hear her assistant manager's boyfriend doesn't have a wanted poster." Zach hoped his slip of the tongue, almost calling Janel by her first name, wouldn't prompt Yeager to ask how well he knew her. If he thought Zach was too close of a friend to remain objective, he might reassign a different deputy to safeguard her.

With nothing else to discuss, they rejoined the others in time to hear Cole telling Janel, "Your former boyfriend hasn't been to the RV park in months."

Confusion flickered through her expression. "Didn't you say he was planning to spend a few days there?"

"That's what his next-door neighbor told us."

"She would know." Janel pushed aside the strands of hair that fell in her face. "There's only one neighbor Todd talks to, and she watches his cat when he's away. He loves his tabby like a child and wants to be reached in case of an emergency."

Zach wondered if the neighbor alerted Todd to the fact the police were asking questions. "Janel, did you get a look at the guy shooting at us today?"

"Not a good one, but I know it wasn't Todd."

"Let's pick your sister up on our way to the ranch." Zach hated to interfere with her business, especially when he knew it was on shaky ground already, but safety came first. "You need to convince Charlene and Karla that their lives may depend on closing the gallery until we lock up these shooters."

"It's for the best," Lieutenant Yeager confirmed before turning to Zach. "Your phone is drenched, isn't it?"

"I'm afraid so." He noticed the dismay registering on Janel's face and wished he could make this all go away for her. She should be able to focus on her business instead of running from gunmen.

Yeager sent a text message before announcing, "A deputy will deliver a temporary phone and vehicle to the ranch."

"Thanks." Zach caught the scent of rain in the air and felt a drop land on his cheek.

"I have the heater turned on high," Cole called out, waving them over to his SUV.

"You don't have to tell me twice." The thought of warmer temperatures put a spring into his step as he escorted Janel to the vehicle.

Once inside, raindrops sprinkled the windshield, and the SUV's air vents blasted Zach's body with a powerful wave of welcoming heat. His skin tingled as the chill faded away. "Warming up back there?"

"Yes. Thank you." The stressors of the day made Janel's voice sound shaky.

They drove to her gallery and found only one parking space available. As soon as the car stopped, she jumped out, leaving the blanket behind, and ran for the glass door. The deputy sitting in the sheriff's vehicle gave a nod when Zach stepped out of the SUV. He returned the greeting.

Tugging the door open, Zach found Karla hugging Janel. Half a dozen customers cast quizzical glances their way, obviously noting their disheveled appearances. A gray-haired couple stopped flipping through the box of matted prints and spoke to one another in low voices, then left. A middle-aged woman finished paying for her purchase, then stepped outside with a man who carried shopping bags.

With the gallery appearing to be safe, Zach took notice of the missing art. When he was there to drop off fall festival materials, he had admired her mother's work. At least twenty Southwestern-themed paintings hung on the walls around the empty spots where the stolen paintings had once been the major attraction. White pedestals of various sizes now held colorful cowboy statues made of resin. They were nice, but nothing compared to the bronze VanZandts that were once displayed in the center of the room.

A tall, clean-cut man glanced at the badge clipped to Zach's belt and stepped forward to offer his hand. "Deputy, I'm Robert Matthews. I volunteered to keep an eye on the place while Janel is having…issues."

They shook hands, and Zach took notice of the man's firm grip, along with his dark blue suit and spicy cologne. "So, Mr. Matthews, you're Charlene's boyfriend."

"Please, call me Robert."

Zach nodded and turned to the petite young woman behind the counter. "Miss Owens, we spoke over the phone yesterday."

Charlene's expression switched from pleasant to troubled. "I wish it had been under better circumstances."

Cole entered, and the appearance of a uniformed law enforcement officer was enough to send the straggling customers out the door. He changed the sign from Open to Closed, and Charlene raised her brows.

Janel hurriedly told everyone what had happened. "With a second shooter to worry about, Karla and I need to go back to Walker Ranch, and…we have to close the gallery."

"No!" Charlene blurted, but then seemed to realize the seriousness of the situation. "Can we at least fulfill our online orders? A dozen came in this morning. Your friends, other gallery owners and collectors around the state, are doing what they can to help, namely buying artwork."

A long pause hung in the air, and Zach offered his opinion. "If you take what you need home with you, there shouldn't be a problem."

Charlene looked hesitant before asking Janel, "Are you okay with me taking paintings and supplies home before I mail them?"

"Of course." Janel's tone held no doubt. "If this gallery is going to survive, we need to work together."

"I'll help." Robert grabbed a roll of tape from a bottom drawer, then Charlene told him where to find the other mailing supplies. Together, they gathered what they needed to complete the orders.

Zach held the front door open while Robert carried a load out to his green Mercedes-Benz. Karla wrapped paintings for transport, and Cole handed them to Charlene's boyfriend when he returned.

Janel stared up at the blank spaces on the wall, and Zach's heart ached for her. He left the door to stand with her.

The last flicker of light dimmed in her eyes. "Seeing my mother's paintings gone is…heartbreaking."

"I'm here for you," Zach said. "No matter what you face." Remembering his ex, he added, "That's what friends are for."

She sent him a gentle smile.

He wanted to kick himself for adding the "friends" part. *Friends.* At this moment, it was Zach's least favorite word. He found it strange that he could risk his life tracking down and confronting murderers, but was unwilling to risk his heart on a rebound relationship.

Janel's eyes soon clouded over as she sat there, staring at the wall for what seemed like an eternity, but was maybe five minutes. She suddenly shook her head as if coming out of a daze. "I just remembered going to the bank yesterday." She glanced at her sister, who stepped closer. "I had to tell the loan officer about the burglary. Putting it off would only make me feel worse."

Karla nodded. "I get it."

Janel breathed in deeply, then exhaled. "I remember crying at the loan officer's desk. She was sympathetic and gave me a box of tissues, but I felt like a blubbering fool."

"About that…" Karla's gaze traveled between Zach, Cole and Janel. Charlene and her boyfriend were working in the back room. "My friend from work called. Frank Hyde, the investigator assigned to your claim, knows about your meeting with the bank and how you used the paintings as collateral to secure the loan."

"I wasn't hiding anything," Janel stated defensively. "I did the responsible thing. My loan papers said they could take the paintings if I defaulted on the loan. Since I no longer had possession of them, I needed to let them know I would turn over any insurance money I receive for the paintings. There was something to that effect in the loan papers. And if it isn't enough to cover what I owe, they'll put a lien on the gallery."

Karla placed a hand on her sister's shoulder. "We know you aren't hiding anything."

"Then what's the problem? Why are you looking at me like a two-year-old who spilled her milk on purpose?"

"I didn't mean to." Karla sighed. "Hyde already thought the burglary was an inside job because your security code was used to turn off the alarm. Once he heard you went to the bank right away, he immediately suspected insurance fraud. He thinks you stole the paintings so you would never lose them."

Janel's jaw dropped. "I…"

Charlene stood near the back door, her hands planted on her hips. "No one in their right mind could possibly believe you had anything to do with the burglary."

"He doesn't know Janel the way we do," Karla calmly explained.

"If I stole from my gallery, why are two men trying to kill me?" Janel asked, her tone incredulous.

Zach had his own theory. "Hyde might think you hired them to steal the paintings for you so the bank couldn't take them, and then you refused to pay for their services. They don't want the artwork. They want their money—or your dead body."

Janel's dizziness began to fade now that she'd showered off the grime from the floodwaters and eaten a few bites of Mrs. Walker's delicious stew. The warm bowl felt good in her hands.

Their small group had gathered at the dining room table. Karla sat next to her while Zach and his sister, Lily, occupied the seats across from them. Mr. and Mrs. Walker had already eaten and were attending to chores, while Cole had returned home to his wife. They had a house on the far end of the property.

An open laptop near Zach displayed security footage of the ranch. The largest box on the screen rotated through each camera every five seconds, giving you one expanded, in-depth view at a time. Seven smaller boxes showed partial coverage of what the remaining cameras filmed.

The view of the horses playing and exploring beneath a magnificent sunset provided a much-needed sense of calm to Janel's turbulent day. She sipped from the water glass, then placed it down next to her bowl. "Lily, thank you again for picking up clothes for us, especially the extra pair of boots. It will take at least a day for my other pair to dry."

"No thanks needed. It was a team effort." In her early thirties, the youngest Walker sibling, with her golden locks, high cheekbones and keen marksmanship skills, was a cross between a cheerleader and a Wild West gunslinger. "Once Jackson and his team determined your house was safe to enter, I just needed to grab Karla's bag and pack one for you, using the list your sister made for me."

"Where *is* Jackson?" Karla asked. "He's done so much to help, and I haven't even met him yet."

"You will." Amusement danced in Lily's eyes. "He drops by the house at least once a day for Mom's cookies. Since finding out they're expecting their first child, his wife, Bailey, is determined to improve their health by turning their pantry into a sugar-free zone."

"A baby. That's wonderful." Janel's smile faded when she remembered Jackson had also built a house on the property. "We shouldn't be here. It's dangerous for Bailey."

"She's staying in town with her best friend for the next few days." Lily reached for a biscuit. "With Jackson working all over Northern Arizona, she doesn't mind. It's like having an extended slumber party."

Guilt gnawed at Janel. "We need to find these shooters so your lives can go back to normal."

It would help if she could remember more about the past few days. She had to be certain that the insurance investigator's suspicions about her were wrong; she didn't hire burglars now seeking revenge. The brief memory of crying at the bank proved she was innocent. Didn't it? Frank Hyde would probably say she was acting. Everything in her insisted he was wrong. But...what if he was right?

Sales had continued to drop at her gallery no matter what she did to bring in more customers. It was only a matter of time before she would default on the loan and lose their mother's legacy. She had been so tired from the doubts, fears and loss of sleep that she was dragging herself into work every day. Could she have become desperate enough to search for someone who would involve themselves in a burglary-for-hire scheme? She pictured herself hanging out in seedy bars, sizing up the men who entered.

No.

Maybe...

I've always tried to follow the scriptures. Could I have strayed?

Dogs barking caught their attention. A cacophony of disturbing pops and crackles mixed with high-pitched horse neighs, followed by the sound of pounding hooves, forced Janel to her feet. "What is that?"

"I can't find anything on the security monitor, but it sounds like fireworks." Zach pushed away from the table and rushed toward the living room windows, with his sister close behind.

Karla peered at the laptop's screen. "The ranch is so big, there are blind spots in the surveillance coverage."

Mrs. Walker appeared in the hallway, hurriedly making her way to the front of the house. "Who set off fireworks in the pasture? They're scaring the horses."

"We don't know for sure." But Janel could guess. The loud

crackling noises continued. She stood, watching everyone take action, wishing there was something she could do to help.

Zach removed a heavy-looking black gun from his hip holster, and Lily opened a cabinet to retrieve a pearl-handled one with a long barrel.

"It has to be a trap," Janel warned. "He wants you to run out the door." The shooter must have followed them, somehow. The lump on her forehead throbbed so badly her eyes narrowed, and her stomach churned.

"We'll be fine." He touched her shoulder before heading out the door. "Stay here."

Mrs. Walker grabbed a rifle from the gun rack mounted to the wall. "I'll guard our guests."

Janel pointed to the laptop. "Karla, if you keep an eye on the surveillance footage, I can look out the window."

Mrs. Walker started to object but appeared to change her mind. "Stand to the side of that window near the corner, and I'll take this one."

Before getting into position, she prayed. *God, please grant us the courage and wisdom needed to fight these intruders. Amen.*

With two fingers, she widened the space between the cream-colored slats to peer outside. Across the ranch, bright lights exploded one after another as they stretched ten to twelve feet into the air. Fountain fireworks. She'd seen a similar display on Independence Day.

Making sure no one had sneaked up to the house, Janel's gaze swept over the porch. A white two-seater swing hung at her end. Two rocking chairs sat in front of the window, with a small wooden table between them. And a cast iron dinner bell was mounted to a wooden pillar near the steps. Nothing out of place or alarming there.

Next, she surveyed the surrounding area. Zach, Lily and Mr. Walker used the corner of the stables, piles of hay and a tractor as shields. But who did they need protection from? She didn't see anyone else. Seconds later, Cole and Jackson appeared from around a tree, guns ready. They must have heard the noise and come running from their homes.

"We have company out back!" Karla pointed to the laptop.

Mrs. Walker and Janel ran to the table to view the security footage. A man wearing camouflage and a ski mask held a gun in a ready position as he crept closer.

"I've got this." Mrs. Walker headed toward the back door.

No matter how good Zach's mother may be with a rifle, Janel couldn't let her face this shooter alone. There had to be a way to alert the Walker family all at once.

Remembering the dinner bell, Janel ran out the front door and yanked the chain back and forth. The loud, repetitive clang caught the attention of everyone on the ranch. She made eye contact with Zach, who took a step away from the stables.

"Behind the house!" She made a sweeping gesture. "Hurry!"

When he bolted in their direction, she ran inside and locked the door. Turning, she found Mrs. Walker standing in the center of the room, aiming her rifle at the closed back door in case the shooter broke in.

Karla stood in the hall entryway, holding a gun she must have borrowed, since she didn't have her own pistol with her. "Are you crazy going outside? You could have been shot."

"But I wasn't." Janel smiled, knowing it was something Zach would say. Peering into the laptop again, she could no longer see the intruder. Did that mean he fled when he heard the bell?

Or was he waiting for the Walkers to come closer?

Fear seized her heart. Did she just send Zach straight into a trap?

Chapter Seven

Scared senseless, Janel forced each breath into her body. She sat on the living room rug behind a wing-backed chair, her legs crisscrossed and her hands holding on to the open laptop. From her position, she could see Mrs. Walker, aiming the rifle at the back door, and Karla, standing in the hall, holding a gun. What she desperately wanted to see was Zach.

Finally, he appeared on the screen. Relief engulfed her. She hadn't sent him into a trap after all.

"Zach and Lily are moving toward the shed." Janel provided a play-by-play account of what she witnessed through the surveillance footage. She anxiously studied the screen, hunting for the masked man. What she would do if she spotted him was a question swirling through her mind.

"What about the others?" Mrs. Walker spared a quick glance in her direction before focusing on the rear entry of the house again. None of them wanted to be taken by surprise.

"Your husband is searching the cars parked near the house. Cole and Jackson jumped the fence where the fireworks went off and are running toward the trees. They must have spotted someone on that side of the ranch." Her chest felt heavy. The second intruder could be the murderer who chased her through the forest.

Janel noticed Mrs. Walker's arms were lower than before and suspected she couldn't maintain her guarded stance for much longer. "Do you want to trade places? I can hold the rifle while you watch the security footage."

"I'm fine." Mrs. Walker kept her eyes glued to the door, and Janel could see Zach in the woman's determination.

Karla sent Janel a grim smile. "Let's hope someone gets arrested today."

"Yeah." The last thing she'd wanted was for the ranch to be attacked. No one near her was safe, no matter where she hid. She checked the laptop screen at the exact second Zach started running away from the shed. Lily followed his lead. "I think they found the masked guy who tried to sneak up on us."

"What do you mean by 'think'?" Karla left her spot in the hallway to join her.

"Zach and Lily are running after someone." Janel pointed to the far end of the screen until she could no longer see them. "Mrs. Walker, your family has chased them off the ranch." Janel wanted to stop worrying but couldn't. These men kept showing up when least expected.

The older woman slowly exhaled a long breath before collapsing onto the sofa. She placed the rifle at her feet. "Just in case," she noted.

After ten excruciatingly long minutes, Zach knocked on the locked door.

Janel sprang to her feet and let him inside. "What happened?" She'd already seen him approaching on the laptop and knew that he and Lily had come back alone. "Did he get away? What about the other guy? Did Jackson and Cole catch him?"

"Yes, and no." Zach sat on the ottoman near his mother, but kept his gaze on Janel. "From the description Jackson gave me, it looks like our fugitive set off fireworks in the pasture to distract us."

"The murderer," Janel muttered.

Zach nodded. "Same black hoodie and mirrored sunglasses. He took off on an ATV parked on that side of the ranch. His buddy—"

"The guy who shot at us today. I recognized the camouflage jacket," Janel noted.

"Correct. He must have figured we would all run toward the fireworks and leave you unprotected."

"Silly man." Mrs. Walker guffawed. "He would have had a surprise waiting for him if he had tried to come through that door."

"That's right." Zach smiled at his mother. "Unfortunately, he had a head start and ran for the ATV he had parked on this side of the ranch."

Karla left the hallway and eased onto the sofa next to Mrs. Walker. "Zach, did your lieutenant find us a safe house yet?"

"We talked." Zach rubbed his chin with the pad of his thumb, thinking again. "They haven't found a safer place for you. No houses are available, and motels have too many people around. At least here we have three law enforcement officers living on the property, and the sheriff will increase patrols nearby."

As if on cue, sirens sounded in the distance. The response time out here was longer than she'd like. Maybe that will improve now. "I don't understand why they are so determined to kill me. I get that I might be able to identify the murderer if my memories return, but they could leave the state, or the country."

"I have a theory," Karla said. "If there are several people tied to the burglary and murder and they all suddenly move, it would be like advertising their guilt when you identify one of them."

"I hadn't thought of that." Janel turned to Zach. "What do you think?"

"She makes a valid point. They could also have a life here they don't want to leave, especially if they have influential careers, a lot of money or strong family ties." Zach's gaze shifted between the sisters. "You two would go to great lengths to protect one another."

"True." Janel recognized the sound of Lily's boots on the back porch. "Just like your family members protect one another."

The door swung open, and the conversation stopped as Lily entered the living room. "The deputies are taking statements. They'll come to the house soon."

Glancing at the laptop once more, Janel counted four sheriff's vehicles parked on the ranch. She wished she could tell them what the murderer looked like. Now that the most dangerous moments were over, her temples throbbed with the onset of another headache. The doctor had warned her to relax. That wouldn't happen until these men were caught.

"We have to get ahead of this," Janel announced.

Lines creased Karla's forehead. "Meaning what exactly?"

Looking Zach straight in the eyes as if she could bend him to her wishes, Janel stated, "I need you to take me to the place where the landscaper died."

"No." His tone held firm.

Karla huffed. "You want to go to a murder scene when masked men are trying to kill you?"

"It doesn't matter where I go, they'll keep trying." Frustrated, Janel bit her lip while she reined in her emotions. "Please try to understand. I need to do this. Zach and I both agree that witnessing the murder could be the emotional event blocking my memories. If I'm there, in person, everything might come back to me."

Lily turned to her brother. "This morning's shooting did trigger her memories of the landscaping truck."

Zach worked his jaw while he remained quiet.

Janel tried another approach. "We all need to get our lives back—sooner, rather than later. Keeping us here has turned your ranch upside down. Lily has had to move her horse riding lessons to other ranches. You can't book cowboy cookouts or hayrides while we're here. You must be losing business. I've had to shut my doors, so I know I'm losing business."

"Your life is more important than money," Zach shot back. "My entire family agrees with me on that."

"What he said." Karla gestured in Zach's direction.

Lily placed a hand on her brother's shoulder. "Zach, hiding here indefinitely could drag this out for a long time. Is that fair to Janel? She's the victim."

After what seemed like an eternity, he exhaled a long breath and relented. "If you're going to remember something important, it will most likely be where this all started. And I prefer to go on the offense, instead of defense. We need to bring Cole, since we all believe the killing and burglary are connected."

Karla crossed her arms over her chest. "I'm going with you, too."

Janel shook her head. "You need to stay here. If a shooter shows up, he might mistake you for me. Somehow, this is all my fault. I'm the one they're after, and I'm the one who must help catch them before someone else dies." Taking on the assertive sister role felt foreign to Janel, but good. She should do it more often.

"None of this is your fault," Zach insisted. "And even I know nothing short of a natural disaster is going to keep Karla from going with us." He removed his phone from his pocket. "I'm calling my lieutenant. If he gives our plan the green light, we'll need to prepare for anything that could go wrong."

The following morning, Zach drove a sheriff's vehicle up the mountain toward the high-end houses where the landscaper had been shot and killed two days ago. He still had reservations about this trip but knew they had to take steps toward ending the madness for everyone's sake. There was the ranch and his family to think about, as well as the twins' safety.

The tension in the cab grew thicker with every mile. Janel

sat beside him, staring out the window, while her sister sat in the back, emailing contacts on her phone.

Karla huffed an exasperated breath. "According to my friend at the insurance company, Frank Hyde recently lost his biggest client. He needs a fast paycheck, so he formed an alliance with the detective working the burglary cases in Scottsdale."

"Frank, the insurance investigator who thinks I'm guilty?" Janel grimaced. "What type of alliance?"

"They're feeding each other information," Karla explained.

"That's not uncommon." Zach turned down a quiet residential road. "And it sounds like they think they're both trying to find the same burglars. As long as they follow the evidence, there shouldn't be a problem. In fact, this Scottsdale detective might convince Hyde that Janel had nothing to do with her gallery's break-in."

"Wishful thinking. Hyde molds the facts to fit his narrative." Karla leaned closer to the front seat and placed her hand on Janel's shoulder. "I won't let him smear your good name. We all know you didn't steal Mom's paintings."

Janel rubbed her temple, and Zach feared her memories of what happened the day before wouldn't come back if she was emotionally distraught over what Frank Hyde might do next.

Zach pulled up to the curb in front of the white Victorian house. After parking behind Cole's SUV, he turned to his passengers. "My mother always says not to borrow trouble. Meaning, let's not worry about what hasn't happened yet. Instead, let's focus on the reason you convinced me to come here."

"You're right." Janel's tone was soft, almost apologetic, as she peered through the window at the stately looking house with blue trim. Two sheriff's deputies and Cole walked the property, ensuring the coast was clear.

"Wait here a minute." Zach scanned their surroundings before walking around the front of the truck to open the door for Janel and her sister. "I want you both to stick close to me or Cole."

"We will," Janel promised. While waiting on the sidewalk for her sister to climb out of the vehicle, she pointed to the asphalt in front of the mailbox. "The landscaping truck parked there Monday morning. I could see it from the corner."

Zach's gaze followed hers to the stop sign down the street. The shooting occurred at least eight hours after the burglary took place. If the two events are related, why did they come here?

She pressed her lips together while looking around. After a few seconds passed, she closed her eyes as if willing her memories to return. The three of them waited. And waited. When she swayed, Zach grabbed hold of her arm to keep her from falling.

Her lids flitted open. "The man in the hoodie and the redheaded one with him grabbed rakes out of the truck and walked that way." She pointed to the open area, at least fifty feet wide, between the Victorian house and its nearest neighbor, a house with a stone facade. Neighborhood doorbell cameras showed two men in the landscaping truck. The murderer had managed to keep his face hidden.

Zach had also learned from his lieutenant that the owner of the Victorian worked for an engineering company and was in Flagstaff when the shooting occurred. He told them the owner of the stone house was spending the holidays in Florida. Not a bad idea, considering the temperature here had dropped to where you could see your breath.

Afraid to break her train of thought, Zach remained silent as he followed Janel with Karla at his side. Cole walked toward the back of the two houses with the younger, taller deputy. The more experienced deputy staked out the front.

The decorative landscape between the houses included lush winter grass, manicured evergreen shrubs and beds of colorful flowers. Nothing seemed to trigger another memory; her blank expression remained constant.

Once she stepped into the clearing behind the houses, they could see the forest straight ahead, bordering both unfenced yards. A ladder at the corner of the Victorian stood beneath newly installed motion detecting lights. Empty boxes littered the grass next to both houses. If anyone returned at night, the area would light up like a football field.

Standing in place, Janel quietly looked around. Yellow caution tape tied to the Victorian's wooden porch posts stretched over the grass to the forest trees, blocking off the crime scene. A blood patch in the middle marked the spot where the landscaper was shot and killed.

Zach studied Janel, hoping for any sign of recognition. She turned toward the backyard of the stone house. Gray-colored covers protected the porch's outdoor furniture. Twenty feet away, Adirondack chairs surrounded a firepit. Her gaze appeared to lock on a casita, which might serve as a guesthouse or mother-in-law suite.

When Karla opened her mouth to speak, Zach raised a finger, stopping her. He wanted Janel to have uninterrupted time to take in the scene.

Cole and the deputy continuously looked out for trouble, reminding Zach of the danger Janel was in just standing here. A pang of guilt struck his stomach. This was a mistake.

"I followed a man with dark hair from Sedona," she blurted and strode straight toward the Victorian house. "I tried to remember why, but there's a mental wall blocking that memory."

Anticipation rose in Zach's chest. "Try to relax. It will all come back to you."

"Eventually," she said, despair hanging heavy in the air.

"We came here for you to remember." Karla took her sister's hand and pulled her away from Zach. "Think. Was the man with the dark hair the guy who chased you through the forest and blew up my car?"

Agitated by Karla's pushy interference, Zach clenched his jaw, but then he noticed Janel's wide eyes.

"Yes," Janel answered. "It was the same man. He drove a silver sedan up the mountain. When he reached the forest, he pulled off the road, onto the shoulder behind the landscaping truck and trailer. He covered his hair with a black hoodie before he climbed inside with the redhead."

"Then you saw his face?" Karla exclaimed.

"No, I didn't. He had his back to me."

Zach tipped the brim of his cowboy hat. "How did you not get caught following them?"

"I hid on the other side of a slow RV when I passed them, then I found a place to park and wait for them to drive by before following again at a safe distance."

"Do you remember the make and model of the silver car?" Karla rubbed her temple, concern flashing through her expression.

Janel shook her head. "You know I'm not into cars."

Zach stepped between the sisters to capture Janel's attention and gestured toward the backyard of the Victorian. "You were walking this way."

"Right." She ambled toward the porch, her expression one of deep concentration. "I... I didn't want them to see me, so I snuck closer and hid behind a tree."

"You parked and got out of the car?" Zach felt like he'd skipped a chapter in a book. He'd found her deep in the forest, far from this location.

"I must have." She touched the white railing surrounding the Victorian's porch on her way to the far side of the yard. Her pace increased until she reached a tree with a large trunk on the edge of the forest. She stepped behind it, then leaned out to face them. "I hid here, watching them."

Zach's gaze shifted from her to the bloodstain on the grass. She was roughly twenty feet away from where the landscaper was shot. "What else do you remember?"

Still gripping the tree, Janel closed her eyes. Soon, she gripped the trunk tighter, her arms shaking, sweat pooling at her brow. She sucked in a raspy breath.

Karla rushed over and pulled her sister into a hug. Janel cried on her shoulder.

Zach turned to his brother, whose expression showed empathy, but he stood back, silently watching. Cole must have felt as helpless as he did in the moment. Then he reminded himself that Janel wanted these memories to return. Nobody forced her. She was stronger than she looked—even now. He admired her for seeing this through.

When Karla glanced up at him, he said, "We need to know what happened next, while the memories are fresh."

Janel lifted her head. "It was horrible. I never saw anyone die so violently."

"I have. You're right. It's horrible. I'm sorry you were here when it happened." Zach tried not to think about the times he had to shoot another human, even if it was to help save his sisters-in-law.

Their gazes locked, emotionally connected by a similar experience.

Janel abruptly jerked around. "I remember parking on that street." She pointed away from the houses. "I cut through this part of the forest. When I got close, I only moved when they made noise, so they wouldn't hear me." She looked back toward the crime scene. "The redhead was a real landscaper. He was doing his job, raking pine needles. The dark-haired man wearing the hoodie played at it. At one point, he went back to the truck for a blue canvas bag."

"What was that for?" Karla asked.

"He didn't say anything to the redhead when he carried the bag over to the casita and picked the lock." She stared in that direction for at least twenty seconds.

When her breathing grew shallow, Zach took a step forward. "You're doing a great job. You've got this."

Drawing in a deep breath as if to summon her courage, she continued. "After the door was open, the redhead pulled a gun out of his pocket. The guy in the hoodie shoved his lock-picking kit into his pocket and told the other guy not to do anything foolish."

Tears flowed down her face. "Before the redhead had a chance to say anything, the guy in the hoodie lifted the gun hidden in his pocket and shot. The redhead fell backward." Her gaze traveled between Zach and Karla. "I couldn't help it. I gasped. He saw me. I… I had to get away."

"And that's how you ended up running far into the forest," Zach concluded.

"I could hear him shooting behind me. I ran and ran and ran." A click sounded nearby, and Janel gasped again.

Chapter Eight

Fear and anxiety twisted in Janel's gut as the back door of the stone house flew open. At the same time, Zach, Cole and Jackson reached for their holstered firearms, keeping their fingers on the handle grips.

A casually dressed middle-aged man stepped out onto the porch, clearly disturbed by the sight of armed law enforcement officers. "What's going on?" He eyed the deputy standing beside the firepit and added, "This is my yard. I heard the shooting happened next door."

"I know him. Mr. Allen is a regular customer." Janel's voice weakened as her confusion grew.

A dozen questions crossed her mind, starting with why would a murderer break into his casita yesterday?

"Do you have identification?" Zach asked, keeping his hand near his holster. "We heard you were in Florida."

"I was until a neighbor called about the shooting. I flew back here immediately to check on my property." Mr. Allen removed his wallet from his back pocket.

Cole checked his ID and nodded. "He's the homeowner."

"Janel, what's going on?" Mr. Allen's gaze traveled between the two sisters.

She didn't feel the need to point out she had a twin. Partly because most people assumed the truth when they saw them together for the first time, but mostly because she didn't know if he had a connection to the men trying to kill her.

Remembering the casita, Janel gestured in that direction, and Zach asked, "Mr. Allen, did you find anything disturbed when you checked your property?"

"Not yet. Why? Did something happen to my guesthouse?"

Zach urged the homeowner to go inside with a sweeping gesture. "You tell us."

Mr. Allen glanced at the caution tape in his neighbor's yard with a wary expression. "I'm granting you permission to search anywhere on my property that you like."

Wise decision. Janel wouldn't want to be the first person to venture inside when the door stood partially open. Who knew what waited for them?

"Stay here. I got this." Cole peered through a gap between the blinds in the casita's side window, then walked around to the front stoop and disappeared inside the small structure. He was most likely looking for a connection between the shooting and the burglary. After several long minutes, he emerged and asked Mr. Allen to join him. The homeowner looked reluctant but cooperated.

Standing next to Zach, Janel wrung her hands while Karla fidgeted with her phone for several minutes.

"That statue is not mine." Mr. Allen's loud voice filled the silence. "I have nothing to do with it being here."

Not his? Janel had to see the statue for herself. She rushed to the door with Zach at her heels.

"I'm coming, too." Karla fell into step behind them.

They stopped at the door, giving Mr. Allen room to exit. Janel entered the apartment-sized living room and took in the decor. The casita was smartly decorated with an off-white loveseat, chair and ottoman. In the center was a black coffee table. On top sat one of the stolen VanZandt statues: a bronze cowboy riding a bronco. Her jaw dropped open. "That's my…"

Cole nodded. "I recognized it from the photos."

Karla nudged her and pointed to the built-in shelves. Her other three VanZandts were all on display as if they belonged here. "They hid them in plain sight. This proves your gallery burglary is tied to the murder outside and the attempts to kill you."

"Mom's paintings…" Desperate for answers, Janel found the bedroom. Above the white goose down comforter hung a painting featuring a field of daisies, one she'd never seen before. Spinning around, she realized the other walls were all blank. Despair fell over her. "Where are they?"

"Keep looking." Karla dropped to her knees and lifted the comforter to peer under the bed. "Not here."

Janel followed her lead and tugged open the other door in the room. The walk-in closet was nearly empty, except for a hotel-style robe hanging near the far corner. She flipped up the wall switch and a single bulb illuminated cylindrical objects stashed behind the robe.

"Don't touch anything. I need to handle potential evidence." Zach pulled a pair of gloves out of a pocket and slipped them on while she moved out of his way.

It took every bit of Janel's self-control to keep from snatching the cylinders and ripping them open. If the statues were in the living room, the paintings had to be close by. She craned her neck, trying to see into the closet.

Karla stepped closer, trying to get a look, as well. "Did you find the paintings?"

"I don't know. Maybe."

Cole joined them in time to watch Zach carry out two mailing cylinders, the type Janel used in her gallery. He set them on the bed and then pulled the plastic seal off the end of the closest tube. Tipping it ever so slightly, a roll of white glassine paper slid out.

"Let me." Cole, already wearing gloves, peeled back one end of the paper enough to reveal the corner of a canvas. His eagerness to reveal the painting lit up his eyes while her pulse soared.

Janel spotted the familiar rust-colored rock formation and teal blue sky featured on the canvas and sucked in a breath. "It's Mom's." She closed her eyes and prayed, "Thank You, God. I feared I would never see them again."

Overwhelmed with emotion, tears streamed down her face. Zach gently placed his hand on her back. She was appreciating the gesture of comfort when her sister ran to the closet.

"Don't touch!" Zach ordered. "Cole needs to transport the evidence to the police station. The burglary is his case."

"I know. I'm only counting," Karla called out from inside the door where they could still see her. Seconds later, she announced. "There are eight more. There should be ten cylinders, not nine."

"They might have rolled two paintings together," Zach suggested.

"I hope not." Janel wiped her face with her fingers. "That could crack the paint." Now that they'd found her mother's legacy, or at least most of it, she hoped they were all in pristine condition.

A deputy stepped inside the bedroom. "We located Miss Newman's car. It's parked around the corner, like she remembered. Halfway down the block between a truck and an SUV." He dangled her keys from the rhinestone heart-shaped charm attached to the ring. "These were in the grass and—"

"I must have dropped them." Janel accepted her keys from the deputy. He also held her burgundy-colored leather purse by the strap at his side, which triggered another memory. "I put my phone in my purse and shoved them both under the car seat before sneaking across the edge of the forest to spy on the landscapers."

After he handed over her purse, she dug inside for her phone and discovered the battery had died. That was probably for the best. If the movies she'd seen were correct, the murderer could use her phone to track her.

"Now that you mention it," Zach said, his tone hard. "Leave the surveillance to the professionals."

"Spying is illegal," Cole pointed out.

"I'm sure she learned her lesson." Karla reached for the keys. "I'll drive your car back to the ranch. You don't want to leave it here. And with that concussion, it's better that you don't drive yet."

An image of her sister being shot struck Janel like lightning. "No!" She held the keys to her chest. "You shouldn't drive my car. You look too much like me, and there are now two men who desperately want me dead."

"We can tow the car," Zach said, agreeing with Janel.

"There's no need for that." Karla huffed. "I'm an investigator, even if I do work for an insurance company. I've had to travel in crime-ridden areas and speak to people you wouldn't want to run into in a dark alley."

"Can you at least wear the hood of your coat to cover your blond hair?" Janel asked, her voice laced with annoyance.

"Sure, if it will make you happy, sis."

With that settled, Zach conferred with his brother. They decided Cole and one deputy would stay behind to transport the artwork to the police station, while the other deputy helped escort the sisters to the ranch.

Before leaving the casita, Zach pointed to the camera positioned in the living room corner near the ceiling. He was familiar with the model and knew a small red light should be glowing. "Cole, can you ask the homeowner which security company he uses and when this camera was turned off?"

"I already did. It was on when he left town, and I found no sign anyone tampered with the power source." Cole reached for his phone. "I'll text you the name of the company."

"Thanks." Zach was interested in knowing if this camera

was shut off remotely without the homeowner being notified. If so, it would show Janel's break-in wasn't necessarily an inside job. He hadn't forgotten the technician who installed the gallery security system may have seen her enter her code and had skills worth investigating.

He wanted to prove her innocence, especially with the insurance investigator teaming up with the Scottsdale detective to make her look guilty. There was also Charlene to consider. She knew Janel was staying at his ranch.

In front of the house, Karla pulled up the coat's hood, hiding her blond hair. "See." She turned to Janel, modeling her new look. "I'm a giant marshmallow."

Janel rolled her eyes. "Please, be careful. And keep an eye out for a shooter."

"I will." Karla looked directly into her sister's eyes. "I promise."

The younger of the two deputies stepped forward. "I can drop her off at the car and stick close to her during the drive back." His tone was professional, but his expression showed he was eager to help. "If I see anything suspicious, I'll hit the siren." He lifted his finger, indicating one more thing. "And before she gets in, I'll check for any devices that shouldn't be there."

Bombs. He meant bombs. The burglars had access to them. A fact they needed to keep in mind.

Janel handed the deputy her car keys, accepting his help. Karla waved and then followed the law enforcement officer to his sheriff's vehicle.

Janel watched them leave. "I wish she would drive back with us."

"We'll be close behind her." Zach admired the way Janel always looked after other people, but the truth was no one was 100 percent safe with two shooters out there—somewhere.

While tugging open the passenger door of the truck for Janel, he heard the soft whir of a helicopter. Peering into the cloud-filled sky, he spotted a blue aircraft. He knew the markings for law enforcement copters. This wasn't one. Maybe a news crew. He hurried his efforts to leave before it flew closer.

His seat belt locked with a click, then he inserted the key into the ignition.

Janel reached over and touched his hand. "There's something I need to tell you."

"Can it wait?" He started the engine and turned on the heat.

"You might want to share what I have to say with Cole before we leave."

What now? Another memory? He leaned back against his seat and waited for her to explain.

"Mr. Allen recently bought a painting from my gallery. He asked Charlene to have it shipped to his house in Florida."

"Did you hear this conversation?"

She nodded slightly, and he began to understand her troubled expression. "Did he tell Charlene that he was going to be out of town for a while?"

"For two months." She pressed her fingers against her forehead. "I know this might make us both look guilty of stealing the artwork and hiding it here, but anyone in the gallery at the time could have overheard him."

"Not just 'anyone' knows your password." Something else came to mind. "Does your security footage also record audio? The security technician might have heard Mr. Allen say he wouldn't be home."

"Not to my knowledge. Do you have a tech team who can figure that out?"

"We have access to one." He let out a long breath, hating to see the toll every twist and turn was taking on her. "You're right, I need to speak to Cole."

She nodded again, then waited while he made a quick call to his brother.

Snow dusted the windshield during his conversation. At least it wasn't another downpour. He was tired of the rain. Before he shifted into gear, he turned to her one more time. "Thank you for trusting me with this information."

"I don't want to keep any secrets from you. Plus, I thought it would be better for everyone concerned if it came from me."

"True, but I know you don't want Charlene suspected of any wrongdoing."

"She's proven to be trustworthy time and time again."

When Janel turned to stare out the window, he made a U-turn on the residential street without expressing his thoughts on the subject. Many people, even trustworthy ones, have committed crimes when faced with dire circumstances. He needed to know more about Janel's assistant manager.

Down the street, Zach spotted the deputy turning right out of the residential neighborhood at the stop sign. Karla followed the deputy in an older model dark blue hatchback, only she ignored the stop sign.

Janel groaned. "I asked her to be careful."

"Does she always disregard traffic laws?" Zach slowed near the corner, stopped, then followed the others onto the main street leading to Sedona.

"Not *always*."

He let the subject drop as he centered his car in the right lane, thirty feet behind Karla. The deputy traveled in the parallel lane on her left side. A grassy median separated them from cars traveling in the opposite direction.

While driving downhill, Zach kept to the forty-five-mile-an-hour limit, and the gap between him and Karla grew. To his surprise, she surpassed the deputy. Speeding tickets must mean nothing to her.

"Slow down, Karla," Janel said, as if her sister could hear her. But Karla's speed increased with each passing second.

"I think there's something wrong." Zach flipped on the siren and pressed down on the gas pedal.

Suddenly, the emergency lights on the hatchback flickered

a warning. Karla sped faster toward the red traffic signal at the bottom of the hill, where a busier street crossed their path.

Janel gripped the truck's grab handle. "There's something wrong with my car."

"Could be the brakes." Zach felt his pulse racing as he shifted into the left lane behind the deputy, who flipped on his siren and drove ahead of Karla, hopefully to block the intersection.

"Do something! Please." Desperation punctuated Janel's words. "She'll crash."

Zach suppressed the emotions Janel's screams brought on and concentrated on the situation. He sped up, closing the gap between them and the hatchback. He grabbed his phone from the cup holder and used facial recognition to unlock it for Janel. "Call Cole."

He tossed her the phone, then pulled up beside Karla and honked.

She pointed down, shook her head and yelled, "No brakes!"

Every muscle in his body tensed. He didn't need to hear her to know what she was saying. With little time to act, Zach laid on the horn repeatedly. Between his horn and the sirens, the drivers up ahead sped out of the intersection, which was about two hundred feet away. The deputy was almost there.

"Cole, it's Janel. The brakes are out in my car. Karla's in danger. We need help!"

With his pounding heart pummeling his chest, Zach searched their surroundings while Janel continued speaking to his brother. If her brakes had been cut, a shooter might be hiding nearby.

The windshield wipers swept away the snow with a loud swoosh, and more sirens sounded nearby. Most likely Cole and the other deputy.

A hundred feet from the intersection, drivers coming from the other direction eased off the gas and began to slow. He hoped their light was yellow and would soon turn red. They might avoid a crash after all.

The deputy entered the intersection and stopped, lights flashing and sirens blaring.

Despite the warnings, a brightly painted preschool van filled with young children didn't slow. The driver entered the intersection and abruptly stopped in front of the deputy, blocking Karla's path forward.

Zach instinctively threw his hand out in front of Janel to protect her as he pressed hard on his brakes.

But Karla had no brakes.

With his breath caught in his throat, he watched in what looked like slow motion as Karla made a sharp right turn before reaching the intersection, avoiding a horrific collision with the preschool van. The hatchback flew over the curb, turned upside down and then landed in a ditch with a loud *thwack*.

Janel screamed. "No!"

Red and blue lights flashed in the rearview mirror. Cole was behind them. He could take care of Karla. Zach's job was to protect Janel. Without saying a word, he drove to the intersection where he turned right to avoid the preschool van.

"What are you doing?" Janel turned to look for her sister. "Go the other way! She could be dead!"

"Cole and the two deputies will take care of her. I have to get you out of here. A shooter might be watching."

"No!" She made quick work of unbuckling her seat belt. "You wouldn't desert your family. Don't expect me to desert mine." She pushed open the door as he slammed on his brakes. They both jerked forward.

"Are you crazy?" He reached across the seat to grab hold of her arm, but she jumped out of the car and ran back to the ditch where her sister had landed.

Chapter Nine

Janel sprinted down the sidewalk, her gut twisting into knots while she prayed her sister was alive. She ignored the pain in her forehead, made worse by sirens closing in, as she focused on reaching the car that had flipped over before landing. If there was a shooter nearby, she'd have to outrun his aim.

After jumping over the curb, she scurried over rocks and down into the ditch. Her boots slipped on the snow, and she gasped as she fought to regain her balance. Steady on her feet again, she rushed toward Karla, who lifted her hand and waved out of the open window.

The second Janel knew Karla was alive, a wave of overwhelming emotion swept over her, threatening to knock her off her feet. But nothing could stop her from reaching her sister, not even Zach and Cole, who kept calling out her name as they ran toward the crash site.

"I'm here." Janel fell onto her knees in the snow beside the upside-down car and grabbed her sister's hand.

The seat belt and airbag pinned Karla in place. The windshield had shattered on impact, and the metal front end of the car had bent inward when it collided with the ditch's dirt and rock wall. "I'm sorry," she mumbled.

"It's not your fault. Are you okay?" Janel's throat burned as the words escaped, and her body sucked in much-needed air. "Does anything hurt?"

"I don't know." Karla sounded weak and scared. "I think I'm in shock."

"Don't move her," Zach warned. "Paramedics are on the way." He glanced about, reminding her of the potential for more trouble. If guns fired from uphill, they'd have to hide behind the car—if they weren't shot first.

"I'm not going anywhere." Karla coughed, then added, "I'm starting to feel pain in my wrist. The airbag hit my hand."

Cole hurried around to the passenger window and peered inside. "I don't see any obvious injuries or blood. That's a good sign."

The two brothers checked out the car, which took Janel's attention away from her sister until Karla spoke. "I should have listened to you."

That was a first. "Can I have that in writing?"

Kara chuckled, then groaned. "Don't make me laugh."

A fire engine and ambulance arrived, and Zach helped Janel to her feet. "We need to get out of their way."

He kept his arm around Janel as they walked over the uneven, snow-covered ground toward a tree growing outside of the ditch. "This is all my fault," she said, watching her step. "I should have insisted we tow the car."

"You were never going to win that argument with her."

Janel sniffled, refusing to cry again. "You pegged her right. She'll wear you down to get her way. I've let her do it too many times."

He pulled her close to his side when the firefighters descended on the scene and worked on freeing her sister from the car. Feeling lightheaded, Janel turned away. "Zach, were my brakes cut? You and Cole checked my car."

"It looks like someone punctured the line. From what I can

gather, most of the brake fluid didn't flow out until after the car was in motion."

He watched over the scene as she leaned her head against his arm. Her sister almost died again because of her. She dared to look. The paramedics were carrying a stretcher to the car. That meant a trip to the hospital. The possibilities spun in her head as the winter cold made her shudder.

"I didn't expect anyone to cut the brakes," Zach said, breaking into her thoughts. "They didn't come back for the artwork, which should have been their top priority."

"Mr. Allen came home, neighbors were on alert and I assume deputies were patrolling the murder scene. My car was around the corner and halfway down the block."

"True. But they should have stayed away. It was in their best interest."

"Their top priority is killing me. Why? He had that hoodie on and sunglasses. I never got a good look at the murderer's face."

"That you remember."

He was right. There was still so much locked away in her mind. She fought to regain those lost memories as the emergency responders lifted Karla onto the stretcher.

With guilt and fear at war to control her emotions, Janel rushed toward the closest paramedic, a tall man wearing a stoic expression. "Is she going to be all right?"

"I'm okay," Karla answered for him as they carried her toward the ambulance. "The only thing that hurts is my wrist. There's nothing to worry about."

"We're taking her to the hospital for testing," the paramedic explained. "Do you want to go with her?"

"No." Karla's tone was defiant. "Stay away from the hospital. Remember the last time?"

The bomb. Janel's gaze instinctively drifted to the hills surrounding them, searching for a reflection of light that would reveal a shooter waiting to attack. "But…"

"You know I'm right." Karla's voice faded as they carried her away.

Janel jogged to catch up. "I'll call to check in on you."

"She'll be fine," Zach assured her. "God is looking out for her."

He was right. She could feel it in her heart. "Can a deputy go to the hospital with her?"

Zach nodded. "I'll make it happen."

Cole walked up, phone in hand. He ended his call and announced, "The insurance investigator is waiting for you at your gallery. He's insisting he speak to Janel."

Dread settled in her gut. "How much worse can this day get?"

Once they reached Sedona, Zach glanced over at Janel's waning features and decided a pit stop was in order. He turned the sheriff's vehicle toward his favorite drive-through restaurant. "I don't know about you, but I need a pick-me-up."

"Can we? The investigator is waiting for us." She straightened, taking an interest in the building with brightly colored posters of burgers and fries.

"Let him wait." Zach's chief concern was Janel's welfare. She'd been beaten down at every turn but still kept going. Aside from keeping her safe, he planned to support her by keeping her energy up. "We'll listen to what he has to say when we're ready and not a minute before."

A faint smile appeared on her beautiful face. "I like the way you think. And thank you. Something to eat sounds good."

After receiving their order, Zach parked beneath a tree away from the street, making them less likely to be noticed by drivers passing by. With the snow falling, the traffic was lighter than usual. He took a sip of his soda, then lifted his phone. "I got the impression your sister doesn't like this insurance investigator. We should learn more about him."

"How?" She glanced up from the drink she held with both hands.

"The internet." He entered the man's name in his phone's search engine and found a website. "Frank Hyde is an independent private investigator who offers his services to big corporations. He used to be a Phoenix police officer."

"Is that good or bad?"

"It depends on how he uses his training. I know someone who might have worked with him." He sent a text to his high school friend asking about Hyde.

"Can you also call the hospital to check on Karla?"

"It's too soon for test results, but I can give her phone number to Lily. She can make calls while we meet with Hyde at the gallery."

Zach wasn't sure if Hyde's name brought on the angst in Janel's features or the fact she didn't know the extent of Karla's injuries. Maybe both. "What's your sister's phone number?"

He sent the text right after she rattled off the digits.

Lily replied right away. "Lily says she heard about the crash and is sorry it happened. And she'd be happy to help by keeping tabs on Karla and bringing her back to the ranch when it's time."

"Thank her for me." Janel stopped eating after three bites and stared at the traffic. He couldn't blame her for losing her appetite. She faced one challenge after another, and there was only so much he could do to help. Something he hated to admit since he was usually a problem solver.

Zach's phone rang. His friend was calling instead of texting. "Nick, how's it going?"

"The kids are keeping me busy, but that's not what you want to know," Nick said. "I heard about the shootings up there, and if Frank Hyde is involved, I feel sorry for you."

"Why? Does he have criminal ties?"

"Nothing like that, but he's a pit bull. He's quick to make judgments and sticks to them even when the facts say differently. He left the force after two years because rules didn't suit him."

Zach loathed the sound of that. The pit bull had decided the gallery burglary was an inside job. "Does Hyde step over the line where rules are concerned or jump over it?"

"He straddles the line while he manipulates other people into breaking rules, laws, norms…you name it. It's only when he can't find anyone to do his dirty work for him that he'll break a law or two. He's smart enough to make sure he covers his tracks."

"What kinds of laws?"

"I hear breaking and entering is his favorite."

Zach caught the worry on Janel's face. "This will help. I owe you."

"And I'll collect one day. Good talking to you." Nick ended the call, and Zach let Janel know what he'd learned.

She pressed her lips together while she considered the news. "Hyde's worse than Karla thought. At least we know what he's like and it won't come as a surprise."

"Are you ready to meet him?"

"No, but we should get this over with." She took a long sip of her soda through the straw, then placed it in the cup holder.

Zach turned the key in the ignition and shifted the truck into gear. He couldn't help but check on Janel often during the drive through town. He cared about her deeply, but he needed to keep his feelings in check. Besides not wanting to risk his heart by playing the role of rebound guy again, he also couldn't be positive Janel hadn't participated in the burglary. Everything in him wanted to believe in her, but he had been wrong about a woman before.

The only vehicle parked in front of the gallery was a black Mercedes-Benz with darkly tinted windows. Zach left three spaces free between them and expected Hyde to emerge from the car. Instead, the gallery door opened, and Charlene ran outside.

Janel rushed to meet her halfway. "What are you doing here? You're supposed to be at home."

"Please don't be angry." Charlene's sweeping gaze included Zach in her plea. "A big order came in and the money was too good to let it slip from our hands, so Robert and I came back for the paintings and shipping supplies. We parked his Mercedes around back in case one of the bad guys drove by."

"And the insurance investigator showed up," Zach concluded. He wasn't thrilled with the idea that Charlene was here. He had hoped to keep the two women separated, but he might as well question her while he had the chance.

"Frank Hyde. He's inside." Charlene grimaced and gestured toward the door. "I already showed him where the stolen art was kept. He's not what I would call a pleasant man."

"I'm not upset that you're here." Janel sounded worried, though. "But next time, I would like you to call me first. Zach can arrange protection, right?"

"Sure." For a limited time. He held the door open for the women. "So, Charlene, do you live close by?"

"About five miles away." She waited for Janel to enter before she followed. "I did have a roommate, but she moved back to Phoenix. I haven't found anyone to replace her yet."

Zach made a mental note to finish their discussion later when he spotted a man standing on a step stool, examining a security camera in the corner. He wore a black T-shirt beneath a gray suit jacket. The kind body builders wore when they wanted everyone to see their muscles outlined by the form-fitting material. "You must be Frank Hyde."

"I am." He climbed down and took in Zach's badge clipped to his belt. "And you must be Deputy Walker."

"I am," Zach mimicked the man, whose attitude was living up to his reputation.

Charlene slid over next to her boyfriend behind the cash register counter and appeared to keep busy while obviously listening to the conversation.

Hyde took in Janel's disheveled appearance. "Miss Newman, I'm here on behalf of your insurance company to investigate your claim. I heard about your sister's accident. Someone else will contact you regarding your vehicle after you file that claim."

When no condolences or well wishes for her sister were added, Janel explained, "The car can wait. My sister's health is my primary concern."

"How noble of you. Detective Walker said someone punctured your brake line." Hyde removed a notebook from his back pocket. "Whose idea was it for your sister to drive your car?"

"Karla's," Zach snapped. Did the guy think Janel tried to kill her sister? "I understand you know her."

"I do." Hyde scowled.

"Then you know no one can talk her out of an idea when she's made up her mind." Zach walked closer to Janel. An unspoken message that he was on her side.

After opening the notebook, Hyde pinned Janel with his stare. "According to the security company, your password was used to shut off the alarm."

"They did say that," Janel admitted, "but there's a chance the man who installed the system watched me enter my password."

His expression turned smug. "But he wouldn't have known your customer was going to be out of town, offering the perfect place to hide the stolen art."

Zach shook his head in disbelief. "How do you know all of this about Mr. Allen?"

"The detective, your brother, if I'm not mistaken—and I rarely am—gave me the address where the art was found. I contacted the owner while I waited for you to arrive."

"The security technician might have an audio hookup here," Zach offered.

Hyde pointed to the camera. "Not up there."

"I'll have the place swept for bugs."

"You do that." He glanced down at his notes again. "Miss Newman, who knew your security code?"

"I created the code." Janel pressed her lips together as if wishing she didn't have to answer his questions.

"And then she shared it with me." Charlene's tone held no fear. "But I didn't steal anything." She looked at Janel apologetically. "Her old boyfriend, Todd, never turned his eyes away when she entered it into the panel."

Hyde lifted a brow. "Did Todd know Mr. Allen would be out of town?"

"No." Janel shook her head. "We broke up a month ago."

Hyde's gaze landed on Charlene's boyfriend. "What about you? Do you know the alarm code?"

Robert pointed to himself. "Me? No. I mind my own business."

"He always gives me privacy when I turn the alarm on and off." Charlene smiled at her boyfriend.

Hyde took down Robert's name, his occupation as a real estate agent and how often he was at the gallery. Then he asked Janel, "I heard there was a shooting next door to Mr. Allen's house yesterday, and the perpetrator chased you into the forest." He quickly explained to Zach, "Detective Walker filled in some of the missing pieces for me."

Janel pressed her lips together again. "Today, I remembered seeing the shooting."

"And that brings us to your amnesia," Hyde said. "Some people might think it's convenient you lost your memory. You can't tell the police why you were at the exact location where the missing art was found."

"That's enough!" Zach's ire was boiling over.

"I never said she was making up the amnesia. I've only been asking questions. Some of the other store owners on this block find the timing of your burglary odd." He sent Janel a smug look. "They say you've lost customers to a bigger gallery." He checked his notes again. "The bank manager said you were two weeks late with your last loan payment."

Janel's face turned red. "We found the artwork. Why are you even here?"

"According to the detective, there's still one painting missing. The most expensive one." Hyde stepped closer. "Did you know insurance fraud is a serious crime?"

"Get out!" Zach gestured toward the door. He'd file a complaint with the insurance company contracting Hyde's services first thing in the morning.

"I'm not saying Miss Newman stole anything. I was wondering if someone might have done it for her. Someone who didn't want her to lose her mother's paintings." He glanced at Charlene, whose eyes grew wide.

"Out!" Zach repeated, wondering if the investigator was purposely being obnoxious to judge their reactions—who looked guilty and who didn't. Or was he taking out his dislike of Karla on her sister?

Hyde strode to the door. Before exiting, he announced, "Throwing me out will not stop me from doing my job. And until I'm convinced that this isn't an inside job, you won't receive one red cent." He took one last look around. "Nice gallery. It's too bad you aren't open for business."

Zach fisted his hand at his side. He'd met men who tested his patience before, but this one was upsetting a woman he cared for, making it twice as hard to control his temper. If the reports about Hyde were correct, the investigator would do everything he could to convince the insurance company that Janel or Charlene hired the burglars. Then there was Hyde, teaming up with the Scottsdale detective. Would they try to blame one of these women for the other burglaries, as well?

A nagging voice reminded Zach he couldn't be positive they were innocent. He had trusted a woman who ran off with her ex. That reminded him they still didn't know if Todd was behind the burglary. Was he hiding? Would Janel go back to him if he declared he did this to show his love for her? The questions never stopped. Neither did the danger. It lurked around every corner.

Chapter Ten

When the door shut behind Hyde, Janel latched on to Zach's
arm. "This situation is hopeless. I can't save my gallery unless I keep it open. And I can't do that unless you arrest those
murderous burglars and prove they acted on their own. So far,
you can't identify them to make those arrests unless I recall
the memories I've lost."

"The doctor said you need to relax if you want to remember," Charlene added. A hint of embarrassment flashed across
her face when they glanced in her direction. "Karla told me."

"Who can relax with a target on their back?" Janel ran her
fingers through her hair. "I'm going to lose everything."

Zach placed his hand gently on her shoulder. "Let's get you
to the ranch. My mother's hot tea and a night away from the
chaos will do you a world of good."

"You're probably right." She was finding it almost impossible not to obsess over the troubles she faced every waking
minute of the day. "Charlene, please lock up as soon as you're
finished here. And don't take too long. I need you to stay safe."

"I promise to hurry." Charlene handed her boyfriend a stack
of mailing labels. "Let's make sure we have everything on the
list I printed."

"Just point me in the right direction." Robert turned to Janel. "We'll do everything we can to help. You only need to name it."

"Thank you. I will." On the way to the sheriff's vehicle, the snow crunched beneath Janel's feet. The cold chilled her to the bone, forcing her to shove her hands into the pockets of her coat.

During their drive, Zach turned up the heater, then asked about her phone. "I think we should charge it to see if you've received any threatening calls."

The possibility hadn't occurred to her. "If so, could they be traced?"

"It's a possibility. Also, voice analysis and background noises might help us find them."

For the first time, she felt a glimmer of hope. "I'll need a charger."

"We have plenty."

After what seemed like a long drive, they turned onto the ranch. She took in the sight of horses frolicking in the pasture, and a smile tugged at her lips. Maybe she could unwind for a few minutes.

Cole met them inside the garage. "How was your meeting with Hyde?"

Zach pushed the driver's side door closed. "He's pretending he hasn't already mentally tried and convicted Janel of burglary."

"That was the impression I got when he called to set up the meeting." Cole shifted his attention to Janel. "I hope he didn't get to you."

"How could he not?" Anger aimed at Hyde twisted in Janel's gut as she rounded the front end of the car. "He's blocking my insurance payment. If I default on my loan, the bank will take the paintings we found. And if I don't have the money for the missing painting, then the bank will put a lien on my gallery. I'm at my wit's end." So much for relaxing.

"We'll do whatever it takes to uncover the truth." Inside the kitchen, Zach removed a charger from a drawer and handed it to her, then hung his coat on the back of a wooden chair.

"Thanks." She placed her purse on the quartz countertop and dug inside for her phone. She plugged it in, then hung her coat on the back of a chair and sat while Zach turned on the gas burner beneath the teakettle.

Cole grabbed a water bottle from the fridge and joined her at the table. The laptop displaying the ranch's security footage was open next to him. "Lily and Mom left ten minutes ago. They're headed to the Flagstaff hospital to pick up Karla."

Finally, some good news. "That means the tests came back okay, right?"

Cole nodded as he swallowed a sip of water. "Aside from a sprained wrist and a multitude of scrapes and bruises, she's fine. She tried to call you, but your phone was dead. I told her you were meeting with Frank Hyde."

Janel would have trouble believing her sister was "fine" until she saw her in person. "When will they be back?"

"My best guess is a couple of hours. It's about a sixty-minute drive each way in the snow. They thought it best to go together. Mom can guard the car against bombers while Lily runs inside to collect Karla."

"No one should have to live like this," Janel mumbled. Glancing into the dining room, Janel noticed the blinds were down. They always covered the windows when she was here. No doubt to keep anyone from shooting at them. Again, she felt guilty for disrupting their lives and putting them in danger.

Zach had tried so hard to turn the ranch around after the local resorts turned to neighboring ranches for hayrides, cowboy cookouts and trail rides for tourists. They couldn't bring visitors onto the property with a targeted witness here. And after so many shoot-outs, how could they rebuild? They might all lose their livelihoods.

The key to ending this nightmare, for everyone's sake, was to remember what the murderer looked like. With fatigue settling in her bones, she rubbed her temples, wishing she could snap her fingers and have her memory back. *If only...*

"I haven't seen Dad," Zach noted. "Where is he?"

"Dusty is limping. The veterinarian agreed to squeeze him into his schedule."

"Horse?" Janel asked, trying to stay up with the conversation.

"Dog," the brothers answered in unison.

"That poor little fellow." Janel always wanted a dog but was never home long enough to take care of one.

The kettle whistled, and Zach opened a box of tea bags. "I guess it's just the four of us for a while."

"Three," Cole corrected. "Jackson is having dinner with Bailey. After last night, she's worried about him, and he wants to calm her nerves. Stress isn't good for her pregnancy. Once she's feeling better, he'll come back to help stable the horses."

"Jackson, a father..." Zach grinned. "That I have to see."

Janel felt she could relate in a small way to Bailey's fears. She wasn't married to Zach, or even dating him, but she worried something would happen to him every time he confronted the shooters. "I don't blame her for being concerned. Jackson should stay home with her. We'll manage."

"You're right. We will." Zach placed the bottle of creamer on the table. "The sneak attack last night failed, so they know we'll be keeping an eye out for them. Plus, there's increased patrol by the deputies on the main road leading to the ranch. You're safe. Focus on relaxing." He handed her a mug. "I hope you like chamomile."

"It's just what I need. Thank you." After half an hour, the laptop screen showed the sun disappearing below the horizon. Janel walked to the kitchen counter and checked at least thirty text messages with her phone still plugged in. Many were from Charlene and Karla on the day she hadn't returned to work. Seeing her ex's name made her stomach flip-flop. "Todd called and texted after he heard a murderer tried to kill me. He wants me to reconsider his offer to reconcile so he can protect me."

Zach worked his jaw, clearly agitated. "Did he say where he's staying?"

"His best friend is getting married, so he took time off work to drive to Colorado for the wedding."

"And didn't tell the cat sitter?" Zach shook his head.

Cole studied his brother's reaction, then turned to Janel. "Do you mind if I use your phone to call Todd?"

"Not at all." She stepped away from the counter. "While you have it, please check for any threats. I prefer someone else reads them."

"Will do." Cole unplugged the charger and carried the phone out of the room, leaving Janel to wonder what he might find.

"How do you feel about Todd texting you?" Zach's tone sounded flat, hard.

"I wish he hadn't." The anger and embarrassment brought on by the breakup stirred inside. "It's a reminder of how gullible I was. Someone I trusted betrayed me. And now, no matter how badly I want to believe it will never happen again, I can't help but wonder."

They sat quietly, sipping their tea, while studying the security footage on the laptop as the largest picture flipped from one camera view to the other every five seconds.

The pounding of hooves and frantic neighs jerked them out of their quiet thoughts. A small picture in the corner of the laptop showed light flying through the darkening sky. Zach double-clicked to enlarge that camera view. Flaming arrows, one after another, landed on the hay inside of a trailer. She couldn't believe her eyes.

"Fire!" Zach jumped to his feet.

Janel's entire body stiffened with fear. "They're here."

Cole ran back into the room and glanced at the security footage. "The fire is too close to the stables. I have to put it out."

"Watch out for the guy shooting arrows. And take a different route across the ranch. Last night, they learned how we react to danger and now they're escalating their attack." Zach pulled on his coat. "I'll deal with whoever thinks they're sneaking up to the house again."

Cole grabbed a coat and rushed to the living room.

"This can't be happening again. Nothing deters them." Watching the flames on the screen fueled Janel's anger. "And I've had enough of this!"

"Good." Zach opened the gun cabinet. "I need to go outside and stop them from setting fire to the house." He handed her a weapon. "If anyone gets past me, shoot him." He headed to the back door. "Lock up after I leave and call 911."

The second after Zach fled outside, Janel pulled the door closed and secured the dead bolt. She turned and faced the empty room. Standing still and listening, the silence grew deafeningly loud. Last night, Karla and Mrs. Walker had been here with her.

She refused to let fear consume her again. Lifting the cold, hard gun, her determination set in. "I won't let them kill me."

Peering out between the blinds, she called 911 and reported the situation while watching Zach. He scanned his surroundings as he inched toward the far end of the porch, climbed over the railing and jumped down. When he stepped out of sight, her heart hitched, and she prayed he would come back to her, safe and sound. And not just because he kept her alive time and time again. She wanted to be near him. Maybe one day, she'd trust her instincts again, and let herself fall in love. Maybe...

The automated floodlights turned on, bathing the yard in a bright glow. Aside from Zach, there was no one out back. Her gaze traveled over the snow, between the trees—oaks that had lost their leaves and a few evergreens—to a metal shed in the distance. Her body tensed as she stared at the structure, expecting the murderer to step out from inside the shed.

He didn't.

With the gun feeling heavy in her hand, she returned to the

kitchen and set it down on the table. She slid onto a chair and pulled the laptop closer to watch the security footage. Cole, revealed by the stable's floodlights, hosed down the hay while two dogs ran around him, barking at the fire.

The next screen showed the horses, agitated but unharmed and gathered at the end of the pasture. She strained to see anyone lurking in the shadows cast by the lights attached to poles along the ranch road.

Seconds ticked by slowly, her nerves twisted into knots. The next screen popped up and a man wearing a black jacket and ski mask stepped out from behind an old truck parked on the side of the house and aimed at Zach.

She flinched. "No!"

Her scream must have reached his ears, even if faintly. Zach spun around and the bullet whizzed by, barely missing him.

The shooter ducked behind the truck. Janel lifted her hand to her head and drew in deep, settling breaths. *God, please protect Zach.*

Another camera angle flipped onto the largest section of the screen. A different masked man, also wearing all black, stood at the opposite end of the house. Zach was right; they had learned from the mistakes they made last night.

Her heart lurched as the intruder held up a gun and crept closer.

Zach needed to deal with his own shooter, who was drawing him away from the house.

Cole needed to put out a fire to save the stables.

And she needed to face a killer—all by herself.

The perpetrator reached out from the other side of an old ranch truck and discharged his weapon. Zach ducked behind Cole's parked SUV. Hearing footfalls, he inched toward the bumper in a crouched position.

A bullet fired from a different direction and shattered the window above Zach's head. He jerked away, his chest tightening with intense emotions. He had to suppress his anger and fear in order to think straight and stay alive—to keep Janel alive. Caught in a crossfire, he leaned against the tire so no one could hit him by aiming under the car.

He held his breath and listened. The familiar sound of a family pickup truck carried over a gust of wind. Straining to see the entrance to the ranch, he spotted Cole racing over the snow on horseback to prevent their father from driving into an ambush.

Zach clenched his jaw while maintaining a secure grip on his Glock.

Another engine roared, and he snuck a peek. The shooter skyrocketed over the snow, driving an ATV. He stopped about fifty feet away to collect his accomplice, a tall man wearing a similar black jacket and ski mask. A crossbow hung over his back. He'd shot the flaming arrows into the hay.

Rushing out from behind the SUV, Zach chased after them, pausing only to aim at the ATV's tire. They jolted forward and his bullet missed. Not by much. Before he could aim again, the man sitting behind the driver reached into his jacket pocket. He held up a grenade, pulled the pin and threw it at him before they took off at high speeds.

Adrenaline shot through Zach's body as he dove behind a copse of oak trees. The ground shook from the blast. Shrapnel, dirt and rock flew through the air. Seconds later, shaken but okay, he pushed to his feet. The debris had fallen short of his body by a mere six feet. Knowing better than to run after men with grenades, he headed home.

Suddenly, gunshots fired in rapid succession from the other side of the house, and a different ATV took off from that area, the driver wearing all black. A third shooter? Where did he come from? This wasn't just an attack, it was an ambush.

Zach raced across the backyard, then stopped to peer around the corner. The barrel of a gun stuck out of the guest bedroom window, firing in rapid succession toward the escaping ATV.

Janel? He did tell her to shoot at anyone who got past him.

If he said anything while outside, she might react before thinking and fire at him. Instead, he ran to the porch and unlocked the door.

"Janel!" He cautiously walked through the living room, the sound of gunshots echoing down the hall. "It's me, Zach! Don't shoot."

Silence.

"Zach?" She emerged from the door, her eyes wide and glassy. The muzzle of the revolver faced the tile floor. "It was him. I recognized the way he walked. He was coming to the house—to kill me."

"You're safe now. They're gone." He holstered his gun, then reached out for the Smith & Wesson. After taking it from her hand, he wrapped his arm around her shoulder. Then, glancing into the room, he spotted four other guns lying on the bed. "Backups?"

"I was afraid if I stopped to reload, he would run to the window and shoot me."

A smile tugged at his lips. "Good thinking. I'm proud of you." The sound of keys in the front door lock told him they were no longer alone. "That would be my dad and Cole."

Zach collected the weapons on the bed while she locked the bedroom window. He wished he hadn't left her alone. His goal was to intercept the intruder before he could get close to the house, and if they hadn't brought more men this time, he would have succeeded.

Tonight, their attackers heightened their efforts. He had to do the same.

They met up with the others in the living room.

"Are you both okay?" Cole asked.

"Terrified, but alive." Janel headed toward the kitchen. "I'm going to make more tea."

Sirens blared, and Zach shook his head. "So much for increased patrols in the area."

"I'll deal with them." Cole stepped back outside with their father.

Tired, both physically and mentally, Zach joined Janel in the kitchen. He would update his lieutenant after he made sure she was truly okay.

Janel turned on the stove beneath the kettle and then slid into a chair. "Do you think they knew most of your family had been pulled away from the ranch?"

He glanced at the charger on the counter. "Your phone wasn't on long enough for them to have used spyware to hear our conversations. They know about cameras. They turned off the one in your gallery."

"If I were them, I would strap one in the trees near the ranch. Maybe more than one."

"You're right. I would, too. They probably knew Cole and I were the only people here to look after you."

She looked taken aback. "I did a pretty good job of protecting myself."

"You were impressive. You're turning into a real cowgirl." He felt his brief smile fall. "Now, let's hope you don't have to do it again." But he knew she might—sooner rather than later.

Chapter Eleven

The next morning, Janel carried a cup of coffee loaded with creamer into the ranch living room for her sister while Zach sat within hearing distance at the dining room table. With Karla's many bruises, aches and pains, it was difficult to believe she only sprained her wrist in the accident.

"A thought occurred to me late last night. Maybe these guys know I have temporary amnesia. One of them could have snooped around the emergency room when I was there."

"It's a possibility." Karla straightened on the sofa and accepted the steaming cup with her one good hand.

"The rapid pace of their attacks feels desperate, but could also be part of their overall plan." Janel eased onto the ottoman across from her sister. "They might be trying to scare those memories deep into my subconscious until they can kill me."

"The doctor did say you needed to relax or you might not remember the events leading up to the concussion." Karla sipped her coffee while worry lines fanned her eyes. "This is your way of telling me you still plan to take another field trip, isn't it?"

"It's more important than ever." She reached out to touch her sister's knee. "My memories are fragile, but vital to ending this nightmare."

"Then I'm going with you and Zach."

"Absolutely not. You need to recover from the crash. And I'm not letting you change my mind this time."

Zach joined them from the dining room. "The purpose of the trip is to jog Janel's memory. That isn't going to happen if she's worried about you."

Karla finally agreed. "Please be careful. Regardless of whether these guys are trying to scare you, they are determined to fight it out rather than leave the state. There's something powerful keeping them here."

"And they have resources. We went from one assailant to two, and now three." Janel chose not to mention the grenade; Karla wouldn't let her out the door if she knew. "But we have God on our side. How else would we keep surviving hit after hit?"

Karla, not a believer, nodded slightly. "Maybe you're right."

Janel's mood lightened. Her sister might come around yet.

Minutes later, Zach drove toward the ranch's front gate in the sheriff's vehicle while she sat next to him, scanning their surroundings for the masked men. The only movements came from the horses grazing in the pasture. The peaceful scene reminded her there were people in this world who went about their days without the worry of being shot.

If only she could turn back time and choose a different path on the day of the burglary. But she couldn't. And now she was more determined than ever to uncover the truth. Why did she follow the killer instead of going back to work after her meeting at the bank? Everything in her said she didn't know the dark-haired man personally. Did that mean she didn't know him at all?

Todd... Did he hire these guys to commit the burglary at her request? At the time, she'd given up hope God had a long-term plan for her and was desperate to keep her mother's paintings. This scenario would explain why her ex thought they had a chance of reconciling. It would also explain why he left the state.

Zach turned onto the road that would take them through Sedona and glanced at her. Concern filled his eyes. "You okay?"

She nodded, despite feeling nauseated by her thoughts. Dark, threatening clouds loomed ahead, a mirror reflection of her mood. "Zach, thank you for taking me up the mountain. I know you don't like leaving the ranch."

"That was before."

"Before?" She raised her brows at his gruff tone.

"Before we met Frank Hyde yesterday." Zach's jaw tightened as he gripped the steering wheel with both hands. "I've met men like him before. I have no doubt this insurance investigator will bend the facts to make you look guilty. We need to do everything we can to mount your defense."

"I hope returning to the spot where the murderer climbed into the landscaping truck with the redhead will help me remember more."

Stealing a glance toward Zach, she wished her life was different. That she wasn't attracting danger, and she felt emotionally strong enough to make wise decisions. She believed he was a good man. He acted like one. But was he the man for her...one day far in the future? If she were found innocent of the burglary? She didn't know for sure.

Raindrops dotted the car as they drove through Sedona. Zach waited until they covered the windshield to flip on the wiper. "I hope the sky is clear going up the mountain."

"Weather shouldn't be a problem." She replayed the recently recalled memory. "I stayed in the car that morning, so there's no need to get out and retrace my footsteps. And who knows? Maybe we'll find his silver sedan parked on the side of the road."

"Probably not, but like you said, who knows?"

Fifteen minutes later, they left Sedona and drove the two-lane road through Oak Creek Canyon. Winter hikers rushed over the snow to their vehicles as sprinkles turned into a down-pour. One car after another passed them on their way out of the scenic area.

Red rocks and oak trees soon gave way to pine trees and switchbacks as they climbed the mountain. The narrow roads made her nervous, especially in construction areas like this one. The drop-off on their right kept Zach driving close to the center line. With the storm sending most people indoors, the traffic thinned and then became almost nonexistent.

Lightning lit up the sky. Through the rain-streaked window, she spotted the blue helicopter she'd seen right before Karla's car accident. A man wearing a black ski mask held a rifle outside the door. He aimed directly at them.

Her eyes widened.

"Shooter!" She heard a pop and felt a sudden jerk.

"He hit our tire!" The sheriff's vehicle swerved. Zach slammed on the brakes while gripping the steering wheel, trying to regain control, but the front end drove out over the side of the mountain, pushing on the orange netting meant to warn drivers to stay on the road.

The car stopped moving. The undercarriage of the car rested on the edge of a cliff, but they weren't tipping—yet. Movement of any kind might send them over. She held her breath, not ready to put her faith in an orange safety net that might not hold their weight. Instead, she prayed.

A vehicle rounded the winding road farther up the mountain, and the *wyump, wyump* of the helicopter's whirling blades faded as they flew away.

"What do we do now?" Pressing her back against her seat, she froze in place. All she could hear was her heartbeat, despite the rain pelting the windows.

Zach looked around, his expression grim. "We can't stay here."

"I vote we do. I'm scared." Her breathing grew ragged, her chest felt heavy and her head throbbed.

"The shooter will most likely come back to see the damage they caused. If we're alive—"

"We won't be for long. I get the picture." She groaned. "And I thought driving off a cliff into a creek filled with raging water was bad."

"You can do this." He reached his hand out to cover hers. "We have to, but slowly."

The warmth of his touch reminded her she wasn't alone. Together, they were stronger. "What happens if we open the doors—slowly—and the car tips over?"

"Jump out. Immediately." His wide eyes and tone demanded she take him seriously. "Ready?"

She barely nodded, still afraid to move but trying to look on the bright side. They had overcome so much already. How hard could this be?

Zach reached for his handle. "Unlock your door." When she paused, he whispered, "Janel, you need to unlock your door."

Biting her lip, she clicked the power button. "Do we open the doors on three?"

"Sounds good. One."

Horrified by what might happen, she screamed, "Wait!"

"Two. Three."

Having no choice, she pulled the handle and pushed against her door when he did. The sky rained on the arm of her coat.

The car creaked beneath them.

Her breath hitched.

Peering down, she eyed the cliff's edge below her seat. She blinked hard, diverting her gaze from where she might fall. Directly in front of her was maybe a four-inch width of solid ground for her to take her first step. Maybe she should crawl out.

The car slid forward another inch.

Her entire body shook.

"Jump!"

His loud, commanding voice propelled her forward. She fell onto her hands, with one knee landing on solid ground covered with patches of frigid melting snow while the other hugged the side of the cliff. Rain, turning to hail, pelted her back.

Zach rushed around the back end. "Are you okay?" He pulled her to her feet as water dripped down their faces.

A sports car, driving down the switchbacks, approached quickly. Zach tried to wave the driver down, but he ignored them and increased his speed, his front tires hitting a huge puddle right next to their car.

Janel instinctively took a step back as the water and slush splashed, drenching them. She lost her balance and screamed as she slipped beneath the orange netting and fell over the side of the mountain. Air whooshed out of her lungs.

She reached for a crevice but missed. Then her fingers skimmed a thick tree root, and she immediately grabbed hold of the hard rope-like feature that looped out and back into the mountainside.

The freezing hail struck her face as thunder filled her ears. Looking up, she found Zach reaching out to her.

With feet dangling below her, she tried to force her hand to let go of the root, but sheer terror controlled her body. Her fingers ached from holding on so tightly. Logic told her she couldn't stay there; she'd grow tired and fall to her death. But she couldn't move, either. Tears clouded her eyes and slid down her cheeks, dropping into thin air. Who knew where they would eventually land?

Was she really going to die—here—after everything she fought against already?

"Janel, grab my hand." He leaned out farther. "You can do this. Trust me."

A gust of wind made her shiver as the torrential rains threatened her ability to hold on. She prayed for help. "God, please don't let me fall."

Fear squeezed Zach's heart as he peered down at Janel. She hung from a tree root on the side of the mountain that had been carved out to keep boulders from falling on the road far below. If she let go, it would be a straight sixty-foot drop onto hard ground. He could not lose her, especially like this.

"Janel, look at me." Stretched out over the muddy ground, with the rain beating down on them, he continued to reach for her. Their hands were roughly two feet apart, and he couldn't move any closer without risking both their lives.

She tried, but rainwater hit her eyes, forcing her to blink and turn away. "I can't." Her entire body shook, then she made the mistake of looking down and began hyperventilating. "I don't want to die," she pleaded.

"I won't let you." He could hear the desperation in his voice. "Please, take my hand."

"I'm afraid to let go."

"You have no choice." He had to make her try. A memory of them talking at church flashed through his mind. "Janel, close your eyes and ask God for help."

"I already did." One hand slipped off the root. She gasped and kicked her boots wildly in the air as she grabbed hold again.

Horror struck him. "Pray for strength!"

"God, please save me!" she screamed and shot one hand up into the air.

Zach grabbed her wrist and pulled her up and over the side. Together, they fell into the mud. He didn't care; she was safe in his arms. Overwhelmed with emotion, a single tear slid down the side of his face. *Thank You, God. Thank You.*

Sobs racked her body as he held her close, patting the back of her coat.

After the worst was over, he helped her up and walked her away from the edge of the mountain. "We need to get away from here before they come back."

A frigid wind swept over them, and she shuddered. "You saved my life—again."

Guilt nudged at him. "We wouldn't have been here if it weren't for me."

"Don't say that. We both agreed it's important for me to re-member why I followed the murderer, and if I saw his face."

"You're right." He had to stop being so hard on himself. Only in a perfect world could she lie low until the shooters were caught. Their situation grew worse by the minute, and he needed her help.

Zach removed his cell phone from his pocket, hoping to call for a tow truck and a ride home. "I can't get a bar. The moun-tain and rain are interfering with the signal."

"Then we walk." She glanced up at the dark clouds, then wiped the water from her face. "Like you said, we don't want to wait here for that helicopter to come back."

After tightening his coat's hood around his face, he reached for her hand, not wanting to risk anything else happening to her. If he kept her close, he could pull her out of danger—in time, he hoped. At least the rain would keep most cars off the road, reducing the likelihood of getting hit since there wasn't much of a dirt shoulder to walk on. The rainwater would also wash away the mud covering them.

Lightning lit up the sky and thunder roared as they strode down the mountain toward a cabin his friend Joe owned, about five miles away.

He looked forward to reaching shelter. Careless drivers and shooters weren't the only dangers they had to look out for. There were still areas on the mountain where rain could dis-lodge huge rocks, sending them down on top of them.

Their eagerness to reach a safe and dry location kept their pace swift and the conversation to a minimum.

After walking for almost an hour, Janel sighed. "Are we there yet?"

He squeezed her hand. "Almost."

Fifteen minutes later, he led her up the muddy, unpaved driveway to a log cabin. The blinds were closed in the win-dows, the porch light was on during the day, and the fact Joe traveled for a living all pointed to his friend being out of town.

When no one answered his knock, Zach reached around a bush for the fake rock that held the spare front door key. "Joe said I had an open invitation."

"How long have you been friends?"

"Twenty years." He unlocked the door and entered first. A quick look around confirmed his suspicions—Joe's razor, toothbrush and comb were missing from the medicine cabinet. "He's not here. I'll leave him a note."

"What about your phone? Can you get a signal?"

Zach checked. "Three bars." His first call was to Cole. The second to his lieutenant, and he emphasized the sheriff's vehicle hadn't gone over the edge of the mountain. His third call was to Lily, who knew the way to the cabin. "We're going to need a ride back to the ranch once the rain lets up."

"I'll text you before I leave." Lily ended with, "Try not to get shot at while you wait."

"That's the plan."

Zach caught sight of Janel hanging her wet coat over the back of a kitchen chair, before grabbing a throw blanket from a recliner and wrapping it around her shoulders. She was beautiful, even with her hair soaked and hugging her face. When her gaze locked on his, he blurted, "I'll light a fire."

"That would be wonderful." She hugged the blanket close before joining him at the stone fireplace.

Once the flames crackled, they sat on the hearth, soaking up the warmth. When she shuddered, he ran his hands along her arms, trying to force the cold away. "Is that better?"

She nodded, looking up at him. "Thank you for telling me to pray when I was hanging from that tree root. I hadn't felt God's presence in a long time, but he was there on the side of that mountain. In that second, I knew without a doubt that I would be safe. He wouldn't let me fall. That's why I didn't hesitate that last time to reach for you."

"I was terrified that I might lose you." Remembering those

feelings lowered his guard, and the reasons they couldn't be together didn't seem so important.

"Lose me?" Her soft, questioning voice pushed any remaining reservations aside.

He stroked her soft jaw. "I feel strongly about you. I know we've been friends for years, but I'm hoping that maybe one day we could be more."

With gazes locked, she leaned closer, and he kissed her. Tenderly at first, then more fully. This moment felt right. They belonged together. Now he held no doubts.

A house-shaking thunderbolt jerked them apart.

Then Zach heard the hum of a car engine outside.

Chapter Twelve

Zach separated the blinds enough to look out into the storm. The hairs on his neck stood on end when a car rolled by slower than the weather called for. "There's a silver sedan outside. The windows are fogged, so I can't see the driver."

"The guy who shot the redhead drove a silver sedan before he switched to the landscaping truck."

"It's gone now." Zach placed his hand on the handle of his holstered gun. "I won't let him come anywhere near you."

"I know." The worry etched into her face remained, despite his reassurances. As if needing to see for herself, she peeked out through the window. "If it's the murderer, he might drive up the mountain and discover we left the car behind."

"He might not turn around and search for us," Zach spoke without taking his attention away from the window. The heavy clouds, rain-soaked trees and deserted road gave off an eerie vibe.

"That might be too much to hope for." She retreated to the dining room table and glanced about. "Would your friend mind if I made coffee?"

"Not at all." He told her where to find a canister of ground coffee and filters.

She took over from there, which gave him time to think about the kiss they'd shared and about how he'd become lost in the moment. He'd wanted to tell her how much she meant to him, and how he wanted to become a couple. But he couldn't. Not yet.

While listening to the coffee drip into the pot, he wondered about Janel's relationship with Todd. They'd dated for years. Were they truly in love? If so, he had to bow out and give her time to recover emotionally from their split...or go back to the man, if that's what she wanted.

But what if she and Todd weren't in love? Was there room for him now? Perhaps her grief over her mother's illness and later passing away were too strong for her to see the reality of the relationship back then. If so, how could she be better off now? The stress over her concussion, memory loss, potentially losing her gallery, her mother's missing painting and running for her life would be too much for anyone to handle.

He and Janel needed to talk about their kiss. Eventually. They were too on edge to have that conversation right now. Minutes later, she carried a cup of coffee for him to the window, where they could see the rain was letting up.

His phone dinged with an incoming text. "It's Lily. She's a mile away." He swallowed several gulps before handing the cup back. "I'll deal with the fireplace."

"I'll clean up the kitchen."

They had just finished when he heard the hum of an engine and car tires crunching gravel. Zach flipped off the inside lights, then made sure it was safe to exit before locking up and leading her to his mother's Cadillac. His sister sat behind the wheel.

They secured their seat belts while Lily announced unsettling news. "Cole says I need to take you both to Janel's house. Karla is already there."

"She's still recovering from her crash." Confusion registered in Janel's expression when she turned to Zach. "Do you know what's going on?"

"No, but I don't like it at all." He clenched his jaw. None of this felt right.

Sitting in the back seat, Zach squeezed Janel's hand several times on the way. She could only muster a partial smile in return. He remembered her telling him about the house she and Karla had inherited and how it felt empty without their mother, especially with her sister working in Scottsdale.

Looking out the windows, he studied their surroundings, keeping an eye out for any shooters. At least the rain had stopped, and the storm clouds were drifting away. That was one thing in their favor.

Driving down her block, he counted five vehicles parked on the curb, two marked Sheriff and one belonging to Cole. The front door opened, and Karla, cradling her braced wrist, marched across the grassy lawn toward them.

"Thanks, Lily," Zach said. "We'll catch a ride back with Cole."

"Anytime. My taxi service is always available." In a more serious tone, Lily added, "I'll pray things go well for you here."

The second the vehicle stopped, they pushed open their doors and Janel rushed to her sister. "What's going on?"

"They have a search warrant." A mask of disgust marred Karla's features.

"Who has a warrant?" Agitated, Janel ran her hand through her damp hair. "There's nothing here worth this kind of effort."

"Zach's lieutenant, his deputies, a Scottsdale detective and that slimy insurance investigator, Frank Hyde." Karla's voice heightened as she rattled off each person. "They think Mom's missing painting is here."

"What?" Janel took two steps forward, then stopped and rubbed the chill from her arms. Their clothing was still damp from their walk down the mountain in the rain. She should change while they were here.

"Hurry," Karla urged. "I don't want Hyde wandering around the house unsupervised."

Zach, with his long stride, beat them to the door while Lily drove away.

Once inside, Cole hurried over. He wasted no time filling them in. "When your lieutenant couldn't reach you, he called me. The guy with the mustache standing next to the dining room table is Detective Everly from Scottsdale. He says he arrested a fence who claimed he's been buying stolen art from Karla for the past year."

"No." Janel shook her head vehemently. "That's a lie."

Her sister's eyes narrowed. "He's lying."

Zach nodded his understanding, although he wasn't ready to make any declarations of innocence yet. He barely knew Karla.

A deputy finished searching the coat closet, and Zach reached inside. "Why search here?" he asked Cole while handing Janel a heavy sweater. "Karla lives in Scottsdale."

Janel hung her damp coat from the closet doorknob. Shrugging into the dry sweater, she stared at a deputy in the living room. He had removed seat cushions from the sofa, and it must have felt like he was tearing her home apart. There was nothing Zach could do about it. He felt helpless.

"The news gets worse," Cole said, jerking Zach's attention back to the conversation. "The fence claimed Janel called him the morning of the burglary, wanting to sell him four bronze statues."

Her eyes grew wide. "I don't know any fences."

Frank Hyde stepped out of the hallway. The smug look he wore said he'd overheard them. "The fence, Axel, was arrested before your scheduled meeting. Otherwise, he would have been caught with the goods."

"I never set up a meeting." Janel glared at Hyde.

Karla fisted her hands and stepped toward him. Zach blocked her path forward. This wasn't the time for a brawl.

"We found something." Voices drifted in from the opened sliding glass back door.

* * *

"The deputies couldn't have found anything connected to the burglary," Janel insisted. "It's not possible." She followed Zach out her back door. The snow around the pavers had turned to slush, so she watched her step on the way to the small art studio. Her mother had built it in the yard after they moved to this community near Sedona.

The lieutenant reached the studio door before them. "Wait here," he instructed. "Detectives, join me inside."

Janel wanted to protest as Cole and the Scottsdale detective were granted access, but not her. This was her home. Karla's, too, if she ever moved here. And their mother's painting space was like a memorial. The two of them had left it untouched, other than sweeping the floor and dusting. Whenever they missed her more than usual, they sat inside and reminisced. The thought that strangers had rifled through every drawer and cupboard made her stomach churn.

A deputy stood guard at the door, blocking the entrance, while Frank Hyde, the independent investigator hired by the insurance company, carried his leather notebook and paced the patio. He wore the same black T-shirt and gray suit he had on the previous evening. Karla glared at him, but he didn't seem to notice.

Zach leaned close to Janel and whispered, "What's in there?"

"My mother's art supplies. And the painting she was working on when she passed away. A rainbow above Cathedral Rock." Growing emotions, caught in her throat, threatened to choke her. She might need a lawyer, but asking for one could make her appear guilty.

"When was the last time you were in there?" Zach placed his hand on her arm, his expression sympathetic.

"Two weeks ago, and everything looked untouched. I don't understand what they think they've found."

After several long minutes, the lieutenant called them inside. The aroma of linseed oil wafted through the room. The deputies must have opened the one remaining bottle. She was glad to see they had put away anything they had searched through.

Fully inside the room, her boot heels clicked on the tile floor as she walked toward the easel that was turned in a different direction. Looking down, she found her mother's unfinished painting resting against the wooden easel leg. Her instinct was to snatch it up off the floor, but Cole stopped her.

"Don't touch anything," he instructed. "We have to check for fingerprints."

Annoyed that her mother's final work would get dirty on the floor, Janel stepped around to the front of the easel to see what was on display instead of the other painting. She blinked, then stared in disbelief at the sweeping swirls of red and orange. *Sun Setting on Rocks.* The missing painting. Her mother's legacy was all accounted for now.

Relief washed over her. "How did it get here?"

Instead of answering her question, Cole asked one of his own. "Are you positive it's your mother's work?"

"*I* am, and it was *planted* here." Karla pointed to Frank Hyde. "You refuse to see that because you want me to go to jail. You're after my job. It's common knowledge at the insurance company. How many times have you dropped hints around my coworkers? Six? Seven? I've got news for you—they will never hire you full-time. They don't like your methods."

Hyde snapped pictures of the painting with his phone, then smiled at her. "They'll like my methods now. And I want you to go to *prison*, not just jail, because you are behind the string of burglaries you supposedly couldn't solve. And now your sister is in on the act. She set up the burglary at her own gallery, and I'm going to prove it."

"The art has been retrieved, so your job here is done." Zach addressed his next comment to the Scottsdale detective. "I don't understand why the judge signed a warrant to search a house in my county. No offense, but this isn't your jurisdiction."

"No offense taken." The Scottsdale detective, a quiet man

with brown curly hair, placed his hand on his hip near the badge attached to his waist. "The fence claiming he bought art stolen from Karla Newman is in my jurisdiction, and her name is on the deed to this house, along with her sister's. Plus, we had an anonymous tip."

Zach lifted his brow. "What tip?"

Hyde lifted his finger, indicating he wanted to talk. "I received a voicemail message saying we could find stolen artwork here."

"That's convenient," Janel murmured, feeling like a spider caught in a web of deceit. Her sister was right; someone planted the painting here. There was no other reasonable explanation, and if these men didn't see that, she and Karla were in a world of hurt.

Anger flashed across Karla's face as she spoke to the detective. "I'm the one who put you on to the fence's trail. *I found* the informant who said Axel was buying the stolen art." Not missing a beat, she turned her ire on Hyde. "Did you ever consider the possibility they broke into my sister's gallery to keep me off the case because I was getting too close?"

"You make a valid point." The Scottsdale detective paused momentarily, as if ruminating over the facts. "I don't know what's going on here. The lieutenant says someone has tried to kill both you and your sister. And now this." He gestured to the painting. "If I were you, I would hire a bodyguard and an excellent lawyer."

"What?" Hyde shook his head. "You're not going to let them walk, are you?"

Annoyance flickered across the detective's stoic features. "This painting is evidence in Detective Walker's Sedona case, not mine. Nothing else was found here. I'm heading back to Scottsdale. Don't call me again unless you personally see proof related to *my* case."

Frustrated, Hyde stormed out of the studio.

Relieved, Janel retreated to her yard. Zach followed her, but then Cole called him back inside.

"I'll wait for you on the patio," she promised. Surely, she'd be safe with so many law enforcement officers on her property. Seconds later, she removed the wet covers from two chairs and sank into thick cushions. Her sister claimed the chair beside her.

Karla snarled. "Hyde always gets on my last nerve."

When Janel studied the fierce expression on her sister's face, she suddenly felt ill. A memory flickered through her mind. The morning of the burglary. In Sedona. Outside of a coffee shop. Karla, looking as angry as she did now, drew back her hand to slap a dark-haired man. He caught her wrist before she could follow through with the motion.

Janel had witnessed this while seated in her car at a traffic light. After leaving the bank, she headed back to work. Karla mentioned that morning that she was coming to town because of the burglary. She must have stopped for coffee and run into this man.

A flood of memories returned, and Janel's pulse raced. Breathing proved difficult as she remembered watching the man turn around. He wore mirror-lensed sunglasses and a black jacket with a hood hanging over his back. The murderer. Nausea struck her, and she felt lightheaded.

Karla, in real time, stood in front of her, waving her hands to capture her attention. Janel closed her eyes, not wanting her returning memories to slip away. *Why did I follow him?*

Suddenly, she pictured this man at her gallery last week. He'd spent at least twenty minutes studying her most expensive pieces, including her mother's paintings that were not for sale. He checked his cell phone between admiring one item after another but didn't buy anything. Had he been casing her gallery?

Her thoughts traveled back to the café parking lot. If asked why she wanted to slap him, Karla would have said it was nothing to worry about. So, wanting answers, Janel decided to follow the man. If he had been casing her gallery and stole from her, perhaps she'd find a clue leading to her mother's paintings.

Once Karla and the man climbed into their own vehicles and departed, Janel made sure she stayed at least two car lengths behind the dark-haired man.

After leaving Sedona and driving up the switchbacks, he left his silver sedan on the shoulder of the forest road to climb into the landscaping truck. That led to the two men parking in front of the white Victorian house. The dark-haired man walked toward the casita where her stolen art was hidden. The redheaded man attempted a double cross but was shot and killed. Horrified, Janel had gasped. The murderer spotted her and the race for her life began.

Then Zach saved her.

Janel blinked rapidly as her mind came out of her daze. A rush of emotions swept over her. She pressed her fingers against her forehead and closed her eyes.

Karla grabbed Janel's shoulders. "Talk to me. What's wrong?"

"I remember *everything*."

"That's great!"

Confused, she looked up at her sister, ready to read her reactions to the truth. "You haven't been up front with me."

"What are you talking about?" Deep lines creased Karla's forehead.

"You know the man who chased me through the forest. You tried to slap him outside of a coffee shop. *I saw you*." Janel now understood why her memories had eluded her. They were too painful to face. Her sister was somehow connected to a murderer.

Karla quietly stared at the ground.

Janel pressed on. "He knew which car was yours when he planted the bomb because he saw you driving it. Why did he try to blow you up? I understand why he shot at me. I saw him kill the redhead. Did you see him kill someone?"

"No. I always turn my car on with the fob, and he knows that. Maybe he was trying to scare you into keeping quiet." Karla glanced toward the sheriff's deputies on the other side of the yard. "I swear I didn't know he was the man trying to kill you until you connected all the pieces just now."

Janel grabbed her sister's arm. "What's his name?"

"Shh. You'll attract attention." Karla jerked free of her grip and then leaned closer. "This is worse than you think. If Hyde persuades a district attorney to arrest either of us for the string of thefts he and his brothers committed, the charges will include accessory to murder."

Hyde could have them arrested for murder? Her mind refused to accept the possibility. She shook her head. "This isn't happening."

Karla pushed out of the chair. "I'll fix this."

Wanting answers, she followed her sister inside the house. "What do you mean by 'fix this'?"

"Exactly what I said." With the law enforcement officers all outside, Karla removed their mother's car keys from a kitchen drawer. "The next time you see me, you won't have to worry about anyone trying to frame us, and Zach can make his arrests. Until then, I need you to keep this between the two of us. If anyone stops me, I can't prove our innocence."

"What did you get yourself mixed up in?" Stunned, Janel stood there, watching her sister exit out the garage door. Could Karla really solve their problems, or was this the beginning of a horrible end for them both?

Chapter Thirteen

Zach had wanted to believe from day one that Janel was innocent, and recent events only confirmed his gut feeling. She was too smart to display a stolen painting on an easel. Plus, she never would have disrespected her mother's unfinished work by leaving the canvas on the studio floor.

He told Cole as much during their conversation in Janel's living room while she'd gone to change into dry clothes. "What do we do now?"

Cole crossed his hands over his chest. "For starters, we can check the gallery's security technician off our list of suspects. He's worked for the company for fifteen years. Respected. No outstanding debts. No obvious suspicious spending."

"Sounds clean to me."

"Another thing," Cole continued. "Remember the casita where we found the other paintings?"

Zach nodded. "The one where the security camera had been turned off."

"The wires were cut. But the cameras attached to the house were still working."

"They must have used jammers to get inside both the casita and the gallery, just like the string of burglaries Karla was investigating."

"My thoughts exactly," Cole shared. "They needed to disable the camera inside the casita because the stolen art was out in the open. The owner could have gone online to check on his property while he was in Florida."

"So, we're dealing with intelligent burglars, who are *not* computer hackers, but did gain access to Janel's security code." Zach rubbed his chin with the pad of his thumb, trying to think of any other leads they may have forgotten to pursue. "Did you ever get a hold of the former boyfriend?"

"No answer. I left Todd a message to call me."

"He could be busy at his friend's wedding." Zach removed his cowboy hat and ran his hand through his hair. He was still a disheveled mess from walking in the rain and hail.

Leaning to the side, Cole glanced down the hall as if making sure Janel wasn't headed their way before he spoke. "What about Karla? She seemed eager to take off. Do you think she could be involved?"

For Janel's sake, Zach hoped not. "It wouldn't make sense for Karla to give information about the fence to the Scottsdale detective if she were the one selling him the stolen art."

"Unless she suspected the detective was already hot on his trail, and she wanted to make sure no one believed the fence if he named her."

Zach blew out a long breath. "I wish you hadn't said that."

"Why?"

"If Karla is involved in these burglaries, including the Sedona gallery, Janel will never get over it. It's her twin we're talking about."

Footsteps clicking on the tile floor ended their conversation. Seconds later, Janel entered the living room, carrying a garment bag. "I figured I'd better bring more clothes back to the ranch. I hope you don't mind."

"Not at all. It's a good idea." Zach strode over and collected the bag from her. "Cole's giving us a lift."

She sent his brother a tenuous smile. "This seems to be a repeating pattern. We get shot at and you drive us to the ranch."

"A pattern I hope to break soon by making an arrest." Cole waved them toward the front door.

Worry lines creased her face.

"You all right?" Zach asked, knowing no one could truly be "all right" when they've endured so much in such a short time.

She nodded, then silently walked to the front door and locked it after they were all outside.

The quiet in Cole's SUV was deafening. No one felt like talking, and if they did, they received one-word answers. They were all tired. It had been a long, overwhelming day.

Zach had so many questions to ask Janel, but he wanted to wait until they were alone. Driving through Sedona, the hum of the engine had almost lulled him to sleep in the passenger seat when he heard the whirr of helicopter blades.

"Is that the shooter? Please tell me it's not him," Janel called out from the back, panic infused in every word.

They peered through the vehicle's windows, trying to spot the helicopter. Cole had to slow down when the light up ahead turned red. They were boxed in by the heavy traffic.

"It's close." Zach rolled down his window to get a better look. Sure enough, a blue helicopter hovered high above them. "It looks like the same one."

Janel leaned closer to the front seat. "He won't shoot with this many witnesses, will he?"

"I want to say no," Zach answered. "But these men are desperate and anything but predictable. Although…" Remembering where they were, he had an idea. "Cole, take us to the police station. Let's see how daring these guys really are."

"You got it." Cole flipped on the siren and radioed the station to alert them to a potential danger.

The helicopter flew off. Zach tried to find identifying marks, but it was too far away. He called his lieutenant, who promised to get eyes in the sky.

The light turned green and the cars ahead of them moved out of the way. Cole sped to the police station, where several officers stood out front, waiting for them.

When the SUV parked at the front entrance, Zach told Janel to wait for him to get out first. When no one shot at him, he opened her door. "Walk quickly inside, then stay away from the windows."

"I'm so tired of being shot at." She unbuckled her seat belt and bolted toward the doors.

"Me, too." He stayed close, his body shielding hers.

"This way." Cole led them to his office, a cubicle in a large room. On his desk was a picture of his wife, Sierra. She had once been chased by a bomber. This was a reminder that good triumphs over evil when God is on your side. Sometimes it took longer to see the results, but Zach always saw the positive outcome in the end.

After Cole left them alone, Zach found another chair and pulled it into the cubicle to sit next to Janel. "This will be over before you know it."

"And then what?" Her eyes pleaded for an answer.

He wanted to make her promises, but he knew he couldn't. "I pray God will put these men behind bars, and soon."

Janel sat silently, rubbing her hands over her crossed arms.

Impatient for an update, Zach checked the window several times. He neither saw nor heard the helicopter. It was long gone.

Every time he sat, he studied Janel, finding her both strong and fragile. She would do what was needed to stay alive, even fire a gun, but she wore her heart on her sleeve. The thought reminded him of their kiss. "Janel..."

"There's something you need to know," she stated, stopping him from exploring where they stood romantically. "When I was sitting on my porch and you were in the art studio, a memory came back to me. I did see the dark-haired man's face, just like you thought. I don't know him, but I doubt Frank Hyde can be convinced of that. He thinks I'm guilty."

"You remember his face, and you didn't tell me?" Zach shook his head in disbelief.

She reached for the barely visible bump on her head. "It just came back to me at the house. So much happened there, and this is the first time we've been alone."

"You could have told Cole and me after everyone left."

"I wasn't ready," she snapped. "I'm sorry. Please forgive me for raising my voice. I'm trying to sort all of this out and needed time."

"I understand." At least, he thought he did. "Did you remember anything else?"

"He was in the gallery last week. I think he was casing the place. He had an eye for valuable art with resell potential. I thought he was interested in purchasing a piece as an investment, but he left without buying anything."

"Is that why you followed him? Because you thought he might be one of the burglars?"

"Yeah." Her gaze lowered to the industrial carpet. "I know it was foolish, but I was hoping he would lead me to my mother's paintings."

Before he could ask another question, Cole stepped inside the door. "False alarm. It turns out the helicopter is owned by a real estate developer. The pilot was carrying a photographer hired to take aerial shots of a property for sale, and the local tourist sites."

Zach glanced up at his brother. "Did the pilot say why he took off so fast?"

"Police sirens." Cole pointed to himself. "My siren. He thought it best to get out of the way in case there was trouble."

"Smart," Janel concluded before her gaze traveled between the brothers. "Cole, I remembered what the murderer looks like."

"That's great! This is the breakthrough we needed." He

rushed behind his desk. "Since I have you here, do you mind looking at mug shots of men arrested for burglary in Arizona?"

"I guess not," she said, but the worry lines on her face said something different.

Zach reached over and squeezed her hand. After everything she'd been through, he couldn't blame her for not looking forward to studying photographs of men with criminal histories, especially when the right one might take her emotionally back to the forest when she was running for her life.

The next morning, Janel entered the bedroom where Karla usually slept, hoping she had returned to the ranch during the early morning hours. There had been no sign of her the previous night.

Janel sat on the blue and white quilt covering the perfectly made queen-size bed and tried to reach Karla again. When the call went to voicemail, she hung up. She'd already left ten messages. How many times do you need to tell someone to call you?

Dread threatened to invade Janel's thoughts, but she wasn't ready to give up hope that her sister had safely returned to the ranch.

She checked the living room, dining room and then the kitchen before finally accepting the fact Karla was still out there somewhere. Doing what? Why did her sister think she could fix this? And how?

"Good morning." Zach stepped into the kitchen, his boots clicking on the tile floor. The woodsy scent of his cologne wafted through the air.

"I'm not sure it is a good morning." Janel sat at the kitchen table and clasped her hands together. "I didn't recognize anyone in those mug shots. All we know about the gallery burglar is he's willing to kill, has dangerous accomplices and could have run into my sister last night."

Zach prepared two mugs of coffee and joined her. "Do you have any idea where she went?"

"I wish I did." She accepted the coffee he offered and tried to draw comfort from its warmth before placing the mug down on the table. "Karla was so angry at Hyde yesterday. He's going after us, and she's determined to stop him."

Guilt ate at Janel for telling Zach a partial truth, but revealing that Karla knew the identity of the murderer and didn't tell anyone would make her sister look complicit in his crimes. And Janel couldn't stab her twin in the back like that.

Besides, Karla needed secrecy in order to prove their innocence. She told her so.

But how could Janel enter a romantic relationship with Zach if she wasn't completely honest with him?

She couldn't. Staring down at the coffee threatening to turn cold in her mug, Janel felt a new hole growing in her heart.

Zach drank his coffee, unaware of the emotional quandary she faced. "How does Karla plan to stop Hyde?"

"By uncovering the truth."

"That's what we want, too." Zach reached across the table to touch her hand, but she abruptly pulled it back onto her lap. He blinked hard before confusion altered his expression. Her reaction was a far cry from the kiss they had shared in the cabin.

"I could be in a jail cell by the end of the week," she said, offering some sort of explanation.

"I won't let that happen."

"No matter how hard we try, there are some things we can't control—even when we pray. Take my gallery, for example."

"Give it time." He leaned closer. "You prayed you'd find your mother's paintings, and you did. They may be in police custody for a while, but you'll get them back."

"Or the bank will. Have you forgotten I put them up for collateral to get my loan? My gallery is closed, and mail orders won't keep us afloat for long. I'll have to work for someone else while I spend the rest of my life trying to find those paintings and hoping I can buy them back. One piece at a time." Her heart ached. "To make matters worse, the murderer or one of his accomplices might mistake Karla for me. My sister is risking her life, trying to prove we're innocent. How much can go wrong all at once?"

"You're right. The future looks bleak right now, but that's when we need to rely on our faith the most." He pulled the laptop closer. "Let's help your sister find the truth."

"How? I already looked at mug shots." Curious, she watched while sipping her coffee again.

"You said the murderer came into your gallery before the burglary. He might still be on your security footage."

Hope lit anew. When Zach turned the laptop toward her, Janel entered the URL address. While waiting for the website to load, she tried to recall the man's face. Closing her eyes, she replayed the scene where she first saw him—with her sister—in the coffee shop parking lot.

Karla had tried to slap him. He grabbed her wrist to stop her. They argued. Karla pulled her hand back.

The man turned to leave, and Janel saw his face. Oval shaped. Clean-cut. Grecian nose. Piercing, angry eyes.

She quickly logged into her account. Scanning the page, she found the link that would show the camera footage for the day she believed he was casing her gallery. "Here we go."

Zach rounded the table to sit beside her. "What time was he there?"

"About two o'clock." She fast-forwarded the video, then slowed its progression. The picture suddenly distorted and turned black. "No..."

"One of his buddies must have jammed the camera." Zach shook his head. "If only... A picture would have gone a long way in identifying him."

Janel slumped in her chair. Suddenly, she remembered another time she saw the murderer, although briefly.

Her eyes widened. "I passed him on a sidewalk." Reenergized, she sat up straight and clicked out of the website. "I was about to enter a gala celebrating the opening of a Scottsdale gallery when he exited through the double doors. We don't know each other, so I forgot about it until now." She grinned. "The gala had an official photographer."

Zach's eyes lit up as he watched her work. "Maybe we'll catch a break after all."

She searched online for the gallery name, then scrolled through a multitude of photos.

Five minutes later, a picture and adjoining caption ignited genuine excitement. She pointed at the dark-haired man, who stood next to a museum curator and a wealthy art collector. "I found him!"

Zach pulled the screen closer to read, "Sawyer Sloan. Does the name sound familiar?"

"No, it doesn't, but then I don't leave Sedona much these days. Too busy working." She typed his name into a search engine and found a business website. "He's an art broker based in Scottsdale. He doesn't have regular office hours. You have to make an appointment to see him."

"Let's schedule one." Zach jotted down the phone number on notebook paper before calling. When no one answered, he left a message. "I'm interested in acquiring your services." He left a Biblical name but didn't mention he was a sheriff's deputy before hanging up.

"John?" she asked.

"My middle name."

"Nice. Can you check to see if he has an arrest record?"

"Sure." After a few minutes, Zach announced, "No prior arrests, but he did file a police report. His personal collection of Southwestern art was stolen a year ago."

"That is when the string of burglaries started."

Zach met her gaze. "The photographs attached to the police report were provided by the same insurance company your sister works for."

Words eluded her. Karla's specialty was art cases. This must be how she met the dark-haired murderer. Why did she try to slap him? Did she figure out he broke into Janel's gallery? If so, how? And why didn't she say anything?

While listening to Zach update his brother and lieutenant, mixed emotions assaulted Janel. A nagging fear ate at her, too. What if she just made things worse by giving law enforcement the name of the murderer? Would these masked men become more reckless with their attempts to kill her if law enforcement zeroed in on them? If so, more people would die.

Chapter Fourteen

An hour later, Zach continued to investigate with Janel's help. She'd fired off emails to the event coordinator in charge of invitations for the gala, and to the two men photographed with Sawyer Sloan, asking what they knew about him. She sat across from him, waiting for their replies.

Meanwhile, Zach discovered that Sawyer, who was an art broker, had two unemployed brothers living in Casa Grande, near Tucson. Oscar, nicknamed Oz, did time for burglary. Mostly video game stores. Larry, who owned a motorcycle, served in the military during his early twenties, which meant he had weapons training. He was involved in a bar fight two years ago, but no one pressed charges, even though the other guy left with a broken arm.

Zach's best guess was Sawyer selected the items to steal. Oz coordinated the burglaries. And Larry led the attacks. It made sense. What he didn't know was how they got Janel's alarm code. He pictured the gallery in his mind. The front was all glass, so the alarm panel hung on an adjacent wall. One of these men could have sat in a car with binoculars and watched Janel or Charlene enter the code.

There were other pressing questions Zach wanted answered.

Did any of the brothers have a pilot's license? Where were these brothers hiding now? And where was Janel's sister? Sawyer had killed one man already. Karla needed to be here, at the ranch, for her own protection and Janel's peace of mind.

Cole's name showed up on Zach's vibrating cell phone. They had been sharing information back and forth since Janel discovered the murderer's name. "Tell me you have good news."

"These are definitely our guys," Cole rattled off. "Oscar Sloan shared a prison cell with our murdered landscaper for a few months. The rest of his time, he bunked with a low-level member of a Mexican cartel, who smuggled drugs into Arizona through tunnels. I'm hoping no one from the cartel shows up around here."

"Me, too. Anything else?"

"An officer in Casa Grande swung by the apartment Oscar shares with the third brother, Larry. According to the manager, they've been gone for a few weeks."

Zach smiled at Janel. "We are so close to making an arrest, I can feel it in my bones."

Cole cleared his throat. "Unfortunately, I also have bad news."

"What now?"

When Janel raised her brows, Zach shrugged.

"That Scottsdale detective called. He's at the gallery with Hyde. They have a warrant and want to see both sisters. It looks like a repeat of yesterday. I'm stuck at the station, so I won't be able to meet you there. Call me later."

"Will do." Zach hung up, anger twisting in his gut. He knew Hyde wouldn't let things drop. He was like a dog with a rawhide bone. "Let's go," he told Janel. "I'll explain on the way."

"What are we driving? We're fresh out of vehicles."

"The sheriff's office towed my loaner off the switchbacks and replaced the tire. Lieutenant Yeager dropped it off while you were sleeping, along with a warning not to drive it into a gunfight."

"As if we did it on purpose." Janel rolled her eyes, then grabbed her phone and purse on the way out the back door.

Checking for shooters and helicopters, Zach ushered Janel to the car, determined to keep her safe. Although, he knew full well her greatest peril today could be the detective waiting for them and the insurance investigator who kept claiming the twins should be locked up.

When they arrived at the gallery, Lieutenant Yeager opened the door and stepped outside. Zach wasn't surprised. Local police usually served search warrants since they had jurisdiction. Janel's gallery was in both Sedona and the county he and the lieutenant worked for.

After removing the key from the ignition, Zach walked around the car to open Janel's door. Her clenched hands showed her nervousness. Once they reached the sidewalk, she stood between the two men.

Zach asked his lieutenant, "Did they complete the search of the gallery yet?"

"They did. There was nothing to find." Yeager addressed Janel. "Miss Newman, where is your sister?"

"I don't know." When he looked doubtful, she repeated more forcefully. "I don't know. And why does it matter? This is my gallery. Her name isn't on it."

Lieutenant Yeager's gaze shifted to Zach. "They have an arrest warrant for Karla Newman."

"What?" Janel jerked back, bumping into Zach.

He grabbed her shoulders to hold her steady. "Let's take this conversation inside."

Seconds later, Zach found the Scottsdale detective and Hyde huddled in a corner beside a collection of framed watercolor paintings. When they spotted Janel, the detective whispered something to the insurance investigator.

Janel's assistant manager stood behind the counter, wrapping up a painted ceramic vase. That explained how the lawmen gained access to the gallery.

Charlene gave them an apologetic look. "I know I was supposed to stay away, but that Hyde guy called and ordered me to come in. Can he do that?"

"We'll talk later," Janel told her.

Zach wondered where Charlene's boyfriend took off to. He was supposed to be her bodyguard.

When the detective crossed the room to speak to them, fury marred Janel's features. "Why are you trying to arrest my sister? She hasn't done anything wrong."

The smug look on Hyde's face had Zach's ire up once more. He reined in his emotions and focused on what the detective had to say.

"I'm sorry to tell you we've found a storage unit in Scottsdale rented in Karla's name." The detective casually placed his hands on his hips. "It contains artwork from each of the burglaries she was investigating this past year, along with printouts from her company showing their insured value."

Charlene's jaw dropped open.

Zach arched a brow. "Another anonymous tip?"

"Just good ole detective work." The detective narrowed his eyes at Zach. "I know how to do my job."

Janel crossed her arms over her chest. "Anyone could have rented that unit in her name, especially if the necessary paperwork was filled out online. It seems like you can do everything online these days."

The detective's features relaxed, as if remembering what Janel had been through recently. "There were containers inside with Karla's prints on them. They were on file because her employer required a background screening when they hired her."

"Tell her the best part," Hyde called out.

The detective sent him a dirty look.

They were playing a twisted version of good cop, bad cop.

"What?" Janel demanded.

The detective spoke to Zach. "I spoke to your brother this

morning. He gave me Sawyer Sloan's name, and I called a gallery owner who was helping me with the case."

Hyde laughed. "Karla's been dating Sloan for a year now."

Zach felt like someone had pulled a rug out from under his feet. He reached for Janel, seeing the shock on her face.

"That's not true. She would have told me." Janel glared at Hyde. "My sister warned me about you. You'll twist the truth until she's out of the way so you can take her job."

"Your sister is telling fairy tales to cover up for her crimes."

"That's enough," Zach snapped at Hyde. "Detective, what proof do you have that they've been dating?"

"I only have the gallery owner's word, but I don't need to prove they were dating when I have her fingerprints connected to the stolen items."

"But not *on* the stolen items," Zach pointed out, "or you would have said so. Her fingerprints were on containers that could have been stolen from her house."

The detective worked his jaw. "I have enough evidence for a warrant. If you see her again, it's your responsibility to arrest her." To Janel, he added, "Just doing my job, ma'am."

"Not good enough." She fumed as she watched the detective head to the door. When Hyde was halfway across the room, she glared at him. "Don't ever come back to my gallery again."

Hyde smirked. "Your sister thinks she's smarter than me, but she isn't. I'm going to track her down and take great pleasure out of watching the cuffs tighten around her wrists. I might even snap a picture and send it to her supervisor."

"Out!" Zach demanded. How many times would he have to say that to this man? "Detective, *do not* bring him back here again."

Lieutenant Yeager marched to the door. "I'll make sure they leave."

Finally alone, except for Charlene, Zach felt a wave of regret flow over him. "Janel…" He looked into her wary face. The last thing he wanted to do was hurt her.

She shook her head, not wanting to hear what he would say, but he couldn't let that stop him.

"The detective is right. If I see Karla, I have to arrest her."

Janel felt her knees buckle beneath her, and Zach pulled her up into his arms. Remembering what he'd said, anger hit her like a punch to the gut. She backed up. "You're going to arrest my sister."

Zach's eyes begged her to understand. "I don't have a choice."

"Everyone has a choice." She spun away from him and marched over to Charlene, needing to be with someone who had her back. "I'm so glad to see you, but where's Robert?"

"He had to show a house in Prescott. He'll be back soon."

Janel couldn't bring herself to look over her shoulder at Zach. Everything was such a mess. He had kissed her and wanted to date, but she was keeping a big secret from him—she saw Karla with Sawyer Sloan, and now she had to face the fact her sister may have dated him. But would she have taken part in the burglary? Janel didn't want to think so.

Her headache returned as her mind spun with conflicting thoughts. Karla knew about Janel's bank loan and was worried about losing their mother's paintings, too. But her sister wasn't even in town when Mr. Allen asked Charlene to mail the painting he bought to Florida. She wouldn't have known about the potential hiding place. And she was too smart to leave a stolen painting out in the open in their mother's studio.

Was Sawyer in the gallery that day? Could he have heard Mr. Allen? Janel rubbed her forehead, wishing the answers would come to her. Instead, she pictured Karla in the parking lot with Sawyer. Why did she try to slap him? They didn't look like two people who liked one another.

Before she dared to speak, she checked to see where Zach stood. He was peering through the blinds, no doubt searching for the Sloan brothers and giving her space to cool off.

Janel whispered to Charlene, "Have you seen Karla lately?"

She glanced at Zach before answering in an equally hushed tone. "She dropped by my house last night, wanting to know where I bought the *malasadas* I sometimes bring to the gallery."

Karla was supposed to be fixing things, and she wanted to know about Portuguese donuts? "Did she tell you why she wanted to know?"

"Not last night. But during one of her visits, I brought in a dozen *malasadas*, and she said a man she occasionally dated had one every morning since his first trip to Hawaii. They're quite popular there. That's where I first tried one."

Zach strode toward the back of the gallery, sending them a questioning look. Janel pushed away nagging feelings of guilt as he passed by. Karla was her twin; she had to keep her out of jail. Whatever it took.

"What did you tell Karla?" Anticipation swelled in Janel's chest. This could be the first genuine lead to finding her sister before the Scottsdale detective or Hyde did.

"Sugary Joy Bakery in Flagstaff."

Janel pressed her lips together, hard. She didn't want to ask, but she had to know. "Did Karla give you the name of the man?"

"No. She only said she met him on a case." Charlene shrugged. "That's all I know."

"Thank you for your help." Janel wasn't sure if she should be relieved or disappointed that she didn't name Sawyer. "Please do me one more favor and don't tell anyone else about the bakery. No one at all. Unless directly asked by someone with a badge. I don't want you breaking the law."

After Charlene promised to keep their secret, Janel looked around, wondering what to do now. Putting all the pieces together, she could only conclude that her sister had sometimes dated Sawyer and planned to track him down using his weakness for *malasadas*.

Janel stepped away and pulled her phone out of her purse. She checked her family locator app for her sister's whereabouts. *No location found*. Karla must have her phone turned off. After texting her to call back, she asked Charlene if she could borrow her car.

"No, you cannot borrow her car," Zach stated from the hallway leading to her office. "Someone is trying to kill you, remember?"

"Zach, what would you do if someone was trying to frame Lily? Would you hide at the ranch, or prove her innocence?"

He expelled a long breath. "I would prove her innocence, but you cannot do that without me. I've been the only thing between you and a bullet since you were running in the forest."

"But you'll arrest my sister."

"I was thinking about that." He drew closer, his presence formidable. "If I see her, I can hand her over to Cole, who doesn't have to call the Scottsdale detective immediately."

Hope sprung in her chest. "Your brother would buy us time?"

"If we're close to real evidence proving her innocence."

The gallery phone rang, and Charlene reached for it.

"We're closed," Janel reminded her. When the machine answered, she waited for a message or disconnect. The room grew quiet, and she heard the hum of traffic and a horn honk in the background.

Charlene read the caller ID. "Unknown caller. It's probably nothing." Her shaky voice belied her words.

Zach marched around the counter and snatched the receiver. "Who is this?" The line died. He hung up, and the message machine disconnected. Next, he tried dialing star sixty-nine. No one answered.

A shudder reverberated down Janel's spine. "Do you think that was Sawyer or one of his brothers?"

"Do you really want to hang around to find out?" Zach didn't wait for an answer. He turned to Charlene. "Leave now. If you're followed, call 911 and head straight to the police station. And don't come back here. *I mean it.*"

"I won't. If Hyde calls me again, I'll hang up," Charlene

promised. She grabbed the box holding the vase she had prepared for shipping and Zach escorted her to her car.

Zach locked the back door and strode toward Janel. "Let's
go."

"To Flagstaff. I have a lead."

Lines creased his forehead. "How did you find a lead?"

"I'll explain on the way."

Letting the subject drop for now, he stepped outside to make
sure the front parking lot was clear. He waved to her, and she
locked the door with swift movements. Seconds later, she was
securing her seat belt in the passenger seat of his sheriff's vehicle.

He turned onto the main street, then spared a glance in her
direction. "Did Karla tell you she was dating Sloan?"

"She usually meets guys online or at the gym. There wasn't
anyone serious, and she only mentioned a guy if she had a
funny story to tell. No one was named Sawyer."

"And Karla never mentioned dating someone she met on a
case?" He glanced in the rearview mirror and then switched
lanes.

"No. I wouldn't have approved if the case was still open."
Janel had always been a rule follower—until now. Technically,
she was interfering with an investigation by not telling Zach
she remembered seeing her sister with Sawyer. But if he knew,
he might assume Karla was guilty and not help prove her innocence.

Janel's stomach knotted, making her feel sick. Then she noticed Zach kept glancing in the mirror. "What's wrong?"

"We have company."

Chapter Fifteen

Alarmed, Janel twisted in her seat to look out the back window and then peered into her side mirror. "The black Ford Taurus? It was parked near the gallery."

"It's Hyde and the Scottsdale detective. They must think we'll lead them to Karla." While remaining in the right lane, he checked his side mirror. "I have a plan."

"That's good. We need one." She turned to face the back window again. There were three cars between them and the Ford. "Do you think they called the gallery to get us to leave? If so, it worked."

"Them or one of the Sloan brothers, trying to find you."

"I'm so tired of all of this. I'll never complain about being bored again."

"I can get behind that sentiment." He checked his mirrors again. "Prepare for sudden moves."

She adjusted her seat belt and reached for the car's grab handle. "Ready."

With the light turning yellow, Zach quickly switched lanes and, after entering the intersection, made a sudden U-turn.

Now traveling in the opposite direction, Janel watched the

cars in front of Hyde and the detective stop at the red light. "They'll be stuck for a few minutes."

"Enough time to lose them."

"Maybe you should drive faster," Janel suggested.

Zach chuckled. "When we reach the interstate." He turned right into a residential neighborhood, left at the next corner and then right again two blocks later. This route took them to a back road. "Where did you plan to go in Charlene's car?"

After a slight hesitation, she told him Karla asked about a special donut. "Someone she occasionally dated has *malasadas* for breakfast every morning."

"You mean Sawyer," Zach concluded.

Janel sighed. "I'm going with that assumption. She wouldn't have gone to Charlene's house to ask about these donuts if some other guy she dated liked them."

"You're right. It sounds like Karla's hunting down the Sloan brothers."

"Yeah." Worry dripped from her one-word answer. Janel looked out the window, keeping an eye out for the Sloans, Karla, Hyde and the Scottsdale detective. She pulled her coat closed, the chill in the air growing as the outside temperature dipped. A light dusting of snow fell on the windshield, and Zach turned up the heater.

While they drove, Cole called with an update. There was an all-points bulletin out for the car Karla was driving. That would make it harder for her to remain free long enough to find Sawyer. Janel felt conflicted. She wanted her sister to find her proof, but being arrested might keep her alive. The Sloan brothers were dangerous men.

Zach glanced her way. Janel frowned but remained silent. What could she possibly say that would help her sister now? Nothing. If she told him she remembered seeing Karla trying to slap Sawyer, it would only make matters worse. It proved they were together in Sedona. If she told Zach her feelings for him were growing, he'd eventually learn she was hiding a memory and accuse her of using him. The best thing she could do was emotionally disconnect from him and focus on finding her sister.

They were entering Flagstaff when she noticed the blue helicopter flying high in the distance. "Not again."

"What?" Zach peered out through the window while the wipers swished back and forth, sweeping away the snow.

"Helicopter." Her tone hitched with fear. "It could be carrying a photographer or—"

"A shooter," he said, completing her thought.

"If they see us go into the bakery, they'll figure out we're close to finding them."

"That could put the employees there in danger. These men kill witnesses." Zach scanned their surroundings. "We need a place to hide the car."

"The university has parking garages."

"That will do." He turned onto East McConnell Drive while calling in another update to his lieutenant. "I need an unmarked car." They coordinated their plan and then disconnected.

The helicopter hovered over downtown Flagstaff. Why? Could the pilot be searching for them? If so, how did he know they were here? What if the Sloans spotted Karla? Would they kill her?

Zach entered the garage and drove up a level to hide his sheriff's vehicle. He parked and turned to Janel. "You okay?"

"I think so." The dread she heard in her own voice told a different story. "How can we put these horrible men in prison before they kill me or Karla if Hyde, a detective and possibly a helicopter pilot are searching for us?"

"One step at a time." Zach placed his hand over hers.

His touch felt warm and reassuring. "You said God sometimes shakes us out of our everyday life to force us to choose a new path."

"More or less."

"When does the shaking part stop?" Her voice cracked as she pushed back tears.

He squeezed her fingers. "You're not alone."

"I appreciate all you've done...even if I don't deserve your kindness." Remembering the secret she kept from him, she felt guilty and pulled her hand back into her lap.

"Janel..." The hum of an engine entering their level forced him to look away. Lieutenant Yeager parked a black SUV behind them and climbed out. Zach turned to her. "Time to go. We'll talk later."

They exited the marked sheriff's vehicle, and the two men exchanged car keys. Zach gestured toward their new ride. "Thanks for this."

"It has four-wheel drive. You might need it if the snow keeps falling." The lieutenant's gaze swept to Janel and back. "Do you want me to take Miss Newman to the ranch so you can follow this lead?"

"No." Janel panicked, taking a giant step away from the lieutenant. "Zach needs my help. Karla stormed out of our house after the search warrant. She won't listen to anyone but me."

"Then find her and talk fast," the lieutenant ordered, as if she worked for him. "Sawyer will do anything necessary to stay out of prison." He turned to Zach. "I paid a visit to his ex-wife. She lives near here. They have a six-year-old son, suffering from severe aplastic anemia."

"That's horrible." Janel couldn't imagine the depths of this woman's fear.

Yeager nodded his agreement. "Sawyer was helping her consult with specialists for the best course of treatment."

"No wonder the attacks have been relentless." Zach's expression filled with sympathy as he pushed back the brim of his Stetson. "When was the last time Sloan visited his son?"

"The day before the burglary at Miss Newman's gallery." The lieutenant opened the door to the marked sheriff's vehicle

Zach had been driving. "I'll give you a head start. Someone might be watching for this vehicle to come out of the garage."

Janel and Zach climbed into the SUV and drove away. Trepidation built by the second. Finding the bakery was the easy part. What happened after that might get them killed.

Zach phoned his brother. "Cole, I need you to meet me in Flagstaff. I'll tell you why when you get here."

Janel lifted a brow.

"We might need backup, and I couldn't ask Yeager. He'd have to arrest Karla and hand her over to the Scottsdale detective."

"I'm surprised your lieutenant didn't mention the warrant."

"Me, too. But then, the burglaries are being handled by detectives outside of the sheriff's office. We want Sawyer for murder, and Karla could make our job easier."

Satisfied with his answer, Janel changed the subject. "I found the bakery on my phone. Turn right on Milton."

They stayed alert for signs of danger and for Karla while Janel navigated. Ten minutes later, they parked in front of Sugary Joy Bakery. The purple building stood out from the pine trees growing in the undeveloped areas around the quaint shop. Snow accumulating on the surrounding landscape and on the half dozen cars in the lot gave the scene a winter wonderland appearance, even though the feeling in the SUV was anything but enchanting.

"I'm going in with you," Janel stated flatly. "No offense, but I think it'll be easier for me to get information."

"No offense taken. Just don't say anything alarming. If Sawyer's been here, deputies will set up surveillance to capture him when he comes back. If the bakery staff looks scared, it will tip him off."

They strode to the entrance through the crisp air, hugging their coats tightly to stay warm. He tugged the door open and held it for her. The neatly decorated cakes in the window and the aroma of baked goods wafting through the air had her stomach grumbling.

They were perusing the offerings in the refrigerated display case when a college-aged teen, wearing pink glossy lipstick, black pants and a purple shirt sporting the store's logo, strolled over.

"Do you have any *malasadas*?" Janel asked, keeping her tone conversational.

"We do." The teen pointed to a tray in the top left row, then suddenly did a double take. "You look familiar. Didn't you buy some this morning?"

"You're thinking of my twin sister. She might have been here with this guy." Janel showed her the picture of Sawyer.

"He's been in here a few times, but they were never together."

"Really?" Janel's mood lightened, and she pointed to the display case. "We'll take half a dozen *malasadas*. Two of each flavor and two coffees."

While the girl bagged their order, Zach joined the conversation. "Did you see which direction he drove from? We're trying to find her sister so we can give her a ride back to Sedona."

"They broke up," Janel explained. "She doesn't want to be near him. You know how it is."

"Been there." The teen snatched two cups and filled them with coffee. "All I know is the man in the picture walked over here from that hotel." She pointed to a building half a block away.

"Thank you for your help." Janel took the bag and cups over to a counter containing creamer and sugar to prepare their coffee. Zach finished paying and then held the door open for her.

Outside, on the way out to the car, she grinned. "Admit it, I did good."

"Yes, you did. Now we call in the deputies." He clicked the doors open.

"Not yet." She climbed inside the SUV and waited for him to join her. "We have to find Karla first."

He met her stern gaze with his own. "What if Sawyer sees *you* first?"

After a fifteen-minute debate, Zach had relented and agreed to finding Karla before they called in the deputies. He parked the SUV in front of a nearby diner to wait for Cole. "There he is."

"Thanks." Janel sent Zach an apologetic look. "I know I'm not making this easy for you."

He blew out a long breath, remembering what his parents always said about looking at a situation from another's perspective. "I have a sister, too, and if Lily were caught up in this mess, I'd do anything to help her."

"I knew you'd understand," Janel said, her tone sincere. "And I pray Lily will always be safe."

Cole parked and walked over to their open driver's side window. It took only a minute to fill him in on recent developments. He whistled and pushed back the brim of his felt cowboy hat. "You're in a pickle. You can't go into the hotel without backup, and we can't leave Janel in the car alone."

"And I promised not to call in the deputies until after we find Karla." Zach frowned, wishing this case wasn't so difficult to navigate. He prayed for guidance, then took a leap of faith. "Let's play it by ear."

"Now, why didn't I think of that?" Cole's sarcastic tone hung in the air.

"We can't make a plan until we see the layout of the hotel, anyway."

"True." Cole opened the back door of the SUV. "We'll be less conspicuous if we arrive in one car."

Zach turned the key to start the engine, then noticed Janel's blond locks. "These guys are less likely to notice you if your hair is inside your coat's hood."

She quickly obliged. "And you two wouldn't stick out from the crowd if you ditched the cowboy hats."

"Good point." Zach handed his hat to his brother in the back seat, then ran his hand through his hair to straighten it out and noticed Janel was watching with interest.

A few minutes later, he drove the SUV around the hotel, a three-story beige building with white trim. The snow-covered grounds appeared neatly kept. Not first-class accommodation, but not run-down, either.

"I'm not seeing any familiar vehicles." Zach scanned the parking lot once more. "Definitely no motorcycles."

"How do you want to play this?" Cole asked.

"I have jurisdiction, so I'll go inside." Zach turned in his seat to speak directly to his brother. "How about you sit up here and watch over Janel? If Sawyer shows up, call me."

After Cole agreed to the plan, Zach flipped Janel's visor down to block part of her face, then handed her the sunglasses he'd stashed in his coat pocket. The car would get stuffy if they couldn't keep the heavily tinted windows open a crack.

Cole took his place behind the driver's seat and opened the bag of *malasadas* sitting on the center console. The enticing aroma wafted through the air.

Zach strode inside the office, where he found a middle-aged woman bundled up in a sweater behind the registration desk. According to her name tag, she was the hotel manager.

"Good evening, Molly." He showed her his badge, then the picture of Sawyer he'd saved on his phone. "Have you seen this man?"

"We run a respectable establishment here." Her voice remained flat as she stared at the picture.

"I'll take that as a yes. Which room?"

"Twenty. Bottom floor on the end." She swiped a key card through a machine and handed it to him. "You can let yourself in."

"When was the last time you saw him?"

"He sped out of here with his buddies about two hours ago." She pulled up the registration information on her computer, wrote it down, including vehicle make, model and license plate, then handed it over.

Zach showed her the mug shot for Oscar Sloan. "Is this one of his buddies?"

She groaned and nodded. "An ex-con. Figures. He shaved off that hideous goatee, but it's him."

"And this one?" Zach pulled up the military picture for Larry Sloan.

"He's with the other two. At least he doesn't have a mug shot."

"Not yet." He wanted to know if Karla and Sawyer were still dating, but he didn't have a picture of her. A thought occurred to him, and he brought up a picture from the gallery website. The sisters looked so much alike that one of Janel might work. "How about this woman? Was she with these men?"

"She showed me a picture of the first guy. Said he was her brother."

"Did you give her a key card, too?"

"Absolutely not. I gave her his room number, nothing else. I don't want any trouble here."

"Let's hope you don't get any." He strode out the door and over to Cole, who rolled down the window.

Janel leaned across the seat. "Did you learn anything useful?"

Zach lifted the key card for them to see. "They're not here." He gave his brother the piece of paper the woman had written on. "If this car returns, don't waste a second calling me. I'm going to check out the room."

He strode across the wet asphalt to room twenty and let himself inside what turned out to be a two-bedroom suite. The living area was neat and clean. Surprising for three criminals. Each bed held open suitcases, packed and ready to go. *Prepared for a quick getaway, or leaving town soon?*

The manager had given him permission to go into the room, but that did not extend to searching through suitcases. Heading back into the main area, he surveyed the couch, coffee table, television and desk. Something felt out of place.

Looking up, he noticed there were two smoke detectors on the ceiling. One above the coffee maker, and one close to the desk. Hotels wouldn't have two detectors in one room.

He pulled out the desk chair and climbed on top, suspecting the detector above was a spy camera. It took little effort to yank it off the ceiling and find the recorder hidden inside. He'd seen one of these before. If Karla planted it, the digital recording would be sent to her phone, or any other device she'd selected.

After placing it on the desk, he called his lieutenant, who enthusiastically reported that he would call for backup and work on obtaining a search warrant.

Zach returned to the SUV and discovered Janel was already excited. She didn't even know about the fake smoke detector yet. "What's up?"

"My sister showed up on my app." She lifted her phone for him to see. "We have to go back to my house—now."

When Zach told them about the recording device, Cole agreed to wait in the office for the deputies to arrive and pocketed the hotel key card. Climbing out of the driver's seat, he added, "It makes sense to take her back to Sedona. Yeager would agree. He told you to keep her safe."

He thanked his brother with a tap on his shoulder and then took his seat behind the wheel.

"Let's hurry." Janel buckled up her seat belt.

"First, tell me how long you've had a location finder on your phone."

When he raised a brow, she scowled. "Don't give me that look. It only works if her phone is turned on, which it wasn't until a few minutes ago."

"Did you call her?"

"I tried. She didn't answer." Janel pointed to the key in the starter. "Let's go before she leaves—or the Sloan brothers find her. Somehow, they know everything."

Chapter Sixteen

Janel warmed her hands in front of the SUV's heating vent. They were ten miles away from her house. "Can you drive faster?"

"The sun's gone down. It's dark and snowy." Zach glanced at the rearview mirror.

"You're right. I'm just so worried about my sister."

"We're almost there. Try focusing on the good news. We have witnesses who can say Karla wasn't hanging around Sawyer and his brothers. The teen in the bakery said they never came in together, and the manager said Karla had to show his picture and ask for a room number. If they were still dating, he would have called her from a burner phone. That puts doubt in the theory that she was in on your burglary."

Janel studied his face as the light from oncoming traffic illuminated his strong features. "Then you believe we were both framed, not just me?"

He spared her a glance before returning his attention to the slippery roads. The windshield wipers swished as they swiped away the sleet. "Yes, I truly believe you're both innocent."

Relief flowed through her. "Then there's something I should tell you. I hated keeping it a secret, but I had to, for Karla's sake. It made her look guilty when I knew in my heart she wasn't."

This time, he kept his eyes on the road. "I'm listening."

Janel couldn't tell from his voice what he was thinking. After hesitating, she decided there was no backing down now. "I remembered seeing Karla outside a café in Sedona the morning the landscaper died. She tried to slap Sawyer. I didn't know his name then. They argued and drove away in separate cars. I knew she wouldn't tell me what happened because she never wanted me to worry. Then I remembered seeing Sawyer in the gallery and suspected he'd been casing the gallery."

Zach pulled over onto the road's unpaved shoulder, and she could sense his mixed emotions through his stiffening posture. "When exactly did you remember seeing this?"

"At the house. After they found my mother's painting." She felt like an invisible wall protecting her from the bad guys was crumbling away. "Don't hate me, please."

"Of course, I don't hate you." He huffed a heavy breath. "And when you confronted Karla, what did she have to say for herself?"

"She said she was going to fix things." Janel realized too late that her statement would erase his belief in Karla's innocence. "My sister *did not* steal from anyone. That predator targeted her to keep tabs on the investigation. There is no doubt in my mind."

"I thought you didn't trust your instincts?"

Anger struck her like lightning. "How dare you throw that in my face?"

"Make me understand, Janel. You withheld vital information. We could have talked to Karla at the house, discovered exactly what we were up against and solved this case by now. You are still in danger because of your sister."

"Don't say that." Conflicting feelings warred inside her. "She's fixing this."

"What else are you hiding?"

"Nothing. I swear."

"Omitting the truth is a lie. You've been lying to me." He

clenched his jaw, then drew in a calming breath and met her gaze. "Didn't our kiss mean anything?"

"It meant everything." She wiped a tear from her cheek. "But Karla is my blood. My twin. I had to know you would believe in her innocence before I could share this."

"What I know is relationships are built on trust. And we don't have any." He angrily drove back onto the main road, not giving her another look.

Her slashed heart sunk irretrievably into a bottomless pit.

"Everyone keeps secrets, Zach. Even you," she shot back. "Your job requires it."

"That's different."

"Not from where I'm sitting. You keep secrets to protect the innocent, and so did I." She stared out the window, wondering how long it would take for Sawyer and his brothers to return to the hotel where they would be arrested. Once that happened, she could return home for good. Not a minute too soon.

She might also have to start attending a new church. Entering through the same doors, expecting to see him and then knowing he didn't want to see her would hurt too much.

God, why is this happening? Please tell me what to do. Show me. I need Your help.

They drove in silence until Zach slowed in front of her house. Her mother's sedan had been abandoned at the entrance to the driveway, the back end still on the street.

"Karla's still here." Janel waited impatiently for the SUV to come to a full stop near the streetlight, then she flung open the door.

"Wait!" Zach rushed around the front of the car, following her.

Janel ran along the bushes lining their large snowy yard, stopping only to inspect the sedan's back tire. Most of the tread was missing. Her sister must have kept driving on the flat to get here, then left it parked over fifty feet from the house. The need to see her sister overtook her. She rushed toward the front door, following the single set of footprints in the snow.

Karla always locked the door, so Janel quickly searched through her purse and retrieved the key. Standing beneath the porch light, she was about to insert it into the lock when she detected the faint scent of rotten egg.

Zach stepped onto the porch, then suddenly grabbed her arm and pulled her into a full run down the driveway.

"Let me go! My sister's in there." Exasperated, she tried to yank free. "Karla!"

Gunshots followed the hum of an engine on the street.

"Down!" Zach pushed her behind the bushes lining the yard and dove on top of her. Snow-covered grass cushioned her face as she listened.

The Sloans were here to kill them.

More gunshots. One took out a window.

The earth suddenly shook below them.

A roar from the house breathed life into an explosion, ripping through the air.

The car sped away, and Zach rolled off her back. She pushed to her hands and knees and stared up at the flames that engulfed her house. Heat from the raging fire flowed through the air above them.

"Karla!" Pushing to her feet, she scanned the yard, desperately searching the shadows for her sister. Tears choked her. She coughed on the smoke and irrepressible misery. "Where are you?"

Zach grabbed hold of her arm. "We have to go!"

Firelight flickered over his face. Janel stared at him, unable to speak or move. Her sister was dead because of her. Everything was her fault. She was the only witness. This explosion was meant for her.

"Janel, they could come back. I'll call the lieutenant, but we have to leave. Now!"

* * *

Minutes after receiving a text from Charlene, asking for their help, Zach parked the SUV in front of her quaint one-story house, only feet away from the concrete driveway where the assistant manager's red two-door coupe sat. Like the other homes in this older neighborhood, a solitary oak tree—missing its leaves—grew in the center of the snow-covered yard.

During their drive, Zach had tried to come up with a scenario where Karla was still alive. "Maybe your sister took a rideshare or walked to a neighbor's house," he suggested, removing the key from the ignition.

Janel continued to stare out the passenger side window, her body limp like a doll. "Footprints. They show Karla walked to the door and never came back out."

She was right. There had been only one set of footprints. They led from the car Karla was driving to the porch. Not back again. What bothered Zach was the amount of gas that had filled the house. Karla would have smelled it—unless she'd been asleep, unconscious or dead. The Sloan brothers could have killed her and then blew up the house to destroy the evidence.

The front door suddenly swung open, and Charlene, illuminated by the porch light, ran outside.

"Something horrible must have happened." Janel sprang from the SUV, then slammed the door shut.

Zach rushed to join the women on the sidewalk. Charlene was talking so fast he couldn't understand what she was saying. "I need you to start at the beginning and speak slower."

Charlene pressed a hand to her chest and inhaled deeply. "I heard someone in my backyard and called Robert, but he's stuck in Prescott. His tire blew out. He told me to call the police."

"Good advice." Zach scanned the front of the house and then grabbed a flashlight before walking over to the side gate to examine the lock. It was still secure. "Could have been raccoons."

She shook her head. "I know the difference between animals trying to get into the trash and a human walking over my backyard river rock."

"What did the 911 dispatcher say?"

"I was on the phone with her when I heard an explosion. I reported that, too. She told me an officer would be out, but I know whatever blew up will probably take precedent. They might not be here for hours." Charlene's brows furrowed when she turned toward Janel, who held fingers over her mouth as tears flowed down her cheeks. "Did something happen?"

"There was a gas leak at her house." Zach placed his hand gently on Janel's arm, but he knew there was no comforting her. Her grief was too deep.

Charlene's eyes grew big. "Your house...blew up?"

Janel nodded. "Karla..." Devastated, she couldn't say more.

"Karla's car was parked out front," Zach explained. "We believe she was inside when it happened."

"No!" Charlene gathered Janel into a big hug. "I'm so sorry. Please, come inside. We can sit while Zach checks my backyard."

"I prefer you both sit in the SUV until I come back." He waited for them to climb into the front seats before he clicked the doors locked with his key fob. His footfalls crunched the snow, and he could see his breath in the air as he strode toward the house.

After pushing the door fully open, he slowly stepped into the living room. A blue sofa, rocking chair and television took up most of the small space. He had to go through the kitchen to enter the backyard. An enticing aroma wafted from the Crock-Pot, reminding him they hadn't stopped for dinner yet. Janel needed to eat something more substantial than donuts before long.

While opening the back door, he discovered it was unlocked. He considered it odd for a woman living alone and hearing noises outside. Concern stiffened his spine as the beam of his flashlight pierced the darkness.

More troubling were the footprints in the snow, leading from the backyard wall to the concrete porch. Zach pulled out his weapon and methodically checked each room of the house, the hairs on his neck standing on end.

No one hid behind a door, under a bed or in a closet. But the room in the far corner of the house felt colder than the others. Gun ready, he pushed aside the drapes covering an open window. On the ground outside were more footprints in the snow. The intruder had escaped over the brick wall four feet away.

Remembering Janel and Charlene were waiting in the SUV, fear pumped through his arteries. He ran down the hall, through the living room and out through the front door.

The women were still there waiting for him. He lifted his finger, signaling for them to wait. He then crept closer to the car in the driveway. Footprints illuminated by the streetlight showed the intruder had jumped from the wall that surrounded the yard, into the snow, then walked down the sidewalk to the street where the trail disappeared, mostly likely erased by neighborhood traffic.

Zach strode over to the SUV. When Janel rolled down the driver's side window, he shared what he'd discovered. "Charlene," he began, leaning to the side to see her in the passenger seat. "When did you hear someone in the backyard?"

"Maybe ten minutes before I texted you two. Why?"

He glanced about one more time. "That was at least twenty minutes ago. Your intruder is probably long gone. Come on in. See if anything is missing."

Back inside the house, Zach and Janel followed Charlene from room to room. It wasn't until she reached the kitchen that she noticed anything odd.

"This wasn't here when I heard the noise outside, and it isn't mine." Charlene picked up the cell phone, protected by a teal-colored case, resting on top of a receipt on the kitchen counter next to the refrigerator. Her motions caused the receipt to fall to the tile floor.

Janel reached out for the device. "It's Karla's." Surprise, then confusion, flashed across her face. "How did it get here?"

He picked up the grocery store receipt and noticed writing on the back. He read it to the others. "'Give my phone to Janel and tell her to avoid the house. Natural gas leak—already reported. PS, I need to borrow your car. Thanks, Karla.'"

Janel's eyes sparked with joy. "That's her handwriting. She's alive!"

Zach was at a loss for words. Relieved, he sent her a warm smile. Apparently, Karla had smelled natural gas like they had. Because of her car's flat tire, she couldn't drive anywhere. "But we didn't see footprints leaving the porch."

"We have pavers between the porch and the water spigot," Janel noted. "We didn't walk over there to check for footprints."

"My car keys are missing!" Charlene stood in front of a Home Sweet Home mail and key holder hanging on the kitchen wall above the light switch.

They all rushed out to the front yard and discovered the red coupe was gone.

"How did we not hear her leave?" Janel ran to the sidewalk and searched the street.

Charlene shrugged. "Karla probably left when my neighbor came home." She pointed to a sports car in the driveway next to hers. "I heard him."

So did Zach, although faintly. Charlene had good insulation in her house.

Janel appeared to accept the explanation, but then her brow creased. "If Karla just left, she was hiding from us. I don't get it." Her gaze locked on Zach's. "Is it because you're here and there's a warrant for her arrest? I mentioned it in one of my text messages."

"I forgot about the warrant." Snowflakes fell on Charlene's

green sweater, and she swiped them away. "Let's go back inside. It's cold out here."

Zach shared his thoughts with Janel as they walked back to the house. "Karla left you the phone for a reason."

"I know her password. Let's hurry." Janel's dedication to putting the Sloan brothers behind bars had returned full force.

"I'll put a kettle on. I have tea and hot chocolate," Charlene offered, not appearing overly concerned about her car. She must have faith she'd get it back.

Inside the warm kitchen, Zach sat beside Janel at a round wooden table while she entered her sister's password. Charlene kept herself busy, pulling mugs from the cupboard and prepping their drinks as if wanting to give them privacy.

"I think I found something." Janel squinted while checking the phone's app. She tapped on one image, then another. "This looks like a recording from the camera hidden in the fake hotel smoke detector."

Zach leaned closer to view the screen. The video started with the profile view of Sawyer Sloan typing on a laptop. A man off-screen groaned. "I don't know why we ever listened to you. Faking a break-in to get close to that woman was the worst idea you ever had."

Sawyer shook his head. "You don't know what you're talking about. Karla was investigating our heists. She told me everything, and I led her in the wrong direction."

"Right," the man scoffed.

"You're an idiot. I was the one who suggested she look into art thieves released from prison over the past five years, especially ones on the East Coast, where there are more museums and wealthy investors. Remember when I told you she thought some guy out of Boston might be guilty?" Sawyer looked up from the screen as if waiting for an answer that never came, so he went on. "Dating her also gave me easy access to her spare house key. You wouldn't have been able to put those bags with her fingerprints in the storage shed if it weren't for me."

"Okay, okay," the man mumbled. "But you shouldn't have killed Red. He was a good guy."

Sawyer narrowed his eyes. "If your prison buddy was such a good guy, why did he pull a gun on me?"

"He doesn't think straight sometimes. You could have just roughed him up a bit and he would've got the message."

"Enough already." The third Sloan brother, Larry, pulled a chair up next to Sawyer at the desk. "We need to transfer enough money for me and Oz to leave the state."

"I'd have it done already if he'd kept his trap shut." Sawyer typed the name of an overseas bank into the search engine, slowly enough for Zach to see each keystroke.

Seconds later, Zach's eyes widened. Stolen art paid well. He grabbed his phone and snapped a picture. He knew Oscar, nicknamed Oz, was a petty thief, but this was a whole new level of criminality. A balance of over five million dollars sat in their account after they transferred three hundred thousand to a US bank for traveling expenses.

"You sure you don't want to go with us?" Larry asked Sawyer.

"I can't. My kid needs me."

The video abruptly ended, and Zach, feeling sorry for the sick boy, contacted Cole to tell him about the evidence they were forwarding from the two phones.

"I was just about to call you." Cole's tone sounded more serious than usual. "According to Hyde, Karla called him, told him about the overseas account and claimed she transferred those millions to the insurance company's bank account."

"Why?" Zach stepped away from the table, not yet ready to share this information with Janel. "What is she hoping to accomplish?"

"Hyde said she called Sawyer and left him a message. She had their money, and they could pick it up at the Mexican border—if they left her sister alone."

Zach pushed the rim of his Stetson away from his face. "Why call Hyde? She claims he's been wanting her job."

"I guess she was trying to prove she was one of the good guys by telling him he could arrange for the police to pick up the Sloan brothers at the border. Also, the insurance company would need to know where the money came from. And one more thing, she also told Hyde that you would soon have access to the video proving the Sloan brothers are guilty, not her and Janel."

"Remind me to thank her." Sarcasm dripped from Zach's words. "The last thing I need is Hyde on my tail." He noticed the impatient expression on Janel's face when he ended the call and told her, "We need to head back to the ranch."

Janel remained seated. "You were talking about my sister. I want to know what's going on."

His trepidation grew with each passing second. "Karla just gave Sawyer and his brothers a good reason to kidnap you—before they kill both you and your sister."

Chapter Seventeen

Janel tried to figure out where her sister would go. She desperately wanted to search for her, rather than drive back to the ranch, but Zach had put his foot down. He was convinced the Sloan brothers would try to kidnap her, and he was probably right. They wanted their five million dollars back from Karla and could use her as leverage.

When they entered Zach's living room, Janel did a double take. Karla sat on the sofa, speaking to Cole, who took notes on a tablet.

Janel felt waves of emotion wash over her: relief, love, joy, anger, then exhaustion.

Karla strode over and pulled her into a hug. "I'm so glad you're okay. Cole said you went to the house. You could have died in the explosion."

She couldn't help but chuckle at the irony of her statement as a tear slid down her cheek. "I thought *you* did."

They hugged again, and Zach cleared his throat. "You have a lot of explaining to do, Karla."

"You're right." Karla stepped back. "I was giving my statement to Cole, but I'll start again."

"From the beginning." Zach's stern tone altered the mood

in the room. He waited for Janel to join her sister on the sofa before he sat across from them, near his brother's chair.

The serious expressions on the men's faces made Janel feel the need to show her sister support. She placed her hand on top of Karla's.

A smile tugged at her sister's lips before she turned to the lawmen. "All right. Here we go, from the beginning. I met Sawyer Sloan when expensive pieces of his art collection were stolen from his house. I thought his break-in might be connected to a string of burglaries I was working on. A couple of weeks later, I ran into him at my gym. He asked me out. One thing led to another, and we started dating once or twice a month. I thought he was being nice when he offered to fix my kitchen faucet."

Janel groaned. "That must be when he stole your spare key."

"You listened to the recording on my phone." Karla's eyes lit with pride. "I knew you'd find it." She turned back to Cole. "Sawyer told me he had two brothers but claimed they lived in Texas. One day, I was running errands and spotted the three of them standing next to an SUV at a gas station. I could see the family resemblance in their nose shape and jawlines. He later lied about where he had been, and my suspicious nature took over."

"You discovered his brother has an arrest record," Zach concluded.

"Yes, for game store burglaries. He never became a person of interest during my initial investigation into the art burglaries, so I didn't memorize his last name." Karla took a sip from the water glass on the coffee table. "I started putting the pieces of the puzzle together, and a picture of Sawyer running a burglary ring with his brothers began to emerge. When the Scottsdale detective arrested the fence, I went to see him. I flat out asked if he bought the stolen merchandise from the Sloan brothers."

"Did you expect him to be honest with you?" Janel didn't

know any criminals, but according to the television shows she watched, they usually lied.

"You never know for sure until you try. Unfortunately, I couldn't get a straight answer out of him, but then I didn't need to because he told Sawyer about our visit."

Janel's head ached again, just when she thought she had totally recovered from the concussion.

"Sawyer confronted me, and we argued. I accused him of using me, and he laughed." Karla shook her head. "He told me what a fool I had been to walk straight into their trap, which he spelled out. They rented a storage unit in my name and filled it with one piece of stolen art from each burglary, plus boxes and bags with my fingerprints and DNA on them. They framed me."

"And if you ratted on them, they'd make an anonymous call to the police," Zach guessed. He rubbed his chin with the pad of his finger. "Only you didn't rat on them, and they made the anonymous call to the Scottsdale detective, anyway."

Karla nodded. "When Janel witnessed Sawyer killing the redheaded accomplice, their plan crumbled. That's why they forced the fence to name both me and my sister as his source for the stolen art. They needed to discredit her before she could finger Sawyer as the killer."

"Which wouldn't have happened if my memories hadn't come back." There were a few times Janel wished she hadn't recalled those horrific moments.

"Sawyer showed me a video of you working at the gallery." Karla's expression filled with angst. "He threatened to kill you if the police ever questioned him."

Janel squeezed her sister's hand. "I don't blame you for not saying anything. You were afraid. I know how that feels."

"The argument I had with Sawyer, the one Janel remembered seeing, was about the gallery burglary. I believe he wouldn't have gone back to the casita for the stolen art so soon after hiding it if I hadn't seen him in town and confronted him." Karla directed her statements to Zach. "When I saw him in the café parking lot, I accused him of stealing our mother's paintings. He must have thought I was wearing a wire because he kept ranting about how I was crazy and probably stole from my sister, and maybe Janel was in on it, too. He knew about the loan and made disparaging remarks about her, so I tried to slap him."

Cole took more notes. "Why didn't you say anything *after* Janel was almost killed in the forest and your car blew up?"

"You were convinced the gallery break-in wasn't connected to the ring of burglaries. I thought you were probably right. Sawyer wouldn't have had Janel's security code to disable the alarm, and to my knowledge, the Sloan brothers never murdered anyone before." Once again, Karla spoke to Janel. "I wasn't positive Sawyer was the one trying to kill you until you remembered seeing us together in the parking lot and told me he was the murderer."

"Then you tried to make it all go away." Janel wished her sister had asked Cole and Zach for help.

"And you thought hiding a camera in their hotel room, which gave you access to their bank password so you could transfer millions out of their account, would fix things?" The remark was less question and more sarcasm. An incoming call on Cole's phone kept him from waiting for an answer.

Janel had to agree it might not have been the best move to make under the circumstances, but Karla did prove their innocence. A win in her book.

Zach scowled at Karla. "Don't you get it? There's no way they will leave the country without their money. And Sawyer won't leave at all. His son is too sick. They will do everything possible to kidnap Janel to force you to give back their money."

"Sawyer never told me he had a child." Karla turned her gaze away from the brothers. "Why would he? I was a means to an end." The hurt flickering across Karla's face made Janel think there might have been a time when her sister thought she had a future with Sawyer—before she realized he was a criminal.

The second Cole disconnected his call, Zach asked, "What now?"

"A no-name caller claims there's going to be an attack on the police station. He didn't say when. The chief asked the sheriff to send deputies over to help defend the place in case it comes to that."

"The Sloan brothers aren't planning to attack the police station," Zach concluded. "They're coming here instead."

"They can do both." The hospital explosion flashed through Janel's mind. "They have bombs."

"And grenades," Zach mumbled. "Probably from their Mexican drug cartel connection."

Cole stood. "Regardless, the priority is defending the police station. We won't get additional officers when we have three living on the ranch."

Janel vividly remembered the fear of running away from Sawyer in the forest and shooting at him from the bedroom window. The idea of facing off with him again sent terror pulsating down her spine. "I need more guns."

Sitting at the dining room table with Cole, Jackson, Lily and their parents, Zach reflected on the business the ranch had lost after his brothers inadvertently brought danger to it. He had been working hard to entice resort managers to recommend their hayrides and cowboy cookouts to their visitors ever since. Now this.

He brought Janel and her sister here because it was the right thing to do, even if another attack might bring their equine business to financial ruin. His unsteady nerves had him clenching his jaw as a solemn mood settled over him and his thoughts wandered.

Tombstone came to mind. Tourists flocked there to see the O.K. Corral. They had a gunfight in 1881 that lasted less than one minute. Admittedly, books and movies about Wyatt Earp made it more famous. Zach didn't see a movie deal in their future, but maybe a public relations person could help turn their bleak financial situation around—if he could find an alternative to bringing witnesses to the ranch in the future. Official law enforcement agencies hadn't made that possible yet.

Lily kept her laptop open in front of her so she could watch the security monitor during the meal their mother had kept warm until everyone came home. His sister could protect Janel and Karla as well as anyone else in the family.

"Zach." Cole placed his cell phone down beside his plate. "I spoke to Sierra, and we both agree you should hide the twins in our house since it's at the far end of the ranch and less likely to be noticed."

"She's sure about that?" Their father reached for a dinner roll. He had been a pillar of strength all their lives, but the years were showing in the wrinkles on his face and the gray streaks in his hair. "I can't believe any woman would want to come back from visiting relatives to find their house full of bullet holes."

"Yes, she's sure," Cole stated emphatically. "Sierra remembers when she needed help and wants to do the same for Janel and her sister."

Their mother tapped her husband's hand. "Where's your manners? Wait for our guests."

"We're going to battle. I need sustenance." He turned at the sound of footfalls in the hall. "There they are." He snatched another roll, and she rolled her eyes.

The twins joined them at the table, both dressed alike in black jeans and black turtleneck sweaters. Karla believed the Sloans wouldn't shoot Janel if they thought she might be the sister who could transfer their money back.

Janel chose the seat next to Zach, but their gazes didn't meet. His heart still struggled over his feelings for her. He meant what he said; he couldn't have a romantic relationship with someone who kept secrets. His ex did so before she went back to her old boyfriend. He refused to go through that again.

"Let's say grace," his mother said, her tone as light as the circumstances would allow.

They held hands, and his father began, "Lord, we ask Your blessing for this food, Your protection as we defend our home and Your strength to win the battle. Amen."

A chorus of "Amen" ended the prayer.

Zach silently asked God for guidance before reluctantly releasing Janel's hand. She was still his friend, and he worried over what the night had in store for her—for them all. "Lily, how does it look out there?"

"Quiet. No sign of trouble." Lily took her eyes off the laptop for five seconds to spoon mashed potatoes on her plate when Cole handed her the bowl.

Jackson stabbed a pork chop on the platter with his fork. "Zach, you're in charge of protecting the twins. How do you want to handle this?"

"I was thinking you and Cole could stay here to watch over the house with Mom and Dad. They'll show up here looking for Janel. The rest of us can go to the other house."

"Solid plan," Cole confirmed, accepting the platter from Jackson.

His brothers had more law enforcement experience, so it meant a lot to Zach that they respected his opinion.

After dinner, Lily and Zach stashed weapons and phone chargers into a duffel bag while Janel and Karla thanked everyone for their help. The four of them then tugged on their coats before climbing into the unmarked sheriff's SUV. Zach drove them down the ranch road to Cole's house, which was nestled in a far corner, surrounded by evergreen trees. He parked inside the garage.

"Ladies, let's keep the blinds closed and the lights off." He pushed open the driver's door and carried the bag filled with guns and ammunition inside.

"Can I at least make coffee?" Lily placed her laptop on the table.

"Please do." Zach placed his arsenal on the kitchen table next to an unread newspaper, then traveled from room to room with a flashlight to reacquaint himself with his new surroundings. Peering out through each window, he was glad to see everything appeared normal. A blanket of snow covered the pasture beneath the starry night, while the horses stayed warm in their stalls. The thought of another assault endangering his serene home made him clench his teeth.

Minutes later, they sat at the table drinking coffee. The caffeine would help keep them alert. The laptop and a kitchen night-light provided minimum illumination. Shadows flickered on the wall, making them all jumpy.

"What do we do now?" Janel hugged the warm cup with both hands.

Her vulnerability tugged at his emotions. "We wait." He pushed a pistol in front of each twin. "Karla, do you know how to use this if anyone breaks in?"

She nodded. "I own a gun but didn't bring it with me."

After three hours and four cups of coffee, they moved to the living room, where they would be more comfortable. He relocated the night-light to the wall behind the dining room table so they could see more from any of the main rooms without drawing attention to the house. Janel placed her weapon on the coffee table, and so did Karla.

"Help me move the sofa away from the window." Zach started pushing once everyone found a place to stand and take hold of the frame. Preparing for another attack felt surreal. He'd spent months helping Cole build this house.

Lily sat on the carpet with her computer while the sisters claimed spots on the sofa. Zach moved an overstuffed chair into the corner and sat where he could see both entrances to the room and all three windows.

Time ticked by slowly. Janel crossed her arms over her chest, hiding her shaking hands. Eventually, she nodded off to sleep, then jerked awake again.

An hour later, Lily handed him the laptop. "I need to stretch."

"No problem." He placed the device on his thighs and took over, monitoring the ranch as his sister walked up and down the hallway.

After she returned to her spot on the carpet, the silence became deafening again.

Eventually, each of the women fell asleep.

Fear and suspense kept him alert.

When the first rays of morning light shone through the windows, Zach heard the whir of helicopter blades. He nudged Lily with her boot. "Wake up." When she peered up at him, he added, "We have company. Call Cole, then the sheriff's office."

Their voices woke Janel and Karla, and he instructed them to stay on the sofa.

Zach stood beside the window, peering out through the blinds at the helicopter flying with its door open over the stables. A man covered in black from head to toe climbed down a rope, with a rifle slung over his shoulder. He jumped onto the metal roof of one of the stables and then scrambled to the snow-covered ground.

"Watch them," Zach told Lily as he pulled out his Glock. "I'm headed to the stables." His gaze met Janel's.

Her eyes grew wide, and she snatched two pistols from the coffee table. He remembered she didn't want to stop shooting to reload.

"I'll be back. Do what Lily says." He grabbed his coat from the kitchen and snuck out through the back door. When he neared the pasture, two ATVs roared across the blanket of white, heading straight for the horses, now galloping out of the stables. The drivers wore helmets that covered their faces, but there was no secret behind who had invaded the ranch.

Zach's ire threatened to take control of his mind and actions. *No.* The voice in his head was his, but the thought felt like God sent it—a reminder to stay on the right path.

When Zach caught up with his brothers halfway between

the two houses, he announced, "I'm going to the stables to deal with that guy."

Jackson slapped him on the back. "We'll take down the other two."

The three brothers ran in separate directions.

Eying Copper, Zach climbed up on the white picket fence and whistled. His quarter horse left the pack and galloped to him. Keeping an eye out for shooters, he climbed on his friend's back. The ATVs had reached the other end of the pasture.

He turned Copper toward the stables, and they took off. The intruder in black emerged through the open doors. Zach jumped off the horse, landed on top of him, tossed the man's rifle into a stall and then ripped off the mask.

"Larry Sloan." That made sense. He must have learned how to propel out of helicopters in the military. The surprised look on the man's face made Zach smile. "We know everything."

Sloan knocked Zach off of him. They pushed to their feet and took turns throwing punches.

Zach took a hard one to the face and stumbled backward. Rubbing his aching cheek, he glared at the man who had shot out their tire on the switchbacks. "I've had enough of you and your brothers."

"Show me what you've got, cowboy." Larry pulled a switch-blade from his pants pocket and danced around like a wrestler. He lunged forward, trying to strike Zach in the chest, but he jumped back. With each swipe of the blade, Zach sidestepped or dove out of the way, then quickly pushed to his feet.

Despite the freezing temperatures, Zach grew hot from exertion. His breathing turned shallow as he evaded another strike. Finally, he spotted a shovel leaning against a stall wall. He ran, grabbed it and turned to find Larry barreling down on him.

With a limited window of opportunity, Zach swung as hard as he could. He hit Larry over the head and knocked him out. "*That's* what I've got. Sleep tight."

Before leaving the barn, Zach grabbed a rope and tied Larry's hands and feet together. Back out in the snow, he spotted his brothers chasing after an ATV. The other vehicle rested on its side, close to Cole's house. *Janel!*

Chapter Eighteen

"There's Zach, coming out of the stable." Relief flowed over Janel as she turned the laptop toward Lily. The two women had been sitting on Cole's sofa, watching the ranch's security footage.

"He's alone," Lily pointed out. "He must have taken out the guy who climbed down the helicopter rope."

Janel read aloud the text she sent to Zach. "'What happened to the guy in the stables?'" Seconds later, she shared his answer. "'Tied up. Stay hidden.'"

"I hear sirens. But they're not close." Karla peered out through the living room blinds. "I don't see anyone."

"That doesn't mean no one's there." Janel knew it was something Zach would say. Thinking of him reminded her to pray.

God, I humbly ask for Your protection and guidance in our time of need. Zach says You have a plan, and I've come to believe that is true. You did send him my way. Please keep us all alive and end this nightmare for good. Amen.

"Do you smell smoke?" Armed, Lily rushed toward the dining room, then down the hall.

Drawing in a deep breath, Janel caught the scent, too. Worried, she pushed off the sofa and snatched a gun off the coffee table. "Karla, keep an eye on the front rooms."

Lily opened one door, then another. Janel ran down the hall and around the corner. Clouds of smoke escaped from under the last bedroom door, stealing both her breath and the limited sense of safety she had minutes ago. She reluctantly tapped the brass knob with her finger.

Heart pounding, she whipped around to stop Lily from getting any closer. "The doorknob's hot."

"We have to get out of here!" Lily spun in the opposite direction.

As they ran, Janel asked, "How did we not hear anything? They must have opened a window to get a blaze going that fast."

"The gunshots and ATVs covered up any noise they made." Lily stopped in the living room. "Karla. Fire. Grab a gun and your coat, now!"

"The helicopter pilot had a bird's-eye view. If he saw Zach coming out the front door, he told the others." Karla set aside the laptop and hurried to the dining room.

They set their weapons down on the table and tugged on the coats they'd left hanging on the backs of wooden chairs.

Janel zipped hers up. "How did they get close to the house without us seeing it on the laptop?"

"They're burglars," Karla reminded her. "They look for cameras and find the blind spots. And they could be out there, waiting for us."

Smoke tendrils slithered into the dining room like a snake.

"That's why we're armed," Lily said before calling her parents to report the fire.

While Zach's sister promised her father they'd head to the main house, Karla removed the tie holding her ponytail and placed it in Janel's palm. "Wear this. They'll think you're me."

"Put your hair back up." She wouldn't let her sister die for her.

"No."

Janel's gaze landed on a rolled-up unread newspaper sitting on the table. She tugged off the rubber band, holding the pages together, and handed it to her sister. In two seconds, they both had their hair secured in ponytails.

The acrid smell of smoke and crackling of the blaze coming from the bedrooms warned them to get out.

"Let's go." Lily opened the door a couple of inches and glanced outside.

Karla grabbed her weapon, then headed out the door after Lily. Her gaze darted about, searching for danger. Janel shoved a gun into her coat pocket to keep her hand warm, hoping she wouldn't need to use it, and followed the others.

They scanned the snow-covered yard and surrounding evergreen trees. The sun's rays filtered through the clouds and reflected off the snow, while a strong breeze whipped around them.

"Won't they burn your parents' house if we go there?" Janel whispered, while glancing over her shoulder to make sure no one followed them.

"We're not staying. My truck's there. If we're fast, we can hightail it away while my brothers keep those guys busy."

Flames engulfed the entire back end of Cole's house. Timbers fell from the burned frame. Janel wished she hadn't been a magnet for trouble. The Walkers were down-to-earth, good, caring people who didn't deserve to suffer through one invasion after another. If only she had turned down Zach's offer to come here.

Lily and Karla had stepped behind a metal shed ahead of her when she heard footfalls in the snow to her left.

"Stop right there," a man's voice commanded.

She froze in place. When she slowly turned her head in his direction, she instantly recognized Sawyer Sloan. He stood roughly a dozen feet away, holding a gun, its barrel pointed at her. Terror exploded in her chest.

"You're coming with me, Karla," he sneered. "I want my money."

He thought she was her sister. If he knew her true identity, he would shoot and kill her. Karla, hidden behind the shed, lifted her finger to her lips, warning her not to speak. They might look alike, but they didn't sound the same.

The wind picked up and whistled through the air vent in the shed. Lily took advantage of the noise to rush forward, spring around the corner and take aim at Sawyer.

Her gun jammed.

Sawyer laughed and shifted the barrel of his gun toward Lily.

A need to protect Zach's sister propelled Janel into action. She dove in front of Lily while trying to rip the weapon out of her coat pocket, but she wasn't fast enough.

A gunshot rang in the air.

Janel felt a sting in her upper body, dropped the gun and fell into the snow. Her mind floated on a haze similar to the one she experienced after hitting her head. She barely recognized the sound of muffled screams. Lying on the cold ground, the flickering image of a man with broad shoulders came into view.

"Zach," she mumbled. She could have been happy with him. "I love you." With that declaration drifting away in the wind, her world turned to darkness.

After Zach had spotted the smoke above Cole's house, he sprinted to the front door and pounded. No one answered, so he ran around to the kitchen door and found footprints pressed into the snow leading toward the evergreen trees. He followed the trail while keeping an eye out for the Sloan brother who had left the ATV and helmet nearby.

When he heard a man's menacing voice, he circled the trees to come up behind him. That's when he witnessed the beginning of a nightmare. Karla lunged in front of Lily as Sawyer fired his weapon.

Karla slumped to the ground and mumbled something.

Reacting instinctively, Zach whipped his gun from its holster and fired at Sawyer. His body jerked, then another shot rang out—this one coming from Lily's direction—and he fell forward, face down.

After snatching Sawyer's gun and discovering he was unconscious but alive, Zach looked up and found Karla lowering her weapon. Her stance looked practiced, like she'd spent hours in a shooting range. He wasn't surprised; she was an investigator.

Wait a minute, if that's Karla... Janel was the twin lying on the ground. His eyes widened. His mind refused to believe it was possible. That's when he noticed both sisters had their blond locks pulled up into ponytails.

He rushed closer. The fear he might have lost his one true love rose in his chest, urging him into a full sprint.

"Janel!" Karla screamed. "Lily, call 911."

Zach dropped to his knees in front of Janel's motionless body. The welcome sound of sirens finally reached the ranch as he held her wrist and searched for a pulse. It felt faint, but there.

Everything after that moment happened in quick succession. Jackson arrived, announcing that he and Cole had repeatedly shot at Oscar's ATV until it crashed. After throwing a few punches, they managed to take down the third Sloan brother and hand him to the deputies, who also collected Larry from the stables. EMTs worked on both Janel and Sawyer. A short distance away, firefighters valiantly fought the flames while Cole watched.

Zach's emotions were all over the place. He was glad the Sloan brothers had been caught, and he felt horrible about the destruction of Cole's home, but all he could focus on was Janel. His heart ached as he kicked himself for being angry at her earlier. He climbed into the back of the ambulance, determined not to leave her side unless absolutely necessary.

The trip to the hospital was a blur. He alternated between praying and watching her intently, hoping for a sign that she'd wake and be fine. But she didn't. Forcing back tears brought on a splitting headache.

When the ambulance's back door opened, Zach crawled out.

He did his best to stay out of the way while watching Janel every second until the doctor told him he had to stay behind. He stared at the closed hospital door, feeling lost and empty. Destroyed.

The bullet had penetrated Janel's body near her shoulder, and she spent hours in surgery.

Lieutenant Yeager ambled into the waiting room, hat in hand. "How's she doing?"

"Hanging in there." Zach shifted position in the uncomfortable chair, wishing someone would tell him she was no longer in danger.

"She's a fighter. I could tell that at the creek."

Zach nodded. "I suppose you want my statement."

"It can wait till morning." Yeager ran his hand through his hair. "Where's her sister?"

"My family practically dragged her to the cafeteria."

"And you didn't go?"

"They've learned to leave me alone when I put my foot down."

"Me, too." The lieutenant smiled. "I wanted you to know Oscar Sloan is already talking. He's been to prison before and knows the advantages of cooperation."

"I hope they all plead out. Janel's suffered enough already. She doesn't need the hassle of a trial…if she makes it through surgery."

"Don't go there. She will. And then her life can go back to normal. The Sloan brothers are no longer a threat, and both her and her sister have cleared their names where the gallery burglary is concerned. Karla still needs a competent lawyer. She broke a few laws while proving their innocence."

Zach knew he was referring to the break-in at the hotel where Karla planted the recording device, then her transferring the ill-gotten gains to the insurance company. "I'll tell her."

The surgeon stepped into the waiting room, his mask dangling from one ear, and called out for the family of Janel New-man.

Zach, fearing the worst, tried to read his face as he walked up to him. "Doc, how is she?"

"The surgery went well. You can see her when she wakes up." The surgeon described the medical aspects of her condi-tion, but Zach couldn't get past the fact she was alive and he could see her soon.

The seconds seemed to tick by even slower after the doctor and lieutenant left. He called Karla to share the good news. She returned shortly with Lily and his parents. They had stopped by the gift shop on their way back.

"We bought candy and games for Janel." Karla lifted a purse-type bag made from quilted material.

"That was thoughtful." Maybe he should have picked up something for her.

His mother gave him a hug and whispered, "All Janel needs is you. Don't let this one get away."

"I won't." Thinking about how close he came to losing her, through both his stubbornness and the shooting, took his breath away. He tightened his grip on the brim of his Stetson. "I'm going to stay here. You should take Dad and Lily home."

After they left, he passed on Yeager's suggestion of getting a good lawyer.

"With what?" Karla answered. "I'm currently unemployed."

"Fired?"

She nodded. "You know, when Janel opened the gallery, she asked me if I wanted to be her business partner. If I sell my house, I could pay back her loan, save Mom's paintings from the bank and hire that lawyer."

"If only you had thought of that before meeting Sawyer Sloan." He sent her a half smile.

"If only…" She scrubbed her face with the palms of her hands. "I do love my sister and never dreamed that anything like this would happen."

He believed that about her. "Everything will work out. God has a plan."

After a brief frown, the lines on Karla's forehead disappeared and her shoulders relaxed. "Maybe it's time I went to church again."

"You have a ride anytime you need one." He knew Janel would be pleased.

Karla slapped her thigh. "That's another thing I need. A new car. Mine blew up."

Charlene arrived, carrying a vase filled with yellow roses, minutes after a nurse told them Janel was now awake but would be groggy. Karla filled her in on what happened at the ranch as they headed to the assigned room together.

Not willing to wait any longer, Zach stepped inside ahead of the others. Janel opened her eyes, and the weight of the world lifted off his shoulders. With emotions threatening to choke him, he cleared his throat and moved closer to the bed. "Hi, there. You gave us all a scare."

"Sorry." She closed her lids, then opened them again. "You know me. I'll do anything to get out of running another festival."

He chuckled. "And here I was thinking we could cochair the next one."

She squeezed his hand, then fell asleep again. He remained at her side, watching her, thanking God for sparing her life.

The next time she woke, Karla spoke to her, then Charlene. "Robert sends his best."

"Thank him for me." Janel was more alert, more like herself. When Zach kissed her forehead, the others left the room, giving them privacy.

He pushed stray strands of hair away from her face. "I thought I lost you forever."

"Does this mean you're not mad at me anymore?" Her voice was faint, but her words packed a powerful punch.

Regret flashed through him. "I was a fool. I shouldn't have

compared you to my ex. You're not at all alike. Your words and actions prove you're a good, caring woman. And you protect your family the way I do."

Janel placed her hand on top of his. "I *should have* kept comparing you to my ex. You two are so different. The truth is, there were signs Todd was no good. I just didn't want to admit it. With all the work at my gallery and then my mother's cancer, it was easier to have a boyfriend who was gone most of the time, but still there when I wanted to call him."

"Do you still want a long-distance boyfriend?"

"No. I want you, Zach Walker."

"I love you." He placed a tender kiss on her lips.

"I love you, too." Her gaze held his. Their connection was undeniable.

The door opened, and Cole poked his head inside, looking sheepish. "Sorry to interrupt, but Zach, there is someone you need to meet. It's important."

He placed another kiss on her forehead. "I'll be back shortly."

When he left the room, Karla and Charlene walked back inside. She'd be in good hands while he was away.

"What's this all about?" Zach asked his brother, admittedly exhausted and wishing he could stay with Janel.

"I received a phone call from a guy who works at the airport. He thinks he knows the pilot who was flying Larry Sloan around. He's on his way over."

"I almost forgot about him." Zach picked up his pace. They had to wait in the parking lot for ten minutes before a man in his late forties pulled up in a white work van.

"You Detective Walker?"

Cole lifted his hand. "I am. This is Deputy Walker."

"Like I said on the phone, my friend told me about a blue helicopter being involved in some shootings. He thought I might know more about it."

"Why would you?" Cole asked.

"I repair helicopters."

Now he had Zach's interest. "I'm assuming you do, or you wouldn't be here."

"I got a call from a pilot who flies for a real estate developer. The landing skid on his blue helicopter was bent, like maybe someone shot at it. He was real nervous. Said it had to be fixed before the weekend. His boss wants a flight back from Phoenix."

Zach tried to act nonchalant while his nerves twitched with anticipation. "Who's this pilot?"

"Robert Matthews."

Charlene's boyfriend. Zach was thunderstruck. The enemy was sitting in their camp the entire time. This explained how the Sloan brothers knew Janel's alarm code. He watched his girlfriend enter it during one of their trips to the gallery.

The man glanced over his shoulder. "I have to get back to work. Don't tell anyone I gave you a name. I want to live long enough to retire one day." With that, he drove away.

Zach turned to his brother. "How does a guy with no record end up flying for the Sloans?"

Cole shook his head. "We should have checked to see if Matthews's path crossed Larry Sloan's during their military days. I'll get an address and find out what he drives."

"No need." Zach's ire returned as he pointed to a distinctive green Mercedes-Benz parked two rows away. "He's here. And he knows Karla can access millions of dollars."

Afraid his universe might crumble, Zach ran inside the hospital, hoping he wasn't too late.

Chapter Nineteen

"How lovely. Thank you." Janel admired the crystal vase filled with yellow roses that Charlene placed on a small round table in front of the window.

"They brighten up the room, don't you think?" Charlene moved to the foot of the hospital bed as Janel nodded her agreement.

"Here's something else guaranteed to put a smile on your face." Karla dug through a quilted bag, then handed Janel a yellow pen with a cartoon head on the end. "You used to have one just like it."

The mop of blue hair and goofy grin on the head made Janel chuckle. "Ah, I did, and if I remember right, you broke it."

Karla pointed to herself, feigning innocence before admitting, "I might have accidentally stepped on it."

"As long as it was accidental," Janel teased as she gestured to the bag she'd never seen before. "What else is in there?"

"Red licorice and puzzle books." Karla placed her gifts on the over-the-bed table next to a plastic water pitcher. Her expression suddenly turned serious. "I'm so relieved the surgery went well. I can't lose you."

Touched, Janel placed her hand over her heart. Before she could say anything, the door burst open.

Charlene's boyfriend rushed into the room. His wild eyes, like those of a trapped animal, made the hair on Janel's neck stand on end.

"Robert! You're back." Charlene lifted her hands to hug him until he pulled a gun out from beneath his coat. Her jaw dropped open, and she backed away from him.

Janel froze as she stared at the barrel of his weapon. The bandages covering her bullet wound grew heavier as the memory of being shot replayed in her mind.

He pointed the gun at Karla. "You're going to give me that five million dollars."

No! God, please don't let anything happen to my sister. Janel had to distract him. "You were in on the burglary. You fed the Sloans information, like the fact we were staying at the ranch and every place we said we were headed to, didn't you?"

"Stop stalling. Your boyfriend is outside talking to his brother. He's not coming back anytime soon." He waved the gun around, and Janel sucked in a breath. When she glanced at the call button, his intense glare bore into her. "Don't even think about it. If a nurse shows up, I'll shoot."

Karla lifted her hands, palms out. "I'll give you the money."

"Wait a minute." Charlene's eyes grew wide with anger as she fisted her hands at her side. "Did you date me to get the alarm code?"

"What of it?"

His attitude made Charlene's face turn red.

"How do you even know the Sloans?" Janel asked, feeling the need to step in between her assistant manager and Robert—verbally, if not physically.

"Larry and I have been friends since we were kids." He pointed the gun at Karla again. "Money. I have an account I want it transferred into."

"That's all you have to say?" Charlene glared at him.

"You should be thanking me," he blurted, his patience spent. "I'm teaching you a valuable lesson. Stop being so gullible." He pointed the gun directly at Charlene. "Enough talking!"

Janel gritted her teeth. The guy was so jumpy he might accidentally shoot someone. He wasn't acting like a man who had military training. Was his friend Larry the type to name accomplices for a lighter sentence? Is that what had Robert so desperate to get his hands on the money to leave town that he would risk coming to the hospital with law enforcement officers on the property?

The door, set back in a six-foot-long hallway, inched open. Janel's pulse skipped a beat.

Zach poked his head into the room. He made eye contact with Janel and held his finger to his lips. Robert had his back to him, and a good dozen feet separated them.

Karla's gaze flitted about the room, landing on Zach at least once. She lifted the quilted bag off the table and stepped back toward the wall. "I need my phone to transfer the money."

Was her sister trying to lure Robert away from the hospital bed? Trying once more to keep Janel out of danger? If so, her plan wasn't working. He hadn't budged an inch.

If Zach tried to shoot him, he could hit Janel by mistake.

Janel fingered the pen in her right hand, the uninjured side of her body. What they needed was a distraction that would allow Zach to rush in and subdue Robert.

When Robert reached into his coat pocket for a slip of paper and handed it to Karla, Janel threw her pen as hard and fast as she could. The cartoon head smacked against the window.

Robert spun around and shot. The sound of breaking window glass held his attention for at least two seconds. Long enough for Karla to extend her foot out in front of him and push hard.

Zach exploded into the room, lunged on top of him and ripped the gun from his hand as they fell to the floor.

Cole opened the door, took in the sight and rushed over to take the weapon. He passed a set of handcuffs to his brother.

"Robert Matthews, you're under arrest." Zach clamped the cuffs around the man's wrists.

Janel finally released the pent-up breath she'd been holding.

"You creep!" Charlene snatched the vase from the small wooden table and dumped the water and roses over Robert's head.

Cole grabbed the crystal vase from her hands. "Okay, that's enough."

She screamed at her now ex-boyfriend. "That's what you get for using defenseless women."

Zach pulled Robert up off the floor and chuckled. "There is nothing defenseless about any of you." He sent Janel a loving smile. "Especially you."

Epilogue

Six months later, Janel sat in the gallery's new café area, watching her sister test the espresso machine. "Make mine a white chocolate."

"You got it," Karla said, grinning from ear to ear. She had sold her house in Scottsdale the first week it was on the market. That allowed her to invest enough money into the gallery to pay back the bank loan and divide the education room into two areas. The café being one of them. They offered coffee, hot chocolate, tea, milk and pastries. And while customers sat at stylish bistro tables, they could watch an artist in residence through a glass wall. Today, their painter, a cowboy with good manners and deep blue eyes, was hard at work in the well-lit studio.

Janel's mood had lifted since the Sloan brothers and Robert signed plea bargains and were safely behind bars. Although she felt badly for Sawyer's son. The lieutenant learned the boy was doing much better after starting his medical treatments, but he would surely miss his father. She would keep him in her prayers.

She sipped her mocha and gave her sister a thumbs-up. "This is better than the café down the street. We should charge fifty cents less to drive traffic this way."

"The best part is no other gallery around here serves food or coffee." Karla slipped into the chair opposite hers. "Sedona Imagined is no longer a threat."

"Do you miss working as an investigator?"

"I thought I would, but I don't. Getting fired was the best thing that could have happened for the both of us." Karla scanned the room with the expression of a proud parent.

Janel smiled as she lifted the warm cup to her lips.

"It's time for me to unlock the front door." Karla marched off, leaving Janel to her thoughts.

Charlene popped her head inside the room. "I'm off to the post office."

"We need more mailing cylinders." Janel waved goodbye, reflecting on how they had made the right decision, giving Charlene a pay raise and putting her in charge of online sales. She had a knack for internet commerce. She was also renting rooms to the sisters while their mother's house was being rebuilt. This time, the insurance company wasn't giving them any trouble.

Janel recognized the voice floating in from the showroom. Her heart filled with joy as she rushed into the main area. She found Zach looking up at the bright swirls of color on *Sun Setting on Rocks*.

"Hi." Was it her imagination, or was he even more handsome than the day she met him?

"Hi, yourself." He reached out his hand, pulling her to his side. "Your mother's painting looks much better here than on a cold backyard studio easel."

"My mom believed all art should be displayed for the public to enjoy. That's why she wanted me to open my gallery."

He squeezed her hand, held it up to his lips and kissed her fingers. "You look happy."

"I was thinking about what you said. God sometimes shakes things up so we'll choose a new path. I think He threw me off my old one." She chuckled. "But life is much better, and not just for me. Karla is an exceptional business partner."

"Only because you bounce ideas off each other," Zach clarified. "Don't underestimate what you bring to the table."

She felt a blush heat her cheeks. "We work well together. Anyway, I was going over the books this morning. The gallery is now officially out of the red."

"That's wonderful."

"If sales keep up, we'll have a record year." She placed her hand on his strong jawline, taking in the woodsy scent of his cologne. "You get some of the credit for our success. You introduced me to your social media influencer. Sarah's a real go-getter."

"That she is." His smile reached his dark brown eyes. "I signed a contract with a new resort this morning while you were balancing your books. You know, I was exaggerating when I asked Sarah if she could make Walker Ranch as famous as the O.K. Corral, but she might just reach that goal as long as Hollywood doesn't make another Wyatt Earp movie within the next few years. Lily is coming up with a speech to give tourists on hayrides, telling them where the shoot-outs happened and what blew up."

"Let's not forget your uncle. The cabin he gave your mother will go a long way in rebuilding your family's business."

"True. No more protecting witnesses on the ranch means no more gunfights." He planted a kiss on her forehead. "No more looking over our shoulders for gunmen. And no more resort managers pulling their business."

"Should we celebrate our mutual success and brighter future?"

"Wonderful idea." He released her hand and then reached into his jeans pocket. "I was going to do this tonight, but standing here, beneath your mother's painting, feels right. You went through so much to save this place, the paintings, your life, your sister's life, and prove your innocence. That struggle brought us closer together—forever, I hope."

She tried to peek at what he held, but he gripped it tightly. Was he going to…?

He lowered to one knee, and her heart leaped in her chest.

Yes, yes, a million times yes. She forced herself to remain silent until he popped the question.

"Janel, love of my life, will you marry me?" Zach held out a sparkling diamond ring. "I want to wake up beside you every morning and grow old with you by my side."

"Yes, I will marry you. The sooner the better."

Grinning, he placed the ring on her finger. A perfect fit.

While the magnitude of this moment swept over her, he stood and pulled her into his arms. "I love you, Janel Newman."

She gazed into the eyes of the man who had made all her dreams come true. "And I love you, Zach Walker. Now kiss me."

* * * * *

Cold Case Disappearance

Shirley Jump

MILLS & BOON

Shirley Jump is an award-winning, *New York Times*, *Wall Street Journal*, Amazon and *USA TODAY* bestselling author who has published more than eighty books in twenty-four countries. Her books have received multiple awards and kudos from authors such as Jayne Ann Krentz and Jill Shalvis. Visit her website at shirleyjump.com, and follow her on Facebook at Facebook.com/shirleyjump.author for giveaways and discussions about important things like chocolate and shoes.

Books by Shirley Jump

Cold Case Disappearance

Love Inspired Cold Case

After She Vanished

Love Inspired Mountain Rescue

Refuge Up in Flames

Visit the Author Profile page at millsandboon.com.au for more titles.

Fear thou not; for I am with thee: be not dismayed; for I am thy God: I will strengthen thee; yea, I will help thee; yea, I will uphold thee with the right hand of my righteousness.

—*Isaiah* 41:10

To the family we have built by finding each other.
It's everything I dreamed of...and even more beautiful
than I could have imagined.

Chapter One

Brady Johnson rolled into Crestville on his first day as the new sheriff of Franklin County, Colorado, a little less bright and shiny and up to speed than he would have liked because he'd spent the last thirty minutes arguing with his fifteen-year-old nephew. Hunter had sent his uncle one last parting shot about how unfair it was to start over in a new school before he slammed the door and stomped toward the brick building of Crestville High. Clearly, not everyone was happy about the move and change of scenery. Brady wanted to pull Hunter aside and tell him that this was for his own good, that all of this upheaval was for one reason and one reason only—so that Hunter wasn't lost to the streets like his mother had been. But Hunter wasn't in a mood for listening, so that was a conversation for another day.

Brady parked his Explorer in the spot designated for the sheriff, grabbed his white cowboy hat from the seat beside him and climbed out of the cranky SUV he'd been given yesterday, when he met with the mayor and formally accepted the sheriff's position. One of these days, the county was going to need to buy the department something newer, but that day was not today.

A clear, cloudless sky and a higher elevation made for a

warmer, sunnier late August morning than he was used to back in Indiana. Deep oranges and purples shadowed the mountain range in the distance, the peaks kissed by golden sunlight that danced off the lingering Rocky Mountain snow, despite the late summer date. He drew in a deep breath of fresh, sweet air, and felt, for at least a second, like he had finally landed where he was supposed to be.

The Franklin County Sheriff's Office was a beehive of activity this Monday morning, as the shifts changed and the day shift walked into the building. Almost the entire force was here, about fifty people who filled the three shifts for the county, both because the meeting this morning was mandatory and because they were curious about the new sheriff. The men and women in this room would be assessing him, weighing whether he had what it took to pass muster. Brady had worked for three different departments before coming to Crestville, so he knew the drill. He also knew the stakes in this job, a temporary position that had the potential to lead to a more permanent post, something both Brady and Hunter needed more than anyone knew.

He was grateful to Mason Clark, an old high school buddy who had moved to nearby Crooked Valley years ago and become one of the Franklin County commissioners. When a slot opened up because of the sudden death of the previous sheriff, Mason called and asked if Brady was interested in the job. The chief deputy, Mason had told him, was going out on maternity leave in a few weeks, which was what had led Mason to think of Brady. The appointment was only for a year, just long enough for the county to elect someone new to replace Sheriff Goldsboro, who had died after what Brady was told had been a pretty bad heart attack.

The job opening had been a blessing for Brady, and he only wished it hadn't come at the cost of the Goldsboro family's grief. Brady prayed they would find comfort after their sudden loss.

The slot had opened up at the same time Brady became desperate to change the situation for his nephew, and just before his friend Mason stepped down from the board of commissioners. Mason had told Brady he'd done his research and knew that Brady was tough on crime. "That's something this county needs," Mason had said. When Brady asked him why, Mason had changed the subject.

Yes, Brady had built a reputation for nabbing criminals and putting them behind bars, doing his best to improve the lives of the people in the community where he lived. He'd been able to save so many—but not the one person who mattered most, his sister. At least this was an opportunity for Hunter to change his path. Brady thanked God for that. One chance conversation, and before Brady knew it, he was loading a U-Haul and setting out for Colorado with a reluctant Hunter in the passenger seat.

As he walked through the squad room, a few people greeted him, but most just watched him pass, silent and guarded. He'd expected a little of that, being the outsider. He poured a cup of coffee from the small station set up just inside the break room door, added a splash of creamer and then headed into the conference room. The coffee was more to give his hands something to do than to wire him up any more than he already was. The last thing Brady needed to do on his first day was let the guys in his department see the new sheriff's hands shaking with nerves.

As the clock inched closer to 8:00 a.m., the officers began to file in and drop into the hard, black plastic seats. There was little conversation, just the screech of chairs against the scuffed pea-green tile floor.

Brady set his coffee on the lectern, then gripped both sides of the wooden stand. "Good morning, everyone. In case you don't already know, I am the new sheriff, Brady Johnson."

A few people said "good morning" back. A few others sat there with their arms crossed, clearly not impressed yet. There was a definite air of mistrust in the room, and a touch of outright hostility. Had the last sheriff been so beloved that an outsider was automatically rejected? Or was this county as bad off as Mason had implied? Brady had done some preliminary research on the crime statistics, and they didn't seem to be much higher than the rest of the counties around here. Maybe the rest of the force simply didn't like change.

"Thank you for your warm welcome to Crestville." Brady waited a beat for the irony to settle in. It didn't. "This place is beautiful and very different from Bloomington, Indiana, which was where I was before I came here."

"A lot different," one of the men muttered under his breath. He was tall and thin, with dark hair and a darker attitude. Wilkins, said the shiny name badge on his shirt.

"I'm looking forward to getting to know the entire department. To that end, I asked Carl to schedule one-on-one meetings with each of you so that we can build a little rapport, see where you're at."

The front desk officer had been none too happy to take on the task of Brady's calendar. Brady figured if anyone would know who was happiest coming into the office at what time, it would be the guy who saw them every single day. He'd also hoped the meetings would feel less forced and more friendly if they were set by a fellow deputy. Apparently not.

"I want to hear it all—the good, the bad, the ugly. I want to know if you're happy with your job or if you think there are some things that we could change."

Someone in the back scoffed, "Nothing changes around here."

"Well, I'm the kind of guy who thinks change is a good thing. Just because something worked for the last few years doesn't mean it's the best plan going forward for everyone." He took care not to disparage the previous sheriff's name, because he sounded like he had been a good guy. Got along well with his deputies, ran a tight ship, but hadn't exactly been a meticulous record keeper. The files in the office were a mess when Brady had stopped in Sunday afternoon to take a look at what awaited him this morning and to pick up the county-issued SUV. "I welcome your suggestions and feedback."

The looks he got in return were still wary, doubting, un-friendly. Not an easy crowd to win over. Not that he'd expected to walk in and be everyone's best friend, but he had hoped for a little more enthusiasm. He pulled out his trump card, the one thing he knew could change those doubts into at least guarded optimism. "And as a way to say thank-you for welcoming me to Crestville, Maria's Bakery will be by in a few minutes with some breakfast treats for the morning shift. The Bluebird Diner will be dropping off a selection of sandwiches for the after-noon shift. Overnight shift—it was a little harder to find a place open that late in a town this small..." He waited, but no one laughed. "So I ordered some pizzas from the Crooked Valley Late-Night Craving pizza shop."

Murmurs that sounded largely positive rolled through the room. The deputies looked at one another, then back at Brady. They were still not certain about him, that much he could see in their eyes, but there seemed to be a slight reduction in the palpable wall he'd hit when he walked into the building. It was a start.

Despite the minimal uptick of the warmth in the room, Brady still had that feeling of being an intruder, as if he'd walked in on something no one wanted him to see. He shook it off. First-day nerves, he told himself.

Through the glass in the door, he saw an older woman car-rying a tower of bright white boxes toward the break room. Yes, Brady was bribing his deputies to like him through their stomachs, but he figured there was nothing wrong with that.

"While Maria is setting up in the break room, let's walk through this morning's reports. Get me up to speed on where we're at with any ongoing investigations." He waved up Chief Deputy Tonya Sanders and then took a seat in the front row.

Wilkins, who had been seated by the chair designated for

Brady, shifted to the right, sending a clear message that there was no amount of pastries and pizzas that would change his mind.

Annie Linscott walked into Three Sisters Grindhouse in Crooked Valley and prayed she looked a lot more confident than she felt. And that the anxiety knotting in her stomach would somehow miraculously pass and she'd get through this meeting without making a fool of herself. She had to make this job work out. Not for the money, but for the answers that she so desperately needed.

Three women turned to look at Annie as the door swung shut. They were close in age, similar in features and were, Annie figured, the eponymous three sisters. Right away, Annie recognized Mia Beaumont—technically, Mia Westfield, after she got married last year—and figured the other two dark blonde women were Mia's younger sisters, Chloe and Julia. Annie had heard all about them on Mia's YouTube investigation channel, when their older sister was solving a crime that had directly impacted her family last year.

"Hi. Um… Mia?" Annie forced herself to add a little more confidence to her voice. "I'm Annie. We talked on the phone last week?"

"Annie! Of course. Thanks for coming here to meet. I appreciate you being on time, too." Mia smiled and came out from behind the counter. She pressed a hand to her back and placed another on the swell of her abdomen. "Sorry. Pregnancy makes me move a lot slower than I'd like and makes me insanely tired, so I'm happy to get this meeting in before the baby needs me to take a nap."

Annie wasn't sure how to reply to that. Should she say *congratulations* or somehow find a way to commiserate, even though she'd never had kids or been pregnant?

"Okay," Annie said, and then immediately regretted the stilted response. Every time she got around groups of people, her tongue seemed to freeze, and any kind of sensible thinking flew right out of her mind. It was part of why she loved her job as an online journalist—very little in-person interaction, just a lot of phone calls and video meetings where the pressure to be socially dazzling was lower.

Mia didn't even seem to notice. She crossed the shop, heading for one of the black wrought iron bistro-style tables, talking as she walked. "The channel has exploded in growth since we solved that murder that happened here in town thirty years ago. Just in time, too, because the cops were so sure my grandfather did it."

"I saw that story. It's what got me hooked on your channel." And had brought her here, full of crazy hope that maybe Mia could succeed where others had not. Mia's grandfather had long been a suspect in the disappearance of his business partner—and the money the partner stole from the company. Despite a few close calls with a gunman, Mia and her now-husband, Raylan, had solved the crime and put the vengeful son of the murdered man behind bars. "You never gave up, and I think the world needs more people like you so that innocent people aren't put in jail. And so the lost can be found."

The bucket of words poured out of her so fast, she was tripping over her tongue as she spoke, which meant she had passed the point of nervousness and was now just filling every moment of silence with speech. Her cheeks burned. *Monopolizing the conversation already, Annie?* Her mother would have scolded her and called her selfish.

Deep down inside, Annie knew that talking too much didn't make her a selfish person, but she couldn't stop those decades-old criticisms from echoing in her head whenever she was nervous or under pressure. Always leaving her feeling like she didn't fit in with the job she was doing or the people she was with. Her mother's constant critique of Annie's every move had caused her to grow up shy and introverted, terrified of making a mistake. Those were great traits for a journalist, but not so good for in-person situations. "Sorry. I, uh, just get really excited about the whole concept of solving crimes."

"Don't apologize for being excited to see wrongs made right or answers brought home to worried families." Mia put a hand over Annie's and gave her fingers a squeeze. "I think everyone should care about those things, and if your enthusiasm comes through on camera, they will."

"On…on camera?" Annie thought back to the job description she'd seen on Mia's website. Research assistant… Help catalog evidence… Develop story ideas. None of that involved a video camera, which was a thousand percent why Annie had applied. She preferred to be behind the scenes, gathering data and facts, not front-facing with sources and the audience. The internet magazine she'd worked for before she came here had operated almost entirely through email interviews, which had kept Annie securely in her introverted box. But an on-camera job? That was so far removed from her comfort zone, it might as well be another continent. "You didn't say anything about that."

"You're right. But I'm sure you'd have a good video presence, because you're earnest and likable. That comes through on camera, and people engage with that kind of rawness. Honestly, I had no intention of having anyone else host the show, but then—" Mia put a hand on her stomach "—the doctor said I had to start taking it easy. I had a few early labor pains—"

"More than a few, and you should be at home with your feet up," Julia interjected from across the room.

Mia scowled. "Bossy sister," she whispered to Annie.

"I heard that!" Julia said.

Annie envied their relationship. The familial connections, the light teasing, the obvious love in their eyes. She'd grown up an only child, with a father who was gone most of the time and a mother who had been stoic and harsh, not the kind who dispensed hugs with abandon or made her a mug of cocoa just because. Annie suspected these three, with their close family bond, one reflected even in the name of their business, had grown up with plenty of hot cocoa moments and bedtime stories and many, many hugs.

She shook off the thoughts. She wasn't here to find a family; she was here to find Jenny, and to do that, she needed to convince Mia that she—the biggest scaredy-cat of all scaredy-cats—could have good "video presence," whatever that meant. She couldn't remember the last time she had even been on video, never mind filmed one. The journalism degree she had meant she could research a story, but talking about it on camera was a whole other terrifying thing.

But if she didn't, where would that leave Jenny's story? Forgotten again, one more unanswered question in a country full of missing women. No one else had the drive that Annie had to solve this crime. No one else would care like Annie did; that much was evident by the way the police and media had kicked this story to the back page before the ink was even dry. Jenny wasn't even a footnote in history—she was a few forgotten paragraphs.

Twelve hours ago, Annie had knelt beside the hospital bed that dwarfed the skinny frame of Jenny's mother, frail, weak and so pale. She had prayed with Helen Bennett and sworn that she would find out what happened to Jenny if it was the last thing she did. When Annie said that, a single tear slid down Helen's face. A tear full of hope and heartbreak, and a ticking clock that Annie prayed she could beat.

No, there was no *could*. She *had* to find her friend before it was too late for Helen.

"Sure, I can do that," Annie said, pushing the words out of her mouth in a fast rush, like a reluctant rocket. Before she changed her mind or let her anxiety pull her right back into that comfortable corner where she'd spent most of her life. "I mean, I'd…"

"Great!" Mia's face lit with relief. "I was thinking we could cover the story about…"

"Actually…" Annie warned herself to be calm, not to betray how much she needed Mia to agree to this plan. "I came prepared with a story. Big overachiever here." She waited, but Mia didn't laugh at the joke. "I, uh, well, I researched the stories that have done the best on your channel, and it seems that cold cases about missing people, especially missing girls, are the best performers. So I thought we could—should—cover this one." She fished a copy of a newspaper clipping out of her bag and slid it across the table.

Sitting here, with the image of Jenny mere inches away, sent a wave of sadness through Annie. Her bright smile, wide eyes, long blond hair, all faded in the clipping, almost as if the memory of Jenny was melting away, bit by bit. It had been ten years since Jenny was last seen, and as far as Annie could tell, no one else was looking for her. The sheriff's office had barely looked for her, and none of the other podcast and vlog hosts Annie had reached out to, hoping they'd take on the story, had been interested. This was, quite literally, Annie's last chance.

Mia studied the image and began to read the article. To keep herself from fidgeting and betraying her nerves, Annie clasped her hands in her lap. What seemed like hours—but was really only minutes—passed before Mia lifted her head. "This is such a sad story. Teenager with a bright future, goes to meet her sort-of boyfriend in Crestville and is never seen again."

"There wasn't any kind of real investigation, either. Her home life was sort of chaotic at the time because she and her stepdad didn't get along, and the police just assumed she ran away. Her mother tried to keep interest going in the case, but she couldn't afford to hire a private investigator, especially with so little to go on. As far as I can tell, there was nothing done, nothing except..." Annie shook her head. "Forgetting that Jenny Bennett mattered to someone."

Mia's gaze narrowed. "Sounds like you know a lot about this case. Almost like it's...personal for you."

Annie swallowed, took a beat and then forced what she hoped was a blank look to her face. One that didn't say, *I've*

*spent the last ten years trying to find out what happened to
my best friend but couldn't get anywhere because the cops
don't hand out evidence to private citizens.* "No, not really. It
just interested me because it seemed so sad." But as she tried
to hold Mia's gaze and pretend the lie was the truth, a rush of
heat filled her face and undid all her careful composure. Lying
was no way to start off this job, and not something Annie did.
"That's not the truth. I do know her."

"Then why would you lie to me?"

"Because I really need this job and really want to solve this
case, and I figured if I told you that she used to be my friend,
you wouldn't hire me." Annie sat back and waited for Mia to
tell her to get lost.

"I just investigated a case centered on my own family. Do
you really think I wouldn't understand?" Mia's features softened. "I totally get that need for justice for someone you care
about. This case has enough interesting tidbits about it and
does fit what my audience tends to like best. You're right, it is
something I would normally tackle. But…"

Everything Annie had hoped and prayed for hung in the
space of that *but*. She needed to say something, anything, to
erase any doubts Mia might have. "I promise, I'll be objective."

"What I was going to say is that the truth can lead you to a
destination you don't want." Mia glanced at her sisters, then
back at Annie. "I got lucky that my grandfather was innocent
of the crime he was accused of committing. I am eternally
grateful I was able to clear his name, even if it meant uncovering some history that people didn't want exposed. Your friend
Jenny could have disappeared for a number of reasons or even
not want to be found. All I'm saying is that you may not like
the answers you find."

"I'm willing to take that chance, if you're willing to take a
chance on me." It was the bravest thing Annie had ever said.
The drive to find Jenny, not to let another month, never mind
years, go by was so strong, it overpowered the anxiety flitting

about inside her. Helen had a few months, maybe as little as a few weeks, and Annie refused to go back to Denver empty-handed. "I'll be impartial, and I'll find the facts, whatever those facts may be."

Mia assessed Annie. A long minute passed where the only sound between them was the soft rock radio in the coffee shop and the quiet clanging of the dishwasher in the backroom. "I can see how much this means to you, and that's the kind of passion that got me to start my channel. I might be foolish to hire someone with no experience in front of the camera, but the rest of your résumé looks good, and if you can bring that passion to the screen, this might just work out. Record a couple episodes, and we'll see. Okay?"

A mixture of *yay-I-got-the-job* and *oh-no-I-have-to-be-on-camera* ran through Annie. She didn't know whether to whoop or panic. "Thank you, Mia. I will. I promise."

"I'll drop off some equipment to you on Wednesday, if you're staying in town, and send you an email with some tips for recording."

"I live in Denver but I'll gladly get a room at the motel while I'm working on the story. Whatever it takes."

Mia held up a hand. "This is not a guarantee of anything. It's a chance for you to show me what you've got. We're going to play it by ear and see how the first videos go. I'll pay you half the going rate for those, and if it works out, I'll bump you up to the full rate we talked about in our emails last week. If it doesn't work out, I'll find someone else. This channel is too important to let it fail."

"I understand that. Making this work, and getting attention on Jenny's story, means a lot to me, too." Annie could barely contain her joy. She'd gotten the job and could finally, hopefully, find out what happened to Jenny, now that she had the credential of a massively popular vlog on her side. She'd reasoned the Crestville law enforcement wouldn't want the bad publicity and would lean toward helping her, because she was a part of Mia's channel. She'd hit a thousand roadblocks trying to get information on her own. Maybe now she had some leverage that could break the case open. If she could bring Jenny home, no matter what that meant, she would give Helen the only thing that Jenny's mother wanted—peace.

Mia got to her feet and pressed a hand to her back. "And with that, I'm going to follow my sisters' stern advice—"

The other two women laughed at that. "About time," Chloe said.

"—and go put my feet up at home. Call me if you have any questions, Annie." She put a hand on Annie's shoulder. "Not all my cases have happy resolutions, you know. I hope you're emotionally prepared for what you might find out."

"It's better than having no answers at all, isn't it?"

Mia's gaze took on a faraway look, as if she was thinking back through the cases she'd covered on her channel. "Sometimes it is, Annie. Not every time."

Chapter Two

Brady stared at his deputy in disbelief. "What do you mean Judge Harvey let him go?"

William Marsh, the deputy standing in Brady's office, was a wiry young man in his early twenties who had about as much intimidation factor as a stuffed bunny. How he ended up in the sheriff's office was beyond Brady, who would never have hired someone so meek. "That's just what I was told." A nervous quiver danced in Marsh's words. "Judge Harvey didn't think there was enough evidence to convict."

"Not enough evidence? I found the stolen jewelry in Anderson's car."

"I don't know, sir." Marsh stood across from his new boss, trembling in place. "Am I…am I dismissed?"

"No. Give me a second to think this through." Brady had been on the job for two days before he was called to his first crime scene in Franklin County. A local jewelry store had been burglarized just after nine that night. Whoever had broken in had also cracked the code to the antique safe and stolen everything inside. The store owner had been in tears, devastated by the loss. Brady and his deputies fanned out, searching the nearby area. An hour into the search, Brady ran into a guy wandering the streets, clearly high and looking for drugs.

Every time Brady came across someone lost like that, it made him think of Tammy, who had made one mistake in high school that sent her down a dark path, nearly costing her everything. Now, his sister was in rehab, and hopefully this time, Brady prayed, she'd find the help she needed.

He'd seen a little of Tammy in this stranger on the street, which might have come through in Brady's conversation with the man, because after a few minutes, the young man seemed to drop his guard a bit. In a hurried whisper, he told Brady that he'd seen someone cutting through the alley shortly after the store alarm went off. As another deputy approached Brady, though, the informant darted away, as frantic as a startled rabbit. All he had to go on was the tipster's name—Frank Givens—and the scant info he'd given Brady.

Brady had listened to the young man and headed down the alley. Under a dumpster and nearly hidden in the dark sat an earring, two pearls and a diamond fashioned into a heart shape. Three blocks from the burglarized shop and far too fancy to be forgotten in an alleyway meant the pieces were likely from the burglary. That evidence led him a little farther down the street to a relatively new sedan that had a suspicious-looking and lumpy bag on the back seat.

Brady knocked on the door of the house where the car was parked, and when he asked the grumpy older man at the door if he could look inside, the owner bolted around the corner. Two deputies tackled the guy, who turned out to be one Edward T. Anderson, known on the streets as "Eddie the Answerman," and arrested him. The search of his car revealed more than half of the goods that had been stolen from the store, a fact the shop's owner corroborated. It didn't get more open-and-shut than that, at least not in Brady's world. Yet the judge had released the car owner anyway.

He turned back to Marsh. "What justification did the judge use to dismiss the charges?"

The deputy flipped through his notebook, his gaze on the scribbled words, not on Brady. "Uh, the, uh, suspect claims someone else planted it while he was sleeping and that he didn't know where it came from. And the snitch—uh, guy—who was the witness is a known drug user no one can find, so the judge discounted his account." Deputy Marsh put his hands up before Brady could ask another question. "I'm just the messenger. Judge Harvey is the one you should talk to."

Something in Marsh's words, and in the way he kept shifting his gaze to the squad room, sent a tingle of suspicion up Brady's spine. He crossed the room and closed his office door. "Is this something Judge Harvey has done before? Dismiss a case at the arraignment?" It was not impossible, but very rare for a judge to override the prosecution's argument for a trial and toss the case before it made it to the docket. Maybe the suspect had a good lawyer, or maybe Judge Harvey was just lazy. Maybe the prosecutor hadn't done a decent job. Either way, Brady couldn't believe such a clear-cut case wouldn't have been pushed through the justice system.

Marsh glanced back at the room full of detectives and officers, then the closed door, then Brady. "Uh, yeah."

"As in once? Twice? More than that?"

"I can't tell you that, Sheriff. I just…" Marsh put up a hand, cutting off Brady's objection. "I can't. You gotta understand, this is a small town, and in a small town, people do things different. They take care of their own."

Brady knew what that meant. Bloomington had a sizable population, but as the smaller sister to the state capital of Indianapolis, it had a decidedly small-town feel in his years there as the chief deputy. He'd known of some backroom deals and good-old-boy networks that protected people who shouldn't have been protected. There were many days over the course of his career when Brady felt like he was fighting an uphill battle for right and wrong. He'd prayed Franklin County would be different, but apparently that kind of corruption had no boundaries.

That feeling that something was not right in this county returned, and he realized he was going to have to spend some time ferreting out wrongdoing within his own department. "Is the judge related to the suspect?"

"No, he ain't related. But Judge Harvey is cousins or something close like that with Kingston Hughes, and Hughes owns about everything around this place, including that diner across the street, so if Judge Harvey wants something to go his way, it usually happens." Marsh shook his head. His demeanor had stiffened, become even more wary and hesitant. He wasn't going to share any more, that was clear. "Am I dismissed, sir? I gotta get back on my shift."

"Fine. Dismissed." Brady opened the door and watched Marsh leave.

The rest of the squad room quieted as the deputy walked out of the boss's office. The department had yet to accept Brady as the new sheriff and were still leery of anyone who worked closely with him. He could see that in the way they avoided him, the harsh whispers when he announced policy changes and the distance they kept from him. That was okay. He was used to being the odd man out. The rest of the department would come around eventually.

Either way, his biggest problem right now was in the form of a lenient judge and a burglar who should be behind bars, all, it seemed, controlled by Kingston Hughes. A quick search on his computer revealed a few facts: Kingston Hughes was the largest employer in the county, employing more than two thirds of the population in his megacorporation that had real estate holdings and, the primary moneymaker, a steel factory. He'd lived in Franklin County for fifteen years, after choosing a vast empty acreage outside Crestville as the headquarters for Hughes Steel.

And he was one of three county commissioners who, along with Mason, had voted in agreement to hire Brady. If he'd wanted a puppet who was soft on crime, one look at Brady's résumé would have told Hughes that the county wasn't hiring someone like that. It didn't make sense that someone running a successful business would want leniency for petty criminals like Eddie. Not unless Eddie the Answerman was doing more than stealing jewels. And how did Judge Harvey tie into all this?

Brady tried talking to the DA's office, but the lawyer assigned to the case said that "getting charges to stick to Eddie is like trying to use wet tape on a wall." Brady could hear the frustration in the prosecutor's voice and figured he needed to go straight to the source for why this was happening.

Brady grabbed his car keys from the dish on his desk. Nothing like paying a personal visit to the judge to get off on the wrong foot—but hopefully get some answers. He would make this a friendly "coincidence." Already from the office scuttlebutt, he knew the judge ate lunch at the diner across the street, often with Hughes. Brady would just "happen" to run into him.

"I'll be back after lunch," he said to Carl, the receptionist behind the front desk, an older man with a full head of gray hair and an uncanny ability to remember every detail about a call. Brady had liked Carl from the second he got here. Friendly but efficient, smart but modest, and on most days ending in Y, just a little cranky. He reminded Brady of his grandfather in a lot of ways.

"It's your hour," Carl said, then went back to his newspaper.

The Crestville office was small, a relic in this age of new and modern buildings. The bulletproof glass erected between the lobby and the station itself was bolted to the floor with unsightly metal T-bars and enormous bolts. The phone system had a habit of freezing when too many calls came in at once, and half the computers in the office were still running Windows 97. Brady made a note to review the budget line items. The glance he'd had at the numbers yesterday said there should have been plenty of money for modernization over the last year or two. Where was the money going, if not to some modern computers and a nice entryway?

Just as he went to push on the handle of the glass door, a woman who was no bigger than a snap pea, as Brady's grandmother would say, was coming up the granite steps. She had soft blue eyes and pale blond hair that was swept into a ponytail, a pretty contrast against her maroon blouse and dark jeans. On her shoulder, she had a massive brown leather tote bag that looked like it might swallow her whole.

He pulled open the door and stepped back to let her pass. "Good morning, ma'am." He tipped his hat in her direction.

"Good morning." She started to walk past him but stopped when she glanced at his name badge. She stood there, halfway through the doorway, which meant Brady couldn't move. "You're the new sheriff, aren't you?"

"Yes, ma'am. Brady Johnson." He shifted to put his weight against the heavy glass door so he could shake hands with her. "What brings you by the sheriff's office today?" He figured he could point her in the right direction, end this entryway impasse and be on his way. He knew Judge Harvey took a lunch break around now and was a man who loved the diner that sat between the sheriff's office and the courthouse. It was a perfect place to catch him for a quick conversation.

"Actually, it's you I'm here to see." She took out her phone and raised it toward his face, pushing a button as she did. "Sheriff Johnson, I'd like to ask you a few questions about the disappearance of Jenny Bennett."

The next thing Annie knew she was staring at the glass door as it shut in her face.

The sheriff had simply said, "Nope," then scooched past her and out the door, just before she stepped back and the glass entry swung closed. Between the backward-facing gold-leaf letters spelling Franklin County Sheriff's Office, she saw the tall figure of the very man she needed to talk to heading for the street.

On any other day, Annie would have let him go. Avoided the confrontation. The rejection. But if she did that this time, how on earth was she going to get the story she needed? Jenny had disappeared in Crestville, ergo the sheriff's department would have the very file Annie had tried for years to get on her own by filing several Freedom of Information Act requests, and been denied over and over again by the previous sheriff under Exemption 6: "Information that, if disclosed, would invade another individual's personal privacy."

Whose privacy? And why?

Maybe now, with a new sheriff in town and her job as a journalist with Mia's investigative channel, she could file another Freedom of Information Act request and hopefully get traction with the better credentials, but that could take weeks—or worse, months—and she would fail at a job that was so new, she hadn't even bothered to print new business cards.

She drew in a deep breath, pushed open the door, ignored the heavy pounding of her heart and went outside. She had dithered too long back in the lobby and the sheriff was already out of earshot. She prayed he didn't get in his car and drive away because there was no way she could close the gap to get to her little Toyota and then chase him down.

He didn't. She saw him cross the street, a tall, handsome man who cast a long shadow as the morning stretched toward noon, and then duck into the Bluebird Diner.

Annie stood there on the sidewalk, debating. Everything inside of her wanted to go back to the car, drive away, hole up in her motel room and do research on her laptop. To use the internet as a way to avoid human interaction and all of the anxiety and stress that caused her. She hated confrontation, hated to hear people yell or even so much as raise their voices. Last week, she'd been in the grocery store and happened upon a couple having an argument and the sound of their angry voices was enough to make her abandon her grocery list and go sit in the car until her racing heart calmed down.

She didn't know the sheriff and had no idea if he was the kind of man who would be irritated or furious at being interrupted. The longer she stood there, imagining worst-case scenarios, the more the nerves in her stomach multiplied, becoming a roar of worry.

Fifty yards to the right sat the quiet sanctuary of her Corolla. A hundred yards in front of her sat the big unknown of the sheriff. The lure of escape pulled her a few steps toward her parking space. Annie opened her bag to find her keys and saw the folder holding the newspaper article about Jenny.

On the front of the folder, she had written three words to herself: What Matters More? It was something Jenny had said a hundred times when they were growing up. *What matters more, Anna Banana? Your life or making other people happy? What matters more? Your grades or this movie?*

Sunshine glinted off the Corolla's windshield, almost as if the car was winking at her, smug in knowing Annie would pick the safe route, the one that afforded no conflicts, no arguments.

And no answers.

Annie drew in a deep breath and turned toward the diner. A man in a three-piece suit had just exited, looking irritated as he slipped into a shiny Lexus.

What mattered most right now was finding Jenny. If she didn't come home with answers this time, how could she ever forgive herself?

Give me strength, Lord, she whispered as she took the first step across the street. *Don't let me chicken out.*

As she pulled open the diner door, the tantalizing smell of burgers spattering on the grill and onion rings sizzling in the fryer hit her first. It had been hours since she'd eaten, and only a gas station granola bar at that, grabbed in her haste to get here from Denver, get checked into the motel and get to work. The last couple days had been a whirlwind, after the meeting with Mia about the job, then tying up loose ends in Denver before finally setting out for Crestville to settle in and start the investigation. She hadn't even had time to play with the video equipment Mia had sent over yet.

A hubbub of activity filled the small space. Dozens of people sat in the bright red-and-white booths or chatted with the wait-staff dressed in white shirts with red epaulets. Oldies played on the jukebox at one end of the diner, a peppy undertone to the easy flow of conversations.

The sheriff was sitting in one of the booths against the windows, deep in conversation with a heavyset man who was ten or so years older, with a short gray beard and a serious scowl on his face.

Annie's steps faltered.

"Miss? Can I get you a table?" a young waiter asked her.

Her stomach said yes, but her head shook no. She could eat later. Jenny mattered more than a burger any day of the week. "No, thank you. I see the person I need to talk to." Then she made her feet move—ignoring the urge to fight, flight and freeze all at the same time—until she was standing right beside the sheriff.

"Judge, I need to understand why—" The sheriff flicked an annoyed glance in her direction. "Can I help you?"

"I'm so sorry to interrupt." Her voice began to tremble and the nerves in her stomach went into full-on riot mode. Annie took a deep breath and plowed forward. "I need to talk to you, Sheriff Johnson, about something important."

"Make an appointment with reception." He thumbed toward the office across the street. "I might have some time next week."

Next week? She couldn't wait that long. Mia was expecting content every week, and a short video saying *I found nothing to report* wasn't going to get this investigation moving anywhere. She would blow her big chance before it even started. Then there was Helen Bennett, slowly dying in her hospital bed back in Denver. She didn't have an extra week—and neither did Annie. "I only need a few minutes, Sheriff. If you could—"

"Take my seat, little miss," the other man said as he slid out of the booth. "I'm done talking to him anyway."

The sheriff half rose. "But, Judge—"

The older man shot the sheriff a glare. "I told you I'm not talking about my decisions. You've been in this town for five minutes, Johnson. You don't know these people like I do. If you want my advice, keep your nose out of our judicial system. You earn that right in this town. You don't demand it. If you don't like what's happening, I suggest you take it up with the DA."

As soon as the other man left, Annie slid into his seat. The vinyl was still warm, the plate of food—a towering stack of onion rings and a heart-attack-inducing triple cheeseburger—in front of her was untouched, as was the sheriff's corned beef sandwich. Okay, so maybe she had interrupted at a bad time. Her nerves threatened to choke her, but she kept reminding herself that this was Jenny on the line, and for Jenny, she could overcome any kind of anxiety.

The sheriff scowled at her as he pulled a twenty out of his wallet and tossed it on the table. "I do not appreciate being interrupted in the middle of something important. Like I said, ma'am, make an appointment at the desk." He slid out of the booth, one hand on his hat, then plopped the Stetson on his head before stalking out of the diner.

Annie scrambled after him—in for a penny, in for a pound, she told herself—and hurried across the street, struggling to keep up with his longer strides, narrowly avoiding being hit by a dark SUV that blew through the intersection. "Sheriff, please, just one minute." At the same time, she pulled the folder out of her bag.

He spun around. Annie and the folder collided with his chest. Annie stumbled back.

The sheriff's scowl only deepened. "I told you. Make—"

"I will. After you look at this." Annie thrust the folder at him. "It's a missing girl, and she disappeared from this town, and no one will give me answers, and I just need you to—"

But he'd already taken the manila folder from her and walked away without a word. She half expected to see him toss it into a trash can on his way into the brick county sheriff's building. The hot midday sun beat down on Annie's head. She'd just made the boldest move of her life—and it had probably ruined everything.

Chapter Three

A can of baked beans simmered on the stove while Brady pushed a couple of hot dogs around in a frying pan. Not the most nutritious dinner on the planet, but the best Brady could do, considering most of his meals were grab-and-go. It wasn't until Hunter started living with him that he realized he'd have to either get a second job to afford takeout three times a day or figure out how to put something together that the kid would eat. So far, hot dogs had made the cut. Salads, not so much.

Brady had to say, he didn't blame the kid. Salads were about as satisfying as cotton candy, and for a man like him, cotton candy wasn't much as far as dinners went. Probably had the same nutritional value as the hot dogs. If Brady could find an extra hour in his hectic days, maybe he'd have time to watch something like the Food Network and learn how to do more than boil water. Given how much work he had to do in order to put the Franklin County Sheriff's Office into some kind of order, since the previous sheriff apparently wasn't much for recordkeeping, Brady doubted there'd be lasagna on his kitchen table anytime soon. "Supper's ready!" he called.

No response. Brady turned off the stove, grabbed two plates from the cabinet and a couple of forks out of the drawer and then set them on the table. All of his kitchen navigating happened in the space of a few feet, a working triangle smaller than most people's closets. From the table, he could open the fridge if he wanted to, or even load the dishwasher. The little cabin he was renting just outside downtown Crestville was cheap and small, but a tad cramped for a grown man and a nearly grown nephew. Eventually, he was also going to have to search for a more suitable place to live.

What did it say about him that he hadn't done that yet? Not in this town and not in the one before. *You're the kind of man who never lets grass grow under his feet*, Cassie, his ex-girlfriend, used to say. For about five minutes, he'd considered getting married to her, settling down, having a family, but then the idea of even setting a date to do all that had him filling out applications in the middle of the night and moving on to the next job. That was what took him to Bloomington, and probably what would have kept him moving until he retired.

Then Hunter came into his life, and Brady realized that he couldn't be living all over the country if he was going to give the boy some stability. So he headed to Chicago, picked up his nephew and drove away from the city where Hunter had begun to run wild, a lost kid who'd been left to his uncle like a family heirloom.

The whole thing had been a whirlwind. Tammy called him one day and said she was heading to rehab and Brady needed to take Hunter before she changed her mind. He asked her how long she'd be gone, and Tammy said, "Until." Until she completed the program, until she had some sobriety under her belt, until she was back on her feet physically, mentally and most of all, emotionally. The kid had been through enough in his young life, and the answer was a no-brainer: *Of course I will*.

But that had meant a change of lifestyle. One that Brady's former girlfriend had refused to make, which ultimately broke them up. Nothing was more important right now than Hunter to Brady.

He knew Hunter would fall down the same dark paths the boy's mother had if they stayed in Chicago any longer, and Bloomington, Indiana, where Brady worked, was far too close for his comfort to the life he wanted Hunter to leave behind. In fact, Hunter, a bright, creative kid, had already had a couple brushes with the law when he was caught at parties where there were drugs and alcohol, and when he was put on academic probation for skipping school for twenty days straight. It was only a matter of time, Brady knew, before Hunter ended up where Tammy was, or worse.

So when the job in Crestville came up, Brady grabbed it. Small town, outdoor living and even better, only a couple hours from the rehab where Tammy was, which meant they could visit her often. A fresh start, he prayed, for everyone.

Brady wandered down the hall and knocked on Hunter's door. A second later, the heavy metal music thudding against the walls turned down a notch. "Supper's ready, Hunt."

"Not hungry." The volume rose again.

Brady knocked again, but this time opened the door and poked his head inside. Hunter was on his bed, a PlayStation remote in one hand, some kind of military game on the TV across from him. "You have to eat."

"Not hungry." Hunter moved right, left, as if he was the character dodging enemy fire.

Brady stood in front of the television. Hunter glared at him. "Supper is not a request. It's a must in this house."

"My mom never made me eat dinner." When he said things like that, Hunter sounded like a petulant five-year-old.

Brady didn't say that Tammy hadn't enforced curfews or schedules because most of the time she was passed out on the couch. She'd been clean and sober throughout her pregnancy, but as Hunter got older and the pressure to provide as a single mother mounted, Tammy had started using more and more.

Brady knew she'd had some troubles staying sober and had talked to her dozens of times about it, but on the surface, she'd seemed to have it together. For fourteen years, she'd kept the depths of her addiction a secret from her brother and everyone close to her. Then she'd been pulled over for driving the wrong direction on the highway while she was high on meth, with a freaked-out Hunter in the passenger's seat, and been given a choice—prison or rehab.

Brady didn't know much about kids, but he did know one thing—structure was good. He'd read somewhere that keeping a baby on a schedule made the child feel secure and safe. If it worked for infants, maybe it would work on an angry, confused teenager.

"Your game will still be there in ten minutes," Brady said. "Let's go. No is not an option."

"Fine. Whatever." Hunter tossed the remote onto his bed and stomped out of the room.

Brady trailed behind him, wondering when his nephew had grown so tall and how he could have missed so many years of this kid's life, especially when he'd lived just a few hours away. If he could have been there more often, maybe seen what was happening with Tammy sooner, maybe made a difference.

Maybe.

Brady filled a plate for each of them and sat down across from his nephew. A sullen Hunter picked at his food, pushing the beans around on the plate. "I thought that was your favorite dinner."

"It was. Until we had it seventeen times in a row."

The exaggeration wasn't too far from the truth. Brady needed to figure out how to cook an actual meal that contained at least a couple food groups. Add that to his list of seven million things to do after taking over as the county sheriff. "I'll make something different tomorrow."

Hunter just shrugged. A heavy blanket of silence fell over the room. The small space seemed to close in on them, making every breath, every screech of a fork against a plate, sound ten times louder. Brady was about as good at small talk as he was with cooking.

"So, uh, how was school?"

"Stupid and boring." Hunter looked up from his plate. "I hate this town. How long are we going to have to live here?"

"We just got here. I took a job and signed a contract. I can't just up and leave."

"Why not? You made me just up and leave Chicago. I was happy there." Hunter pushed back from the table and got to his feet. "I don't want to live in this stupid town. I don't want to eat hot dogs and beans ever again, and I don't want to live with you." He stormed down the hall and slammed his bedroom door as a nice little exclamation point at the end of his words.

Brady sighed. He picked up both plates, scraped the dinner he hadn't really wanted to eat either into the trash and then ordered a pizza delivery. He wasn't naive enough to think that one pepperoni pie was going to make a dent in all the anger and hurt swirling inside his nephew, but at least it would be something the kid might eat.

Brady sank onto the sofa and put an arm over his eyes. Today had been an epic fail on every level. The guys in the department didn't like him, the county justice department seemed to be on the side of the criminals, he had a pesky reporter who wanted information he didn't have, and his nephew was miserable. Tomorrow had to be better because there was no do-over for today.

He allowed himself a five-minute pity party, then he went back into the kitchen to do the dishes. As he took out the trash, he noticed the folder that reporter had given him sitting on the front seat of his squad car. By the time he came back from the trash can, the natural curiosity that had brought him into law enforcement made him retrieve the folder from the car and bring it inside.

Just as he opened the front door, a pair of headlights swung past his stoop, lingering for what seemed a second too long.

Brady shielded his eyes against the light, thinking maybe it was the pizza delivery or a lost Amazon driver, but the car sped off. Maybe they'd gone to the wrong house. Brady closed and locked the door, just in case. If there was one thing he'd learned over the years, it was that he could never be too careful.

The file inside the folder was, sad to say, a run-of-the-mill missing person case. Young girl, seventeen, with a little trouble at home between her and Mom's second husband, who had driven to Crestville from her house in Denver to meet up with a sorta-boyfriend that her stepfather had forbidden her from seeing. Just before she got to town, her car broke down, leaving her stranded. A couple people in town reported seeing her walking into town, then again outside the Bluebird and farther down the street later, trying to wheedle the Crestville Motel owner into giving her a free room for a couple nights. There was one other report of seeing the girl on a street the day she disappeared. That was it.

When Jenny Bennett didn't come home or call, her mother reported her missing, filing a report both in Denver and in Crestville. According to the newspaper, there hadn't been much to go on to find her, and the trail had soon gone cold. Brady was just about to put the article back in the folder when a sentence buried in the last paragraph caught his eye.

A witness said she saw local resident Eddie "the Answerman" Anderson talking to Jenny outside the Bluebird Diner. Anderson, who has been previously investigated for solicitation of a minor, denies seeing the girl. The Franklin County Sheriff's Office had no further comment.

Twice in one week, Brady had come across Eddie Anderson's name in connection to a crime. Granted, the events were ten years apart, but that seemed to be more than a coincidence. Twice in one week, he'd seen law enforcement and the judicial department fail to bring charges or investigate Anderson in any way. One time would be a fluke. Twice in one week—

That sure seemed like a pattern to Brady. Brady had a hunch that there was more to dear old Eddie than met the eyes. And he always listened to his hunches.

Chapter Four

Annie fiddled with the vlogging camera that Mia had given her. An empty tripod sat a few feet away, waiting for her to mount the Sony on it and record her first video for the channel. She had promised Mia she would send it over by the end of the day on Friday, which had suddenly arrived before she had anything recorded. An overly ambitious promise, it turned out, because not only did Annie have zero evidence, she was more than a little terrified of speaking into the big plastic eye of the camera. What on earth was she going to say?

A part of her wanted to leave Crestville, drive over to Crooked Valley, hand all the equipment back to Mia and tell her that she couldn't do the job. She'd bitten off more than she could chew, as her grandmother would say, and it had been foolish to think she had the chops to do this. But then her gaze caught on the picture of Jenny that she had taped to the mirror in her motel room, and the urge to throw in the towel was replaced by guilt.

No one was looking for Jenny anymore. No one cared if Jenny was alive or dead. Except for Annie and Jenny's dying mom. And if Annie stopped looking, Jenny would be forgotten forever. A girl like Jenny, with her contagious smile and dorky jokes and warm hugs, deserved to be remembered. She deserved to be found.

Ken Lincoln, the reporter at *The Denver Post* who had written the original article on Jenny's disappearance, had been little help. "Sorry," he said when Annie called and interviewed him earlier today. Annie wished she had had the courage to call Ken years ago, when his memory would have been sharper. Her own doubts of her abilities had put her so far behind on this case, and had cost them valuable time.

"After I retired," Ken said, "I tossed a lot of my notes. The wife wanted to make room for a craft table in my home office." A little snort of derision said loads about how he felt about *that*.

"Can you start with what you do remember about the case? Any kind of detail can help." Annie hoped that letting him ruminate would jog his memory.

"It's been, what, ten years? I've covered a lot of news in the time since, and I've gotten older, so my memory isn't what it used to be." He chuckled, then paused for a long moment. "I remember talking to her mother and seeing how distraught she was. Made me feel bad for her. What a rough thing to endure."

"That's why I'm doing this story. For Jenny's mom. She's very, very ill, and I just want to get her some answers before… Well, before it's too late."

When Ken spoke again, his voice cracked a bit. "That's a good thing you are doing. All who are missing deserve to come home."

"Amen."

"I don't know how much help it can be, but I probably still have some notes on the rough draft of the story on my computer," Ken said. "If you can hold on a minute, I'll dust off the keyboard, power it up and see what I've got."

"That would be terrific. Absolutely." Annie fixed a cup of tea while she waited, just to keep her nerves in check and her optimism from getting too high.

It didn't take long for Ken to come back on the line. "Okay,

I've got a few things but not much, because I liked to write things down as opposed to typing them up. Helped me remember better, which is why tossing those notes was… Well, it doesn't matter now. Anyway, I did keep some notes in the margins of the story as I wrote it. I have some information on the boyfriend and one of the witnesses."

Compared to what Annie had so far, that sounded like a gold mine of information. "That's terrific." She scribbled quickly as Ken gave her what he had, including where Jenny's boyfriend, Dylan, worked at the time of the disappearance and the name of the witness who had seen Jenny outside the Bluebird. "Do you mind emailing me a copy of that rough draft, too?" she asked.

"Sure. Don't see what it can hurt. I wish I could give you more than that, but maybe one of those people will remember something."

"If they cared about Jenny, then I hope they do, too." Annie thanked him again and hung up.

The story arrived in her inbox a couple minutes later, along with some hope that maybe this case wasn't going to be a total dead-end after all.

The first person she set to tracking down was Jenny's boyfriend, Dylan Houston, who thus far had refused to speak to her every time she reached out. This time, she'd updated her information on him by doing a search for his name and employer. Maybe now that more time had passed, Dylan would want to talk to her. To finally bring closure to Jenny's disappearance.

Annie's hopes sank when she saw that the cement factory Dylan used to work at had been shuttered for more than a year. She tried again, putting his name and Crestville into a new search. She came back with an old address for an apartment on Hyde Street and not much else. Just a couple of very old social media posts tagging him at local bars and an employee of the month award from the cement factory. As far as Annie could tell, Dylan no longer lived in Crestville.

She expanded the search to the entire state of Colorado and

finally received a long list of hits on four different Dylan Houstons, a name she hadn't expected to be popular. Two of the people that came up in the search matched what Annie thought might be Dylan's age. Annie had only had bare details from Jenny, and Jenny's mother hadn't remembered much about him, but had remembered that a big part of her argument with Jenny about the boyfriend was the ten-year age gap between them. These two men were twelve and fifteen years older than Jenny would be.

The other information Ken gave her was a little vaguer. A busboy named Marco at the Bluebird, who didn't want to be named in the article, remembered seeing Jenny at the diner. In the margins, Ken's comment on his story said simply, *Possibly looking for a job?*

It was something. Kindling to the fire Annie wanted to light beneath the search for Jenny. She needed more information than this, which meant she had to go to the one person who held the match.

Ten minutes later, Annie was parked in the lot outside the Franklin County Sheriff's Office. She'd already scoured the archives of the local paper a few weeks ago, hoping for an update story or another article she might have missed in her first search years ago. The only coverage about Jenny's disappearance had been reduced to a couple of paragraphs buried on a back page and a grainy photo from Jenny's yearbook that her mother must have sent in. Ken's story in *The Denver Post* had the most coverage, but there'd been no follow-up stories, probably because there'd been bigger headlines to chase.

The sheriff's department, however, would have the case file, which would have names, dates, times. Whatever they had could only augment what Ken had given her, particularly contact info for Dylan and the busboy. The trick was convincing Brady Johnson that making Annie jump through hoops to get the file would only delay a process with a very short timeline.

Inside the sheriff's office, the wizened gray-haired man behind the desk in the lobby scowled at her. "I thought the sheriff refused to talk to you the other day."

This must be the aforementioned receptionist and appointment-maker, whose first name was Carl, according to the nameplate on the desk. Annie forced a smile to her face. Pushed herself a couple steps closer. She couldn't let a little brusqueness dissuade her, even if everything inside of her was a quaking, nervous mess. "He said I needed to make an appointment and that you were the one to talk to about that."

"He doesn't have any openings." The man stared straight at her, without ever glancing at the calendar she could see open on his computer screen.

"Actually, I see an opening right there." She pointed at the screen. "At 10:30 today, which is perfect. Since that's only twenty minutes away, I'll sit right here and wait, if you don't mind." She dropped onto the wooden bench before her unsteady legs broadcast her sheer terror at being so bold. Annie plunked her tote into her lap, wrapping her fingers around the leather handles, tight enough to stop them from trembling. *What matters most, Annie? You can do this. Be brave.*

"He usually runs late."

"That's fine."

"What are you? A reporter?" The older man nodded at her bag. "Sheriff Johnson doesn't talk to reporters. That's the community relations department, and I'm sorry to say they're not in today."

Awfully convenient that no one was here when she needed to talk to them. She wondered if Carl was telling the truth or throwing up roadblocks to drive her back out the door. "I'm not here for the newspaper." Not really a lie, not if the receptionist wanted to draw a conclusion from it that was slightly wrong.

He gave her a once-over, then harrumphed and went back to his work.

The hard wooden bench underneath her had a curve that pinched her thigh and she was pretty sure was going to leave her with pins and needles, but she stayed where she was, afraid that if she moved, Carl would change his mind about letting her stay in the lobby.

Precisely at 10:30 a.m., the receptionist picked up a phone, punched a button and a second later said, "You have a visitor waiting for your 10:30 slot." A pause as whoever was on the other end said something. "She's claiming you told her to make an appointment. And she did. I told her she was wasting her time. Apparently she's got a lot of time to burn in her life." Another pause. "Will do." The man hung up the phone and got to his feet. He swiped a key card over the lock for the door leading to the squad room and ushered her forward. "His office is at the back on the right. I'd wish you good luck, but this probably isn't going to go the way you want anyway."

Annie hesitated. The noise coming from the squad room was an off-key symphony of hunt-and-peck typing, phones ringing and voices climbing over each other. "Why not?"

"Sheriff's in a bad mood today. I don't know why. My job isn't to ask questions." A sarcastic smile spread across his face. "If you get a word out of him that's not sending you packing, consider that a victory."

Great. She'd hoped that it being a Friday would bode well for a meeting. Everyone was happier on Fridays, right? A beautiful weekend was mere hours away, and when she'd met him, she thought the tall, fit sheriff looked like the kind of guy who loved the outdoors. He was all rugged and strong and...

What was wrong with her? Annie shook her head as she navigated her way through the puzzle pieces of desks and chairs and cubicles before she reached a glass door that said simply Sheriff in gold leaf, with the faintest remnants of a previous name ghosted below it. Brady Johnson had been written on a piece of paper and taped below that, a temporary nameplate for the door.

The sheriff was at his desk, reading something in a file folder. The pair of reading glasses perched on his nose somehow made him look even more attractive. She liked dating men who read, because she was, of course, in a world of words, and just watching him do that made her melt a little inside. Not that she was dating Sheriff Johnson or even thinking about such a thing, of course. That was a preposterous idea. Yet an image of him sitting in the threadbare armchair in her living room with a book in his hands and a yellow Lab at his feet came to mind all the same. For a second, she felt like she'd stepped into an alternate reality where she was more at home than she'd ever felt in her life.

Annie sucked in a deep breath and rapped on the wood frame. He jerked his attention to the door. She'd startled him. Hopefully that didn't make him even more cranky than what the receptionist predicted.

He waved at her to enter, so she opened the door and slipped inside, shutting the door behind her. In an instant, all the noise of the squad room disappeared, replaced by something soft and instrumental, a melody as enchanting as a dream. Surprising.

"*You* like Schumann?" she asked. He wore a cowboy hat, looked like a movie star and listened to classical music? Who was this guy?

A smile curved across his face. "You recognize the piece?"

She closed her eyes for a second and let the music wash over her. A piece she'd heard at least a thousand times. "'Träumerei' from *Kinderszenen*. In English, *Notes from Childhood*. It's my favorite of his pieces. The entire set is, really. It's so…cheerful. Gentle. Almost like watching little kids dance in the rain."

She'd spent so many afternoons practicing Schumann. As a kid, she hated the intricate piano pieces, but as an adult, hearing or playing them reminded her of meeting Jenny, of long summer afternoons by the creek, laughing and getting muddy. The notes of *Kinderszenen* were as light and bright as their friendship had been. The melody glided through the room with sweet melancholy.

"That's a lovely way to put it." He turned the music down a

little, then got to his feet and came around his desk and sat on the corner. He gestured toward one of the two black leather visitor chairs. The tension she'd seen in his shoulders, the irritated wrinkle across his forehead, had eased. Maybe because of the music, maybe because they had this in common? "I don't know if I've ever met anyone who loves this piece as much as I do."

"I grew up in a piano-playing house, and I played Schumann many, many times. It was my mother's favorite, too." And the one she had been the most critical of when Annie played. The only one to gush over her performance at recitals had been Jenny, while Mother had been critical, nitpicky, judgmental. *You play like a happy bird singing,* Jenny had once said. Somewhere along the way, that happy bird had lost its notes. It had been a long time since Annie had sat before a piano. Everything she associated with that instrument came with a side of heartbreak. Until right now.

"Now I'm even more impressed," the sheriff said. "Played it many times? I can't imagine playing something this complicated even once."

A flush raced to her face. "Oh, it's nothing. I wasn't really that good, and well… I'm not here to discuss pianos."

"You want to know what we have on the Jenny Bennett case." The change of subject brought with it a seriousness in his features, a shift in the tone of his voice. This was the sheriff side of Brady Johnson, the side she'd come to talk to.

"Yes." She pulled her notebook out of her tote bag, opened it to a blank page and clicked her pen. She ignored the flicker of disappointment that he had switched gears so easily. This was what she wanted, she reminded herself. "The newspapers barely covered it, and I need more information to go on. I did get a name on her boyfriend and something about the witness—"

"Why?"

"I need to talk to them because I'm doing a vlog on it and—"

"A vlog? What is that?"

"It's a video blog. Sort of like a written blog, except in—"

"Video." He nodded. "Okay, and who is this vlog for?"

She checked her irritation at his impatience and slowed her words, stowing her nervous rush to make her point. "I'm working for a channel called Missing Voices, run by Mia Beaumont, who lives in Crooked Valley. She investigates cold cases and just solved the Richard Harrington disappearance and murder. Maybe you heard of it?"

The sheriff shook his head.

Annie paused. She had the distinct impression the sheriff would be less apt to talk to her if she went on and on about subscribers and reach. He didn't seem the type to want global publicity.

He crossed his arms over his chest and leaned back, assessing her. "I don't talk to press."

"I don't need an interview." Although she would love to get one with him because it would give the vlog episode more credibility, but she kept that tidbit to herself. "I just want the police report and whatever the sheriff's department gathered for evidence."

He pushed off from the desk and went back to his chair. Across the thick oak surface, he seemed less friendly, more distant. "Your best bet is to go through the Freedom of—"

"I don't have time for that." She caught herself and let out a breath. "I'm sorry. It's just that Jenny's mom is dying, and all I want to do is bring her some answers and some peace. Doesn't she deserve that after all the pain she has gone through?"

The sheriff didn't say anything for a long moment. Annie resisted the urge to again fill the uncomfortable silence with worthless chatter. As a journalist, she knew that giving a conversation space to happen was often more effective than asking a lot of questions.

"Her mother is dying?"

Annie nodded. Tears burned at the back of her eyes. Once Jenny's mom was gone… "She only has a few weeks. Pancreatic cancer. Stage four." His features softened so Annie leaned forward, closing the gap between them by a few inches, latching onto that flicker of compassion. "I looked you up online, Sheriff, and you have a track record of closing cold cases. In fact, you said to the *Bloomington Herald-Times* that 'cold cases deserve as much effort as current cases.'"

"You've done your homework."

"It's pretty much my job."

He chuckled. "If you've done that, then you also know I've been in this town less than a week. I'm still figuring out where the coffeepot is. I can't invest my resources in a cold case right now."

"I'm not asking for your resources. Just a few minutes with your copy machine."

His dark gaze swept over her, considering, weighing. "I can't let you do that because technically this is still an open investigation—"

"Open?" She snorted. "No one has looked for Jenny in years." The interruption was so out of character that Annie leaned back and flushed. "I'm sorry. I'm just emotional about this."

"And that was going to be my second reason for saying no." He leaned forward and laced his hands together. "Trust me, you don't want to be emotionally invested in an investigation. It skews your perspective and keeps you from seeing the truth."

"You're impartial. You could help me." She gave him a half smile. "After you find the coffeepot, of course."

For a second, she thought he was going to order her out of his office. After all, he had no reason to help her. He didn't know her from a fencepost and had never met Jenny. The towering piles of folders and notebooks on his desk all said he was far too busy to help a stranger with a case that had gone cold before it even started.

"Well, thank you for your time," Annie said as she gathered her things and rose, turning toward the door. "Sorry to bother you."

"You're going to let go that easily? I thought this girl meant something to you."

Annie wheeled around. A rush of frustration, anger and grief ran through her, escaping in the sharp notes of her voice. "Jenny means everything to me. I'll do whatever it takes to find her. So no, Sheriff, I'm not giving up that easily. I'm just giving up on this conversation for now. I have witnesses to track down. So thank you for the time, and I'll see myself out."

"That," the sheriff said, pointing at her, "is exactly the kind of attitude you're going to need if we're going to find out what happened to this girl."

It took a few seconds for his sentence to assemble in her brain. "You're…you're going to help me? Why?"

"Because I had a mother once, too, a mother who died without…" He shook his head, erasing the whisper of emotion on his face. "Doesn't matter. This case is too important to let it sit another day. Why don't I meet you at the diner at noon? I'll bring the case file. I'll share what I can, but not so much that it could damage whatever case we may have against whoever did this."

All these years, all those closed doors, all those fruitless efforts to figure out what happened to Jenny, and now between what Ken had sent over and what the sheriff promised to share, she could get the information she needed. Finally. *Thank You, God. Thank You so much.*

"Yes, of course. Noon is perfect. Thank you, Sheriff Johnson." Then she hurried away before the big, strong sheriff saw the not-so-tough reporter start to cry.

Brady didn't know what it was about that reporter but every time she looked at him, he could barely concentrate. The fire in Annie's eyes, the earnestness in her voice, all reminded him of his early days as a deputy when he'd start every day all bright-eyed and ambitious, thinking he was going to single-handedly rid the world of crime. Of course, it hadn't worked out like that at all. He couldn't even keep crime out of his own family, never mind the world.

But Brady wasn't a quitter, and he refused to dwell on the impossibilities. He liked to focus on the opportunities. Solving a cold case in a town this small would be a nice way to start off his tenure here, especially after what happened with the burglary. And if Eddie Anderson did turn out to have something to do with Jenny Bennett's disappearance, then Brady would take it as an opportunity to put that miscreant behind bars.

His priority, though, was getting to the root of the problems within his department and how Kingston Hughes's influence might affect them. This cold case could provide some insight into what was going on, and possibly lead Brady to more answers.

As Brady crossed the room toward the door, he nodded hello or said something to each of the deputies he passed. Their replies ran at a lukewarm temperature. The pastries and pizza had been a temporary panacea and had done little to increase camaraderie with the team. He'd scheduled a department barbecue for this afternoon, but no one signed up to bring a dish except for Sanders, the chief deputy. Brady opened his Uber Eats app and scheduled some side dishes to go along with the ribs order he'd placed earlier.

The entire department had this insular quality about it, an ice floe of deputies floating an ocean away from the sheriff's iceberg. They were polite enough, did their jobs well enough, but rarely engaged with him. Maybe all the department needed was more time to get used to him? Or maybe his personality wasn't meshing for some reason?

"Sanders," Brady said to Tonya, who was standing beside Wilkins's desk, talking to the other deputy. Both of them instantly stopped chatting, giving Brady the feeling he had interrupted something they didn't want him to overhear. "I'm heading to the Bluebird for a meeting. Should be back in an hour."

Tonya nodded. "No problem. If anything happens—"

Wilkins scoffed.

"I'll come find you," she finished, with a sharp glance in Wilkins's direction.

"Nothing ever happens around here," the other deputy said, "at least nothing that needs your attention, Sheriff."

An odd comment, Brady thought, but one he'd address later. He was still in the process of going through each staff member's files, what cases they'd handled, how they'd buttoned them up, if they had at all. He wanted to be careful, though, about jumping to conclusions. He wasn't about to bring a world of hurt down on fellow law enforcement officers if there was nothing there. "See you both at the department barbecue?"

"Uh…" Wilkins shifted his weight. "I was—"

"Great," Brady cut in before Wilkins could bail on the event. "See you both there."

He arrived at the Bluebird Diner a few minutes before his meeting with Annie, giving him time to look over the file on Jenny Bennett. There wasn't much, in fact only a handful of pages and not a whole lot more details than the newspaper article had run. A missing person's report, an interview with the girl's mother, another with her boyfriend and a couple of witnesses who "might" have seen something but neither seemed certain about who they had seen. There was one witness, a young man named Marco, who was nervous about talking to the cops because he was an immigrant who was afraid his visa would be revoked, who had told detectives he saw a young girl who looked like Jenny talking to a man outside the diner. Not exactly a lot to go on. Not a big surprise the investigation had gone cold.

He turned to the pages that recapped the interview with Jenny's boyfriend, Dylan Houston. Houston described a short, tumultuous relationship that came to an end before Jenny showed up in town. From Houston's perspective, Jenny was a desperate ex who wanted them to have a second chance, and he wanted nothing to do with that. "I basically just told her to get lost," Houston told investigators. "I didn't mean it literally."

An interesting comment, Brady thought. One that merited more investigation, to be sure. He called over to the office and asked one of the detectives to run a check on Dylan Houston. Brady read off the data on the photocopy of Houston's driver's license, attached to his witness statement. Shouldn't be too hard to find him.

The article Annie had given him yesterday sat beside the folder. *The Denver Post* had described the relationship as "troubled" but that Houston had asked Jenny to move to Crestville so they could "have a fresh start." Why would Houston tell the police and the media two different stories? Either he was hiding something or...

He was hiding something.

That left the busboy at the Bluebird, an elderly woman named Erline Talbot who saw a scuffle by a car and an elderly man named Stan who lived in the apartment on the second floor of the building across from the diner. Erline said she'd seen someone who matched Jenny's description arguing with a man beside a dark sedan. That, Brady realized, could be anyone. Stan reported seeing her talking with a short youngish man outside the diner. Two more names to add to his list of people to talk to.

Then there was the requisite criminal background check, which turned up a speeding ticket when Jenny was sixteen. Nothing out of the ordinary. Nothing that said for sure she'd run away from home but also nothing that said she was a murder victim. It was as if she'd...vanished.

He made a note to request whatever cell phone data her provider still had available. After ten years, he wasn't very hopeful that the records still existed, but better to check than be sorry he didn't. Sometimes the lead he least thought would pan out turned into the one that solved the case.

Brady's gaze drifted back to the only suspect named in the

Post article. Eddie Anderson. Whose interview was—surprisingly—not in the police report file at all. There was a note about the interview, time, date, officers present, but none of the testimony Eddie had given was attached. No recording, no notes. Why?

Maybe Anderson had nothing to do with it. And maybe he had everything to do with it. That meant the person the cops had talked to about the disappearance of Jenny Bennett was the same man Brady had arrested the other day. Maybe Eddie "the Answerman" ran with a bad crowd or maybe he was exceedingly unlucky. Or maybe—and this was the conclusion Brady leaned toward—Eddie Anderson was involved with more than just burglary. But how? And why? And were the police protecting him? Or had the department just been lax in their recordkeeping?

A movement outside the window caught Brady's attention. He saw two things at the same time—a black SUV creeping down the street, pausing a little too long at the four-way stop, at the same time Annie started to cross the street. The vehicle waited for Annie to get from one sidewalk to the other but then didn't move through the intersection. Even though the driver had done the right thing by giving a pedestrian the right of way, there was something off about how long the black vehicle stayed at the stop.

Brady shook off his suspicions. There could be a hundred reasons why the driver didn't move right away, many of which began and ended with a distraction from a cell phone. He could only be grateful the driver got distracted while he was stopped, not while the vehicle was moving. Another car came up behind the SUV and honked, which spurred it into moving.

Just then, Annie walked into the diner, setting off the bell over the door and distracting Brady in a whole new way. Her blond hair was swept into a clip today, with a few runaway tendrils skating against her neck. She looked rushed and anxious, at least from where he was sitting, but then she turned and caught his gaze, and everything about her seemed to shift into something as calm as the Schumann piece they both loved.

"Thank you, Sheriff, for meeting me," she said as she slid into the booth.

"First off, it's Brady." Her perfume—something light, floral, as springlike as she was—danced into the air. "You're not my deputy."

"But I'm not your friend, either."

"Good point." He liked women who were smart and who didn't try to play games or flirt to get their way. Annie seemed to be a straight shooter, which was exactly the kind of person Brady liked best. She was also beautiful in an understated way and clearly unaware of the effect she had on a man when she walked into a room. "Maybe we should remedy that."

"You want to hire me as a deputy?"

He chuckled. "No. But I think we could be friends. I mean…" And now, it was his turn to feel flustered and out of sorts. Since when did he ask a woman to be his friend? "I just mean, if we're going to work together on this case, we should, well, we should…"

"Get along." She cocked her head to one side and studied him. "I don't know that we'll be friends, exactly, but I can call you Brady, as long as you call me Annie."

"Deal." He put out a hand. Her delicate fingers slipped into his and sent a little shock wave through him. Every time he saw her, he grew closer to her, learned more. He liked that. Liked the complexities and layers each conversation uncovered.

She pulled her hand away. A faint touch of pink flared in her cheeks. "Um, what's good to eat here?"

"The burgers are a heart attack on the plate but amazing. I also love the Reubens and the Philly cheesesteaks."

"With extra mayo?" She grinned.

"Always."

A slim young girl stopped by their table, a pen at the ready to take their order. "Let me guess, Sheriff. A large Diet Coke, a Philly cheesesteak with extra mayo and extra-crispy fries."

"Have I become that predictable already?" He liked this town. Liked the sameness of it, the community that felt like friends. Bloomington had some of those same features but in a less-connected way, maybe because the population was seven times larger. "Yes, that would be great. Thanks, Lisa."

"You got it." She wrote the order down on her pad and turned to Annie. "What can I get you?"

"Actually, what he's having sounds fabulous. Same for me. Thanks." Annie gathered both their menus and handed them to Lisa. "Does a guy named Marco work here, by chance?"

Lisa shook her head. "I don't think so. But I've only been here a couple months. You might want to ask the manager, George, when he comes in after two."

"Thanks. Will do."

Brady chuckled. "Always working. I might resemble that remark myself a little."

"That's how cases get solved. Or at least, that's what you said in your interview in the paper back in Indiana." A smile lit her face and eyes.

He didn't know whether to be flattered or suspicious that she was quoting him word for word. "That is true."

There'd been a hint of amusement in her face earlier, but now her features shifted into all-business, serious mode. "So, about the case…"

"Ahem, yes." What was it about this woman that kept distracting him from his job? "I looked through the file, and you're right, very little investigating was done. Maybe because she wasn't a resident, maybe because there wasn't much evidence. I don't know. It's hard to tell all these years later. But it sounds like you know a lot of what I know."

"I talked to the reporter at *The Denver Post* who wrote the original story. His wife threw away his notes, but he did remember his conversation with Dylan Houston and Marco, the busboy. But that's about it." She nodded at the file. "Did you have more than what Ken did?"

"Not much. A witness statement from an Erline Talbot, who saw a 'suspicious car' pull up beside a person she thought might be Jenny. There's a later note in the file that said the car was more likely the neighbor's brother, visiting for a few days."

"She gave enough detail about the car that they could tell that's what it was?"

"I assume so. The report doesn't say much. Just describes it as a dark sedan."

"That's what Ken had, too. There must be hundreds of thousands of dark sedans in Colorado."

"And maybe a couple dozen in Crestville, so it's not out of the realm of possibility that it was the neighbor's brother."

"No, but..." Annie shrugged. "Maybe we should talk to Erline again. Or that Stan who saw her at the Bluebird."

"Stan died three years ago," Brady said. "Sorry. From what I saw in the file, he didn't really see much."

"All the more reason to go talk to Erline."

"Well, the thing with Erline's testimony is that..." Brady stopped. How much did he really want to share with Annie, who was clearly deeply emotionally invested?

"That was what?"

He hesitated but decided telling Annie the truth would be the best policy. He'd warned her that an investigation could lead to answers she didn't want to hear. "Well, where she lives—it's a known hangout for drug dealers, according to the deputies I asked about the location."

"Jenny didn't do drugs. She was adamant about that. She'd seen what happened to other people we knew, and she had no interest in that."

"Doesn't mean she didn't try them. Or fall in with the wrong crowd."

"Jenny didn't do that. She wasn't like that. Yes, she had a fight with her mother and stepfather the day she left, but she was heading to something—well, someone—not running away."

"Kind of sounds like the same thing."

Annie shook her head, adamant. "Jenny and I were one week from graduating when this happened. She texted me when she left town. Said she was going to go see the guy she'd met. I was at work and asked her to wait for me, but she told me she couldn't stand being around her stepfather one more second. She promised to be back later that night."

"How do you know she didn't lie to you?"

"Because she had no reason to. We were best friends, Sheriff—" She corrected herself. "Brady, and we told each other everything."

He chewed that over in his mind for a while. "Then why are there reports about Jenny talking to Marco at the Bluebird? His testimony sounds like she was asking about getting a job."

"Maybe it was a temporary thing? I don't think she had much money. Plus Jenny texted and told me that her car broke down just after she got here. Jenny's mother said they fought when Jenny called her, and she refused to pick her up or send her money. Her mother hoped taking a hard line for a few days would teach Jenny a lesson she said, and it all went so horribly wrong." Annie shook her head. "The next day, Helen changed her mind and called Jenny, but Jenny never answered her phone."

"What do you know about this boyfriend she was going to see? Did you know him?"

"I never met him. She met him on a dating app, and they talked by text and on the phone but never met in person. When she had the fight with her mother and her stepfather, and I was at work, she decided that would be a great time to come here and meet this guy."

Brady thought back to the write-up of the interview with Dylan Houston. He'd said that Jenny and he had "dated for a bit" but then broken up. Wouldn't that imply they had met in person already? Once again, he wondered what the ex-boy-friend could be hiding. "What else do you know about him?"

"Not much. She said he was sweet and sounded like a good guy. Although I'm not sure how much you can judge someone you only talked to on the phone. I wish I'd asked her more questions, but we hadn't seen each other in a couple days and..." Annie shook her head. "I have ten million things I'd do over again if I had a chance."

"It's not your fault, Annie. You know that, don't you?"

"I know I should have blown off work and gone with her. Because then she wouldn't be missing."

"It's not your fault that you didn't go. She made the choice to go alone. You need to understand that."

"I guess I do, in some ways, but in other ways, I don't know if I can forgive myself."

"Well, none of us can truly know what was going on in Jenny's head. She could have decided to run off with him or not. We need to find him and talk to him." The police report differed from the news reports and from what Annie herself knew. That alone was a reason to find out who this boyfriend was—and where he was when Jenny disappeared.

"I know her better than you do. How she thinks—thought—and what was going on in her head when she left Denver. If this—" she waved between them "—whatever it is, is going to work, you have to trust me on that."

"If there's one thing I've learned in twenty years in the sheriff's office, it's that nothing—and no one—is what you think they are."

Including, quite possibly, the woman sitting across from him. Brady would do well to remember that.

Chapter Five

The sun climbed over the Rocky Mountains, washing the valley town of Crestville with soft shades of orange, almost as if someone had spilled a glass of juice along the range, letting it trickle down the streets, over the rooftops and onto the lawns. Annie sat in one of the rickety metal chairs outside her motel room, her hands wrapped around a cup of coffee and a blanket over her shoulders to ward off the morning chill, and watched the day begin.

Finally, they were inching forward with Jenny's case. After their lunch, Brady had done as he promised and tracked down Jenny's boyfriend, Dylan. He'd texted her later that afternoon and asked if she'd like to take a drive over in the morning to Golden and interview him together.

She was up before dawn, had her camera gear, notepad and notes all packed up and ready to go in a bag sitting at her feet. It seemed to take a hundred hours between then and when Brady was due to arrive, but finally, just before 8:30 a.m., his SUV swung into the motel parking lot.

Annie ducked back into her room, set the coffee cup on the small table by the door, then grabbed her bag and headed over to Brady's vehicle. The interior was warm, a nice change from the chill in the morning air. Annie climbed into the passenger seat and settled her tote bag on her lap. "Thank you for taking me along on this. I'm dying to get an interview with Dylan on tape."

Brady held up a hand. "Not without my say-so. We're going to run this interview my way. If Dylan says anything incriminating, I don't want it coming back on us in court."

He had a point. The last thing she wanted to do was prevent the arrest of whoever had made Jenny disappear. Brady backed out of the space, then headed down the road and onto the highway, his profile a study in concentration and determination. She liked this side of him, the dogged detective who would get the answers they needed. It was part of what others had admired about Brady Johnson, in the articles she'd read. He seemed like a stand-up guy, and someone she could depend upon. Which was good, because Annie didn't depend on many people, least of all men. She prayed she was making the right choice in relying on Brady for this investigation.

"What if he agrees to be videotaped?" Annie asked.

He considered that for a moment. The cars on either side of the sheriff's vehicle hung back, like flanking soldiers afraid to zip in front of the officer. It made for a slight roar of traffic as they drove. "I think that can work. As long as you promise not to use any of the footage before I give you the okay."

"I won't. You can trust me."

He flicked a glance in her direction. "Can I?"

"I was wondering the same thing about you a moment ago. I don't trust many people, and I doubt you do, either."

He mumbled something about people letting him down. "That's true."

"To me, it's all about faith. Having faith in each other and faith in the process. Faith that Jenny will be found, if we don't stop looking."

He scoffed. "Your faith in others is a lot stronger than mine."

The admission seemed to soften the air between them,

stretch a thin thread of commonality across the vast interior of the SUV. "That's okay," Annie said quietly. "Because I'm sure there will be a time when your faith is stronger than mine."

He faced her for a moment. "And I'll be the one who's telling you it's going to work out."

A soft smile stole across Annie's face. She was beginning to like this sheriff. A lot. "And I'll appreciate it more than you know."

A smile flickered across his lips but disappeared as soon as he turned back to the road. They passed the rest of the miles talking about the case, sharing notes on the evidence each of them had. "Dylan Houston hasn't been in trouble with the law in almost a decade," Brady said. "He had a couple drug charges when he was younger, but for the past nine years, he's had a decent job at an automotive shop, got married and divorced and has two kids. He's paid his taxes and child support and, from what I can see, has been an upstanding citizen."

"Which could also be a cover for the crime he committed ten years ago when Jenny came to town."

"Talking to him should give us the answers we need." With that, Brady switched on his blinker and swung the SUV into the lot of Lenny's Auto Repairs.

One of the two bay doors was open. A sedan was up on the lift, with a man in dark blue coveralls beneath it, working on the engine. When Brady and Annie got out of the vehicle, she fully expected someone to hear them, but instead the sound of their doors shutting was covered by a radio playing some very loud country ballad.

"Dylan Houston?" Brady said as they approached.

The middle-aged man under the car spun around. His eyes widened, and he dropped the wrench in his hands. Then he darted out a side door and around the back of the building.

Brady broke into a run, taking the ground twice as fast as Annie could, with his longer legs and clearly fit build. He caught up to the young man in a matter of minutes, grabbing him by his coveralls and pressing him against a junk car. "We just want to talk to you."

"I have nothing to say to the cops." A sullen expression filled his face.

Annie stumbled up to them, heaving in deep breaths. The first thing she noticed was the name Dylan embroidered across the pocket of his coveralls. His features matched the image in the driver's license photo she'd seen. Forgetting her agreement with Brady, she fumbled her camera out of her bag, then flipped it to Record. "Dylan Houston?"

"Get that camera out of my face! I got nothing to say to you."

Brady motioned to Annie. She sighed and lowered the camera. "We just want to talk to you about Jenny Bennett," Brady said to Dylan. "You're not under arrest. We're just here for information."

Dylan looked between each of them, his gaze wary, assessing. "That's all you want?"

"Yes," Annie said. She stepped forward and held out the camera but kept the lens pointed away from Dylan. "I'm an investigative reporter—" even saying that sounded weird, but good to Annie "—and a friend of Jenny's. I'm doing a videocast about what happened to her."

A few feet away, Brady was clearly irritated, given the scowl on his face and the way his eyebrows had knitted together. "Maybe we don't drop so much information on Mr. Houston here so quickly," he said to Annie.

"No, no, it's cool." Dylan's posture relaxed. "I can tell you what I know about her, which isn't much."

"Then why did you run from us?"

"I, uh, had a little too much fun at a party last weekend and got into a fight. Broke some furniture. Cops busted it up, but we all scattered. I figured you were busting me for that." The story didn't ring true, but Annie didn't confront him. It seemed as if Dylan was leaving out a detail—or ten. Was he involved in something criminal?

"Not my jurisdiction," Brady said, "and not my case. If you'll help us with Jenny, I'll forget you ever told me that."

"Whew. Yeah, sure. What do you want to know? Like I said, it isn't much. Barely knew the girl."

Annie asked if Dylan minded if she taped the interview and he agreed. The three of them settled around a picnic table set up behind the auto shop. The wooden surface was pitted by the weather and the marks of old cigarettes. The benches had warped and buckled, pulling against the few nails that remained. Annie set her camera on top, aimed it toward Dylan's face and prayed the table held out long enough to do the interview.

Brady started questioning first, as they'd agreed in the car. He ran down the details of Dylan's name, address, how long he had lived in Crestville before coming to Golden and then, finally, how he had met Jenny.

"One of those online dating things," Dylan said. "I was looking for a..." He glanced at Annie.

"Just tell us what you know," Annie said. "Every little bit can bring us closer to finding out what happened to Jenny."

Dylan nodded. "I was just looking for a girlfriend for the night, you know? Not a relationship. Came across this Jenny girl and thought she was cute, so I messaged her. We talked a bit on the app. She told me she was twenty years old, but turns out she wasn't even eighteen yet." Dylan put up his hands. "That was too young for me, and I told her so."

"How'd she take it?"

"Kinda hard. We'd been talking for a couple weeks, off and on. She was a back pocket girl, you know?"

"Back pocket girl?" Annie asked.

"The one I kept in my back pocket, case the others didn't work out. I like to keep my options open."

"Oh." Annie ignored the nausea in her stomach. Jenny had been far too sweet, too innocent, to be anyone's back pocket girl. "Then what happened?"

"I told her eighteen was too young, but she said she felt a 'connection.'" He put air quotes around the word. "You might think I'm a jerk—"

I do.

"But I didn't feel any kind of connection with this girl, 'specially after she lied to me. I like people who are straight-up. What you see is what you get, you know?"

"And she didn't take the rejection well?" Brady asked.

"Girl went nuts on me!" Dylan had the decency to look ashamed for a second. "Sorry, but she did. She was all, 'I thought I was falling in love,' and all that kind of thing. I don't know what she thought was going on between us after a couple phone calls, but she was determined to meet me. Said I'd change my mind when I saw her."

"She was going through a lot at the time," Annie said. Although, why hadn't Jenny told her about lying to Dylan and falling in love? It seemed the kind of thing a friend would tell another friend. Was Dylan telling the truth? "Fighting with her mother constantly about the mother's new husband, who wasn't the best guy. Jenny used to say that there was a fairy tale out there for her, and she just needed to find it."

Dylan plucked his coveralls from his chest. "Do I look like anyone's fairy tale?"

"Maybe you did to a girl who was very unhappy." Brady gestured to Dylan to keep going. "So when she showed up in town, what did you do?"

Dylan splayed his hands on the table and leaned toward Brady. "I had nothing to do with her disappearing. I wasn't here when she vanished. You believe me on that, don't you?"

Annie didn't know what to believe. Brady's features were unreadable. "Then tell us what happened," she said.

"I didn't tell the cops this back then, and I didn't tell that reporter nothing, either. I was kind of a troublemaker back then, and the last thing I needed was the cops breathing down my neck about some girl I barely knew." Dylan waited a beat, then went on, "She did come to see me. Found me at the grocery store I was working at. I almost got fired over that little scene she pulled. She said that I had to help her, that I owed her for stringing her along."

Annie didn't say she agreed with Jenny about that. Everything Jenny had told her about this mystery guy sounded romantic. He'd clearly been saying all the right things to *keep his options open*, as he'd said.

"Anyway, I told her she couldn't come at me when I was at work like that. I promised her I'd meet her after work, down by this place on Pierce and Main, this little restaurant I knew."

"And did you meet her?" Brady asked.

"Nah, man, it was all a way to get rid of her. I figured she'd get mad that I stood her up, and my problem would be solved."

Annie bristled at the thought that Jenny would be considered a problem by anyone, especially a man who could so easily discard her. "Do you know if she showed up?"

Dylan shrugged. "I was at a bar with my friends by then. I never heard from her again, so I figured she gave up. Then the cops come knocking on my door a few days later. That's the first I knew she was missing, I swear."

Dylan's story had a lot of holes in it, from Annie's perspective. He seemed almost *too* eager to share and be helpful. If he'd been a possible suspect would he be so willing to talk? "You didn't see any of the media coverage? The missing posters her mom put up?"

He shook his head. "I had moved on by then."

"Seems odd that you wouldn't hear something, given how small this area is," Brady said.

"I didn't know anything about it, not till the police showed up and started asking me questions." Dylan put up his hands, in a gesture that seemed to suggest surrender. "I had nothing to do with her going missing. I'll even take one of those lie detector test things to prove it."

Annie and Brady pressed Dylan a bit longer, but there was

little more to gain from the conversation. Either Dylan really didn't know, or he was pretending not to know.

But when Annie produced the waiver allowing her to use his likeness on the podcast, he didn't hesitate to sign. He even asked a few questions about when the episode would air and how much of the interview would be featured.

"Thank you for the time, Mr. Houston." Brady extended his hand and with it a business card. "If you think of anything else, call me. Day or night, I'll answer the phone. I'd like to bring this girl home to her family."

Dylan tucked the card into his shirt pocket. A smear of grease from his fingers smudged the edges. "Sure thing." He motioned toward the car on the lift. "I gotta get back to work before the boss fires me."

Annie and Brady thanked him for his time, then headed back to the SUV. As they pulled away, Annie watched Dylan lope into the garage, disappearing inside the dark interior. "Do you think he was telling the truth?"

"I think he was telling his version of it."

"What do you mean by that?"

"You know how they say there are two sides to every story? I think there are three. The versions we convince ourselves are the truth and then the real story. Dylan might not have all the facts straight, but this is what he thinks happened."

"So you think he's being honest." A note of disappointment hung on Annie's words. She'd had the unrealistic hope that Dylan would finally give them the closure everyone needed. All Dylan had done was leave her with more questions and fewer answers.

"I didn't say that. I do think he's hiding something, but whether that has to do with Jenny or not, I'm not sure." Brady took the ramp to get on the highway and pressed the gas pedal, making a swift merge with traffic. "Either way, I'll be keeping an eye on him and digging a little deeper into his background."

"Thank you. That makes me feel better. If you find out anything, will you share it with me?"

He arched a brow and didn't reply.

"I know it's an ongoing investigation, but even a little bit of information on the podcast can—"

"I've done more than I should letting you come along on this interview, Ms. Linscott."

The curt admonishment chilled the air in the vehicle and sent a reminder that the sheriff held many more investigative cards than she did. That meant Annie had to work harder and ask more questions if she wanted to solve this crime.

Brady steered the conversation toward hiking in Colorado for the rest of the ride back to Crestville, an obvious effort to take the disappearance of Jenny off the table. By the time they pulled in front of the motel, Annie could almost feel the wall of distance he'd erected.

"Thanks for today," she said.

"You're welcome. I hope it helped some."

"Can I share what I learned on the channel? Dylan signed the waiver." She held up the piece of paper with his signature. A couple greasy fingerprints darkened the border.

Brady considered that for a moment, his features cold and hard, almost clinical. "Just highlights for now. I'm not a hundred percent convinced Dylan isn't involved. Nine times out of ten—"

"It's the spouse or the boyfriend. I get it. I'll send you the clips I'm going to use before I air them."

The olive branch did its job. The tension in Brady's shoulders eased, and so did the scowl on his face.

Back at the motel, Annie poured a new cup of coffee from the ancient machine in the front lobby, then headed back to her room to go over the photocopies of the case file that Brady had given her yesterday one more time. Maybe there was something she'd missed, some clue that seemed miniscule but wasn't. A little after three, she called the Bluebird, but the manager had gone home for the day, and the server who answered the phone refused to give Annie the manager's home number. She said, "Call back tomorrow," and then hung up. Another dead end. For now.

Out of the three tips called in when Jenny disappeared, there were only two she could follow up on: Marco Gonzalez, the busboy at the Bluebird Diner, and Erline Talbot, the neighbor. She decided to start with Marco, who no longer worked at the Bluebird, but after a deep internet search, she found an address for him in Illinois and a landline number.

When she called and explained who she was, he at first claimed not to remember Jenny. "Lots of girls come to the Bluebird," Marco said. "And they talk to a lot of people. I don't remember her."

"Yeah, but only a few of them disappear. You must have seen the news coverage."

"I just do what the boss says. I don't want any trouble. Sorry, miss."

She sensed he was about to hang up. "Wait, wait. Please, if you have anything, please tell me. Her mother is dying, and I need to bring her some answers."

Marco hesitated a long time. "The boss makes all the decisions on who comes to work for him. You best talk to him."

"The manager at the Bluebird?"

"He's not the real boss. You need to find the real boss. I already said too much." He hung up, leaving Annie with a big question mark on her notepad.

Who was the real boss at the Bluebird if not the manager? She made a note to do some more digging—who owned the diner? That left following up with Erline Talbot, the woman who had seen a "shady-looking guy" on the street where Jenny was last seen. It wasn't much to go on, but she'd found answers with less.

Annie debated calling Brady for a good five minutes before deciding that if Brady had wanted to interview Erline himself, he would have mentioned it. The notes in the police report made it sound like what Erline had seen could have been anyone or anything, and there was probably a good chance that Brady wouldn't bother with such a vague witness all these years later. But it was all Annie had to go on.

She checked the case file for the woman's address and plugged it into her phone's GPS, then set out in her car. The route took her away from the quaint downtown area and into the shadows of Crestville, filled with dark alleyways and run-down homes that had probably been abandoned after the auto manufacturing factory shutdown, leaving thousands of people unemployed.

Cardboard boxes lined one alley, along with shopping carts stuffed with bags of belongings, discarded blankets and a towering stack of trash overflowing the lone dumpster. Heartbreaking stories of loss and poverty filled that narrow street, scenes Annie knew well from her childhood. After this interview, she'd return with some sandwiches from the deli and some toiletries from the general store to hand out to the half dozen homeless people she saw tucked in the doorways and huddled around trash can fires.

Erline Talbot's house sat between two dilapidated homes with overgrown shrubs that hulked across the walkways, like shaggy green monsters. The tiny bungalow, with its sagging porch, raggedy chair and missing shutters, had an air of sadness about it, almost as if the little home had given up on standing proud.

Annie parked, grabbed her notepad and pen and headed up the weed-splintered walkway. The stairs let out an eerie, ominous creak as the wood bowed beneath her weight. There was no doorbell, so Annie rapped against the steel door as hard as she could. The door and its three locks appeared new, a retrofit for the cracked frame.

No response. "Ms. Talbot? If you don't mind, I'd like to talk to you about my friend Jenny. You saw her on the day she disappeared. I know it was years ago, but I could really use your help."

Nothing.

"I'm not with the cops. I just want to talk to you, Ms. Talbot."

The door was thick, making it almost impossible to tell if anything was happening on the other side. To her right, Annie saw a curtain flicker, a face appear for a second.

She knocked again. "Please, Ms. Talbot? You're the only witness I have right now. I need to know what happened to Jenny because…" Annie's voice cracked a little. "Because I'm afraid her mother is going to die before I find her."

Just as Annie was about to give up, she heard the click of a dead bolt being turned. Another. Then the metal-on-metal screech of a door swinging open. Standing on the other side, in the dim light of the house, was a scarecrow of a woman with frazzled grayish-brown hair. "I can't help you."

"Maybe, maybe not. But you're all I have to go on, and I'm hoping if we chat, maybe it will jog your memory."

Erline gave Annie a side-eye. She had to be at least seventy, and a good three inches shorter than Annie, who was just five-four. "Only for a minute. I have a busy day."

As she stepped inside the house and looked around, Annie wanted to ask with what, given the state of the house. Piles of dishes and newspapers topped nearly every available surface amid a thick coating of dust. A couple cobwebs hung from the corners of the living room, one reaching all the way to the threadbare faded sofa that had once been cranberry and was now more of a faint rose.

Judging Erline would do no one any good. Annie didn't know the other woman's circumstances or challenges, and she knew full well that if Erline took a peek inside Annie's constantly revolving mind, she'd find a cluttered mess of anxieties and doubts. "Thank you for whatever time you can give me," Annie said.

Erline gestured toward the cobwebby sofa. Annie perched

on the farthest corner, the only part of the couch that wasn't covered in newspapers and pillows—and didn't seem to have a spider on the cushions. Erline lowered herself into an old armchair with a faded floral fabric that had worn through so much on the armrests that the bare wood showed in several places, a situation Erline had fixed by wrapping the armrests with dishtowels and rubber bands. She put her feet up on a matching stool, sliding them into the narrow gap between a stack of *Reader's Digest* magazines and a can of soda.

Annie opened her folder and pulled out the article with Jenny's image. "If you don't mind, tell me exactly what you saw that day. If it helps, I have a picture of Jenny to help jog your memory."

Erline looked at the photograph for a long moment. "This was a long time ago, you know. My memory's not what it used to be."

"That's okay. Take all the time you need." Annie flipped to a fresh page of her notebook and clicked her pen. A minute passed. Another.

Erline sighed and pointed at the picture window behind the sofa. "It's not much, but that's my view, seven days a week. Some folks think I'm a busybody, but I can't help what they're doing right under my nose. I sit in this chair, and I watch my shows, and I watch what's going on out there. Some people are up to no good, you know."

"I'm sure the neighbors are glad you are so involved."

She waved that off. "Neighbors want everyone to mind their own business. If I did that, who would call the cops when there was something suspicious going on? Who would let them know when John Richards leaves his trash can in the middle of the road? Someone could get hurt if they hit that thing and—"

"Ms. Talbot, let's circle back to the day Jenny disappeared. When you called the police station, you said it was early evening."

She thought for a moment. "That's right, I think it was just going on dusk."

"And you saw what? Exactly?" Annie shifted a little closer. "I know you told the police all of this years ago, but maybe you've remembered more since then."

"I told the police exactly what I'm going to tell you now, and you know what they did? Nothing. No officer came to talk to me, no one called me back. They plain didn't care. She was just another piece of trash in the street to them."

Annie winced at the harsh words. "I agree they should have followed up more. That's why I'm here. To try to figure out what happened. Please tell me whatever you remember."

"I saw that girl walking down the road. She was so beautiful. Hair the color of sunshine. But I could just tell she wasn't from here. She stuck out like a thumb in a picture. That's why I noticed her right off."

"Do you remember what she was wearing?" Helen had told Annie what she'd seen Jenny wearing the day she left. If Jenny got trapped here in town for a couple days without any money, chances were good she'd been wearing the same thing that day.

"Jeans and..." Erline tapped on her chin as she thought a bit. "One of those shirts you kids get when you go see a musician. The kind that looks all worn out before you even put it on."

"A concert T-shirt? For maybe...the Grateful Dead?" Jenny's favorite band. She'd spent years collecting every vintage Dead shirt she could find at flea markets, garage sales and on eBay. Jenny's mom had said that her daughter had on her favorite Dead shirt that day, a faded rainbow-colored T-shirt from a 1978 concert that she'd found at the Denver Goodwill store.

"Maybe. I don't know music like you kids do. Anyway, she was walking down the street like she was lost. You know, looking all around and checking her phone every few feet."

"And then what happened?"

"This car comes cruising down the street, slow as molasses on a summer day. When I see a car like that, I know it means trouble. Drug deals and such, because that's all it seems like this neighborhood does anymore. Nothing but trouble, I tell you. I got my phone and kept it close, in case I had to call the police."

"Do you remember what this car looked like?"

"Something brown and fancy, because it had those shiny wheels and such. You know, like those whisky bottles idiots pay way too much money for." She shrugged. "I don't know cars much."

Annie nodded and wrote down *brown* and wondered how she could get more of a description from a woman who didn't know cars and had memory troubles. "Did the person in the car talk to Jenny?"

"He pulled up alongside her, and he rolled down his window. I couldn't see his face because he was leaning across the seat to talk to her. He said something, and she was shaking her head. Then he got out of the car and got real close to her face, but she kept backing up, like she didn't want to talk to him."

"Did it..." Annie almost couldn't push the question past her lips "...look like they were trying to kidnap her?"

"I didn't think so at first. She kept walking a bit, and they went past my window. My show was on, you know, and I had to wait for a commercial to go see what happened. When I got up to look again, I saw the girl way down the street and over by those shrubs there, so kinda out of sight a little right there, and she was being pushed in the car by some guy. Then he ske-daddled around to his side and took off."

That sure sounded like an abduction to Annie. Poor Jenny. How terrifying. Whoever had kidnapped her hadn't done it for a ransom, which told Annie there had to be a more sinister reason at hand. She shuddered to think of what that might be. Annie asked Erline for a description of the guy, but Erline didn't remember much more than the fact that he wore jeans and had brown hair. "How can you be sure he was pushing her?"

"Well, he could have been helping her in," Erline admitted. "I couldn't quite tell from here. They were all the way down at

the corner of Maple. I don't see that well when the sun starts
going down, so I don't really know what was happening."

Annie asked a few more questions, but it was clear she had
exhausted all the information Erline had, which was, as Brady
had said, not much and not worth a whole lot. A guy who may
or may not have pushed a girl who may or may not have been
wearing a concert T-shirt into a car that may or may not have
been brown.

Annie flipped her notebook closed and got to her feet, pulling out an old business card with her cell number on it. "Can I
give you my card? If you think of anything else?"

"I'll take your card, but, honey, at my age, I'm forgetting
more than I'm remembering." Erline stood up and walked
Annie to the door. Just as she turned the handle, she said, "I
do remember one thing. The guy, the one who was talking to
your friend? When he got out of the car, I noticed he was wearing black leather boots with shiny things on them. I remember
thinking that was odd at that time of year. Colorado can have
some cold mornings, but our summer afternoons are hot." Erline shrugged. "Or maybe they were tennis shoes. I'm not so
sure anymore. In fact, I'm not so sure about anything anymore."

That makes two of us, Annie thought as she headed out to
her car.

Chapter Six

Hunter sat on the bench outside Brady's office with his arms crossed and a scowl engraved on his face. Wilkins had brought him, another young man named Chip and Eddie Anderson into the station an hour ago that Sunday afternoon, picked up on suspicion of intention to distribute drugs.

Brady bit back the urge to punch Eddie for being anywhere near Hunter. That guy was bad news, in a hundred different ways.

Church this morning had been a nice reprieve from all of this, and when Brady had left the building, he'd felt like things were looking up. He'd seen Annie leaving and had stopped to say hello to her. He'd debated asking her to lunch, but the decision was made for him when Wilkins called him about Hunter.

Hunter, thank God, hadn't had any drugs on him, but just the fact that he'd been in close proximity with Eddie the Answerman—who seemed to be everywhere criminal in this town—and another young man who was carrying enough Oxy and meth in his pockets to start a pharmacy, didn't bode well. How did Hunter end up mixed in with Eddie and what was clearly one of his henchmen?

Brady had left Hunter outside his office while he started with the seventeen-year-old who had been standing beside Eddie. Brady had hoped that the kid would be quick to break and admit what was going on, but instead, the teenager, who looked terrified, had called for a lawyer and clammed up.

Frustrating but understandable. The kid didn't want to get in trouble or admit to anything that wasn't his fault. Chances were good that "the Answerman" Eddie was also the mastermind behind the activities on the corner of Hyde and Perkins, in the rougher part of Crestville. The intersection was just two blocks from where Brady had found the jewelry, and the same car that Eddie said someone had framed him with for the burglary. Brady didn't believe that any more than he believed that the Rockies were just big hills.

Brady walked over to Sanders's desk. She was in the middle of cataloging the drugs they'd found on Chip. He could see her typing up a report. Two evidence bags sat on her desk, one filled with round white pills and another filled with tiny packets of powder. The amount they'd found on Chip was significant enough to warrant a trafficking charge, but not enough to charge Eddie who was sticking to his story of just happening to be standing beside a suspected drug dealer or whoever had hired Chip. What Brady wanted to get was the kingpin of all of this, not some scared high schooler. "What have we got?"

"We have about twenty-five grams of Oxy, enough to put the kid away for seven years." She put down her pen and sighed. "This kid is only seventeen. It seems they get younger every year."

"Every year?" Brady's interest piqued at that. "Have you arrested kids with Anderson before?"

The chief deputy dropped her gaze back to her work. "We only have about fifteen grams of meth. Not enough to really charge him with trafficking on that one."

"You're not answering my question."

"Because it's the same answer in towns everywhere, Sheriff. Drugs are ruining small towns and lives across the world. Why should Crestville be any different?"

He had the distinct sense she was leaving something out of the conversation, a detail that would tie all these crimes together. Crimes that seemed attached to Eddie at every turn, who was then protected by the system and let off scot-free. That was not a coincidence in Brady's mind. He sat on the corner of her desk and leaned closer, lowering his voice. "Sanders, you're not telling me everything."

"There's a lot you don't know, Sheriff. Spend enough time in this town, and you'll figure out why."

That statement set off alarm bells in Brady's head. "I think I could do my job better if you told me more."

Sanders scoffed, then cleared her throat and glanced around the room before she spoke again. "I can't tell you more. There are some people in this town who can do what they want, sell whatever illegal things they want, set up whoever they want to take the fall—" she nodded toward the interview room where Chip was sweating bullets "—and nobody's going to do nothing about it."

"Because?"

A pained look filled her face, the kind that begged him not to press the issue. "Just keep spending your lunch hours at the Bluebird. You'll figure out how this town works real quick that way. And that, sir, is all I can—and will—say about that."

He could have written her up for insubordination but suspected coming down too hard on Sanders would only make her more closemouthed than she already was. He let the remark slide.

The implications were clear, though, and ones he had seen far too many times in his years in law enforcement. The kid, Chip, was working for someone—maybe Eddie, if he was reading what Sanders left unsaid correctly—and Eddie was working for someone above him, because there was always a head on top of a snake. That was who Brady wanted to nab. Cut the supply off at the source, and maybe they could clean up the rest of the mess in town. Maybe then the shops downtown wouldn't get robbed by desperate people looking to make money.

Brady opted to try another tack. "We have a lot of crime for such a small town. Just a few days ago, Eddie Anderson broke into that jewelry store—"

"Allegedly. He wasn't charged."

Brady scowled. "Just because he has a friend in judicial doesn't mean he didn't do it. Everywhere I turn, this Anderson guy is mixed up in something illegal. Seems to me, maybe he's in debt to someone higher up the food chain. Maybe that's why he needed to fence the jewelry."

The chief deputy's face paled. She stopped writing for a second. "That's a mighty big assumption."

"And judging by your reaction, probably close to the truth of what's happening with the drugs in this town." Brady leaned closer to her, studying the other deputy's face as he spoke. "Why is everyone in this department too scared to actually do their jobs?"

Sanders's brown eyes were wide. A muscle ticked in her jaw. She bit her lip and shook her head. "I don't know anything, Sheriff. Sorry."

Frustration boiled inside him. "What is going on here? Tell me, Sanders. I can't make it right if you don't tell me."

"I don't know anything, Sheriff. Sorry." Her gaze darted to the other desks, then back to Brady. Without looking down, she nudged the last of the tiny packets of meth in his direction. "I gotta process this evidence, but I'm going to leave it here a sec, if you don't mind, uh, watching over the evidence bags. This baby is pressing on my bladder like a sledgehammer. I'll be right back." She scooted out of her chair and hurried across the room.

Brady rose, putting his back to the squad room. He'd done so many individual meetings with the members of the department but the results were always the same. People were either afraid to talk or being intimidated into not talking.

What was going on in this town?

He picked up the packet of powder and flipped it over. A tiny silver sticker held the tab of the baggie in place. No logo, no writing, just a circle of silver.

A clue of some kind, but what kind, Brady had no idea. Nor did he know enough to fill in the blanks his chief deputy was leaving in the conversation. He put the packet back on her desk, and when she returned to finish her report, he said simply, "When you're ready to talk more, I'm ready to listen."

Whatever was happening in this town somehow all came back to Eddie, but how and why, and who was pulling the strings... That was what Brady was determined to figure out.

Brady headed for his office instead of Room 1. Letting Eddie stew some more in the interrogation room might make the other man frustrated and more ready to talk, or at least that was the play that Brady was going to use.

"Hunter, come in here please," Brady called.

With an irritated sigh, Hunter pushed off from the bench and stomped into Brady's office. He slumped in one of the visitor's chairs. "I told you and the other cop guy I didn't buy any drugs."

"I know, and for that, I'm grateful. But you can't hang around with people like that, Hunter. Why were you with them?"

"Chip is the only person who has been nice to me ever since you made me move to this stupid town." Hunter studied one of his nails, avoiding Brady's gaze. "I don't have any friends at all. You can't expect me to just go live like a hermit with my uncle every day. That is beyond lame."

"That's not—" Brady cut himself off. Arguing would do nothing but inflame an already tense situation. "Please don't hang out with Chip or his friends." If that was what Eddie was, although Brady doubted it. Seemed more like Chip's employer. "You'll end up—"

"Like my mother?" Hunter scoffed. "Of course you'd think I'd be just like her. You're such a cop."

Brady ignored the jab. "What I meant to say was that you could end up in trouble or getting caught up in some bad decisions that they make. It can happen so easily."

He knew that because he'd seen it in his own life. When Brady was fourteen, he'd caught his sister taking some pills that a friend had given her during a sleepover—the pills that started her downhill fall. Tammy had sworn up and down she'd never become an addict, and yet here they were, her in rehab, and her son uprooted from his life. Brady knew too well that even the best of intentions sometimes ended up failing. All he could do was be the safety net that Tammy and Hunter needed. And pray really hard neither of them needed it down the road.

"Did Chip or Eddie try to sell you drugs?"

Hunter shook his head. "Not Chip. That other guy. He just asked if I wanted to try something fun. He never said drugs."

All Hunter had to do was say yes, and Eddie would have sunk his criminal claws into him. Was his nephew in danger of going down the same path as Tammy? It would break Brady's heart—and destroy Tammy—if that ever happened. The last thing she wanted was for her son to repeat her mistakes, which was why she had entrusted him to Brady's care.

And so far, Brady was failing at that job. Big time.

"Can we go?" Hunter said. "I have homework."

Outside the glass door, Wilkins signaled to Brady. "In a minute. I have a little more work to do."

Hunter let out a long, dramatic sigh that Brady ignored.

"Stay in my office. You can start your homework here."

"But—"

"I'll be back. Wait here." Brady headed out to talk to Wilkins.

Wilkins nodded toward the door to Room 2, which was open, with Chip and a female in a suit standing inside, clearly about to leave. "That kid has a public defender. He swears he was just hanging out with Hunter, no drugs involved, so maybe your nephew is telling the truth."

That was a huge relief. Chip still had a potential trafficking charge against him, but maybe he had, as Hunter had said, just been talking to a friend from school. "Good. What about Anderson?"

"Getting antsy. Says he doesn't know Hunter or Chip and we're idiots for dragging him in here. He's talking about calling a lawyer but hasn't asked to use the phone." Wilkins shrugged. "I know that guy. He's a lot of bluster and bluff."

"That's what everyone seems to say, and yet every time I turn around, there's trouble, and there's Eddie the Answerman. I don't know why I seem to be the only one in this department that finds that fishy, Wilkins."

When the deputy didn't respond, Brady headed down the hall to Room 1. Through the small glass window, he could see Eddie Anderson, leaning back in the chair, one knee crossed over his opposite leg. He wore nonchalant boredom on his face, but the frantic tapping of his fingertips on the desk painted that as a lie.

A surge of anger rose in Brady's chest. This man, who had robbed a local shopkeeper, terrifying the poor man, potentially been involved with Jenny's disappearance and, now, tried to sell Hunter drugs, needed to be behind bars. What was it going to take to make that happen?

Wilkins came up behind him. "It's probably a waste of time to talk to him, boss. Eddie says he was just passing through and those kids harassed him."

"Including Chip, who very likely works for him?"

Wilkins shrugged. "Kid never said he did, Sheriff."

"Is this entire town blind? Of course he does. Why else would Chip be standing on a corner known for drug deals in broad daylight with Eddie just a few feet away?"

"Anderson might not be the best person in this town, but he's never been convicted of anything. Innocent until proven guilty. Every single time." But Wilkins wouldn't look at Brady as he said the words.

"What do I have to do? Actually catch Anderson on video robbing a jewelry store or selling drugs?" Brady gave Wilkins a hard look. No one in his department was being honest about "how this town worked," as Sanders had said. How it worked, Brady could already tell, seemed pretty corrupt. The other man shrank back, avoiding Brady's gaze.

Brady had been down this path before, heard every imaginable alibi there was for a drug dealer and had seen how easily one question could lead to decades of bad decisions. If Hunter had…

But he hadn't, thank God. And the only way Brady could ensure he was never tempted with drugs again was to rid this town of the problem in the first place. Granted, getting rid of the drug trade was like playing Whac-A-Mole, because as soon as he hit one problem, another sprouted in its place, but he had to start somewhere.

Wilkins handed him a folder labeled Anderson, Edward. "Like I said, he doesn't really have a rap sheet. Been picked up a few times for suspicious activities. He was found with drugs a couple times, but never enough. You know what I mean? It's always just a lot of questioning with Eddie, which doesn't make him guilty. And means there's not much reason to hold him any longer."

The more Wilkins insisted on Brady letting Eddie go, the more Brady wanted to find a way to keep him locked up. Either Eddie had a lot of friends high up in the county or he was the do-gooder the rest of the department painted him as being.

"Why is everyone protecting this guy?" Brady asked.

"Let's just say some guys are more valuable out of prison than in it," Wilkins said.

"Valuable to who?"

But Wilkins had already left.

Brady had no doubt the guy's rap sheet was nonexistent because no one in this town wanted to charge him with anything. What had Sanders meant about spending time at the Bluebird? The diner where the judge often dined had also been part of the missing girl case. How did a place that sold really great hamburgers figure into all of this?

Either way, there was something about Eddie, something Brady didn't like. And didn't want to see in his town—or anywhere near his nephew. Clearly, Sanders, Wilkins and Judge Harvey were protecting Anderson. But why? And who else was in on this scheme?

Brady grabbed a cup of coffee, just to make Eddie sweat it for a few more minutes, then headed into Room 1. The red light on the camera above the door meant the interview was being recorded. Good. Hopefully Anderson said something useful.

"So, Eddie, how are you today?"

Eddie popped forward in his seat, the move as fast as a snake in the grass. He steepled his fingers and leveled his gaze on Brady. "Let's skip the pleasantries, shall we? Waste of everyone's time. We all know you and I are never going to be friends."

"Why would you say that?" Brady kicked out the visitor's chair and sat. He paused to take a long sip of bitter, hours-old coffee. Maybe it hadn't been such a good idea to figure out where they coffeepot was, because this beverage couldn't even be classified as coffee. "I barely know you."

"And yet you're trying to pin stuff on me that ain't my fault. I didn't sell drugs to anybody. I don't even use drugs." Eddie crossed his arms behind his head, all casual and carefree. "We got nothing to talk about today."

"So you're saying you hang out with kids twenty years younger than you all the time?"

"What? There's a law against being friends with people in this town?"

"Not at all. We encourage healthy friendships. Makes the whole town nicer, don't you think?"

"I dunno. You tell me, Mr. Sunshine."

The little dig betrayed a moment of irritation on Eddie's part. Good. "How do you know Chip anyway?"

Eddie shrugged. "It's a small town. Everybody knows everybody. Doesn't mean I'm friends with them. Just acquaintances."

Brady flipped through Eddie's folder. A couple speeding tickets, one drunk and disorderly, two times he'd been caught with some drugs. There were a few scribbled notes about calling him in for questioning a few times, and a single sheet of paper recounting the jewelry store incident. But not much else.

Including Brady's own notes about finding the jewelry in Anderson's vehicle. How could those disappear? And why? He made a note to ask Carl. Maybe the papers had been misfiled. Or maybe something more was going on in this town.

"So, Eddie, do you owe somebody some money or something?"

The change of tack caught the other man off guard for a second, but Eddie recovered quickly. "You been looking at my bank account, Sheriff? Not going to lie, I do like to party from time to time, but my bills are paid."

"Then why are you robbing jewelry stores and making high schoolers sell drugs for you?"

Eddie's smile curved across his face, slow and sure. "I didn't rob no jewelry store. Even Judge Harvey said so. Someone framed me. And I wasn't selling drugs. That kid was. I just happened to be standing beside him."

"Either you have the worst luck in the world," Brady said, "or you are lying to my face, Eddie. Which is it?"

"You show me what you can prove, Sheriff, and I'll be glad to fill you in on the details." Eddie tipped back in the chair again, as relaxed as a man on vacation.

Brady probed a few different ways, but Eddie never even came close to losing his cool again. He had an answer for everything, and like Wilkins said, they couldn't hold him for being on the sidewalk at the wrong time with the wrong people.

The door behind him opened, and a skinny guy in an expensive suit strode into the room. "My client is done talking to you, Sheriff." He handed Brady a business card. "Raymond Harrison, Mr. Anderson's attorney."

"He hasn't been charged with anything. No need for a lawyer." Especially one who clearly charged several hundred dollars an hour, Brady thought. Eddie hadn't asked for a lawyer and didn't look like the kind of guy who could afford that kind of legal help. So who had called this one in and was paying the bill?

"There is a need for lawyers in a town that seems determined to harass my client," Harrison said. "Come on, Eddie, we're leaving."

Brady had no choice but to let him go. He watched Eddie get to his feet, a self-satisfied smirk on his face.

"Nice to chat with you, Sheriff," Eddie said. "Oh, and great to meet your nephew. Hope I see that boy around again. Seems like a decent kid."

Rage flooded Brady's vision. He curled his hands into tight fists and did his best to keep his emotion under control. "My nephew is none of your business, Anderson."

Raymond put a hand on Eddie's elbow. "Come on. Let's go."

"Nah, but he is one of my new friends, and I do like having friends with people in high places. Like you, Mr. Lawman." Eddie grinned, an evil sneer that darkened his entire face. "See you around, Sheriff." Then he walked out of the room, his heels smacking against the tile floor like hammers driving his menacing point home.

A half hour later, Brady finished up his paperwork, clocked out early and drove Hunter home. They turned off the main street where the sheriff's office was located and down the back roads that led to the outskirts of town where Brady's rental cabin was located. At the same time, a black SUV turned onto the same road.

Brady made a mental note of it but kept driving. He was

more interested in trying to get Hunter to talk to him, but every conversational tack he tried, Hunter either ignored or gave a one-word answer. Brady flicked on his directional to turn down his street, and just as he did, the black SUV roared up behind him. Brady floored the pedal, turning onto the street at the last second. The SUV braked hard, then the driver yanked it into Reverse and took off.

Jerk driver. Some people just shouldn't get a driver's license, he thought. He considered going after the car to get his plate and write him a ticket, but they were already home, and delaying the return to video game paradise would only make Hunter more irritable. Not to mention, taking his nephew on a potential car chase was an exceedingly bad idea. Brady let it go but remained a little shaken by how close that car had come to hitting them.

As soon as they walked in the door, Hunter stomped off to his room and slammed the door. Brady sighed as he pulled up the pizza app and placed another order for junk food. Days like this, he missed his mother's home cooking. Maybe if he'd settled down and gotten married when he was younger, he'd have a wife beside him right now, someone to commiserate with about how hard it was to raise a teenager and someone to kid him gently when he burned the steaks.

But he didn't, and that wasn't a situation he could change right now, so thinking about it was a waste of time. That was how he lived his life—tabling anything that remotely resembled an emotion for some unnamed time in the future. Like after he retired.

A text message appeared on the screen, overriding his pizza order before he could press the last button. He was about to swipe away when he saw a name that made him pause. *Annie.*

Brady, it's Annie. Sorry for bothering you—

He wanted to tell her she was never a bother. That she'd lingered in his mind all day.

Just wanted to let you know that I went to Erline Talbot's house today and have some information I'd like to share with you.

He should tell her to conduct her own investigation. That he had far too much going on at the sheriff's office already to get wrapped up in a case that wasn't even his, a case that had gone cold a long time ago, and that he had more than enough to deal with in his personal life right now, too. He glanced at the closed door to Hunter's bedroom, thought of another lonely night in front of the television while his nephew played video games in another room and texted back, How do you feel about pizza?

I think it's an underrated and necessary food group. But only if there's pepperoni on it.

He chuckled. I wouldn't have it any other way. He started to type *already home with my nephew*, but stopped himself. The whole situation with his sister and the temporary custody, and the why behind all that, was too complicated to explain in a text.

I just ordered an extra-large pizza. I'm stuck at home for the night so if you'd like to come to my house, we can talk about the case.

He decided against adding, *just as friends, not as a date*, because that would sound like overexplaining and trying too hard. Because this was a just friends meeting. Nothing more.

Just as friends, I assume? she replied, as if she'd read his mind.

Of course. He dropped his address into the chat, then went

back to the pizza app and added the double-fudge brownie dessert. Even if she was coming as just a friend, it didn't hurt to make everyone happier with a little sugar.

Chapter Seven

Three times she glanced in her rearview mirror, and three times she saw the exact same car behind her. Maybe she was just being overly suspicious after her talk with Erline, but seeing a dark SUV following her as she wound her way through Crestville and toward the address Brady had given her didn't exactly make Annie feel safe.

There were millions of dark SUVs in the world, surely hundreds in this little town. People ended up behind other people for miles all the time. There was nothing to worry about here. But as she made the final turn down Brady's driveway, she saw the SUV slow to a roll. It lingered at the top of the drive for a few seconds, then zoomed away. Most of the license plate was smudged with mud. By accident? Or on purpose?

Annie took a couple deep breaths to calm her racing heart, then gathered her tote bag and headed up the stone steps to Brady's front door. Before she could hesitate or question the wisdom of spending time alone with the handsome sheriff, she rang the bell.

The door opened, and a lanky teenage boy stood on the other side, leaving Annie speechless for a second.

"Uh…am I in the wrong place? Is the sheriff here?"

"I thought you were the pizza." He frowned. "Uncle Brady, some lady is here." Then he turned and walked away, leaving Annie standing there, unsure of whether she should go inside and shut the door against the chill in the air or wait for Brady to appear.

A second car swung down the driveway, its headlights flashing across the stoop and into the house.

Hunter spun and dashed out the door, a cheetah running past her. Annie leaned back, out of his way. "Pizza's here!" he called over his shoulder as he trundled down the stairs.

Brady appeared at the door with a towel in his hands. "Sorry. Spilled something in the kitchen and didn't hear the door. I see you've met my nephew, who is always grumpy unless there's food around."

"I can relate to that." She grinned and followed him as he beckoned her inside.

Hunter followed a second later with a stack of boxes that he dropped onto the kitchen table.

"We have a guest, Hunt, so let's not tear into the pizza like a couple of wolves."

"So don't act normal?"

Brady rolled his eyes and ruffled Hunter's hair. The young man ducked away and grabbed a plate from the cabinet. A flicker of hurt ran across Brady's features, and a veil of irritation dropped over Hunter's face. A thousand little moments happened in those couple of seconds, hinting at a history that Annie had no business asking about.

Hunter loaded his plate and then gave Annie a nod. "Catch you later."

"Uh. Yeah, uh, catch—"

But he was already gone, down the hall and into what she assumed was his room. The door shut with a heavy thud.

"Sorry about that. He's not the most friendly kid."

"None of us are at that age." She put her tote onto one of the bar stools. Now that it was just the two of them, the tiny kitchen seemed even smaller. Her mind attuned to every detail about Brady—the five-o'clock shadow on his chin, the rumple in his gray T-shirt, the dark scent of his cologne. It had been a long time since she'd dated anyone, and for some reason, this moment had her more distracted than she'd expected.

"Hey, uh, we should have some pizza." Brady thrust a plate at her.

He seemed as nervous and discomfited as she felt, which was impossible, because Annie Linscott had never been the type of woman who made men trip over their words or stumble into a streetlight. They didn't get distracted by her or stunned by her beauty. She was an ordinary woman from an ordinary small town who had never quite mastered the art of mascara or dressing for her body type. She had limited dating experience, absolutely no flirting abilities and got tongue-tied in the most ordinary of moments.

In other words, not the kind of woman who would make a man like Brady Johnson anything other than bored.

She chose two slices of pizza and put them on her plate. "Do you have any salt?"

"A fellow carb salter." He grinned. "Already on the table, because I, too, salt my pizza crust."

She smiled back, oddly touched they shared a habit. Not that it meant anything, of course. But they did seem to have a few of the same favorite foods and favorite music, which was nice. For building rapport, nothing more. She was only here for Jenny.

But as Brady sat down across from her and their small talk rolled like a river into music and films, she began to sense that something more was dancing under the surface between them. Something she couldn't yet quantify, and maybe, didn't want to.

"So, the case." Brady got to his feet, reloaded his plate and offered Annie a couple more slices. "What did you want to tell me?"

She nodded her thanks as he put them on her plate and tried not to feel a tiny bit disappointed that the casual, friendly conversation time was over. "Um, well, let's see." It took her a second to get her head wrapped around the shift in topic. "I went to see Erline Talbot, and she gave me a few more details than what was in her witness statement."

"I've met Erline myself. She called the office again yesterday, complaining about one of the neighbors. Apparently he was sitting in his car in his driveway a little too long, and she found that suspicious. From what I hear, Erline calls in a tip at least once a week."

Annie could hear the doubts in Brady's voice. He was already dismissing Erline's eyewitness account without even hearing what she had to say. "Just because Erline calls the sheriff's office a lot doesn't mean that she can't be trusted with her memory of what happened to Jenny."

"Fair point."

A flush filled her cheeks, and she glanced away. "Sorry. I just got riled up about that because this case matters so much to me."

"Hey." Brady waited for her to look at him. "Never apologize for standing up for what's right. I was wrong for discounting Erline just because she's a bit of a busybody. What did she tell you?"

Annie gaped at Brady for a second. Had he just apologized and encouraged her to be strong? How many of the people in her world, besides Jenny, had ever done that? All her life, she'd been told to sit still, be quiet, not to poke her nose where it doesn't belong. To have someone in authority listen to her and validate her points emboldened Annie a little more. "She saw a fancy brown car, and she saw the man briefly." Annie recounted what Erline had told her.

"That's not much to go on," Brady said.

"I know it's not, which is frustrating, but it's at least a beginning."

He chuckled. "Are you always this optimistic about a cold case?"

"I try to be optimistic in general. Life's too short to be looking at your days through a gloomy lens."

"Wise advice and something I need to remember from time to time." His gaze went to the closed bedroom door in the hallway. The *rat-a-tat* and *ka-pow* sounds of a video game came from the other side. Every once in a while, Hunter said something to the game or whomever he was playing.

"So, how come your nephew lives with you?" As soon as she asked the question, she realized she'd gone too far. She had no business asking this man about his personal life. "Sorry. That's the reporter in me. I didn't mean to treat you like a source."

"It's fine. Really. I should talk about him. Talk about anything, really. If my mother was still here, she would have told you that I'm as buttoned up as a coat in January."

Annie laughed. "That sounds like something my grandma would say. She was Southern and had a simile for every occasion."

"I have no idea what that means, but I can say that you seem to have a smile for every occasion." He cleared his throat. "Uh, sorry. Don't know where that came from."

Something that bordered on joy danced inside her. When was the last time a man had said something so sweet to her? "It's…it's fine. And if I'm blushing, it's because I'm usually the 'Oh, Annie' girl.'"

"What is an 'Oh, Annie' girl?"

"The one that no one notices." She glanced down as she went on. "'Oh, Annie, I didn't see you there' or 'Oh, Annie, where have you been hiding?' That girl."

"I don't know how anyone could miss you when you're in the room." He got to his feet and crossed to reach for another slice of pizza, but the box was empty. All the movement and avoidance seemed as if he was feeling shy or nervous, both of which surprised Annie. "I think the pizza has me in some kind of food coma where I say completely the wrong thing over and over again."

"Maybe we should order a second one." Who was this flirty version of herself? Brady just seemed to bring out a layer of

Annie's personality she didn't even know existed. Distracting her, knocking her off course.

What matters more? Jenny's words came back to her and reminded Annie she had a ticking timeline here. Helen deserved answers before she died, and Annie couldn't waste a second on flirting with the handsome sheriff while Jenny was still missing.

"I, uh, really should get going." She put her plate in the sink and grabbed her tote bag. "I have to record a vlog for tomorrow." She'd told him all she knew from her Erline interview, so there was no reason to linger.

"Absolutely. Let me walk you to the door."

Her feet moved slower, in shorter steps, her whole body rebelling against the idea of leaving. At the door, she turned back to him, catching a whiff of his cologne, a closer look at the stubble dusting his chin. Brady seemed…comfortable in that moment, like someone to come home to. Annie shook her head and searched for the tidbit she'd meant to say. "This is probably nothing, but it seems like I was followed when I came over here and when I went to Erline's. I mean, it's silly. This is a small town, so you're bound to run into the same people multiple times in a day."

"True. But still, maybe I should get some details from you. Hang on a sec." He crossed back into the kitchen and grabbed a notepad and pen. "Did you get a license plate? Make and model?"

"Black Explorer, I think. It's hard to see in the dark. And I only saw a portion of the plate when I turned in here. It was a Colorado plate, starting with—I think—an AZ or A2. I'm not sure. There was a lot of mud on it. I'm sorry, I'm probably not much help."

Brady's face had paled. "How sure are you about the type of car?"

"Kinda?" she said. "I mean, it was dark, and I was probably making a big deal out of nothing."

"I don't think you are, Annie. Not at all." He grabbed his coat from the hook by the door and his keys from the dish. She heard him call out to Hunter that he'd be back in a little while.

"What are you doing?"

"Making sure you get home okay. I'll follow you." He opened the door and followed her down the stairs. "Too many weird things are going on in this town, so I'd rather err on the side of caution."

She didn't ask him what he meant, because she had a feeling he wouldn't tell her. But as she headed back to her motel room, she thanked God for Brady's thoughtfulness, because whatever was going on in Crestville was starting to make Annie nervous, too.

Dragging a teenager out the door a half hour early to go to school, Brady realized, was akin to trying to drag a tractor trailer down the road with a spool of thread. "Hunter, come on, let's go!"

From the bathroom there was a grunt, which Brady took as proof of life—and hearing his words. He gave it a couple more minutes, then wrapped up the pancakes he'd made in a napkin and pounded on the bathroom door. "Time's up. Let's go."

Hunter yanked open the door. "Why am I going to school early? Isn't it enough that I have to go at all?"

"Because I have to meet someone." He thrust the napkin into Hunter's hands, then started walking through the house, grabbing car keys, a water bottle and Hunter's backpack as he did. His nephew ambled out of the house, slow as molasses.

"Someone?" Hunter said once they were in the car. "Like that Annie last night?"

"Yeah, but not because of what you think. I hear the tone in your voice. We're not dating, in case you think that's what this is. We're working on a cold case together, nothing more."

"Uncle Brady, it would be totally cool if you started dating, you know. I mean, this is your life, too. I may not want to be here…" He sighed as he looked out the window at the mountains passing by them, such a different sight from the skyscrapers and concrete of Chicago. "But I am sorta grateful you, uh…" His voice trailed off into a mumble.

Brady cupped a hand around his ear. "What's that? Did I just hear you thank me?"

Hunter scowled and sat back in the seat, arms crossed over his chest. "No. Definitely not."

Brady grinned. He gave Hunter's knee a shake. "I'm glad you're living with me, too, kid, even if you hate me for bringing you to school early."

Silence filled the car for the next couple of miles as the highway curved around the Rocky Mountains and the sun climbed the highest peaks, glinting off the snowcapped ridges.

"Do you think she'll make it?"

Hunter's quiet question was the same one that kept Brady awake at night, and he knew instantly who Hunter was referring to—his mother. "I don't know, Hunt. But I do know your mom is one of the toughest people I've ever met. She loves you and wants to be with you, so I'm sure she's doing everything in her power to make that happen."

"I hope so," he said quietly.

Brady was about to reply when he noticed a car appear in his rearview mirror. A black SUV, trailing him, one car back, the same one that had nearly hit him yesterday and, he was sure, the same one that had followed Annie. As Brady shifted lanes, the SUV did the same. When Brady flicked on his blinker to take the exit toward Hunter's school, the SUV followed suit. Brady slowed and pulled into the breakdown lane, then turned to see if he could get the SUV's plates, but the other car had already darted into the passing lane and taken off.

"Hey, Uncle Brady, school's up that way."

"Yeah, yeah. Sorry." Brady started driving again, wondering if he was being paranoid about the SUV or if he had good reason to worry. It was, after all, a small town, and seeing the same car multiple times was not unusual.

Hunter was already unbuckling his seat belt as Brady pulled in front of the school. Brady put a hand on his shoulder. "Come to the station after school, okay? No hanging out anywhere."

"What? Are you kidding me? Why would I want to hang around a bunch of cops?"

Brady almost corrected him and said *deputies*, then figured that would only add fuel to the fire. "It's just for a few days. I, uh…" He tried to think of a plausible reason for his concern and realized lying wasn't going to gain Hunter's trust. "I'm worried about you, kid, and I'd just like to spend more time with you."

Hunter let out an exasperated grunt and climbed out of the car. "Whatever. Fine." He slammed the door and stormed into the school, the moment of détente short-lived and as elusive as smoke.

Chapter Eight

The text from Brady had been waiting on her phone as soon as Annie woke up. At some ridiculously early hour of the morning, he had sent her a message that said simply: I'll pick you up today. Wait for me.

Underneath that handful of words was a subtext that said he believed her about being followed and he was worried about her. She didn't know whether to be flattered he cared or insulted he thought she couldn't take care of herself—or relieved that she had a tall, strong sheriff backing her up.

Either way, if it brought her closer to finding Jenny and bringing closure to Helen before she died, then it would all be worth it. She'd called Helen last night and given her an update on what Erline had said. She left out the conversation with Dylan, because it hadn't added much to the investigation and Annie didn't want to saddle Helen with her own suspicions about the ex-not-really-a-boyfriend. There wasn't much more information, but it was enough to raise Helen's hopes and bring some positivity into her voice. There was no way Annie could let her down.

Even though she had only the barest fragment of a clue to go on after her conversation with Erline, that tiny detail was enough to fill the air with possibilities for Annie, too. Maybe today she'd be one step closer to—finally—finding Jenny.

She waited on the office stoop for the white, green and gold Tahoe Brady drove to pull up to the motel. A couple of people at the motel gave her a curious look, as if he was here to arrest her. The idea was laughable. Annie had never been in trouble for so much as a late library book in her life. A rule-breaker she was not.

He parked, leaned across the seat and opened the door for her. "I was going to do the gentlemanly thing but figured people are already wondering what you're doing with the sheriff. Maybe not a good idea to give the gossips more to whisper about."

"Smart thinking." The idea of Brady being a gentleman, picking her up as if they were on a date made her wonder what dating him would be like. Definitely not a good train of thought.

"I still don't know for sure if anyone is following you," Brady said, "but I'd rather be safe than sorry. If you're game for a stop on the way to the station, there's someone I wanted to talk to, and he said he's only around right now. We can ride together from here."

"Is this someone who is connected to what happened to Jenny?"

He glanced over at her. "I know how much you want to find your friend, Annie, but not everything that happens in this town is part of her disappearance. Yesterday, someone tried to sell drugs to my nephew. Everybody lawyered up, including Eddie. He and the alleged dealer both used the same lawyer, a guy who's usually a corporate lawyer."

"Isn't that unusual?" she asked. "Wouldn't they want a specialist in this type of crime?"

"You would think. But maybe this was just the first lawyer in Eddie's contact list." She could tell the information bothered Brady, nagged at some instinct deep inside him. "Either way, whatever is going on here very likely has a connection to something bigger, maybe a major drug-dealing ring. I just need more information."

"What? Wow. Even in a small town like this?"

"That kind of thing happens everywhere. Even in a place as beautiful as this." His voice took on a faraway sound, as if he was thinking of something beyond the limits of this town, beyond, even, the limits of the mountains.

But it wasn't Annie's place to ask, so she didn't, even though the back of her mind wondered about this layered, caring, gentleman sheriff. "You're probably right. Jenny wasn't doing drugs, so I don't think what happened to her had anything to do with drugs anyway."

"People you love can do a lot of things that you don't know about, Annie. Just because you didn't see her do drugs doesn't mean she didn't use them."

She bristled. "I think I know Jenny better than you do. And when I tell you she would never do drugs, I mean it. We had a close friend who'd overdosed at the beginning of senior year. It was the most traumatic thing we had ever been through. We both vowed that day to never, ever do drugs."

"And yet, she ran away from home."

"No, she had a fight with her stepdad and got stuck here when her car broke down. There's a big difference."

He drove for a while, his fingers tapping against the leather steering wheel. "Did she date anyone other than Dylan? Tell you or her other friends about other guys in her life?"

Annie shook her head. "I asked everyone I knew. No one ever heard her mention anyone other than Dylan. Plus, the app was on her phone, so there was no way to go back and figure out who it was. Her phone disappeared with her."

"I did call her cell provider," Brady said. "They told me they don't keep text messages or data for phones that old on their servers."

Annie sighed. "Another dead end."

"Maybe. Sometimes it helps just to retell the story. I know

you've probably done this dozens of times, but tell me as much as you remember about this part of Jenny's life."

Annie sat back against the leather seat and allowed her mind to reach into memory, to spiral past the years of working, of college, of graduation, of all those moments that Jenny had missed. All those holes in her life without her best friend beside her. "She disappeared on a Sunday. Like Dylan said, they'd met online, talked some, and I guess she thought it meant more than it really did. She was totally infatuated with him and said he was 'special' and she couldn't wait to meet him. I was working at the ice cream shop that night, so I only got a few minutes to talk to her during my shift. She came in and ordered a double caramel crunch... Sorry. I got distracted by the details."

"The details are what we need. Keep talking. Maybe something will come up."

In her mind's eye, Annie could see Jenny's bright blond hair and her contagious smile, hear the excitement in her voice about this new guy. Jenny had dated a couple of other guys in their class briefly, but none of them had worked out, and none of them had treated her well, not until Dylan. "She said he was so sweet to her. Telling her she was beautiful and smart and his dream girl."

"Those kinds of lines still work?" Brady shot her a grin.

"I think every woman wants to hear nice things." Which made her wonder if Brady would say something like that to her. Someday. "She did say he drove a really cool car. I should have asked Dylan about that when we saw him. Erline mentioned seeing a fancy brown car when Jenny disappeared. Do you think it's the same car?"

"Maybe. We can always interview Dylan again and press him on his alibi. What kind of car did Jenny mention?"

"I don't know, but I remember the color, she said..." Annie sat up straighter "...it was something that was like an alcohol."

"Color like an alcohol?" Brady thought for a second. "Wine? Merlot? Chardonnay?"

"No, something like a bourbon or whiskey or something. I don't drink, so I don't really know."

"Cognac?"

"Yes! That's it. Cognac. That color is like a..." Something dark and heavy sank to the bottom of Annie's stomach. "Is like a brown."

"What did you remember?"

"Do you think Dylan was the one who was actually behind her disappearance?"

"I'm not sure Dylan's car would fit that theory. But Dylan did seem a bit off when we interviewed him, so I'm not ruling him out." Brady swung the SUV into a parking lot, stopped and pulled out his notepad. He flipped back a few pages. "I ran his license and registration when we were looking for him, and when Jenny disappeared, Dylan owned a 2009 brown Porsche, which if my car geekiness remembers right, was called cognac back then. I don't know if anyone would confuse a Porsche with a regular sedan, no matter how nice that car was. Even if you don't know car models, the Porsche is pretty sporty looking and distinctive."

She sighed. "Another dead end."

Brady tucked his notepad away. "Maybe. That's a pretty expensive car for a guy that young to own. Especially one who said he was working in a grocery store at the time. Where did he get that kind of money?"

"I don't know. Jenny never mentioned anything about it."

"Another loose end then. We also still don't know if Dylan was the only man in Jenny's life. I know you think he was, but it's possible she was talking to someone else, too."

"True. And the guy we met doesn't fit what I imagined back when Jenny told me about him." Annie closed her eyes, searching for the exact words her friend had used that night, the snippet of a sentence Annie had caught above the sound of the mixers and other people at the ice cream shop. "He told her he made really good money, and he wanted to treat her to an amazing night on the town."

"Then maybe we need to take another look at Dylan. Or get more details from Erline about this car she saw. Either way, we have a starting point." Brady held up a hand for a high five. Annie slapped his palm with her own. "To teamwork."

Annie scribbled some notes on her pad as Brady drove through town. This detail made for great content for the vlog. If Jenny had met another man, or even if she had gone around town in Dylan's cognac Porsche, that was the kind of car that someone would remember. Someone who might know what happened to her.

Even as she wrote it down, her mind kept circling back to what Brady had said about Erline's neighborhood and what Erline herself had said about the kind of people she saw outside her window. Could Dylan have been a lot more trouble than anyone knew?

"There's a lot of money in drugs, isn't there?" she said.

"More than you can imagine, which is why it's such a hard crime to stop. The drug trade preys on people's desperation."

"Enough to pay for a Porsche for a guy in his twenties."

Brady nodded, connecting the dots with her train of thought. "Indeed."

"I talked to that busboy, the one who saw Jenny talking to someone at the Bluebird? He wouldn't tell me anything. Just kept saying I needed to talk to the 'real boss' of the diner, which might be the manager, but I can't seem to pin him down, no matter how many times I call or stop by."

"Unless he means Kingston Hughes, who owns the diner itself. And a lot of other stuff in town. And before you go down that road, I looked into Kingston myself the other day. No criminal record, no ties to anything criminal."

"That's just what it says on paper. I'm a hundred percent convinced it's all connected somehow."

"It usually is," Brady said. "But for now, let's leave the

Kingston Hughes thread out of it. Owning a diner doesn't make him involved."

Annie thought a little more, trying to assemble the myriad of pieces she had into some kind of sensible narrative. None of it fit together neatly. "This guy we're going to talk to, how is he connected to the drug deals in Crestville?"

Brady turned down a street that Annie recognized as one of the side streets close to Erline's house. "He's the one who snitched on Eddie Anderson with the jewelry store robbery. He's not a dealer but a user, and he knows a lot of the players around here simply because of that."

"Eddie Anderson? The guy who was named as a suspect in Jenny's disappearance? Is it the same guy?"

"I think so. It's a common name, but not so common there would be two Eddie Andersons who have a criminal tendency living in this town."

"Then maybe what happened with your nephew is connected to what happened to Jenny."

"That's a pretty big reach, Annie. Jenny disappeared ten years ago."

"If a crime is profitable, it never goes out of business."

"Good point. Maybe Jenny saw something she shouldn't have, and maybe Mr. Fancy Car wasn't the dream guy she thought he was." He glanced over at her as he slowed down. "Maybe. But not definitely. This is my guy to question for a crime that's happening right now. A couple hours ago, I thought it would be a good idea to have you at the interview, just in case all this is connected somehow. But now... I'm rethinking that. So maybe I should drop you at the diner first—"

"No. Please don't. If these two things are in any way connected to Jenny, I have to know."

"You'll have to know later. You can wait in the car, but you're not interviewing my witness. Are we clear?"

She nodded. Even as she prayed that God would get her and Brady the right information somehow. Annie knew God could nudge people—like the sheriff—in the direction of the truth. Maybe He had a plan to help them find out what happened to Jenny, only if they were smart enough to read the signs He was setting before them.

Brady stopped in front of one of two matching and faded duplexes covered with peeling green paint. Two shutters hung askew on the first one, like the downturn of a frown. The lawn had yielded to knee-high weeds that all but hid the front steps.

A scrawny guy in a flannel shirt and torn jeans got to his feet and trundled down the wooden steps. The piercings on his face reflected the sunlight, a stark contrast to the dirty, grungy mop of hair on his head. When he got closer, she could see the pockmarks in his face, the glassiness in his eyes, and she sent out a silent prayer that this troubled man could find the help he needed.

The sheriff got out of the SUV. The younger man's gaze darted down the street, then back at Brady. He nodded toward the side of the house, and the two of them traipsed through the weeds and into the shadows of the narrow space between the two duplexes.

Annie sat in the truck, a nervous ball of energy. She had a bad feeling about this meeting and not just because the man looked like he was on drugs. Surely Brady wouldn't mind if she just listened in on their conversation? Maybe she'd hear a clue that he missed. She got out of the SUV and sneaked down to the space between the duplexes, hiding behind a bush close enough to hear the two men talk.

"Man, let's hurry this up," the scrawny guy said. "I don't like you coming here during the day. They're watching, Sheriff. They're always watching."

Those words sent a chill down Annie's spine. She glanced over her shoulder, half expecting to see that black SUV sitting there, idling, just waiting. But the street was silent, not a soul in sight, not even a bird chirping or a breeze rattling leaves in the gutters.

"Nobody's here now, Frank," Brady said. "I only need to ask you a couple questions."

Frank's gaze darted to the street again. He scooted deeper into the shadows of the house, to where a shrub blocked half of the view, and waved Brady forward with trembling, hurried gestures. Annie had to lean toward them and strain to overhear. "I don't owe you nuthin'. We're square after the other thing."

"We are, but maybe you might want to put a favor in the bank, should you decide to take me up on my offer to go to rehab. I know a place a couple hours from here that would take you in. I called them this morning, Frank, and there's a bed if you want it."

Frank scoffed. "Nobody wants to take me anywhere, and nobody cares if I get clean." He fidgeted, picking at the skin on his arm while he shifted from foot to foot. "But…maybe. Maybe one day."

"That day can be today, Frank. Just say the word."

He shrugged, a gesture that was almost a nervous tic. "What do you want to ask me about?"

"Who do you know that drives a black SUV around here? And why would they follow me?"

The question startled Annie. They were following Brady, too? Why?

When Frank didn't answer, Brady pressed him. "You know something. I can see it in your eyes."

"I know a lot of somethin's," Frank said. "But not things I should tell you. They'll come after me, Brady."

"Tell me this, then. Who marks their drugs with this?" Brady held up his phone with what Annie presumed was a picture.

It seemed like the question sent a river of pure terror through Frank's entire body. He stiffened, his eyes wide, his breaths coming fast and hard. "Your car's been out front way too long. They're gonna come knocking. I gotta go, Sheriff."

"Wait." Brady grabbed his arm. "Who is it, Frank?"

"You're new in town, so I'm gonna tell you what my brother

told me, just before he was killed. To these people, we're just ants inside one of those plastic things with the sand. If a few ants die, they make the other ants carry out the bodies, and they just go buy new ants. I don't want to be one of the dead ants, Sheriff. I may be killing myself a little at a time, but I don't want them to be the ones pulling the trigger. So quit asking me these questions." Frank yanked his arm out of Brady's grasp. "I been talking to you too long."

"That offer still stands, Frank. You could go to rehab, get out of this place and away from whoever's bothering you, get clean, start over."

Frank didn't say anything for a long time. He stood in the shade and shivered, a kind of shiver that ran the entire length of his body and came from something other than the temperature. "I miss my life, Sheriff. Miss my kid."

"Then go. I can take you right now."

Frank looked around. "I need to do a few things first. Maybe this afternoon."

"Okay. But I'm going to hold you to this afternoon. I'll pick you up later and take you there myself. Like I said, there's a bed waiting for you. It's covered by state insurance, so you can go and get help for free. You deserve to have your life back, Frank. To see your kid."

Frank swayed side to side, considering. Wild hope danced in his eyes, then yielded to sad resignation, before sparking with another flicker of optimism. "You swear you'll be here?"

"I will. I promise. I'll pick you up at two. It's a couple-hour drive each way, and I'll stay with you until you get checked in. My sister's there, and has thirty days clean so far. This place is good, Frank. It's exactly what you need."

She'd learned so much about Brady in the space of a few minutes. Her heart softened toward this man who was clearly committed to always doing the right thing.

Frank nodded finally. "Two o'clock, Sheriff. And once I get out of that rehab place, I ain't ever coming back here. I can't.

They'll get me if I do." Frank let out a long, sad sigh. "Like I said, I know a lot of somethin's." Then he darted behind the house and disappeared. A second later, Annie heard the slap of a screen door shutting.

As soon as she turned to run back to the SUV, she saw Brady standing two feet away with a glare on his face. "I thought I told you to stay in the truck."

"And I thought I was the only one being followed by those guys. Seems we both have something at stake in this investigation, Sheriff." She parked a fist on her hip and raised her chin, filled with a sudden wave of defiance. "I think it's best if we keep on working together, so that both of us can find some closure."

"One of us needs to find some safety first." He thumbed toward his vehicle. "We'll talk about the rest later."

There was no sign of the black SUV all morning, and as much as Brady would have felt better keeping Annie close, which was why he'd offered to have her go with him in the first place, she insisted on going back to the motel to work on her vlog episode. She'd be safe there, he told himself, behind the locked door and with a manager on duty just a couple doors away. Brady had a stack of calls to return and reports to go over anyway, so he headed into the office and tried to forget about Frank's warning or his own growing misgivings about the entire situation.

Although he'd gotten involved in Annie's search for Jenny out of compassion for the missing friend's dying mother, he now was convinced even more that the cold case was tied to deeper problems in Crestville.

There was an undercurrent in this town, a darkness that seemed to infiltrate every corner. Brady wasn't naive enough to think there was no corruption in a small town, but it seemed particularly insidious in Crestville. Someone was hiding something—or a lot of somethin's, as Frank had said—and it was up to Brady to figure out what those were. He didn't know his deputies well enough to know who he could trust and who might be involved, so for now, he decided to keep his suspicions close to his chest and nose around on his own.

He ran a DMV report on black SUVs in the area. A couple dozen came back, all registered to people who seemed like regular folks who clocked in and out and mowed their lawns on Saturdays. He expanded his search to include neighboring towns, which added a couple hundred black SUVs to the list. The data took hours to sift through, this search to find a needle in an automobile haystack.

Then, three pages into the list, he hit gold. A black SUV, reported stolen a week ago. He hadn't been close enough to the car following him to know for sure what make and model it was, but the description of this one—a Ford Explorer with tinted windows and the tow package—seemed to match the beefy car he'd seen on the road this morning and the one that Annie had described.

So who was following them? And why?

He opened up the police report about the theft just as his office door opened and Wilkins popped his head inside. "Sheriff, we got something you might want to see."

Brady glanced at his watch. Almost two o'clock. He needed to go pick up Frank. Thank God the other man had decided to go to rehab. Brady was determined to keep his word. "What is it, Wilkins?"

In a couple hours, Frank could be at the same place as Tammy and be one step closer to reclaiming his life. Brady knew the relapse rates and knew that only a strong faith would keep Frank from falling back into his old habits, but it made him feel good to be able to provide this chance. If Brady could have, he would have found beds for every person like Tammy who had made a few bad decisions and gotten caught in something far more powerful than themselves.

"Shooting, maybe ten minutes ago, over on Hyde Street,"

Wilkins replied. "One man down and looks like DOA on the scene, and some windows shot out of the houses next door."

Brady had dealt with murders before but hadn't expected one so quickly in Crestville. Once again, he wondered about such a small town with such a high crime rate. Something wasn't adding up. "All right. I have to go in that direction anyway. Let's go check out the crime scene."

He took nearly the same route he'd taken that morning to get to Frank's house, winding through the weedy streets and past rundown houses, before he hit an intersection just a block from Frank's duplex. An intersection that was completely blocked off with yellow crime scene tape. An intersection holding a body in the center of the crossing, like a giant X across the tar.

The details filtered in before they made sense to Brady: a red flannel shirt, untucked, flapping in the breeze. Torn denim jeans, now stained crimson by a spreading pool of blood beneath the body of—

Frank Givens.

Brady was halfway out of his car, ready to yell at Frank to wake up, to stop playing around. To remind Frank today was the day he was checking into rehab, the day he was changing his life, getting a second chance. But there was no movement coming from the body on the ground, just a misshapen circle of dark red blood that slowly got bigger and bigger.

Wilkins had pulled up right behind Brady. He spent a couple minutes talking to the detective on duty, then returned to Brady's side. "Probably a drug deal gone wrong," Wilkins said with a clear note of disgust in his voice. "Someone gunned him down while he was crossing the street. Wherever he was going, he isn't going to make it now."

"No. He won't." That empty bed at the rehab would go to someone else, and Frank would never see his kid again. Brady's heart fractured at the futility of all of it. Why was he fighting so hard just to watch the very people he tried to help die in front of his eyes? "Any witnesses?"

"Marsh and Dexter are doing knock-and-talks right now. But you know this neighborhood. Nobody sees anything, so we don't know much. Around 1:30 pm, the neighbors saw a car rushing down the street over there at the same time Givens was crossing the street." Wilkins pointed. "Guy in the car rolled down his window and started firing. It was over almost as fast as it started."

A handful of shell casings littered the road at the center of the intersection. One of those shell casings had come off the bullet that killed Frank. The sight of it made Brady angry and hurt and a thousand other emotions he didn't have the luxury to feel right now. "What kind of car?"

Wilkins flipped through his notebook. "Uh, black SUV. A Ford, one of the witnesses said. His brother has the same car, just a different color." The deputy closed the small book and tucked it back into his pocket. "That's all we have so far. Do you need anything else, Sheriff?"

Whoever was driving that black SUV was doing more than just tailgating now. The danger level for the investigation had leaped ten times. "Yeah," Brady said. "More answers. Before someone else gets hurt."

Like Hunter. Or Annie.

Chapter Nine

Annie pressed the upload button and watched the vlog she'd just made populate the screen on YouTube as it went live on the channel. For way too long, she'd fussed with the most miniscule of edits, trying to come close to Mia's easy, conversational style and rapid cuts between scenes, all designed to keep hooking the viewer and encourage engagement. From the outside, the process seemed easy, effortless, but once Annie got deep into the editing software and began building the episode, she realized all that outward "natural" style required an incredible attention to detail.

Her first episode, recorded and loaded a few days ago, had featured a nervous wreck Annie and barely garnered any views. Mia had given her several tips about recording for this second episode, and Annie had paid attention, determined to get it right this time. All she could think about was the possibility of someone recognizing that car and making a connection that could break this case wide open. She'd included snippets of her interviews with Dylan and some outward shots of Erline's house as well as the street where Jenny disappeared.

Mia had watched the second episode before Annie made it live, and praised Annie several times. She also had several pointers on including more B-roll, looking into the camera more often and adding hooks and rehooks to keep the viewer engaged. Annie made even more copious notes and prayed she'd learn quickly. The last thing she wanted to do was fail at this task before she found Jenny.

In the newsroom, the computer that had separated Annie from the people she was interviewing had eased her social anxiety and provided a certain remove that made her job easier. Ironically, once she got used to the camera being there, it was just like talking to the computer screen, and a hundred times easier than in-person interactions because it was almost like talking out loud to herself. She could get used to this, a fact that was as much a shock to Annie as it would be to anyone who knew her.

She'd closed the drapes while she was editing to make it easier to see the screen. She got to her feet and pulled open the ugly brown blackout curtains, revealing a crystal clear blue sky, a flock of hungry pigeons in the parking lot and in the far corner of the lot, near the dumpster—

A black Ford Explorer.

A chill ran down her spine. She tried to read a plate, but what was there was covered with mud and illegible. She backed away from the window, an inch at a time, reaching behind her for the phone she'd left on the bed. She patted behind herself for it but didn't find it, and just as she took her eyes off the Explorer to notice and grab the cell, the Explorer gunned it and started careening straight for her motel room.

Annie shrieked and climbed onto the bed, sure the truck was going to come through the window. Instead, the driver veered left at the last second as he lowered the window and threw something at Annie's door. It hit the metal security-type door with a tinny thud. There was a screech of tires, and a second later, the SUV was gone.

She sank onto the mattress, clutching her phone with both hands. Who were these people? Why were they targeting her?

What had Jenny gotten involved with that would make someone stalk and terrorize Annie just for looking into her friend's
disappearance?

As much as she wanted to know what the driver had thrown
at her door, she knew it was safer and better to call Brady first.

He picked up on the first ring, and it was all she could do
to get the words out in a stuttering rush. "The car...here...
scared me... I saw him, and I thought... But he didn't. He
threw something, and I don't know, I don't know what it is,
and I'm afraid to look."

"The black SUV?" Brady muttered something under his
breath. "Annie, stay where you are. Take a breath. Tell me
where you're at." His calm, deep voice washed over her. "I'll
come to you, but don't move until I get there."

"I'm in my room. I was too afraid to open the door and see
what he threw at it."

"Good. Leave it for the deputies to process. I'll be there
in..." a pause "...ten minutes at most. Don't move. And don't
worry. We're on his trail."

He hung up, but Annie stayed where she was, gripping the
phone like a life preserver, until her heart rate slowed and the
scene outside her window went back to the birds looking for
scraps and the occasional car passing on the highway. No SUVs.
No threat. Not right now.

Curiosity nudged her out of the bed and over to the door. She
unlocked the dead bolts and slowly pulled it open, half afraid
that whatever the SUV driver had thrown at her room was a
bomb. But nothing exploded, she heard no sounds of ticking
or clicking, and when she finally dared to poke her head outside, she saw a brick with a note wrapped around it and secured
with an elastic band.

Annie retrieved a pen from her bag and poked at the rock,
tipping it over a couple of times until she could read the entire typed note. It was only a few words, printed in a massive
font, clear enough for her to see even from inside the doorway

where she was crouched down and doing her best not to disturb the evidence:

Leave Now or End Up Like Her.

Annie rocked back onto her heels, wrapped her arms around her knees and began to cry.

Full lights and siren brought Brady to a screeching halt outside Annie's door in eight minutes flat. He saw the open door, Annie crumpled on the floor, and shoved the transmission into Park so hard he was surprised the truck didn't break. He dashed over to her, his gaze sweeping her body, looking for blood— *please, God, not her, too*—an injury, anything. "What's wrong? Are you hurt?"

The tearstained face she turned up to greet him nearly broke his heart. "I'm… I'm okay. Just shaken up."

"Then why are you sitting here?"

She pointed at a chunk of stone a few inches away. "Because I read that and now…" A sob caught in her throat. "Now I know Jenny is gone."

"We don't know that for sure. Let me check this thing out. Get back into the room, just to be safe." Brady took a couple photos of the rock, then pulled out a pair of latex gloves before picking it up, carefully removing the rubber band around the single sheet of paper and unfolding it.

The handful of typed words leaped off the white page and dropped a weight of foreboding over Brady's shoulders. He put it all back together and set the rock where he had found it, noting the triangle-shaped dent in the metal door. If the person sending this message had wanted to hurt Annie, he could have thrown it through the window at her. Whoever had done this was sending a warning.

The kind of people who did this kind of thing didn't send second warnings. Brady needed to figure out who did this and figure it out quickly. But what did he have to go on? A stolen car, a typed note, a rock and a few shell casings? Until now, he'd wondered if Jenny's disappearance had anything to do with the drug ring in Crestville, but now it was abundantly clear that whatever Annie had reopened was linked to the criminal circles of this county.

"Did you see the man who threw this at the door?"

She shook her head. "He had on a ski mask. And his windows were tinted."

As she described the SUV, Brady knew without a doubt that it was the same one he had seen. The same one following him and Hunter the other day. And very likely the same one whose driver had murdered Frank.

"Here, let's get you inside so the techs can do their job." He motioned to one of the members of the forensics team and handed off the note and rock. He doubted there'd be any fingerprints or DNA to recover. If this man was smart enough to wear a ski mask, drive a stolen vehicle and get away without being caught, he was surely smart enough to wear gloves when he handled the note. Still, a small chance was a chance Brady was willing to take.

He went into the room with Annie while another tech crisscrossed the parking lot, just in case the car had left any other clue besides twin black streaks of burnt rubber. "Tell me again exactly what you saw."

She went through the account a second time, then a third, but there were few details to go on, because it all happened so fast. "I just uploaded the vlog a minute before he did this, so there's no way whoever that was saw my episode yet."

"This is the one where you talked about your interview with Erline?"

Annie nodded. "But it just hit the internet, and I don't even know if it has any views yet." She swiped open her phone. "Wow. Two thousand views in the last thirty minutes. There are even a dozen comments."

"Can I see?"

The two of them scrolled through the list but didn't see anything out of the ordinary. Just the same fans raving about the new case, positing their own theories and critiquing the video. Any hope that the murderer had posted on the channel disappeared.

The SUV had been waiting for her to open the blinds, Brady was sure of that. He doubted this attack was related to the vlog she had just released, but more likely the one the other day. "Were there any comments on the first vlog?"

"Let me check." She swiped on the screen and brought up the other episode. "This is the one where I talk about the basics of the case. When Jenny disappeared, the boyfriend she had, stuff like that."

"But you didn't mention the car because you didn't know about that yet, correct?"

"Exactly." She showed him the screen. "And none of these comments seem threatening. A lot of these people are regular followers of the channel."

"Then whoever it is isn't necessarily a viewer of the show. But rather..." his gaze connected with hers and he suddenly wished he could clone himself so he never had to leave her side "...a watcher of you. Whatever nerve you touched by reopening this cold case has some people very angry with you and trying to keep you away from something."

A visible shiver ran through Annie. "When you said you were on his trail, does that mean you know who it is?"

He shook his head. The whole thing frustrated him. He knew he was missing some connection, something that would tie the SUV, Frank's death, the drugs and Jenny's disappearance into one neat bow. "No, but I'm doubly determined to figure it out now."

"Do you think what he said in the note is true? That Jenny's dead?"

He took her hand in his, praying that whoever this was

would leave Annie alone and stop scaring this sweet, wonderful woman. "The note doesn't say anyone is dead. Let's not assume the worst yet."

Tears pooled in her blue eyes but didn't spill over. She was strong, Annie was, and he admired her so much for that. "There aren't a lot of other assumptions we can make, though, Brady."

He gave her hand a squeeze, more as a measure of comfort, support, but still, his heart did a little gallop. "I'm going to keep you with me twenty-four-seven, Annie. I want to know that you're okay until we catch this guy or you decide to go back to Denver."

"Which you know I won't do until I have answers about Jenny. It's impossible to stay with me twenty-four-seven, Brady. You have Hunter and…" she pulled her hand out of his when he tried to interrupt "…and a full-time job figuring out what is going on in this town. I'd be nothing but underfoot. Let me stay here, do my research, keep looking for Jenny."

"I'd feel better if you did that research at the sheriff's office. We have a conference room you can use. Just for a couple days. Let us find this guy and get him off the streets."

"And what if you can't find him? Can't get him off the streets?"

"That's not a word in my vocabulary, Annie." He got to his feet and plopped his hat back on his head. "And I know it's not one in yours. So let me help you and protect you while you look for answers."

"Come on, Uncle B. You guys have got to be dating or something," Hunter said, more or less under his breath, as Brady dropped some pasta into the boiling water.

At the table, Annie pretended she hadn't heard Hunter's question while she made notes and went through the small stack of case files Brady had brought home from the office. She'd agreed not to use any of the information she saw without talking to him first, one of many compromises they'd made today. The first being the fact that she was here at all.

Eventually, she'd seen the wisdom of staying close to him, at least until they found the SUV driver. The rock had made enough of an impression in the door—and in her stubbornness—that she'd agreed to spending the daylight hours with Brady and moving to a different room at the motel, one that was even closer to the manager's office and hopefully less exposed. Instead of the parking lot, the new room's door faced the tiny hall beside the vending machine and the ice maker and sat directly across from the glass window of the manager, who would be able to see if anyone came to Annie's room. A bit noisier location but far less vulnerable.

Hunter glanced back at her and then raised a brow in his uncle's direction. "Dinner twice in one week? You haven't had dinner with anyone twice in one week."

Annie leaned her head ever so slightly toward Brady to, yes, eavesdrop, without one bit of guilt about doing it. They were, after all, talking about her.

"I've had dinner with you every night for a month, and keep your voice down."

"Well, do you want to be dating?"

A pop sounded behind her as Brady wrestled the top off a jar of spaghetti sauce and dumped it into a waiting pot. "We are working together, Hunter. Nothing more. Now will you set the table please?"

"Whatever you say." He shot a grin at his uncle as he put out plates and silverware.

Annie just kept herself buried in work, because that was far more productive than thinking about dating the handsome sheriff. Who had made it clear just now that they were only friends.

Yet as the three of them sat around the table—Hunter choosing this time to eat dinner with Brady and Annie—and traded jokes while they passed heaping bowls of spaghetti and pasta sauce and ripped off chunks of Italian bread that they slathered with butter, Annie began to feel a sense of family, of camaraderie. It was like being in the center of a hug, which had awakened a need deep inside her that she thought she had gotten over a long time ago.

For a moment, she allowed herself to imagine sitting here at this table every night, with the two of them as they teased and talked. Building memories and moments, things that she had so little of in her memory vault.

Hunter pushed off from the table. "I have homework."

"Which is code for someone waiting for you to get on your PlayStation and take out the bad guys."

"Maybe." Hunter winked at Annie as he picked up his plate and put it in the sink. He returned to the table to grab the leftover food and begin dishing it into plastic containers.

"You're cleaning up?" Brady said. "Did you fall and hit your head today?"

Hunter scowled. "I can help out. I helped my mom all the time. Which really means I did almost everything while she was…"

The easy mood in the room evaporated, replaced by a heavy cloak of history and sadness. "It will be better, Hunt, I promise."

Hunter just shrugged and turned away, busying himself with shoving the storage containers into the fridge. Then he ducked down the hall and into his room.

Brady sighed. "I said the wrong thing. Again."

"What, when you teased him about helping out?" Annie rose at the same time he did, the two of them working in concert to do the rest of the cleanup. "You were just teasing him. I don't see anything wrong with that."

"His mom—my sister—is a really sensitive subject. Normally, I try to avoid it because it just gets him upset."

"Avoiding things just makes them bigger in your mind," Annie said. "That's something Jenny's mom used to say. She was like Yoda."

Brady laughed. "Sounds like it. What do you think Jenny's

mom would say about this situation?" He gestured between Hunter's closed door and himself.

"That he's going through a lot. And that you simply being here is telling him that he is loved and protected. And that you should keep talking."

"Ha. I'm good at law enforcement, not so good at talking about my feelings and all that stuff."

Annie started the water and loaded the dirty plates into the sink. Brady took up a station next to her, drying as she washed. From the outside, they could have been any ordinary married couple on any ordinary weeknight. "Join the club. I'm not good at it, either. I'm always afraid I'm going to say the wrong thing or embarrass myself or just... I don't know, mess things up."

"You've done pretty well with me."

"We're working together. That's different. If we were dating..." She let the words trail off as her face heated. Why did she say that out loud?

"If we were dating, what would be different?"

Annie dropped her gaze to the pot she'd already scrubbed, a pot that was already clean, a pot that she kept on circling with the sponge so she didn't look directly at Brady while she spoke. "I haven't dated a whole lot. My mother said I was shy, but I think it was more that I was always afraid I would mess things up. I saw what a disaster a relationship could be when I looked at my parents, and I figured I'd end up the same way. I saw it with Jenny's mom and her stepdad, too. He was like a dictator with her and that caused a lot of unhappiness for Jenny and for her mom. Them getting divorced five years ago was the best thing that could ever happen. Those were my role models for relationships. What you see, you repeat."

"Not always. I've seen people with the best of childhoods end up in rehab..." and the way he said it, Annie knew he was talking about his sister "...and people who have come up hard and lived great lives. I think you choose the kind of life you want."

She rinsed the pan, set it in the strainer and pulled the

plug. As the water drained, Annie put her back to the sink and chanced a glance at Brady. "So what kind of life did you choose?"

"When I first got on with the sheriff's department, I was so gung ho and ready to save the world. But there was more crime than I had time to conquer, and I found myself putting in more and more hours after the hours I was paid for because I was so determined to make a difference. Before Hunter came along, I was the classic definition of a workaholic. Seventy, eighty hours a week, barely any time for dating, never mind thinking about my future. I was miserable, but I kept working harder so I didn't think about how miserable I was."

"And then?"

"And then my sister called me and said I had to pick up Hunter so she could go into rehab. All of a sudden, I was a stand-in parent—who had no experience parenting, mind you—who needed a change of scenery so that Hunter could be close to his mom and away from that environment that had been so toxic to both of them." He dried the pan and stowed it in the cabinet. "To be honest, as much as I intended for things to be different, I'm doing the same thing as I did before. Staying so busy, I don't have time to think about what I want or the things I'm avoiding thinking about, like whether my sister will make it."

"I get that." She shifted her weight and looked out at the cozy cabin where Brady and Hunter lived. A hodgepodge of belongings and life peppered the space—a denim backpack, Brady's cowboy hat, a gray hoodie, a couple pairs of boots. "I avoid my feelings as much as possible, too. When I was a kid, feelings were a weakness, a vulnerability, that could be exploited to control or guilt me into doing what my mother wanted. She was, I'm sorry to say, a master manipulator who now lives a very sad, solitary life because she refuses to see that she did some terrible things. So I shut down and shut off my feelings so that no one can see past that kinda flimsy armor I have."

It was the most she'd said to anyone other than Jenny in a

long, long time. She waited for Brady to judge her or say some-thing sarcastic, but instead, he just moved an inch or two closer.

His brown eyes softened with understanding and compas-sion. "We're two peas in a pod, doing the same thing for dif-ferent reasons. No wonder we became friends."

There was that word again. *Friends.* She'd never disliked that word as much as she did right now. A single noun and a harsh reminder to get back to the main reason she had come here.

"I, uh, wanted to show you something in the reports from Jenny's case that you gave me the other day." She pushed off from the counter, away from him, erasing the disappointment in her chest and replacing it with work. "I went through the news database Mia's vlog subscribes to. It gives me access to past news stories, which definitely isn't every crime against women that has happened in this town, but it's a start. These three cases are very similar to what happened to Jenny." She shuffled the printouts around and handed him a stack she'd set aside earlier.

Brady turned to the first one, the oldest file that Annie had found, a disappearance that happened about a year after Jen-ny's. "Eighteen-year-old girl, possible runaway, last seen on..." he glanced up at her "...Hyde Street."

The same road Jenny had been walking down just before she got into that sedan and was never seen again. "Look at the next one. And the third one, which happened just two months ago and was never solved. Did anyone mention these cases to you when you became sheriff?"

"This is the first I've heard of any missing girls besides Jenny, and you were the one who told me about her. It could be unrelated, Annie. But I'll look at them." He read each of the three news reports. Like Jenny's, they were short and sparse on details, but there was enough there for Brady to put the pieces together. She watched the light of realization dawn on his face, just as it had for her. "All of these girls were around the same age and disappeared within a quarter mile of each other," he said. "In a town this small, how has no one noticed that kind of coincidence?"

"Because I don't think it's a coincidence. I think we've stumbled upon something that someone doesn't want us to find." Who that someone was, she had no idea, but somehow, it was all connected. The SUV, the rock, the shooting…everything pointed to one central cast of characters who were growing increasingly panicked by whatever Annie and Brady were uncovering. Panicked people made desperate, sometimes fatal decisions. She sensed a ticking clock in the background, a tension in the air, as if a Category 5 hurricane was bearing down on this tiny town.

"You need to go through the police reports in Crestville and see if there are more missing girls no one is looking for. We need to look harder, Brady, before someone else's daughter is taken."

Chapter Ten

At roll call the next morning, Brady placed a pile of folders on the table at the front of the room, taking his time laying them side by side. He'd come in early today and, with Annie, had gone through the police reports for the three missing girls she'd alerted him to and then scoured the database for more reports. Another young woman had come up in Brady's search, fitting the same general description and facts that the others had. With Jenny, that made five missing women in one small town.

Annie was safely ensconced in his office, doing her own research, while Hunter was safe in school. The threat from the SUV had all three of them on edge and made Brady wish he could keep Hunter and Annie right by his side. Even ten feet away seemed too far.

He hadn't told Hunter much, to keep his nephew from worrying. He'd simply warned him to be on the lookout for any kind of car that seemed out of place.

Right now, though, the best thing Brady could do was find whoever was behind these disappearances. He stood beside the lectern and waited for the deputies to swing their attention toward him, then he clicked on a presentation he'd made the night before, dimmed the lights and waited for the murmur of conversation to die down.

"Kaitlyn Brown." An image of a brown-haired girl with big green eyes and a gold-and-black shirt appeared on the screen. The most recent victim, missing for two months.

He clicked the next slide.

"Marcy Higgins." A younger girl, with lighter hair, in the middle of a flower garden. Missing for under a year.

Click.

"Pauline Rivers." A brunette, standing on the steps of the nursing school, beaming as she held her diploma above her head. Missing for two years.

Click.

"Hailey Wicker." The image of an ebullient high school graduate tossing her cap in the air filled the screen. Missing for nine years.

One more click. "Jenny Bennett." He let the screen linger on Annie's friend, with her wide smile and pale blond hair. Her eyes were so intense, she seemed to be asking each of them why she had been forgotten for a decade.

He turned back to the room. "Does anyone in this department know what these girls have in common?"

Not a single soul spoke up or raised a hand. Brady's gaze landed on the people who had been here the longest, the ones who had ten, fifteen, twenty or more years in the sheriff's office. Men and women who had been here when these disappearances had happened, who would at least have a passing familiarity with the cases. None of them met his eyes or said anything. There was an uncomfortable cough, the scrape of a chair.

"I find it hard to believe that in such a small town, where the county sheriff's office is headquartered, that none of you have heard anything about these five young women who disappeared."

The tension in the room was as thick as fog. Brady's gaze

swept across the deputies, most of whom looked away or down at their notepads. Avoiding him. Avoiding the conversation. Why? Didn't any of them care about these young women?

"I expect an answer, Deputies." He stared hard at the leaders of the department. "I am tired of everyone dancing around the answers, and I suspect, the truth. No matter what, I intend to get to the bottom of what is going on in this town. Including what happened to these girls. It's time to decide, Deputies. Are you with me or against me?"

"Sir." Wilkins raised his hand. "I worked the Wicker case. That girl was a runaway. Even her mother said so. I'm pretty sure I heard the same about the others."

"So you *have* heard of these cases." Brady crossed to the light switch and brightened the space again. Then he walked among the rows of chairs, talking as he moved. "If Wilkins has, then so have many of you. For whatever reason, no one wants to share what they know or volunteer any information. That's fine. However, to refresh your memory…" he grabbed a stack of copies beside the folders "…I'm handing all of you a sheet that has these young women's photographs and the stats on their disappearances. These are someone's daughters. Sisters. Friends. They matter, regardless of how they ended up here. I trust that you all will keep that in mind as we reopen these investigations and find them."

"Kids run away all the time," another deputy said. "These girls did the same thing."

"If you look at the sheet, Deputy Wallace, you'll see that all five of these young women disappeared within a three-block radius of each other. That's not a coincidence. That's a clue. This week, I want you all to put noncritical cases on hold and do what you can to work these cases again. The investigative unit will assign the patrol officers to do knock-and-talks, internet research, phone calls. I want a full report on each of these young women by EOD Friday."

"But, sir, we have other work to do. Setting that all aside... That's impossible." Wallace sputtered.

"No, Wallace. That's your job." His gaze swept across the room, sending the same message to all the other deputies. "Dismissed."

Later that morning, the station hummed with activity, mostly deputies on the phone, tracking down leads. Or at least, that's how it appeared at first glance. As Brady made his way through the room, he realized most of the deputies were barely putting in any effort at all. They were dawdling on the phone, making small talk, not writing down notes. It was almost as if they didn't want to do the job. What kind of force didn't want to look for missing young women?

He pulled Tonya aside a little before eleven. The chief deputy had just a couple days left before she began her maternity leave, and he could tell by her face that she was tired, cranky and uncomfortable this close to giving birth. "You didn't speak up in the roll call meeting this morning."

"I've only been with the department for a few years, sir. I wasn't familiar with those cases."

Seemed to Brady that any deputy interested in being promoted to chief deputy and eventually sheriff would spend some time looking into the unsolved files in the department and definitely would have heard about the more recent cases, particularly Kaitlyn. Sanders seemed like someone who worked hard, cared about the Franklin County citizens and who would want justice to be served. Why wasn't she on top of these missing person cases? Or at least riding the deputies to make sure they were putting in a hundred percent effort? "Is it just me or does no one seem to be working very hard on these cases?"

She glanced away and fiddled with the pen in her hand. "They're cold cases, Sheriff. Not much challenge in them."

"Every case is a puzzle. And if there's one thing law enforcement loves, it's puzzles." Brady shifted farther down the hall, a little more out of earshot of the squad room. "So don't tell me that there's no challenge to a cold case, because we both know there is. The Kaitlyn Brown case is so recent, it's barely cooled off. I'm stunned the department doesn't have detectives working that case around the clock. What is really going on here?"

"I…" She rested a hand on her belly, and for the first time since he'd met her, Brady saw something foreign in the chief deputy's eyes—fear. Sanders lowered her voice so much, Brady could barely hear her. "I can't tell you. You'll have to ask someone else."

"Can't? Or won't?"

"I… I can't." She swallowed hard. "I have a family, Sheriff. A baby on the way. I can't get involved in this."

"Get involved in what?" His frustration pitched his whisper sharper. He'd come to the Franklin County Sheriff's Office thinking he could make a difference in this area and a difference in Hunter's life. Yet he was stymied at every point, because there was something sinister lurking underneath this town, something that was trying very hard to suck Annie and Hunter into its vortex. How was he supposed to stop these people if his own deputies wouldn't investigate?

"Listen, there's a reason Judge Harvey let your guy go. A reason none of us touch because, like you said, this is a small town in a good-size county, and what happens here…" she glanced around them and made sure no one was nearby "…goes way above my head or yours. So you'd do well to just let it go."

"How can you live with yourself? How can any of them live with themselves if they're ignoring women being abducted or murdered?"

"There is a lot of money and connections at play here. I joined this office six years ago, and I learned pretty quickly what happens to people who decide they should push an investigation that should have been left alone."

"What? What happened?"

She was shaking her head. "I have less than a week until my maternity leave starts. I'm not going down this rabbit hole. I know too many people who didn't come back out of it. You'd do well to remember that, Brady."

Then she walked away, putting as much distance between them as she could in fast, short steps.

Annie had spent hours in Brady's office, researching the other four young women who had disappeared. She'd called family and friends, contacted witnesses and even called old employers and high school teachers. She debated going back and interviewing Erline again or asking Dylan for another interview. There had to be a clue she was missing, a person she had overlooked. She had amassed a pile of notes but not a lot of leads. All of it was eerily reminiscent of what had happened to Jenny. Troubled girls who disappeared. Throwaway women no one seemed to care about finding.

There was one person she had yet to talk to. The only person named as a suspect in Jenny's disappearance. Eddie Anderson. She did a quick Google search and confirmed that he still lived in town. Maybe it was time to pay Mr. Anderson a visit later today and see what he knew.

Her stomach rumbled, and she decided to ask Brady if he wanted to grab lunch—something that had become a rather regular thing over the last few days as they discussed the case and learned about each other's lives. Another woman might read something into that kind of standing meal date, but not Annie. No, that would be foolish.

Yet a part of her was falling for this determined, strong sheriff with his earnest desire to make things right, his protective spirit and most of all, the glimpses of vulnerability he had shared when he talked about Hunter and Hunter's mother, Brady's sister. One of these days, her investigation in Crestville would come to an end, and she would have to go back to her life in Denver. She hoped that day didn't come anytime soon.

Annie logged onto the page for the vlog and began reading through the comments on the last couple of episodes. She'd loaded a short one just a few minutes earlier, sharing the names of the other missing young women and a few details, then imploring the public to help. The women's images had flashed on the screen one at a time, each photo like a gong tolling the truth.

Someone was hurting or taking these women. It was simply too many in one small town. Was it Dylan? Eddie? Someone else?

Annie scanned the comments beneath the videos, hoping someone had some kind of witness statement. The views were up, which was great, because it meant word was spreading about Jenny's case. The comments ranged from hopeful to pessimistic, with people speculating about a serial killer and one person positing that the women had been picked up by a spaceship. But no one mentioned knowing anything more about the cases. At the bottom of the page, Annie saw a request from a television reporter in Denver. DM me about doing an interview, the reporter had written. This needs to get out in the world.

Annie sent the private message, and within ten minutes, the reporter had messaged her back and set up a video call for that morning. They did a quick interview over Zoom, just enough to get the bare bones of the story out there. "If something develops," the reporter, a young, eager man in his late twenties, said, "let me know, and I'll come out there to do a follow-up. Sadly, we get a lot of this kind of story and most of the time, nobody cares. Your investigation, especially if you find anything, gives me a reason to do another piece."

"Are you saying there has been a lot of missing girls?" Annie said.

He nodded. "Not all of them are runaways, although that's easier for people to think because these girls often have had tough lives and made a few mistakes. But nine times out of ten, it turns out to be rural human trafficking, which is becoming a big thing these days. Cities are getting wiser to the practice, which is forcing these syndicates out into small-town America."

"Rural human trafficking? That's horrible."

"You said your friend responded to a guy on some dating app? Lots of girls end up kidnapped and forced into the trafficking world through those apps. It's the equivalent of the lost puppy sign for a child predator." He sighed. "I wish law enforcement would do more to catch these guys, but the girls just...disappear. No witnesses, no cases."

Could that mean Dylan had been part of some concerted effort to kidnap girls? That his profile had merely been a front? Had he met any of the others?

And what about Eddie Anderson? How did he figure into all of this?

"Either way, we have to draw attention to these cases so we can find them. When will your story air?" Annie asked a few more questions and promised to follow up with whatever she found out, after she aired it on the vlog. Maybe by working together with the Denver TV station, she could get these women the news coverage they deserved.

Brady rapped on the door frame. "I need to get out of here for a bit. Want to get some lunch?"

"I'd love to. The Bluebird again?"

"No. Let's try a different place. How do you feel about burgers?"

"That they should also be their own food group." She grinned and then grabbed her tote bag. The two of them walked out of the station and climbed into Brady's car.

A few minutes later, he took them through a drive-through to order some fast food. She'd expected a different restaurant or maybe even one of the cute little places downtown, but this was the kind of fast-food place that lined highways all throughout the world. Maybe he was just a big fan?

"So we're eating in the car?"

"Yes, so that we can accomplish two things at once." He handed her the bag of food, then pulled out of the lot. "Because I want to head over to Hyde Street. See what's going on, if anything, over there."

"You're not worried about the black SUV following us?"

"I'm always worried about that SUV, but I have an APB out on it, and if whoever stole it is smart, they'll lie low for a bit and not follow the sheriff around town." Brady flicked on his directional and turned right, deeper into the belly of Crestville.

"I want to run something by you," Annie said. "Something a reporter for a Denver TV station mentioned today."

"Shoot."

"He said the disappearances might be tied to rural human trafficking and that the dating profile Dylan had was a way to lure them in."

Brady's jaw hardened. "That could be true. Maybe we should go talk to Mr. Houston again."

"What about that Eddie guy that was named in the file? Should we talk to him?"

Brady didn't reply to that. He slowed the SUV as they approached the corner of Hyde and Perkins. A young blond man stood on the corner, while an older man sat on a nearby bench and smoked a cigar.

Brady let out a frustrated sigh. "They're back at it. I don't know why I'm surprised."

"Who is that?"

"That man with the cigar is the man you were asking about. This is Eddie 'the Answerman' Anderson. I've arrested him for burglary, but he seems to have friends in high places who had the charges thrown out of court. And beside him is his corner kid."

"Corner kid?"

"The kid who actually gets his hands dirty and does the sales. The lowest man on the totem pole, and the one people like Eddie Anderson are willing to sacrifice because they are a dime a dozen to drug dealers."

"That's horrible. I can't believe people are so expendable."

She thought of Jenny and the other missing girls. "Then again, it sadly doesn't surprise me. So many people hurt, in such a small area."

"I know. It all feels...suspicious." Brady stopped alongside the road, watching Eddie and the kid.

Eddie ignored Brady but even from here, the tension in his movements belied his calm.

"I mean, I've worked in big cities before, and it's not unusual to have a spate of crime, especially when someone is running drugs through the area, but Crestville is not a big town, and Franklin County isn't even as populated as Bloomington was. To have this many disappearances, and judges who overlook felonies, all just feels too..."

"Neatly connected." She glanced again at the men on the corner. "Can we talk to Eddie?"

"I think we should try." Brady put the SUV into Park and shut off the engine. "But no notes, no camera. This isn't a formal police interview, and I don't want him to think it's an exposé for *Dateline*, either. More like a...feeling-him-out, easy conversation. I don't want to spook him."

Another reporter might balk at Brady keeping the interview under wraps for now, but everything about this man seemed genuine. He had a good reason for keeping this off the internet, and she was going to respect that, if only for the good of the relationship.

Relationship? Where had that word come from? She didn't have time to even let the word wander in her mind because a second later, they were out of the car and crossing the street to where Eddie was sitting on a bench.

"I got nothing to say to you," Eddie said before Brady even reached the sidewalk.

"I'm not grilling you, Eddie, just making conversation."

The other man snorted. "Cops don't make conversation without an agenda." He turned to Annie, and a spark of interest lit in his eyes. He took a puff of the cigar while he watched her.

"And who do we have here? I've seen you around town. Living here or just passing through?"

Annie started to answer. "I'm—"

Brady touched her arm, cutting off her sentence. Then he took in a breath and steadied himself, erasing the irritation that Eddie was prying into Annie's presence from his voice. "You like this corner, don't you? Second time I've seen you here in the last couple of weeks."

"Didn't know there was a law against sitting on a bench and enjoying the sunshine." Eddie leaned back, spreading his thick arms across the back of the wooden seat. He had the self-satisfied grin of the Cheshire cat.

"As long as that's all you're doing," Brady said. "Not running drugs or women or anything else illegal."

"You know me, Sheriff." Eddie took a long drag on the cigar. A curl of oak-scented smoke rose in the air. "I'm never in trouble."

"The last time I was here, Eddie, I saw a dead man in the middle of the street. Know anything about that?"

Eddie shifted his weight and looked away. "I don't make a habit of being around dead men."

"Even ones that die suspiciously not far from where you and I are standing?"

Eddie's jaw rose and his gaze narrowed. "You accusing me of something?"

"Where were you on Monday afternoon. Around two o'clock?"

"Just minding my own business," Eddie said. "I told you. I don't hang around dead men."

"Let's keep it that way." Brady nudged Annie's elbow. "See you around, Eddie."

"Not if I see you first." He winked, then shot a smile at Annie. "I do hope I run into you again, pretty lady."

Brady mumbled something like "over my dead body" as he hurried back across the street with Annie walking double time to keep pace. Once they were back inside the SUV and on the road, he let out a sigh of frustration. "That guy is up to no good. I know it, he knows it, the whole town knows it."

"Then why isn't he in jail?" The way Eddie had been so chill, so nonchalant, told Annie he was the kind of guy who taunted lawmen, who thought he was above jail time. He gave her a bad vibe, but then again, a lot of places and people in this town were beginning to do the same thing.

Five missing girls. One small town. There had to be a connection.

"Eddie has friends in high places. I can't pin anything on him. Not the robbery, not the drugs. Nothing." Brady took a right, then turned down Hyde and then onto Columbus before parking across the street from Erline's house.

It struck Annie how close geographically everything was in Crestville. Dylan's old apartment, Eddie's haunt, the shooting of Frank, Erline's house. Jenny's abduction site. A very small circle of places that had an awful lot of links.

"Are we talking to Erline again?"

"Not today." He turned off the car and unbuckled his seat belt. "Take a walk with me."

She followed him, not even questioning where they were going. Had she really gotten to that point with Brady already? Where she trusted him implicitly? *Where you go, I go?* Well, that was more like a verse for wedding vows, and she was definitely not going down that path. Still, as she walked beside Brady down the street, it all felt so comfortable and right and natural, as if they had been together forever.

They walked a little way past Erline's house before Brady stopped. "This is where."

He didn't even have to finish the sentence because Annie knew what *where* meant. She could see Erline's raggedy chair on her porch just thirty yards away, the weed-cracked driveway where Annie had parked a few days ago and, ahead of her, a trash-filled desolate stretch of road. This was the place Erline had described, the spot where Jenny had gotten into someone's car and disappeared.

"She was right here." Annie stood on the pavement under a warm early fall sun and wished she could get some kind of sense of what had happened to Jenny, where Jenny had gone. What exactly happened in this space so she could know which direction to look, like rewinding a tape to the beginning. *Lord, please help me to see. To know.*

But of course, this wasn't a sports game, and there was no auto replay of the moment Jenny disappeared. There was just a bunch of overgrown shrubs, some scattered trash and a cracked road that probably should have been repaved years ago and probably never would be repaired. This part of town was clearly not a priority, not to the town or the county. She could see the intersection where Frank had been killed just a block away.

Annie and Brady walked down the street, undoubtedly retracing the steps Jenny must have taken. Trash and decrepit homes surrounded them on all sides. Annie did a slow circle, turning toward where they had come from, and saw only a sad cloud spreading a shadow over the street. What had her friend been thinking? Why would she come here?

Crowded branches hung like reaching arms, thick and gnarly. Broken, empty houses peppered with the detritus of the people who had once lived there. In a couple of blocks, Crestville went from Small Town America to a lost, depressing and forgotten pocket. Had Jenny seen that and thought she needed to leave quickly? Maybe that was why she took the first ride that came along?

Brady came up beside her. "What are you thinking?"

"That this view would have scared Jenny, especially toward the end of the day. She would have known it was getting dark and would have wanted to get out of here. Maybe that's why she accepted that ride. But it still doesn't make sense that she would be here to begin with."

"So you think she went into the car willingly?"

Annie thought about it, imagining herself in Jenny's shoes. Annie had always been the cautious one, the one who thought ten times before making a move, ninety-nine percent of the time. Jenny was more impetuous and spontaneous, reacting out of emotion more than analysis. That knee-jerk response to a fight with her mother had caused her to end up…somewhere. "I don't know. It really doesn't seem like her to accept anything from a stranger. She was a tough cookie all on her own."

"Well, it's too bad she didn't leave a clue for us to find."

"I know." Annie sighed. She walked around the space, poking here and there, praying for a miracle. It wasn't like she thought there'd be a treasure map that pointed to Jenny's location. It had been ten years. What could possibly be left behind that the police didn't find? "Brady, do you know if there was a search done of this area? Did they mention that in the police report?"

"As far as I know, there wasn't. The officer who took Erline's statement didn't seem to think she was very credible."

That spiked a tiny ray of hope in Annie—and frustration that the police hadn't been thorough when it could have made a difference. "Then maybe there is a clue left behind."

"After a decade?" Brady shook his head. "Very unlikely."

Annie kicked at a container from a chicken restaurant that had begun to erode and mildew. "Judging by the age of some of this trash, it's not impossible."

"But that's the problem, Annie. Pretty much everything you see around here is trash. It could belong to anybody."

"Maybe. But we won't know if we don't look." She ducked behind the shrubs that Erline had pointed at the other day, *kinda out of sight…right there*, parting the thick branches, ignoring the scratches they left on her arms, almost as if the bushes didn't want her to disturb their secrets. She tried to estimate how much they would have grown in ten years, but she had no idea if any of the neighbors or the town department of public works might have done some trimming at some point. The

only way to see if anything had been left behind was to actually dive right in. So she took a deep breath and did just that.

"Annie, what are you doing?"

"Praying." She pushed farther into the interior of the shrubs,
even as the branches grabbed at her, a wall of thick nature she
had to force her way past. They tugged at her hair, scraped
her arms, pulled at her jacket. Then, just as she was about to
give up, she saw a flash of something dirty, dull pink, barely
visible among piles of trash. Old newspapers. Empty bottles.
Crumpled cigarette packets. And one thing that seemed like
it didn't belong.

Annie shouldered her way farther into the brambles, no longer noticing how they pushed back, trying to keep her out. A
long branch ran a scrape down her cheek, but she didn't feel
it. Her gaze remained on the only thing that mattered, covered
partly by dirt and leaves and time.

Jenny's sneaker.

The once-bright sneaker sat on the dark brown leather dash
of Brady's SUV, an impossible miracle found ten years after
the fact. If Jenny Bennett had been running away, she certainly
wouldn't have done it wearing only one shoe, would she?

He trusted Annie's belief that it was her friend's shoe. The
white canvas Converse low-top had been decorated by hand, the
body of it once painted a bright fuchsia that had turned a dull
pink and bedecked with sparkling rhinestones. Only a handful
of the plastic gems remained, but it was enough to identify the
shoes as Jenny's when Brady compared them in an old photo
that Annie had of her friend.

The shoe had been found near a small handbag that had been
caught in the branches of a shrub. It was tiny, one of those zip-
pered bags that couldn't hold much more beside a phone and
a wallet. Neither of those things were still in the bag, but they
had found a lip gloss and a receipt from a convenience store just
outside Denver. The second Annie saw the bag, she knew it was

Jenny's—because she'd given it to Jenny the Christmas before she disappeared. The concrete proof both broke her heart and gave her hope that maybe they were one step closer to Jenny.

"All this says to me that she was kidnapped," Annie said. "She didn't go anywhere willingly."

"It definitely appears that way." Too many signs pointed in that direction for Brady to chalk this single shoe and purse up to anything else. "The problem is by who and taken to where?"

Annie dug in a small side pocket of the bag and pulled out a slim white-and-silver object. "What is this?"

Brady turned it over in his hands. A matchbook for the Rook and Pawn, a restaurant he had driven by a dozen times on his way to work, with a shiny logo on one side and details about its location and hours on the other. "I've seen this place. It looks like it's been closed for a while. And the matchbook could have come from anywhere or anyone."

"True, but it was in Jenny's purse. I feel like that's not a co-incidence and that God is trying to tell me something." Annie pulled out her phone and did a quick Google search. "Maybe this place is a clue." She searched for a second, then sighed. "This says the restaurant has been closed for three years, like you said. It's owned by Hughes Properties. Is that anyone you know?"

"Kingston Hughes. One of the county commissioners and the biggest employer around." Something nagged in Brady's memory, but whatever it was, he couldn't grasp it. "Remember, I told you he owns the Bluebird Diner?"

"And you don't find that suspicious?"

He chuckled. "It's not illegal to own a lot of businesses, especially in the same industry, like food. I told you, I looked into him. He came up squeaky clean."

"True. But now there are two things tying him to Jenny. This matchbook, and her being spotted at the diner."

"That's a pretty thin thread. More like a dream of a thread than a real connection."

"I know, but I just have this feeling." Annie stared at the image of the restaurant with its chess-themed logo and had the distinct sense there was something she was missing. "All the other girls who disappeared were all in this town, not far from this restaurant when they vanished. Or this neighborhood. That's too much of a coincidence for me."

"Whoa, whoa. You are putting way too much conjecture into one sentence. The matchbook could have blown in there anytime over the last decade. We don't know how it got in that purse or if Jenny ever even had it in her hands. And yes, Kingston owns the diner and restaurant, but—"

"Brady, there is no *but*. I think he's got something to do with all of this, and if he doesn't, then he must know someone who does." She plucked the matchbook out of his hand and held it up. "We need to talk to him. If only to clear him from having any involvement in this."

Brady's gut had been nagging him for a while about Kingston Hughes. The man who had some kind of influence in "fixing" Eddie's case. The same man whose name kept coming up, over and over again.

Brady hadn't dug that deep, because it seemed incredulous that the man who had hired him would be involved in underhanded dealings.

Unless Hughes was that sure of his power in Crestville that he wasn't bothered by a new sheriff in town.

Either way, maybe it would set Annie's mind at ease if they did talk to Kingston Hughes. It couldn't hurt, that was for sure. But Brady doubted highly that the man who had hired him— knowing the kind of straight-arrow law enforcement officer Brady was—would have anything to do with the disappearance of five young women. If a quick conversation could take that possibility off the table, then maybe Annie would feel better, and he would know he'd exhausted every possible outlet.

"I think I might know a way to do that." Brady grinned. Maybe they'd get lucky and they could have another nice meal together, and run into Kingston, who seemed to be at the diner most days. "You up for a second lunch? Even though we just ate these..." he nudged at the wrappers from the fast-food place "...not-as-delicious-as-I'd-hoped burgers?"

"Have you met me? I'm always up for food. Even better if it's served with a side of sleuthing."

As they walked up the sidewalk toward the Bluebird Diner, Annie glanced at the plate glass windows, catching a faint echo of her reflection. She pressed her windblown hair into some semblance of smoothness and debated reapplying some lip gloss, then chided herself for caring what she looked like. They weren't going to lunch as a couple. She was going as his witness and sort-of deputy, both of them determined to find out what had happened to those young women.

The air had warmed enough that Annie draped her coat over her arm and soaked up the sunshine as they walked. She spent way too much time indoors, because the sun felt like a gift from God. A soft breeze danced around them, whispering across the sidewalk and the skinny saplings. A flock of birds, scared by the beep of a car, burst from the branches of an oak and left with an angry squawk.

"It's so beautiful here," Annie said just before they went inside the diner. "It's hard to believe so many awful things happened in this town."

"Beauty can often be a mask," Brady said. "I've seen that firsthand way too many times."

"And yet, you don't seem jaded to me."

He grabbed the handle of the door but didn't open it yet. "I think my faith in God and in other people keeps me looking at the glass as half full. But trust me, there are days when that glass is a bottomless pit, too."

"Understandable. Working in the news, I go through much the same thing. You see the lowest levels that human beings can stoop to, but also the highest and best that they can be. Every day brings something you didn't expect—and you didn't think was possible, good and bad."

He held the diner door for her, and as she passed by him, she caught a whiff of his cologne with its dark, woodsy notes. Had he worn that just for her? Or was she foolish to even speculate in that direction?

He nodded toward the booths at the front of the diner. "Let's grab a table by the window. Before you know it, winter will be here, and the view might not be as pretty."

"I think snow can be just as gorgeous as sunshine, Mr. Empty Glass." She shot him a grin—a borderline flirty grin, which was impossible because Annie didn't have a flirtatious bone in her body—and then headed toward the only empty booth at the front of the diner. She turned back, expecting to see Brady behind her, but he had stopped at another table and was talking to two men, one of whom she recognized as the judge Brady had been talking to the first day she arrived in town. The other man was the one in the suit she'd seen leaving the diner her first day in town. The discussion seemed heated, tense.

Annie made her way back toward the other table. The closer she got, the more she could catch snippets of the conversation between the three men. The judge, a burly guy with a beard and no-nonsense attitude, was the loudest talker.

"This town sits smack-dab on the intersection of two major highways, Sheriff. Lots of kids come through here, looking to escape their lives. We might as well put out a sign saying Runaway Junction. California this direction, Canada that direction."

"Bunch of losers," the other man muttered.

"Not every kid that disappears here is a runaway, Judge Harvey and Mr. Hughes," Brady said. "We all know that. What I want to know is why no one is investigating these disappearances."

So, the infamous judge who had let Eddie "the Answerman" go free, even though Brady had had a pile of evidence to convict him of robbing the jewelry store. Sitting with Kingston Hughes, as Brady had thought he would be.

Annie pulled out her phone and read over the corporate page for Hughes Properties, the company that owned the restaurant on the matchbook and the very diner they were standing in. The biggest employer in the county. A headshot of Kingston Hughes matched the man sitting across from a very likely a corrupt judge. Didn't mean Hughes was corrupt, too, she reminded herself. *Judge not*, her grandmother used to say, paraphrasing the Bible passage, *until they prove their colors.*

"Sheriff, your term is up in less than a year," Hughes said without even looking up from his menu. "Why don't you just do your job instead of questioning how everyone else does theirs?"

Anger flared in Brady's features. He opened his mouth to say something just as Annie caught his arm. Igniting an argument between Hughes, Harvey and Brady wasn't going to get them any answers. It would only lead to stonewalling and resentment. "Our table is ready," she said.

"Perfect timing," he grumbled. "Have a good day, gentlemen."

She waited until they were seated to speak again. "What was all that back there?"

"That is what you call small-town politics. Kingston Hughes seems determined to back up Judge Harvey, who is determined to let the criminals I arrest go free. And every time I question him about crimes around here, he basically tells me to mind my own business."

"But solving crimes *is* your business." Not the judge's.

"Exactly. It'd be nice if the judge remembered that and backed me up. Or Hughes, who's the one who hired me in the first place." Brady nodded as his gaze went to the other table. "As one of the county commissioners, he also has the power to fire me."

"For doing your job? That makes no sense."

"None of this makes any sense, Annie, which is why I need

more answers from the judge and from Hughes. The check I did on Hughes came up clean, but you know what they say about birds of a feather…" Brady ran a hand through his hair. "I lost my cool when he implied he might fire me. I already lost my cool back with Eddie. I can't do that. This job is more than a job for me, it's a way…"

"A way to save Hunter. I get it, I do. We both have a lot of emotion tied up in all of this, and it's understandable that you would get upset when Hughes said that. Or when Eddie was flippant toward me." His protective spirit was part of what she loved—*wait, loved?*—about him.

No, love wasn't possible. She'd only known Brady for a few days. It was simply all the emotion tied up in these events. It was easy to mistake that for feelings, wasn't it?

He had his head down, studying the menu, his dark brown hair a wavy riot when he didn't have his cowboy hat on. He had a nice profile, a chiseled jaw, broad shoulders and…

Whoa. Not productive, Annie. Not at all.

Thankfully, the waitress came by just then to take their orders—a small bowl of soup for Annie and a hearty cheeseburger for Brady even though they'd just had that fast-food lunch—and when she was gone, Annie refocused on the reason she was here. Jenny. Not a romance with a sheriff who was clearly trying to get his own life together.

She pulled her notepad out of her tote bag. "While you're planning what you're going to do next, I wanted to show you this. I found something interesting with these disappearances. It could be nothing, but I wanted to run it by you."

"You're a smart woman, Annie. If you say you found something, I doubt it's nothing."

The compliment warmed her and for a second left her at a loss for words. The waitress dropped off two glasses of water, giving Annie a second to reorient herself and stop dwelling on the fact that this handsome sheriff had noticed her intellect.

"Okay, so these two girls…" she pointed to Kaitlyn and

Marcy "…were friends in high school. In fact, Kaitlyn was looking for any trace of Marcy when she disappeared. And here's what's even more interesting. I didn't find that information in the case notes. I found it on their social media. As far as I can tell, they didn't know the other two, Pauline and Hailey, but all four of them had one thing in common."

"What's that?"

"They worked right here." Annie pointed at the scuffed tile floor. "At the Bluebird. Kaitlyn and Marcy had photos of themselves in the diner on their social media. There was a note in Pauline's and Hailey's files that they worked in a diner. Look around this town, Brady. Do you see a lot of diners in Crestville? I told you Kingston is somehow wrapped up in this."

"Wait…all of them worked here or at some diner?"

Annie nodded. "Don't forget Jenny was thinking about working here, too, or at least, asked Marco about working here. When she texted me about her car breaking down, I tried to convince her to let me bring her back home, but she was insistent that she didn't want to go back to her mother's house and to her controlling stepfather. She still wanted to meet Dylan, she said, and she told me she'd be fine.

"I offered to pay to fix her car but the repairs she needed cost more than I had available. She told me not to worry. She said something about maybe getting a job to help pay for the repairs on her car and how excited she was because I think she meant to start a new life here, away from her mother and stepfather. It was just a text, so she didn't send many details, just promised to tell me later when we talked. But she disappeared before we could chat."

Across from her, the gears were turning in Brady's mind as he took the puzzle pieces she'd laid before him and assembled them into the germ of a connection.

"Don't you think it's awfully convenient that no one realized all these girls are connected to this diner?" Annie said. "Did anyone even check to see if Dylan or Eddie was, too?"

"There's a lot of things that department has overlooked, it seems," Brady said under his breath.

She could tell he was shocked by the information, by the realization that no one in the department had put this together and realized all of the girls were in some way tied back to this very diner. And the man sitting a few tables away with a judge known to be way too lenient on crime.

"I'll be right back." Brady slid out of the booth. Frustration and tension lined his face. "I'm going to ask nicely if the manager will share his employment records with me."

"Nicely might work better than yelling." She grinned, easing the mood because she could hear the frustration in his voice. "Just sayin'."

"I'll keep that in mind." He leaned down, close to her ear, close enough for her to catch a whiff of his cologne again. "I have an idea, if you're game, that might help a bit with the investigation. Switch seats with me while I'm gone and let me know what the judge and Hughes do."

"Does this mean I'm deputized?"

He chuckled. "No, but I can get you a toy badge down at the five-and-dime if it makes you feel better."

She watched him go, a man on a mission, and thought how much she enjoyed this repartee they had. All of it was as foreign to her as pineapple on pizza. She'd always been the friend to the guys she knew, the one they confided in about relationship problems or asked for help on their homework. The few guys she'd dated had been bookish and quiet, much like herself. This...playful tension between herself and Brady was new and, well, wonderful. She prayed it never ended, even as she knew, eventually, it would. The case would come to some sort of close, she'd go back to Denver, and these lunches in the diner would be a memory.

She sipped at her water while she googled Kingston Hughes and watched the other two men talking, their heads close together, their body language tense and stiff. A few minutes later, the judge got to his feet, tossed a twenty-dollar bill on the table and stomped out of the diner. Whatever had been brewing between them had not ended well. Were they arguing about Brady's questions? Or something more? The glass door swung shut behind Judge Harvey, who disappeared around the corner of the building, in the direction of the courthouse.

Next, Annie saw Hughes get to his feet, pull out a thick clip of cash and peel off some bills. Who used cash anymore? Much less carried around so much of it? She had a thousand questions for this man who somehow, she knew, was tied to all of this.

Before she could think better of it or, worse, let her own anxieties talk her out of acting, Annie got to her feet, heading down the aisle and toward the ladies' room that was just past the cashier station. Hughes turned at the same time, and Annie stumbled into him.

Accidentally. On purpose.

"Oh, I'm so sorry," she said, then paused for a second. "Wait, you're Kingston Hughes, right? The owner of Hughes Steel?"

Kingston was tall where the judge had been squat, with a well-tailored suit and a thick head of salt-and-pepper hair. Everything about him seemed to shine, from the pinstripes in his pale gray jacket to the tops of his leather shoes. His ice-blue eyes narrowed with suspicion and annoyance. "Yeah. So? Don't people say excuse me anymore?"

"I, uh…" She hadn't rehearsed what she was going to say; she'd just acted impetuously, and now, she said the first thing that came to mind. Never a wise choice. "I was just reading about the dip in the steel industry this quarter. That must have been tough on your bottom line."

He scowled. "What do you know about bottom lines or steel? Just get out of my way."

He started to brush past her, but she dug in her pocket and pulled out a business card, one of the ones from her previous journalism job. "I'd love to interview you about how you built success in an industry that is struggling, because from what

I've seen, Hughes Steel has continued to run in the black when everyone else didn't.''

Appealing to his ego worked. Hughes turned back, accepted the card and glanced down at her name. A smile flickered on his face. "Annie Linscott. Seems I've heard your name before. What kind of interview are you thinking about?"

"I work for a number of online publications." Better to remain vague than to promise an article she probably wouldn't write. She wanted an interview—just not about steel.

Her quick research a minute ago told her that Hughes Steel was a major player in Crestville—nearly seventy percent of the people in this town worked for Hughes or lived with someone who did—and that meant Kingston Hughes was undoubtedly a power player in the area. "And I'm also one of the hosts on a popular vlog. Social media is the way to fame, as we all know."

"A vlog? What kind of vlog?"

She didn't want to tell him it was a cold case vlog, but she also didn't want to lie, so she settled on, "Local news. And I'd love to be able to put up an interview with you so people can see how Hughes Steel has made an impact on the community. If you ever want to sit down for an insider interview, just let me know." She purposely left off the words *witness* and *business* before *insider* so that she was more or less telling the truth about what she wanted. Annie turned and started to walk back to her table, moving with a lot of manufactured confidence.

"How's tomorrow afternoon?" Hughes called after her. "Say four o'clock? My office is—"

"I know where you're located. I read all about you." She gave him a nod and hoped the excitement she felt didn't show up on her face. "See you tomorrow, Mr. Hughes."

Chapter Eleven

"You did what?" The next afternoon, Brady paced his office, crossing between the desk and the door, over and over again. He'd finally been able to secure what little there was of the Bluebird Diner employment records—the manager was not going to win any awards for tax compliance or human resources organizational skills anytime soon—and had planned on going through them when he got back from lunch today, looking for the names of the other four young women.

Until Annie told him she had set up a meeting with Kingston Hughes for that afternoon. She'd set it up the day before and he had no doubt she'd waited to tell him until now so that he couldn't talk her out of it.

"I thought if I interviewed him, I could find out more about how he is or isn't involved with all of this. Brady, he *owns* the diner all of these girls worked at and the restaurant on that matchbook. He has got to be connected."

"If your theory is right, then that man is dangerous, Annie. He could be the one behind the SUV following us. The same SUV that threatened you. You shouldn't go alone."

"I can't exactly waltz in there with the sheriff by my side.

That would be like hanging up a neon sign saying he's under investigation. Besides, it's a public space, and I'll be fine."

He could hear the slight tremble in her voice, the flicker of uncertainty in her eyes. Annie wasn't any more confident than he was that this meeting was a good idea. "I still don't like the idea. I can't prove anything but it seems to me that Hughes is involved in all of this somehow. Lunches with the judge, the matchbooks, threatening to fire me…there's a connection I'm just not seeing yet."

"Exactly. He's a shady character in general."

On that he would agree. From the minute he met Kingston Hughes, something about the man had seemed…off, suspicious. "Which is the main reason you shouldn't go alone."

She rolled her eyes. "I am a grown woman, and I have interviewed hundreds of people in my career. I'm pretty sure I can handle this."

He paced some more, but that didn't change the situation or the valid points Annie had made. He was probably overreacting because of the encounter with Hughes yesterday. Even if Hughes was the one following her and threatening her, it was highly unlikely that he would do anything inside the offices of Hughes Steel with hundreds of employees around. But that didn't make Hughes any less of a suspicious character. To tell the truth, Brady had been a little disconcerted by the threat to fire him for questioning Judge Harvey's decisions.

"Either way, you don't get to make the decision, Brady. I do. I promise to call you right after I'm done and—"

"No need to do that. I'm going with you." He put up a hand to stop her objections. "I'll wait in the car, but I don't want you driving out there alone. Remember, that black SUV is still out there. We haven't caught that guy yet."

"I—"

There was a knock at the door, and Wilkins popped his head into Brady's office. "Sorry to interrupt, Sheriff, but we have a…" he glanced at Annie "…situation that you need to be aware of." A situation Wilkins clearly didn't want to discuss in front of a civilian—or a reporter.

"I'll be right back. Don't go anywhere. Especially not to Hughes Steel." Brady ducked out of his office and shut the door. "What is it?"

Wilkins shifted his weight and lowered his voice a little. "You told us to tell you if we came across anything that might be related to those cases, and I'll probably get in trouble with my superior officer for saying anything, because he said this was nothing..." Wilkins glanced around the office. "We just got a report of a missing person, a female, eighteen years old, last seen heading down Hyde Street. My sergeant said to let it go. Probably another runaway. She had a fight with her parents, so she could be a runaway, but—"

"It's probably not a coincidence." That made six girls in the last ten years, all gone in the same geographical area. Either there was some kind of black hole in the middle of Crestville, or someone was purposely luring and abducting these girls. But who? And why? Brady shuddered to think of a serial killer being in their midst but knew that anything was possible. All he could do was start investigating as fast as possible. Maybe this girl had left a trail of some kind. "Why did you come to me if your superior officer told you to let it go?"

"I didn't like you much when you first came to work here. But I'm not big on change, so that might be part of it. We've been doing things the same way in this department for years. Maybe decades." Wilkins glanced over his shoulder again. "I've decided that doesn't mean it's the right way to do things."

"I couldn't agree more. Let's go, Wilkins. I want to see the scene myself. Let me just grab my keys." He'd deal with Willkins's superior later.

Brady hurried back into his office, where Annie sat in the visitor chair, still fuming from their conversation. She was right; she was an adult and could make her own decisions. But he didn't think she understood the violence and evil that lurked underneath the world, the parts that the general public saw peeks of here and there, but law enforcement had seen close-up. Until he could clear Kingston Hughes himself, he didn't want her alone with the guy. "I have to go to a crime scene. Is there any way you can postpone the interview with Hughes until I get back?"

"If I do that, I'm afraid he'll bail. Him agreeing to do this was a spur-of-the-moment thing."

"Well, try. I'd feel much better if I went with you." Brady grabbed his keys out of the dish on his desk. "I don't know how long I'll be."

"What happened?"

He debated telling her the truth, but then again, this could just be a runaway situation, and Brady could be reading things into the sergeant's reaction that weren't there. That area of town had its own set of troubles, which meant a kid taking off after a fight at home could be nothing. Better to find out first and then let Annie know if—and that was still a big if—it was tied to her friend's disappearance. She wasn't, as he'd told her at lunch, a deputy.

"Nothing to worry about," Brady said. "I'll catch up with you later." He avoided looking at her as he passed by and headed out to his car with Wilkins.

Two deputies were already on the scene, knocking on doors and talking to the neighbors. The Hyde Street area wasn't one where residents were especially forthcoming, and virtually every person told the deputies they hadn't seen anything. That was possible, Brady theorized, but improbable, because this was also the kind of neighborhood where people—like Erline—watched everyone around them to make sure they didn't end up like Frank.

Just the thought of how quickly and easily Frank's life had been cut short filled Brady with a sense of outrage and injustice. If only he'd made plans with Frank to leave town one hour earlier, or if he'd insisted Frank go and get help right that second, maybe Frank would still be alive and that much closer to seeing his child. Brady made a mental note to find out where Frank's family lived and take up a collection for his child. It wasn't much, but it was something, and sometimes something was all he could do.

Brady paused as he crossed the street. The crimson stain of Frank's blood had faded some, between the sunlight and cars driving over the spot where he died. In a few weeks, maybe a few months, there would be no trace of Frank's life left in this neighborhood. Brady could see all of Frank's possessions sitting on the lawn outside the duplex where he had lived, probably evicted by the landlord five seconds after word of the shooting got out. Someone else would live there, someone else would buy drugs from the shady guys on the corner and someone else would undoubtedly die because of that.

Brady closed his eyes and drew in a deep breath. These were the moments when he wanted to quit, take early retirement, go work any job that didn't revolve around crime. The same kinds of crimes that had invaded his life, his sister's life, Hunter's and Annie's. If there was some remote planet he could whisk them all away to, a place where drug dealers, kidnappers, burglars and murderers were not allowed, Brady would move there in a heartbeat.

"Sheriff?" Wilkins tapped his shoulder. "Uh, you kind of zoned out there for a second."

"Sorry. Just thinking about the case." Brady cleared his throat and shook the cobwebs from his mind. Dwelling on what-ifs wouldn't get him anywhere. "What have you got for me?"

Wilkins flipped through his notebook, scanning what he'd written down when he talked to the other two deputies on the scene. "One of the neighbors who works at the Bluebird said he saw the girl at the back door around lunchtime. He was taking out the trash and saw her just hanging around, looking like she was waiting for someone."

The diner sat smack in the center of every one of these disappearances. How? Why? Maybe Annie's theory was right. "Go on."

"Then that lady who lives over there…" Wilkins pointed to a house on the corner "…said the neighbor's dog started barking his head off around one o'clock. She looked out the window to see what had the dog all worked up and said she saw the girl getting into a black SUV."

"Willingly or unwillingly?"

Wilkins shrugged. "It's Erline Talbot, you know? Who knows what she saw. Jensen ticked her off, so that's all she'd say. You know how he is when he interviews people. If you want more info, you can talk to Erline yourself, but I'll warn you, she's a nutty old bat who complains if the wind blows the wrong direction, so she's never much help." Wilkins pulled out his cell phone and tapped it. "Also, the DMV sent over the girl's driver's license record, so now we have a photo of her. I'll text it to you."

Brady thanked his deputy, then called Jensen over. The younger deputy repeated the same story he had just heard and reiterated that Erline had stopped talking to him and slammed the door in his face after he questioned her reliability. No one else in the neighborhood had anything to report, or else the other officers hadn't done such a thorough interviewing job, which made Brady think of the caution flag Sanders had thrown up about how this town protected its own.

A town this small, seemed like the residents would be more chatty or gossipy, ready to tell the sheriff's department what they'd seen. But everyone around here seemed to clam up when it came to whatever was going on that made judges release criminals without a trial.

Everyone, it seemed, except Erline Talbot.

Brady headed up to Erline's house. She was sitting on the porch in an old, tattered armchair, watching the deputies sprawled out through the neighborhood and the crime scene techs searching for clues. "'Bout time you came by, Sheriff," she said. "I was afraid you'd be like all the rest."

"What do you mean by that?" Brady leaned against one of the porch posts—a little surprised the decrepit thing held his weight—and set his cowboy hat on the railing.

"Just that nobody in this town seems to want to clean it up. All kinds of trouble has been happening for as long as I can remember." She waved off a fly. "If you really want to know what's happening around here, you gotta go to the source."

"What source is that?"

Erline eyed him up and down, and he could feel the weight of her assessment. "You'll know it when you see it." She got to her feet. "I'm done watching this foolishness. You better find that girl. Since the lot of you didn't bother finding the other one." Her door slammed behind her, conversation over.

Brady headed next door, to where the dog had been barking, and knocked on the door. The grumpy man who answered had a newspaper in his hands while a TV blared in the background. The dog—probably the best witness on this street—was a shepherd mix who went berserk when Brady knocked but turned into a total marshmallow once the door was opened and the mutt had a chance to make friends.

Brady followed up with the second deputy doing knock-and-talks and came back with the same results of a whole lot of nothing. He called up the picture of the girl that Wilkins had texted him. Long, light brown hair, wide, deep green eyes and a smile that had probably cost her parents a fortune at the orthodontist. Ginny Breakstone had a sweet face, the kind that reminded him of every young girl he'd ever met. Friendly, smart, too pretty to end up on the street where Frank had been gunned down in broad daylight. *What happened to you? And how am I going to find you?*

The clock on the wall in Brady's office ticked the time away. Annie fidgeted in her seat and stared at her phone. If she called

Kingston Hughes and rescheduled, she had no doubt that he would cancel entirely. She'd managed to work up just enough feminine wiles to convince him to do an interview; she wasn't so sure she had enough left in reserves to do it again.

At 3:30, with no sign of Brady, she made an executive decision to go anyway. She'd interviewed far scarier people than Kingston Hughes in the past. She didn't need the sheriff around to make sure she asked her questions and spelled his name right in her notes. Annie grabbed her jacket and headed out of the sheriff's office.

"Carl, if Brady asks where I am, tell him I went to my interview." She'd sent Brady a text, too, but hadn't heard back. He must have been busy with whatever they were investigating.

"Be careful there, miss," Carl said as she pushed on the lobby door.

"Of course."

"No, I mean it. You didn't hear this from me, but another girl disappeared today." He shook his head. "I'm just telling you because you never know what might happen. Be aware of your surroundings, miss."

"Another girl disappeared?" She crossed to the reception desk. "Who was it? What happened?"

"I am not giving out details to a member of the press. You can find out yourself when the sheriff makes an announcement. If he makes one. This town is chock-full of runaways, too." Carl scowled. "I'm just telling you to pay attention. That's all. Forget I said anything."

From where she was standing, Annie could see the APB and photo on Carl's screen. Ginny Breakstone, eighteen years old, abducted today from the same place as all the other girls. Another one? Who was behind this? She knew Carl had no answers, so she thanked him and headed out the door.

She kept glancing behind her and down the side streets as she walked. Thankfully, the motel was only a few blocks over, close enough for her to walk and grab her car, since Brady had been her personal chauffer and guardian ever since the incident with the black SUV. She picked up her pace, that ticking clock sounding in the back of her head, alongside Carl's warning. She'd GPS'ed the route earlier—even driving fast, she would need twenty minutes to get to Hughes Steel. Add in time to find a parking space, check in at the front desk… She was barely going to make it on time.

Annie drove as fast as she dared, all the while checking her rearview mirror for the black SUV. There was no sign of it, and she wondered if whoever had been following her had simply given up. Maybe he'd realized that her search for Jenny had nothing to do with him and just let the whole matter drop. A little nagging feeling in the back of her head doubted it.

She pulled into the Hughes Steel parking lot at 3:57, found a parking space in the front visitor lot and snagged it. Just as she hit the lock button on the car remote, she noticed a familiar vehicle in the next row, about ten cars down.

A black Ford Explorer.

No. It couldn't be the same one. There was no way.

The SUV was too far away for her to read the plate, even when she zoomed in with her phone. She was tempted to get closer to snap a pic of the license plate, but she was already cutting it too close on time, and the SUV was in the opposite direction of the front door of the building. When she left, she'd check out the Explorer. Chances were it wasn't even the same car. Hadn't Brady said there were something like a hundred black SUVs in this area? That car could belong to anyone.

As Annie walked into the lobby, she saw Kingston Hughes coming down a sleek glass-and-chrome staircase. Another man walked beside him, someone slightly younger but worn harder by life. She couldn't quite make out who it was, with his craggy face and rumpled suede jacket and a ball cap pulled down low. Or maybe it was just that Kingston, with his immaculate, tailored suit, shiny, expensive shoes and perfectly styled hair, seemed to live on another planet from the guy he was talking to.

They reached the bottom step just as Kingston glanced over and saw Annie standing by the door. Was she mistaken, or did she see a flash of alarm in his features? Whatever it was, the look disappeared, and he broke into a wide smile. He walked away from the other man without so much as a goodbye, Kingston's wide frame blocking her view of him as if by design, and put out a hand in greeting. "Annie Linscott. Welcome to Hughes Steel."

"Thank you for giving me some time this afternoon. I promise to make this as quick and painless as possible."

He chuckled and gestured for her to walk with him. The other man had disappeared in the few seconds Kingston spent greeting her, but she had the weirdest feeling that he was still around, watching her, and that she knew him from somewhere. She shrugged it off and followed Kingston up the same stairs he'd just descended, down a long hall of cubicles and glass and toward a conference room with an expansive view of the Rockies.

"Make yourself at home." Kingston waved toward the table. "There's water and coffee for you. And I'll have Bridgette bring in some pastries."

"Oh, I'm fine. Thank you."

"Great. Let's get to work then, shall we?" He smiled again as he crossed to the conference room door. The office-facing walls were glass, offering a full view of the people in the cubicles and a perfect view for them if they cared about what happened in the conference room, almost like Annie was an animal on display in a zoo. This was a safe space, wasn't it? All open and visible like this?

Kingston swung the door shut, and it settled into the pocket with a soft click.

A shiver ran down her spine. She felt like she had just been shut into a cage with the tiger.

By the time Brady got back to the station, the weight of the day slowed his steps and had dampened his usual belief that all things could be solved, with God's help. He'd interviewed Ginny's distraught parents who said it wasn't like their daughter not to check in with them. The disappearance of Ginny was looking more and more like it was a repeat of the other disappearances, which meant he had a problem on his hands.

A huge one.

The fact that no one wanted to talk to law enforcement wasn't surprising; that often happened, particularly in areas where crime ran rampant. No one wanted to be the snitch who set off a war in the neighborhood between deputies and criminals. But the closed-mindedness and refusal to prosecute among the judicial system—that did surprise Brady. Doing a favor for a friend, assuming Eddie was a friend of Judge Harvey's or even Kingston Hughes's, that could be understood. Not condoned but understood. Brady had a feeling, however, that whatever was going on here extended beyond Judge Harvey. How, he had no idea.

He was tired of not getting answers. With another young woman gone, it was high time someone talked to Brady and told him the truth.

He greeted Carl, who returned the *hello* with a grunt and a nod, and headed into the squad room. His gaze skipped over the deputies working at their desks and went straight to the glass door of his office. No Annie. Was she still talking to Kingston?

He pulled out his phone to text her when Sanders, the chief deputy, came up to him. A fine layer of sweat had broken out on her forehead. Shadows under her eyes spoke of the exhaustion she was clearly feeling late in her pregnancy. She was fiddling with a folder in nervous, jerky movements.

"No offense, Sanders, but you don't look so good."

She'd been the one to mention the threat to officers who stuck their nose where it didn't belong. If anyone knew what was going on, it was Sanders. Any other time, Brady would have waited until she was back to work, but this issue couldn't wait. Not with Ginny's disappearance so fresh.

"According to my doctor, I need to put my feet up." She placed a hand on her abdomen, which barely fit the maternity uniform this close to her due date. "He wants me to go on maternity leave a little early because my blood pressure is kind of high. And I'm just feeling woozy."

Brady was no doctor, but even he knew high blood pressure could be dangerous for mom and baby. "Absolutely. We can cover things here until you get back from leave."

"Actually, I wanted to talk to you about that. Do you have a sec?"

"Sure. And good timing because I wanted to talk to you, too. If you're up to it." Brady gestured toward his office. "As long as you sit down while we're talking. Don't need you passing out on me." He chuckled, but she didn't laugh in return.

Sanders didn't say anything until the two of them were in the room and the door was shut. Even then, she kept her voice so low, Brady had to strain to hear her. "I want to tell you something, but you can't tell anyone else."

"The truth about what's going on here? Because that is something I need to know, Sanders. I don't care what other people have told you or how they've warned you. I can't run a department this way." Sanders had seemed to be a good officer, smart and driven, popular with the other deputies. She seemed to have a good heart and, maybe, a strong conscience.

"Maybe it's time." She glanced over her shoulder at the squad room, then back at him. "Because I'm not coming back from maternity leave. I'm going to use that time to find another job, somewhere far, far away from here."

"Really?" That shocked him, especially because she had done so well in Franklin County. "The sheriff's job will be open once you're back from maternity leave. Not saying I want to leave, but by then, you'll have the necessary years of experience, and I'm sure the commissioners will be glad to appoint a local."

She snorted. "Yeah. They do like keeping locals in power. But I'm not going to be their puppet. I'm done with that."

"Who is pulling those strings, Sanders?" Their conversation a few days earlier had been cut short, but Brady had a hunch that if he pushed her just a little more, Sanders would tell him what was going on. She didn't seem any happier about what was happening than he was.

"You know who. It's not a secret that the person with the most money wields the biggest stick." She shook her head in disgust. "Listen, you getting hired was supposed to be an easy, back-to-the-way-things-always-are decision. When Sheriff Goldsboro died, they lost a lot of control over the county. They wanted to hire someone they could control, and Mason Clark convinced Hughes you'd be a good soldier."

Mason knew Brady better than most people. He knew Brady wasn't the type to fall in line with what some oligarch wanted. Was that Mason's way of making a change in this county before he stepped down as commissioner? Knowing his friend, that was very likely. Mason had seen what was going on in the county and had found a way to hire the one law enforcement officer he trusted to uncover the corruption. "So Hughes went along with it?"

She nodded. "And then he told me in not so many words to let the other deputies know that they should keep you out of the loop. Make your job a little harder. That's why no one warmed up to you in the beginning."

"Is that why the evidence for the jewelry store robbery disappeared? Why there is almost nothing in the files of those young girls who disappeared? Why my deputies aren't asking the questions they're supposed to be asking?" He could feel his frustration rising. A corrupt system, growing more corrupt by the day.

"Pretty much. But there's a few of us. Me, Wilkins and a few others, who are tired of kowtowing to Kingston Hughes. But before we make any waves, we need to know you have our back."

"Of course I do. You tell me what you all need, and I'll support you. Corruption like that should not be allowed to stand."

"I'm leaving, so it doesn't matter to me, but the other guys need to know they'll have a job the next day, no matter what happens with…" She shifted her weight and chewed on her bottom lip, clearly debating what to tell him.

Brady gave her room to talk, leaving a gap in the conversation. It was a tactic that worked in interrogations and, he'd found, in talking to people in general. Sometimes the other person needed space to compose their thoughts, decide on a tactful approach or, in Sanders's case, maybe get up the courage to put the words out into the world.

"There will be repercussions, Sheriff," Sanders said. "For you, for the others, for everyone who so much as writes down a witness statement. Serious repercussions. Just ask Goldsboro. Oh, you can't. Because he's dead."

"I thought he had a heart attack."

"That's the story." She put up a hand that said she refused to go into more detail. He noticed her hand shaking. With fear? Nerves? "Here's the thing. Goldsboro didn't have heart issues. The man ran five miles a day. His 'heart attack' happened after a lunch meeting across the street with a couple people high up the Franklin County food chain. I'll leave you to fill in the blanks about the timing of that heart attack and the fact that he was cremated before an autopsy could be done. The coroner called that an oops."

"That kind of mistake shouldn't happen."

"And yet, in this county, lots of mistakes like that happen. I can't prove anything, but there is more to his death and to most of what happens around here than anyone knows. Wilkins and I have been gathering evidence a little at a time. Because we don't like the way things are any more than you do." She slid the folder across the desk to him. "This might not prove anything, either, but I took a huge risk in having this done, because

I'm tired of what's going on around here and who's pulling all of our strings."

Brady opened the folder. Case report after case report, with notes attached that showed each of the criminals who'd been let go or whose crimes had gone uninvestigated. People who were each, in some way, tied to Hughes, whether as an employee or a friend or a known associate. Beneath those, a stack of disciplinary reports for deputies no longer on the force, who had been fired for insubordination, which Brady suspected was code for *asking too many questions.*

He sifted through the papers and found the money trail, a stack of bank statements that Goldsboro had been sending to the office, maybe to keep the truth from his wife. The statements showed numerous deposits into the late sheriff's account, just a few thousand at a time, but a lot more money than any sheriff would ever make. Who in town would have that kind of money to give to Goldsboro? And whose best interests would it be to keep Goldsboro on the payroll?

All the answers pointed to one person. Kingston Hughes.

At the back of the folder, he found a stack of witness statements and crime scene photos. All of the evidence that had been missing in the folders for Hailey, Kaitlyn, Jenny and the other girls who had disappeared. There'd been a reason their folders were so thin and the investigations seemed cursory—because all of the meat in the investigation had been removed. But not destroyed. "You saved all this?"

"A rainy day always comes along," she said. "I was ordered to destroy it all, but instead, I kept it in a safe place. Now I'm giving it all to you. And I hope you do something with it."

He kept turning pages, and just like Erline had told him they would, the pieces clicked into place, as if they'd just been waiting for someone to flip them over. He reached the last set of crime scene photos, from the kidnapping of Kaitlyn Brown. He could have been looking at the scene where Jenny's shoe had been found. Similar scuffed earth, another discarded purse, its contents strewn across the grass. And a very familiar small white object. "Kingston Hughes is the root of it all, isn't he?"

She didn't nod or shake her head. She stood stock-still. "Like I said, there is more than what anyone knows."

"Then why not stay here? Fight the corruption from this very room?" He pointed at the desk, the chair where she could be sitting when his temporary slot was open.

"Because I've been trying to fight it ever since I got here, Sheriff, and I'm tired of fighting. I have bigger things to worry about. This folder is the best I can do." She cradled her baby bump with both her hands. "More important things to protect. I can't risk…" The sentence trailed off, and she shook her head. Tears glistened in her eyes. "I'm giving you this information so you can make your own decision. But if you know what's good for you and that nephew of yours, Sheriff, you'll find a job somewhere else, too."

"Sanders—"

She had her hand on the doorknob but didn't turn it. "One more thing about those girls. All of them came here because they believed there was something better in Crestville than where they were living. Think about what would tempt a young woman to leave a city like Denver, or any of the places around here, and come to this dump of a town."

"The two biggest motives in the world. Love or money." He thought of Dylan Houston and the dating app. The way he'd brushed off Jenny. Was he part of this, too?

Kingston Hughes thought the smartest person in the room—maybe even on the planet—was himself. The more questions Annie asked him, the more he expounded on all of his *amazing* and *incredible* and *showstopper* achievements. He used words like *industry leader* and *trendsetter* as if he'd invented steel and every product that used it. Within five minutes of starting, Annie wanted to leave and wash the disgust of Hughes's braggadocio off her skin.

The tape recorder she had placed on the smooth walnut surface of the conference table whisper-whirred as it recorded the interview. She'd started with softball questions about how he got started in the steel industry, what his biggest challenges were as the company grew, how he made his mark in the world. Each one opened up another door for him to wax poetic about his own brilliance.

And not give her any kind of entry into asking about the girls who had vanished, his connections with Judge Harvey or why that black SUV was in his parking lot.

"So, why locate your business in Franklin County?" she asked. "Crestville is such a small town and not especially close to any big towns or cities, so how were you so sure you'd find enough of a workforce?"

"Crestville needed me to come in and build this factory," he said, sitting back in his chair and crossing his leg over his knee. "I did it for the town. Judge Harvey and I go way back, and when he said Crestville needed business, I came, I saw and I built."

The little reference to Julius Caesar seemed ironic and, sadly, a true reflection of Hughes's personality. Not to mention how Caesar had ended up—was that where Kingston was heading? Betrayed by his pal? "How do you know Judge Harvey?" Annie put her pen down, as if they were just two friends chatting now.

"Frat brothers. Both of us went to University of Colorado. I was there for my MBA. He was there for his JD. His law degree," Kingston added with a little condescending lilt.

"It's nice to have that kind of history with people." She made sure to smile through her irritation. "I'm sure that makes doing business in Crestville matter all the more."

"It does indeed. It's like extending a helping hand to a family member. I look at everyone in this town as part of my little Hughes Steel family." He opened his arms wide, as if Annie should embrace his faux generosity as much as he did.

She had read the numbers and knew Kingston Hughes was

an extremely wealthy man. He lived on a hundred acres about a half hour away from town, with a custom swimming pool shaped like an H and a nine-hole golf course in his backyard. He'd never married, never had children, but there were rumors that he hosted extravagant and very hush-hush parties for his wealthy friends. She had gleaned that much by searching through the newspaper archives and reading virtually everything she could about him before this meeting.

She'd had more than enough of his grandiose accounts of himself, so she shifted gears and hoped she wasn't making this move too soon. "I'm sure this crime wave in Crestville has concerned you, given how much you care about the town."

He blinked. "Crime wave? In this sweet little burg?"

Yeah, like she was going to fall for that wide-eyed innocent look. He was friends with a judge; he knew exactly what was going on in this town. "There was a murder in broad daylight a few days ago, and a girl was abducted today down on Hyde Street." Annie didn't actually know where the girl had gone missing, but when she said Hyde Street, Hughes visibly blanched and backed up a few inches.

"Well, that crime wave is nothing more than the fallout from drug users," Hughes scrambled to say. "My sources say that murder the other day was more of a drug buy gone wrong. These drug dealers, they come down from the cities and try to corrupt the citizens. I wish the sheriff's department did more to stop them."

"And what about all the girls who disappeared?" Annie leaned forward and decided to take a risk, expose a few more of her cards, link everything together, even though she had no firm proof it was all part of the same story. "Not just one or two, but six. All from this tiny town, over the last ten years. That seems like an awful lot to me."

"Well, ten years is a long time." He pulled a handkerchief out of his pocket and dabbed at his forehead. "Six girls... Are you sure they weren't just runaways?"

"You know, everyone keeps saying that, but if you ask me, that's an awfully big coincidence. Especially here." How she wanted to leap across the table and demand he answer her.

Instead, he seemed to recover some of his bravado. "Coincidence. We're near a major highway, and we get drifters all the time coming in off of I-70. Lots of those kids are just stopping here for a minute before they move on to greener pastures in places like California."

Annie bit back the urge to yell at him and tell him that not all of those young women had been runaways. That some of them had had plans, dreams, families, friends. Things too important to leave behind. "That's a pretty big assumption." She kept her voice level, calm.

"Trust me," he said, leaning across the table and giving her a knowing, creepy grin, "some of those girls were trash. They weren't worth the clothes they were wearing. And they'd do whatever it took to pay for those clothes, if you know what I mean." Then he sat back and had the audacity to wink.

Annie rarely got angry. But right now, she felt a white-hot rage so intense, she was surprised she didn't explode right in that expensive leather chair. "I don't think any woman deserves to be defined like that."

"Some of them ask for it with the way they act. Crestville's better off without girls like that wandering the streets."

Jenny wasn't wandering the streets. Jenny wasn't looking for trouble. Jenny wasn't trash. "Mr. Hughes, you are—"

The glass door burst open. "I told you that you can't go in there!" the receptionist yelled just as Brady stormed into the room and disrupted everything.

Chapter Twelve

No one could say that Sheriff Brady Johnson didn't know how to make an entrance. The shock on Kingston Hughes's face was well worth storming past the reception desk and bursting into the conference room. The frustration on Annie's face, maybe not so much.

"Kingston Hughes, I am arresting you for bribing a police officer," Brady said as he pulled a pair of handcuffs from his duty belt and quickly recited Hughes's Miranda rights. "And I don't trust you not to book a flight to a country with no extradition before we have a chat, so that means you're going to have to wear the law enforcement bracelets."

Hughes scoffed. "I have done nothing wrong. You have nothing on me. And you would be a fool to detain me. I'll have a lawyer here quicker than you can sneeze."

"I have no doubt you will. But until then, you're mine." Brady slapped the first cuff on Hughes's wrist.

Annie sat in the chair opposite, watching the whole thing in shock.

The file Sanders had given him had been the link in the chain that Brady needed. It might not be enough to stand up in court, but it was certainly enough to bring Hughes up on charges, and, maybe, get him to confess. Either way, it gave Brady what he needed to get a warrant for the rest of Goldsboro's bank records—and the trail of where the deposits originated. "You liked to give the girls a little something with your number on it, didn't you? I called the number on those matchbooks, and what do you know... It didn't go to a closed restaurant. It went straight to voicemail. For a phone number owned by your company, Mr. Hughes. You have an explanation for that?"

A flicker of something Brady hoped was fear ran across Hughes's face, then disappeared just as quickly. "I had nothing to do with the disappearance of that girl today. As you can see, I've been in my office, talking to this nice young lady. A friend of yours, I believe, Sheriff?"

"Wrong answer, Hughes. But thanks for verifying exactly what I suspected. I didn't tell you anyone disappeared today, and yet somehow you knew about it."

"Your girlfriend here told me about that poor girl." Kingston nodded at Annie.

Didn't mean that Hughes wasn't connected to the girls, or to the corruption in this town. Brady clicked the second handcuff onto Hughes's wrist. "Let's go to the station."

"Now that, my friend, would be a colossal mistake on your part." Hughes's icy blue eyes met Brady's. "As the county commissioner, I have the power to hire...and fire you."

"You're one of three, Hughes. You can be outvoted."

"How confident are you that the other two commissioners will side with you, an outsider, over the person who employs the majority of the people in this town? The same man who brought Crestville back from the dead?" A crafty smile curved across Hughes's face. "I'm sure you think you hold all the cards, Sheriff, but the fact is, your deck is blank."

"Yeah, well, tell that to the judge. And not Judge Harvey, by the way. I'll make sure he's not there to help you out of this." Brady leaned in, closer to Hughes's ear. "You might have thought I'd be your lapdog when you brought me on, but you were wrong."

* * *

Annie picked up her phone, which she had silenced during the interview, and flipped through the two photos she had taken that day they'd been on Hyde Street. Jenny's shoe and the matchbook from her purse. She realized why the logo for the Rook and Pawn had seemed so familiar. The same image was etched all over Kingston Hughes's corporate headquarters. Everywhere she looked in the conference room and the Hughes Steel building, the reflection of his ego stared back in silver backgrounds, on everything from the company name to the light switch panels. Hubris… The downfall of so many, from Macbeth to Kingston Hughes.

She mouthed a single word to Brady. *Jenny?*

He nodded. His face somber, apologetic, but confirmation that Annie's instincts had been right.

"Come on, Hughes." Brady grabbed the other man by the shoulder and started leading him out of the room, ignoring Hughes's protests and the outraged sputtering of the receptionist.

Just as he reached the front door, the radio on his shoulder squawked. "Sheriff, you better get over to Kent Street right away. It's your nephew."

He clicked the mic. "What happened?"

"Probably nothing, Sheriff. Erline Talbot," the deputy said, the sarcasm clear in his voice, "called in a minute ago and swore she saw a kid that fit your nephew's description get into some kind of truck or something. He was there with that Chip kid we picked up the other day. She said it looked, and I quote, suspicious. But this is a woman who thinks a Domino's guy driving down the street looks fishy, so like I said, probably nothing."

"Okay. I'll try calling him. Send some guys out to the location anyway." He tugged Hughes through the door. Annie followed behind them, using her phone's camera to capture some footage that she hoped she could use later, if this arrest led to the solving of Jenny's case.

"I hope you find your nephew, Sheriff." Hughes flashed him a faux frown of pity. "It is mighty disturbing when our children go missing, isn't it? What a shame it happened to your family. Such an emergency is surely worth attending to right away, isn't it?"

Brady ignored Hughes's chilling words, but they lingered in Annie's mind as she watched the sheriff lead the other man away and put him in the back seat.

Annie agreed to meet Brady back at the station and headed out to the parking lot to grab her car. When she got to her car, she stopped. A shiver ran down her spine, a tingling that told her something was wrong. Annie spun around, expecting to see someone there, watching her, waiting to attack. There was nothing but a sea of cars as far as she could see. Red, green, gray, blue...

No black SUVs.

That was what was missing. The black SUV was gone. A coincidence, after the radio call to Brady about Hunter? *It is mighty disturbing when our children go missing, isn't it?*

There was no reason for Hunter to be kidnapped. It had to be a mistake. But she couldn't shake the feeling that the man she'd seen talking to Hughes, the black SUV and Hunter's disappearance were all connected.

Her phone rang just as she was getting into her car, and she saw it was Mia. "Hi, what's up?"

"Great job on the vlog! I saw that the Denver TV station ran a story about it on the noon newscast. They said they'd run a longer interview on the six o'clock news. Vlog traffic has doubled."

"That's awesome. I'm so glad." Maybe that meant someone would comment who had information about Jenny, or at the very least, more people would care about what had happened to Kaitlyn, Marcy, Pauline, Hailey, Jenny and now Ginny, because of the news coverage. Those young women would no longer be statistics who had been forgotten.

"Keep up the good work. And when you're done in Crestville, let's talk about your next assignment." Mia and Annie talked a little bit more about the vlog and other stories that Mia had waiting in the wings.

When Annie hung up, she expected to feel elated. She'd done it. Overcome her anxieties, filmed a successful show and brought attention to cases that had been swept under the rug. But as she flipped through the video and photos on her phone, all she could keep coming back to was the image of Jenny's shoe. That flash of pink against the earthy brown and the open purse a few feet away.

Annie studied the photo of the matchbook. The phone number on it, Brady had said, went to a line Hughes owned. Why would Jenny have this? There was nothing especially unique about the matchbook. Run-of-the-mill, a logo for the restaurant on one side, hours and location on the other side. The silver color winked back at her under the interior lights of her car, almost mocking her.

Jenny had been with someone associated with that restaurant and phone number, that much was clear. The Rook and Pawn had closed down years ago, so whatever tie had existed was probably no longer there. Still, it seemed as if this picture, this clue, was a nudge from God, telling Annie to push her investigation one step further.

What were the chances the egotistical Kingston Hughes would blurt out a confession? Zero. The man was going to lawyer up and stonewall Brady as long as he could. Without more concrete evidence than a matchbook, Jenny's fate would still be unknown. There was no way Annie wanted to go home to Denver and tell Helen Bennett that she'd failed to exhaust every single resource she had. The Rook and Pawn might be a dead end, but it was the only end she had right now.

She brought up her text messaging app, wrote a few words and sent the message off to Brady. He couldn't be mad at her for pursuing this one last lead. Surely, with Kingston Hughes in custody, there was nothing to worry about.

Maybe.

The empty spot that had held the black SUV told her some-one was still out there. Someone who had warned her to drop the investigation.

Someone who might have taken Hunter.

That fact spurred her into action. She drove across town, to a location about a mile from Erline Talbot's house. She thought again of how close geographically all of these locations were. The Rook and Pawn sat on the corner of Pierce and Main, in a prime location. She could imagine that back in the day, the res-taurant had done well, especially being so close to the highway. With that kind of setting, why would it have closed? Maybe the pandemic, which had put so many other food service compa-nies out of business, had been the final straw.

The lot was empty, save for a pile of trash overflowing the dumpster and a rat that scurried behind the green metal bin as soon as Annie stepped out of her car. She walked around to the front of the building and peered inside the small square window on the dark blue door that sported a circular silver sign, with the chess pieces of a rook and pawn underlining the name of the restaurant.

The dim interior was full of neatly stacked tables and chairs, all pushed to the sides, leaving a clear and wide path down the middle. It reminded Annie of the end of the school year, when the teacher would ask them all to do the same, so the janitor could mop and wax the entire floor.

But if the restaurant knew it was closing, why would Hughes spend the time and resources on polishing the floor? He didn't strike her as the kind of person who chased losing propositions with more money. Maybe he'd intended to put the building on the market?

If that was so, why had it sat unoccupied for the better part of three years?

Annie videotaped with her phone as she walked around the outside of the building, peeking in the windows and seeing pretty much the same thing from every angle. No activity, nothing that suggested anyone had been in this building in the last few years. She sighed. What had she really expected? For Jenny to just pop out from behind the door and say, *Surprise! This was all a bad dream*?

Annie headed back to her car but stopped when she saw a small white door just to the left of the dumpster, with a little sign above it that said Rook and Pawn Loading Area: No Parking. As she crossed toward the door, she noticed something that made her blood run cold.

Scuff marks.

Disturbances in the dirt.

And a lump of dark denim she had seen before.

Annie bent down to take a closer look, zooming in with her phone to document it all. She was just reaching for the backpack when she heard a sound behind her.

And then the world went black.

It took an agonizing fifteen minutes to get Hughes back to the station and set him up in an interview room before Brady had a second to check on Hunter. First, he texted his nephew, but the message went green and said Undelivered. He tried phoning, but it went to voicemail. Brady sent out a call to the patrol officers, but no one had seen him.

It wasn't unusual, he knew, for a teenager to ignore an adult, especially an adult uncle in law enforcement. He got that it was completely uncool to have a pseudo-parent who was also a sheriff, but that didn't mean Hunter could just drop off the face of the earth.

Every single time Brady dialed, his nephew's phone went straight to voicemail. At first, the annoyance had originally frustrated Brady as the antics of a teenager who wanted to be left alone, because it was something Hunter did from time to time when he wanted to avoid a lecture. When his calls skipped the ringing and went to Hunter's voicemail, he thought of Tammy and her silent phone whenever she went on a bender. His sister had avoided truth and consequences by simply being unavailable, unreachable and invisible. And very nearly died because of that. That possibility scared the pants off Brady.

Brady got in his truck and spent an hour searching the streets of Crestville for Hunter. School had gotten out three hours ago, so he couldn't be there, but Brady still checked. He asked the patrol deputies to do another round, but no one found any trace of Hunter. The report that Brady had chalked up to another one of Erline Talbot's cranky calls was quickly becoming something much worse.

He stopped by the older woman's house. After giving him an earful about how long it took him to believe her, Erline told Brady that between episodes of *Judge Judy*, she'd seen a dark SUV roll down the street, stop to talk to two young men who sounded a lot like Chip and Hunter, and then leave again with only Hunter inside. "That boy didn't look none too happy about going in that car, I tell you," Erline had said. "His friend took off right quick after that, too. Whole thing seemed suspicious."

A little more prodding and questioning, and Erline remembered the SUV being black, boxy, big. He showed her a picture of a Ford Explorer, and she verified that was what she'd seen. A black SUV. Just like the one that had tracked him. Just like the one that had thrown a threatening note at Annie's door. And very likely the same one that had whisked Hunter off to God knew where. Brady called into the station and asked them to track down Chip and Eddie.

It wasn't until Brady went into his phone for the twentieth time to call Hunter that he realized he had one unread message from Annie.

Went to check out Rook and Pawn. Will text when I'm on my way back. It's Taco Tuesday, BTW. Want to get tacos with Hunter later? My treat.

Brady dialed Annie's phone, which also went to voicemail. The lack of ringing sent a foreboding rumble through his gut. Both Hunter and Annie gone and their phones off? If that was a coincidence, it was the worst of all coincidences.

Back at the office, he heard the rising crescendo of voices and a crowd gathering around Sanders. Had she gone into labor? He hurried over to the group and pushed his way through them. Sanders sat at a desk, her head in her hands, tears streaming down her face. "What happened?"

"My sister's gone." The words were a whisper. "I told you he'd retaliate. I never should have gotten involved. And now…"

"There will be no 'and now,' Sanders. We will find her." He glanced up at the deputies around him. "This is one of her own. We are not going to let this happen in our town, are we?" Before they could respond, he barked orders, sending a group of deputies out to search for Sanders's sister, Beth, and another group to follow up on where she was last seen and anyone who might have talked to her.

"Thank you," Sanders said.

"I won't let anything happen to anyone in my family," Brady said. "Every one of you deputies is family. We take care of each other, because that's the only way good wins."

She nodded, tears streaming down her face. "I hope you're right."

"Sheriff?" Wilkins came running up to Brady, partly out of breath. "Someone here wants to talk to you."

"I don't have time, Wilkins. I need—" Then he saw who was standing in the lobby and cut off the sentence. "I have time for this."

Twenty minutes later, it all made sense.

When Annie came to, all she saw was darkness. For a second, she thought she still had that hood or bag or whatever it was around her head, but no, the scratchy fabric was gone, and she was in an incredibly dark room. She heard a sound beside her, someone coughing, then someone else crying softly.

Her eyes slowly adjusted to the space, and the outlines of things came into view, barely illuminated by a sliver of light coming from the door across from her. A single cot. A bucket. And two women.

"Hello?" Annie said softly. "Where are we?"

"Shh. They'll hear you," said the woman closest to her. "And then they'll come."

The other woman started crying even harder.

Annie shifted, trying to get comfortable, but the ropes holding her in place cut into her wrists. Her feet were bound together, making it impossible to do much more than just bend her legs. The wall behind her was cold, metallic, the floor hard concrete. Where was she? "Who are you?"

"Shh." The other woman's whisper was harsh and sharp.

A sniffle, then, "Ginny. Ginny Breakstone."

Ginny? The girl who had disappeared earlier today? "Hi, Ginny," Annie said, trying to keep her voice from betraying the terror that had a chokehold on her throat. "People are looking for you, so don't worry, I'm sure we'll be out of here soon. In the meantime, I'm Annie Linscott."

"Nice to meet you, Annie," Ginny said, then she snorted. "I take that back. I don't want to meet anyone—"

"Will the two of you shut up?" The first woman again. "I don't want him coming in here."

"Who?" Annie asked.

Just then, the door opened, a heavy metal door that screeched on its hinges, flooding the space with light. The kitchen beyond the door was full of stainless steel and a faded green tile floor.

A man stood in the doorway. A man Annie recognized from that day in Brady's car. The man who had been standing on the corner with the kid selling drugs. The same man, she realized, who had been on the stairs earlier today, talking to Kingston Hughes, with a ball cap pulled down over his long, dark hair.

Eddie "the Answerman" Anderson.

He stalked forward, his boots slapping the concrete floor, and the woman beside Annie, the one who had kept warning them all to be quiet, shrank away from her, letting out a little shriek as she leaned as far away as she could. Ginny started crying again.

Annie opened her mouth to say something just as Eddie reached down and yanked her up by her hair, sending a sharp pain searing across her scalp.

"Shut up!" he screamed in her face. "All of you! Shut up before I make you shut up forever!"

"Wh-wh-what do you w-w-want with us?" The words stammered out of her. Her pulse roared in her ears and her arms burned where the ropes pulled her back.

"It's not what I want." And then Eddie smiled, a sinister curve of his face that sent waves of nausea through Annie's gut. "Gotta keep the merchandise in good condition."

Had he just said what she thought he said? This was worse than anything she could have imagined, worse than the drugs, worse than Kington's obvious greed. She thought of the conversation with the Denver television anchor about the rise in rural trafficking. Young girls lured in by fake boyfriends and fake job offers, only to be forced to work in the sex industry. She thought of Dylan Houston, saying all the right words to Jenny, the words that lured her to this small town. To this same room?

Was that what had happened to Jenny? Kaitlyn? Marcy? Pauline? Hailey? Was that where she and the other women were going? To be sold somewhere and for who knew what? *God, help us, please help us.* She had to find a way out, a way to get all of them out. But all she saw was the cold metal walls of what had once been a walk-in cooler, an impenetrable tomb where no one would hear them scream.

The silver toes on Eddie's boots gleamed in the darkness, and she remembered Erline's words. *He was wearing black*

*leather boots with shiny things on them. I remember thinking
that was odd at that time of year.*

The man who had taken Jenny had on boots like that. Whatever had happened to her friend was going to happen to every
single one of them in this room if Annie couldn't get free. She
fought against his grip, every movement sending another searing pain through her scalp. She needed to buy time, to get him
talking, to let him know she knew the truth so that maybe he
would make a mistake.

"Where is Jenny? Kaitlyn? Marcy? Pauline? Hailey? *Where
are the others?*" She raised her voice as loud as she could, praying someone, anyone, would hear her outside the restaurant.
A feeble, wasted prayer, but the only one she had right now.

"You don't listen too good, do you?" Eddie yanked her hair
again, pulling her body forward so hard and so quick, he nearly
dislocated her shoulders. "You didn't listen when I warned you
that you would end up like her. So now you'll find out the answers yourself."

The woman who had shushed Annie began to cry. She leaned
toward Ginny, the two of them pressing their shoulders together, two terrified young women who had no way out. Just
like Annie.

She heard a sound coming from the opposite corner, the
part of the walk-in cooler that was still in shadows, out of the
cone of light coming from the kitchen. "Stop! Let her go!" the
voice said, hoarse and raspy. A figure moved, then sat up, and
a pair of terrified brown eyes met hers.

Hunter.

Oh, God, no, not him, too. They were going to need a miracle to get out of this. A miracle even Annie, with all her faith,
doubted would be here in time.

Brady drove faster than he'd ever driven in his life, lights and
sirens on, squealing his way through the intersections, fishtail-

ing as he made a hard turn. An overwhelming tidal wave of fear and worry roared inside him, pushing him to go faster, harder.

Just before he got to the restaurant, instinct took over, and he slowed the car. He couldn't go in there guns blazing if he didn't know everything he was dealing with, or if they were even inside the building. A few minutes ago in Brady's office, a nervous, contrite and penitent Dylan had assured him that it was shipment day and all the major players would be here as part of the trafficking ring that had taken Jenny and the others, a fact Dylan had lied about before.

Dylan had let his fear of Hughes run his life for a long time. Hearing Jenny's name again reminded him that he needed to— finally—do the right thing and connect some of the dots for the sheriff's department.

For the four millionth time, Brady glanced over at the silent iPhone beside him on the seat, a phone that had not been able to reach either of the people he loved. Neither of them had called or replied to his many texts. He had the sinking feeling that when he found Annie, he'd also find out what had happened to his nephew.

Brady parked a block away from the restaurant, stashing his sheriff's vehicle behind a small building, out of sight of anyone who might be inside the Rook and Pawn. Then he drew his gun and crept down the sidewalk, being careful to stay out of sight, to dart from space to space, to use the early evening shadows to hide his approach, until he was against the brick exterior wall of the restaurant. He peeked in the windows. Furniture piled up, covered in cobwebs. No activity. No people.

But then, he saw a small circle of light spilling into the room from behind a pair of swinging doors. The kitchen. Someone— or maybe more than one someone—was in the back.

Brady ducked around the back of the building to where the dumpster was, out of sight of the street, hidden in the shadows beside a taller brick building that had once been a warehouse of some kind. That was when he saw Annie's small gray Toyota, and he knew without a doubt that she had never made it out of that building. He bent down beside her car, duckwalking past it to the door. Just before he got there, he saw a flash of denim on the ground, and a Chicago Bears key chain hanging off the zipper.

Hunter's backpack.

Brady didn't take time to process that or to allow any other feeling other than calm rationality to enter his brain. He couldn't get overwhelmed by what-ifs right now. He had to keep proceeding as if this was any other crime with any other victims. Even if his heart knew otherwise.

He listened at the gap between the door and the jamb, and could barely make out the murmur of voices, too muffled for him to hear what they were saying. He needed to find a way inside that restaurant without those inside detecting him. But how?

He could see why they'd chosen this spot. With the restaurant and warehouse closed, there was not a lot of traffic in this area of town. The road led to the more desolate area where Brady lived. And without much business in the area anymore, there were few people driving by or even in shouting distance. Not to mention, people in this town had a habit of not reporting crime—so that they wouldn't be the next victims. Brady was on his own with this one.

The front door was too obvious and gave whoever was inside an advantage to shoot first, because they would be able to draw before Brady could get across the length of the restaurant and into the kitchen. Opening the back door put him at a different disadvantage because he didn't know where the bad guys were in relation to that door, how many of them were waiting or whether anyone was armed. For all he knew, Annie could be on the other side of this door, a human shield who would be expendable to people like this.

That meant he needed another way in. In other words, a miracle.

Chapter Thirteen

Eddie dropped her onto the floor like a sack of garbage and stormed out of the room. Annie crawled a few feet in Hunter's direction, stretching the ropes as far as their limited reach allowed. It still wasn't enough to do more than stare at him from a few feet away. She could see the fear in his eyes, in the way his body trembled, and wished so badly she could hug him, comfort him. "Are you okay?"

"Yeah, I think so. Where are we?"

"I think we're in the walk-in cooler at an abandoned restaurant." Annie shifted to relieve some of the pressure on her arms. Behind her, Ginny had started crying again while the other woman had gone silent. "How did you end up here?"

"I went to hang out with Chip, and as soon as I got there, these guys grabbed me. I think Chip set me up because they knew where we were. They blindfolded me and threw me in the back of some kind of SUV, and then put me in here."

"He's going to come back," the other woman said. "Don't make him come back. Please."

"Hang on, Hunter. I'll think of something." Annie crawled back to the two women.

Ginny had her knees drawn up to her chest, her head resting on top. The other woman glared at Annie.

"I get that you're scared," Annie said. "I'm scared, too. But we have to work together if we're going to get out of here."

The other woman scoffed. "How? We're all tied up. We're locked in a *refrigerator*. No one will hear us scream. There's no point in even hoping to get rescued."

"Hope is the whole point of life," Annie said and wished she believed that a little bit more right now herself. She was struggling to keep her optimistic attitude and could barely hold on to the belief that somehow Brady would find them all in time. "What's your name?"

The other woman sighed. "Beth."

"Good. That's a great start. Beth, Ginny, the young man over there is Hunter. He's the sheriff's nephew."

"The…" Ginny gaped. "But why would they kidnap him?"

"I think to send a message about who controls this town." Kingston's threats came back to mind, the way he'd seemed so sure that Brady would let him go. Brady's story about the judge who refused to prosecute, the department that seemed afraid to enforce the laws. Kingston Hughes clearly ruled this area and wanted to make sure both Annie and Brady knew it.

She'd sent that text message to Brady telling him where she was. She could only pray that he had read it and realized she hadn't come back and was either waiting outside or on his way. Then again, with his nephew missing, following up on her daredevil expedition might not be his highest priority right now. That meant they were on their own. "We may be tied up, but I'm sure we can do something to get loose if we put our heads together. There's got to be something we can use."

"Listen. Annie, is it?" Beth asked. "This is not some movie where I'm magically going to produce a pair of scissors in my pocket. None of us have phones, weapons or anything that can get us out of this. The best we can do is cooperate with that evil man until someone realizes we're missing. I'm at least three hours late for brunch with my sister, so maybe she's looking for us."

"Who is your sister?" Annie asked.

"Chief Deputy Sanders."

"I can't believe they kidnapped two family members of the sheriff's department. They've got to be stupid or really confident," Ginny said.

"I think they took me to send a message, too," Beth said. "Because they said my sister would leave them alone after this."

Had Kingston Hughes put this kidnapping into motion after Annie questioned him? Was this his way of making sure the sheriff's department dropped the case? Hold Sanders's sister and Brady's nephew until they dropped the charges?

And what was their plan if Brady refused to let Hughes go?

"Listen, we can't think about any of that right now. We can't let them take us out of here, to whatever the next place is." Annie shuddered at the thought of where that could be. How terrified Jenny must have been, or any of the young women who had been kidnapped like this. She didn't even want to picture what her friend had gone through. "If we have to go, fine, but I'd rather go there fighting, wouldn't you?"

"I want to fight back," Ginny said. "If you fight with me."

"We all will," Hunter said, his voice strident now, the trembling gone. The confident, cocky teenager she'd met was front and center. Good. They were going to need that kind of strength from everyone in this room if they were going to survive.

"But how?" Beth shrugged her shoulders, making the ropes behind her tug against the metal bar that was mounted to the wall. "How are we going to get out of this?"

"By using the one thing they didn't take away from us. Our brains." A pair of scissors would definitely have been a better plan, but like Beth said, this wasn't Hollywood. She had nothing to work with but herself. Annie scooted around and turned her back to Beth. She wriggled her fingers and brushed against the ropes binding Beth's arms in place. "Come closer. Let me try to untie you."

"These ropes are too thick. You'll never be able to do it."

"We won't know unless we try, will we?" Annie met Beth's gaze and saw the frailty of a terrified human inside her eyes. "Let's try together."

It took a second, but finally, Beth nodded. Resolution edged a little of the fear out of her features.

Brady ducked back behind the pharmacy next door to the restaurant. He hid behind the corner of the building, in a place where he could see any activity in the restaurant but be out of earshot of anyone inside that building. This was not a bust he should make alone. But whether any of his deputies were willing to go up against Hughes and his gang was another story.

He clicked his radio. "Johnson to Base. I have a ten thirty-three, I repeat, a ten thirty-three," he said, giving the code for an emergency. "My nephew and at least one female have been kidnapped and are being held inside the Rook and Pawn. I suspect Sanders's sister may be here, too." He gave the address and repeated the information. "I need all the backup I can get. All deputies report to this location immediately."

There was no response for a long second. Then Wilkins. "Repeat, Sheriff? I think you broke up."

He said it all again, his voice more urgent this time, more commanding. "I need backup, repeat. Backup. Send all available deputies."

Another moment of silence, and in that soft hiss of the radio, Brady heard the unspoken message coming across the line. They were all afraid. They'd seen what Hughes and his people had done to Goldsboro, to Brady's family, to Sanders's family, to so many young girls, shop owners and others in this town. Those who resisted were punished, and like Sanders, none of them wanted to put their families at risk. Not if they would end up disappearing. "I know Hughes has a chokehold on this county and on your jobs. I know you're all scared of crossing him. Scared for your families. Scared for yourselves. But his men have my nephew and Annie in there and very likely have Sanders's sister, too. I'm not going to let their threats keep me out. If that was your son or your wife, what would you do?"

Again, nothing from the radio. "I'm going in. If the rest of you are tired of being controlled like puppets, you'll know where to find me. I have your backs."

Then he clicked off, turned down the volume of the radio so the sound wouldn't broadcast his arrival and began to creep around the brick building to what he hoped was an entrance that would give him the upper hand.

"It's not getting any looser," Beth whispered. "This isn't going to work."

Annie refused to admit Beth was right, but she'd made almost no progress in getting them untied, either. The ropes were thick, wrapped several times, and her fingers were barely able to reach the knot. "There has to be a rock, a piece of glass, something we can use to break through the ropes. Ginny, Hunter, look all around you." Annie began patting the ground behind her blindly, shifting to cover every square inch.

Beth shot her a look of jaded disbelief but began doing the same. A few minutes passed, agonizing and terrifying. Those men could come back at any second.

"I found something. I think." Beth scooched up to Annie and pressed a piece of glass into her fingers. "Will it be enough?"

"I hope so." Annie put her back to Beth's again, but before she could begin sawing away at the rope, the door opened again. Annie darted back into place, and shifted her butt over the piece of glass.

"You." Eddie pointed at Ginny. "You're coming with me, because you're the prettiest. I have a special order for a girl like you." He crossed the space in three strides, whipped out a massive hunter's knife and cut the rope between Ginny and the pole on the wall. It released with a terrifying *snick*. "Come on, I don't have all day." He yanked her to her feet.

She let out a little cry—of pain, of terror—and stumbled a couple steps forward, then began to crumple.

Eddie yanked her up again. "Don't even think about playing damsel in distress. Get moving, or this will get a lot worse for you." He spun back, dragging Ginny with him as he did. "As for the rest of you, don't be jealous of this one here. It'll be your turn in just a couple minutes. We're taking you to the next place very soon. Call it our distribution center." His gold tooth shone like a dagger in the dim light.

"No!" Hunter shouted. "Don't take her." He tried to get to his feet, to bust through the ropes, but Eddie felled him with one wide kick. Hunter crumped to the floor with a thud. The heavy door swung nearly shut, leaving Beth, Annie and Hunter alone.

"Hunter!" Annie cried, but there was no response. "Hunter! Are you okay?" She strained at the ropes, but there was no way to get close enough to check on him. She scrambled back to Beth, picked up the piece of glass and went back to work on sawing at the thick bindings. Nothing from the boy. "We don't have much time."

Beth cast a worried look at the door. "I think we're already out of time, Annie."

"Have faith," she whispered and prayed she would be able to do the same.

Brady found two cement blocks, just high enough to get him to the bathroom window. He pushed on the bottom panel of the window, slowly, carefully. It let out a creak of complaint, and he eased up, pushing it a millimeter at a time. Each second that passed was agony to him. His brain kept thumping, *Get in there, get in there, get in there.*

With Hughes hopefully still detained at the sheriff's office, the rest of his men would be desperate, maybe even chaotic in their choices because their leader was unreachable. Desperate people did stupid things. Like kill innocent hostages.

He strained to hear the sound of sirens, but the air was eerily quiet. He refused to believe that when push came to shove, his deputies would let Sanders's sister become another victim. He remembered his conversation with Tonya when they'd talked about what would lure a young girl like Jenny to a place like this.

Love or money, Brady had said to Annie. Brady had to pray the power of love was a lot stronger than the lure of money. Or the threat of violence.

Finally, the window was open enough for Brady to squeeze through. He hoisted himself up, wriggled through the narrow opening, using the panels of the stall to stop his body from falling and to help ease his way down to the floor. As soon as his boots met the tile, he took out his gun and froze, listening.

He could hear voices now. A man. A woman. She was crying, begging for her life. The man was laughing, taunting her.

Rage pounded behind Brady's eyes, but he held his cool. Thinking with his emotions would cause him to make a misstep. He had to take all thoughts of Hunter and Annie out of the equation so that he could think like a sheriff, not a worried uncle and boyfriend.

Wait, *boyfriend*? That was a status he would define later if— no, when—he had Annie safely back in his arms. Because he knew without a doubt that he loved her, and he would do whatever it took to save her and the little family they had created.

Brady crept toward the bathroom door and slowly pushed it open, into a little hallway that provided some cover between him and the kitchen. He slipped into the hall and pressed his back to the wall, taking a second to orient himself to where he was. Dining area to the left. Kitchen to the right. A rough pale gray wallpaper behind his back, soft black carpet to deaden the sound of his boots.

He crept down the hall, taking slow, measured steps, even

as the sound of crying urged him to go faster. He came around the corner, leading with his gun, and saw Ginny Breakstone, bound to a chair, sobbing, her shirt torn, her hair disheveled, and Eddie the Answerman with a large knife in his hands. The blade glinted in the light, lethal and terrifying.

"Freeze! Sheriff's Department!" Brady stepped into the kitchen, widening his stance, planting his legs and aiming his gun at Eddie's head.

The other man took his sweet time turning a slow semicircle. "So glad you joined the party, Sheriff. Too bad you won't be here to see how it ends."

In his opposite hand, Eddie held a gun, now aimed at Brady. Another man stepped out from behind a row of shelves and trained his rifle on Brady's chest. Brady was outgunned, outmanned and out of time.

"Go get the rest of them," Eddie said to a third man who appeared from around the corner. "So the sheriff can see what we do to nosy women like his girlfriend."

Shouting. Screaming. Then more shouting. What had happened to Ginny? What was going on outside this door?

Eddie had left the door to the walk-in refrigerator ajar when he dragged Ginny out, allowing a line of light to creep into the room, but not enough for Annie to see the entire space or what she was doing. It was like being in a tunnel with a partial blindfold. She could hear things happening but not enough to put them together into some semblance of awareness.

"Are you done yet?" Beth whispered. "I hear footsteps out there."

Annie did indeed hear the heavy clomps of someone coming closer. Eddie again? To grab one of them next? To take Hunter? She tried to see the boy across the room, but all she could make out was a slumped form. "Hunter? Are you okay?"

No response. Nothing at all.

Annie shifted, trying to wedge the slice of glass deeper into the rope. She could feel pieces of it fraying, slowly unraveling, one thread at a time. "I'm getting it. I don't know if I'm getting close, though."

"Let me check."

Annie pulled the glass back, tucking it into her palm as Beth wiggled her fingers into the space and felt along the edge of the rope. "What do you feel?"

"I think you're halfway through. Hurry, Annie."

Across the room, Annie heard Hunter moan and groan. Thank God he was conscious. "What's going on?" he asked.

Annie slid the glass back into place, but the harder she pressed, the more the sliver cut into her palm. Warm blood dripped down between her fingers. The tight ropes on her wrists were cutting off her circulation, making her fingers less and less useful with every passing second.

"I've almost—"

The door burst open, and a short, squat man in a leather jacket strode in. Someone new, which meant there were at least two people out there they had to get past. Every passing second made the situation seem even more futile. "Time's up, girls. Let's go."

He yanked at the rope tying Beth to the pipe, so hard she let out a cry of pain, and used his knife to slice through it. The knife gleamed in the dim interior, almost as if it was taunting Annie with its efficiency. If she could somehow get that knife…

The man grabbed Beth by one arm and yanked her to her feet. She glanced at Annie, at the same time Annie shifted her foot forward. Beth read the unspoken message in Annie's face and crumpled to the left, causing the man to step just far enough to the side that Annie could trip him. He fell to the floor with an angry thud. The knife bounced out of his hands and skittered across the concrete floor.

"Hunter, get the knife!" Annie yelled.

Hunter swung one leg out in front of him and toed at the knife, which was just out of his reach.

The man began shouting as he got to his feet. "You're stupid, worthless!" He kicked Beth in the side, and she curled into a ball, trying to protect herself from the blows.

Annie lunged at him with the lower half of her body, swinging out both legs, aiming for his knees, but she was too far away, and her kick barely glanced at his calf.

Still, he roared in rage and turned on her. "I'm going to kill you!" He was on her in seconds, a gun pressed to the soft space beneath her jaw, the metal hard and cold and terrifying.

"No!" Hunter screamed. "Leave her alone."

"Maybe I'll kill you first. I never wanted to take you anyway. Too much trouble."

She heard the terrifying click of the hammer cocking into place and then—

Shots.

Brady had fired his service weapon on the job only a handful of times in his years in law enforcement. Despite what people saw on TV, the life of law enforcement wasn't one huge car chase or standoff with suspects. Until today.

Eddie and two of his men stared at Brady, their weapons steady on his chest and head. Brady had worn his Kevlar vest, but that would do nothing to stop a bullet in his temple. And even at this close range, a bullet hitting his bulletproof vest could cause serious damage or incapacitation.

"Get them out of here!" Eddie called to someone in the back. "If any of them resist, kill them. Starting with the sheriff's girlfriend."

"I have this place surrounded, Eddie." It was a lie that Brady prayed was the truth. "You're not going to get anywhere."

He scoffed. "Really? I don't see a single cop outside this place. Maybe because the entire department is in Kingston's back pocket. When you pay people enough, they'll do about anything you ask."

"Is that what all this is about? Money?"

"Money, power, control, name your poison." Eddie shrugged. A chilling, easy gesture that spoke volumes about how he eyed the victims in his hands. "Me, I'm in it for the money. Kingston always finds a way to keep his people in line. Whether that's a shiny new car to pay you for bringing us a pretty young girl or a stack of cash when you teach a jewelry store owner a lesson." He took a step forward. "Just like how we're going to keep our new sheriff in line by using his nephew and girlfriend as leverage."

Brady forced his face to remain passive, to keep the icy fear in his chest from showing and giving Eddie even a moment of satisfaction. "What are you going to do to them?"

"The same thing we did with all the others. Put them out on the streets and let them earn. Ain't no free rides around here. Right, guys?"

The man standing behind Eddie didn't respond; the other one was still gone, dealing with the hostages. There was a movement in the back of the kitchen, and Eddie glanced over his shoulder. It was a split second of distraction, but enough of an opportunity for Brady to fire at the taller of the two men and then lunge at Eddie.

The other two men fired at him, but Brady had already tackled Eddie to the floor. He put a gun to the other man's temple. "Either one of you move, and I'll kill him. Put down your weapons."

The taller of the two men stepped forward. "You think we care what happens to him? He's just another cog in the machine. If he dies, that's what I call a promotion." The man laughed, then raised his gun and—

An explosion of gunfire roared through the kitchen, followed by chaos.

Chapter Fourteen

Annie wrapped the thin navy blanket tighter around herself and hovered as close to Hunter as she could get. While the EMTs tended to their injuries and checked them over, Ginny and Beth remained a couple feet away, with Beth ensconced in an endless hug from her sister, as if all of them couldn't bear to let the others disappear for even a second. They'd endured a trauma very few people went through, and it had bonded them all for life.

Just a few minutes ago, there'd been a swarm of sheriff's deputies filling the back room of the restaurant. She'd heard sirens in the background as more joined them. Two of Hughes's men shot at the cops, but both were taken down by shots from the deputies, leaving only Eddie standing.

Brady had walked up to him with a grin on his face and a pair of handcuffs at the ready. "And you are under arrest, Eddie. Just like Kingston and Dylan and every single person who has ever been a part of this crew."

"You've got nothing on me!" Eddie screamed, repeating the words over and over again as he was led out of the restaurant and into a waiting squad car.

At the last minute, the deputies had taken Brady's call to action and responded in force, led by Chief Deputy Tonya Sanders, who wasn't about to let her sister become a victim. "Seems I had one more thing to take care of before I went out on maternity leave," she said to Brady after it was all over. "How can I ever thank you for finding Beth?"

"By staying on the force after your maternity leave is up," he said. "I'm going to need someone to help me clean up this town."

"I think that's a job offer I can't refuse." She gave Brady a smile, then went off to join the other deputies.

The deputies had arrested Eddie and his men and sat them on the sidewalk, while crime scene techs scoured the restaurant for any remaining evidence. The files Brady had from Sanders were enough to put Eddie and Hughes away for a long time. Dylan Houston would get some credit for coming clean and admitting that he'd used the dating app to lure Jenny here.

"What made Dylan come to you?" Annie asked when Brady walked over to them. He'd told her all about his surprise visit from Dylan when he'd rescued her.

"He watched your vlog. His conscience got to him, and he said he couldn't let Jenny's mother die without knowing what happened. He was also worried that Kingston was going to get rid of him, as yet another loose end."

"Too bad it took him so long to tell the truth." Tears shimmered in Annie's eyes. "Maybe we could have found her earlier."

"She could still be out there. They all could be."

It seemed unrealistic to believe that Jenny, Kaitlyn, Hailey, Pauline and Marcy could all be rescued, but...who knew? God could work miracles, and maybe He had one more left. "I won't stop looking."

"Correction. *We* won't stop looking." He gave her hand a squeeze.

Annie's heart soared, but she didn't dare speak the words rolling around inside her. Instead, she turned to Brady's nephew. "You sure you're okay?" she asked Hunter. His wavy brown hair was a mess, he had a couple scrapes on his cheek and his jeans had a rip by the knee.

He grinned. "You've asked me that like thirty times, and my uncle has asked me about a hundred times. I'm fine. I'm good. And hungry."

Brady laughed. "That's a sign that all is good if I ever saw one."

"Well, good, because I'm hungry, too," Annie said as she leaned into Brady's warmth, the safety of him. Her gaze met his and held for a long time. She could get used to looking into his brown eyes. Very, very used to that.

"I'm, uh, going to go over and talk to Ginny," Hunter said. He shrugged off his blanket and left the two of them alone. A second later, he and Ginny were sitting on the bumper of an ambulance and chatting like two old friends.

"He told me he wants to help girls like her," Annie said. "I think it's his way of giving back and helping young women from ending up like his mom."

"Hunter's a great kid. And however he wants to get involved, I'm a hundred percent behind it." Brady's attention zeroed in on her face. A slow smile curved up his face. "Maybe it's a story we'll tell our grandkids someday."

"Our...what?" Had she heard him right? Maybe all the chaos today had caused him to have some kind of a brain lapse. "Did you say *our* grandkids?"

Brady came around to the front of her. The blanket slipped off Annie's shoulders, but she barely noticed. The evening was settling in, and the air around Crestville was cooling, as the mountains wrapped the valley in a deep darkness, but in the space between her and Brady, everything was warm and comfortable.

He took her hands in his, his grip solid, firm, dependable. "If there's one thing I've learned through this whole thing, Annie, it's that I'm tired of not going after the life I always wanted.

Everything I ever wanted was waiting right in front of me, and I almost lost that today. I won't let that happen again because I want that life. I want you in that life."

"I thought you were a determined-to-stay-single bachelor."

"I was. Until I met someone I truly wanted to spend a lot of time with. Maybe even marry someday." He tucked a lock of hair behind her ear, the touch tender and sweet. "I think I fell in love with you the first time you stormed in on my lunch with the judge, all sassy and demanding."

She mocked outrage. "I was no such thing."

He pressed his temple to hers. The dark, woodsy scent of his cologne drifted between them, wrapped with another scent, one she had never really known before. The scent of home. Of being in exactly the right place at exactly the right time.

"That determination to find the truth and solve what happened saved four lives today," he said, "and countless others down the road. I think you are amazing, Annie Linscott, and I want to spend the rest of my life with you."

"But I… I thought we were just friends." The first words that popped to mind probably came out as dumb as they sounded in her head. The man was telling her he wanted to spend his life with her, and she was trying to get a relationship definition?

"We *are* friends. And that's a good thing, in fact, my favorite thing about us. But I don't mean… I'm getting this all wrong." He shook his head.

"No, Brady, you're getting it all right." She cupped his jaw, loving the feel of his stubble against her palm, the signs of a man who would spend all hours and move mountains to protect the ones he loved. "That's part of what makes being with you so perfect. We started as friends and now…"

"And now, we can be something more…" he caught one of her hands with his own "…permanent. I love you, Annie. Will you marry me?"

"I couldn't imagine anything more perfect than saying yes." She raised on her toes and pressed a kiss to his lips, then whispered the words her heart had held in secret all this time. "I love you, too."

He kissed her back, long and sweet, until one of the deputies whistled. Annie blushed, but Brady just wrapped an arm around her and watched as the deputies investigated the scene. "Do you think you got all of them?"

"No." He sighed. "But it's a start. Hughes has a spiderweb of criminal enterprises spread all the way from here to California. Eddie, however, is jockeying for a get-out-of-jail-free card, and he's already spilling the beans on every part of Hughes's operations."

She was not surprised. Eddie had seemed like the kind of person who would do whatever it took for him to come out the winner. "Would you really let him go for turning over evidence?"

"Not a chance." Brady grinned. "But I'm not worried about Eddie. I'm worried about you. Are you okay? You're sure you're not hurt?"

She laughed. "Now I know how Hunter feels. Yes, I'm fine." The squad cars pulled away from the curb, leaving just the crime scene van and a handful of forensics people. "But I still don't know where Jenny is. That's the whole reason I came to this town."

"And what if you never find her?"

She watched the car holding Eddie "the Answerman" disappear down the road. "I think there's one person who knows that answer."

"And I intend to keep on asking the question until he tells me." Brady drew Annie against his chest and placed a kiss on her forehead. "Until then, let's grab Hunter and head home."

"Is there going to be a pizza waiting there?"

He chuckled. "Absolutely."

Epilogue

Brady and Annie held hands as they stood in the hallway of the hospital, giving Jenny and her mother as much privacy as they could. Once Eddie started talking, he didn't shut up and eventually gave up the location where some of the young women had been sent over the years, a brothel in Nevada.

Brady had contacted the local PD there and within minutes, they had raided the place and brought the women to a motel for processing and statements.

Brady, Annie and Hunter had hopped in his SUV and driven out there the minute they had the information. Annie held her breath, afraid that they would be too late, but as soon as she walked in the door, she recognized her dear friend. Jenny was dazed, muddled by drugs and looked like life had destroyed her. She'd dyed her hair purple and become so gaunt, Annie was afraid the next breeze would knock her over.

It took a minute for Jenny to believe that Annie was there, in the flesh and that Brady wasn't there to arrest her but to help her get back home. "I thought no one would want me back after what they made me do," Jenny said, over and over again, between tears. "I'm such a terrible person."

"No, they're the terrible people who took you away and convinced you that you were trash. Jenny, you were never anything other than the amazing person who was my best friend. I never stopped looking for you," Annie said, pulling her friend into a tight hug. "Or loving you."

Jenny blinked back her tears. Mascara was smudged on her face, and streaks ran through her makeup, almost as if the tears were washing off the life she'd had in Nevada. "You... you still love me?"

Annie pulled back and held her best friend's gaze. "Yes, very much. And so does your mom, Jenny. We've all been waiting a long time to see you again. What do you say we go home now?"

Jenny slept the entire drive back to Colorado, as if the last ten years had suddenly caught up with her. A few miles before they reached the hospital where her mother was, Jenny woke up and started talking. The whole story poured out of her, a tidal wave of abuse and fear. The abduction, the beatings, the constant moving from place to place, then the drugs they forced on her until she was hooked, which made everything easier and harder all at once. She gave them even more details about Hughes's operation and how it worked, especially how Dylan had used the dating app to lure her to town.

When she was done, Brady made a phone call and got Jenny a bed at the place where Tammy was being treated. "When you're ready to go, it's there for you. It's time you started a new life," he told her. "And live it to the fullest, for the people who can't."

Annie knew he was thinking of Frank and of Pauline and Kaitlyn, who they learned had died at the hands of the people who abused them. They'd managed to track down Marcy and Hailey at another brothel in Nevada and were working with local programs to get both of them into therapy that helped re-introduce victims of trafficking back to the world.

Now, Annie watched Jenny reconnect with her mother. There were a lot of tears and even more hugs. It was a bittersweet reunion, but Helen's spirits were bright, and the doctor had said anything could happen with Helen's renewed zest for life. Maybe they'd have far more time together than anyone expected. If one miracle could happen, surely another one could, too. Jenny waved at Annie and mouthed that she would meet them in the car.

"Are you guys ready?" Brady asked.

At the end of the hall, Hunter, who had been playing a video game on his phone, got to his feet and joined them.

"I am ready. For whatever is coming next." Annie slid her hand into Brady's, and they began strolling down the hallway, with Hunter close behind.

Brady glanced over his shoulder at his nephew. "After we're all done here today, I think it's time Hunter saw his mom, and my *fiancée* met my sister."

She laughed at the emphasis he put on the word *fiancée*, something he'd been finding a way to work into conversation at least a hundred times a day. "I think you just like saying that word."

When she looked back, she could see Hunter's face light up at the prospect of seeing his mom.

When they reached the rehab a few hours later, they were welcomed with good news again. Tammy was doing well and would be released to a halfway house in another week. Jenny was inspired by Tammy's progress and eager to settle in and "get back to myself," as she told Annie. After a teary hug, Annie watched her best friend get a second chance at a new beginning.

On the drive back to Crestville, Annie and Hunter had talked about how difficult it was to grow up in a tough situation, him with a mother who was a substance abuser and Annie with a mother who was loveless and distant. They'd found common ground in the things they had missed from childhood and an understanding of what made each other tick.

In the couple of days since Brady rescued the two of them from that walk-in cooler, Annie and Hunter had built a kind of friendship that wasn't really parental and wasn't really peers. It was something in between that worked for both of them.

Secretly, Annie loved having this instant family with Brady, even if it wasn't conventional or perfect. From that first pizza, it felt like she fit into their world as if she was meant to be there. It made her want to start playing piano again and allow the music she loved to heal her difficult past so she could build a bridge to the future.

"You know, I like saying fiancée almost as much as I like saying the word *wife*. Which hopefully, I'll be saying very, very soon." Brady took her hand in his and kissed their joined fingers.

Hunter rolled his eyes but grinned at their goofy antics.

"That's something we can do as soon as we are home, my love." But as she leaned her head on his shoulder, Annie knew, deep in her heart, that she was already home.

* * * * *

Romantic Suspense

Danger. Passion. Drama.

Available Next Month

Colton's Deadly Trap Patricia Sargeant
The Twin's Bodyguard Veronica Forand

 LOVE INSPIRED

Hostage Security Lisa Childs
Breaking The Code Maria Lokken

 LOVE INSPIRED

K-9 Alaskan Defence Sarah Varland
Uncovering The Truth Carol J. Post

Larger Print

 LOVE INSPIRED

Defending The Child Sharon Dunn
Lethal Wilderness Trap Susan Furlong

LOVE INSPIRED

Cold Case Mountain Murder Rhonda Starnes
Christmas In The Crosshairs Deena Alexander